Secret Seekers Society

WRATH OF THE WENDIGO

J.L. Hickey

Black Rose Writing | Texas

ISBN: 978-1-68433-213-7
PUBLISHED BY BLACK ROSE WRITING
www.blackrosewriting.com

Printed in the United States of America
Suggested Retail Price (SRP) $20.95

The Secret Seekers Society: Wrath of the Wendigo is printed in Palatino Linotype

Dedicated to my beautiful family, my amazing three boys, Wyatt, Cass, and Finn. May adventures be born into your blood!

To the love of my life, my wife, Tesia, who supports and believes in this crazy dream of mine.

To my niece and nephew, Hunter and Elly, who are the stars of the book, and who the original book was written for.

To my mother and father, who blessed me with such passion for the arts.

Secret Seekers Society

WRATH OF THE WENDIGO

PREFACE THREE YEARS AGO UNDISCLOSED LOCATION

It was three in the morning when esteemed "insert doctor title here" Dr. Johnathon Osborne's front door was kicked in. It sounded like an explosion went off in his living room, awaking the Doctor and his wife, Jenny, from the dead of sleep.

"Jesus!" Jenny grabbed his arm as tight as she could.

"What the hell was that?" Dr. Osborne grabbed his glasses from the night stand, turning on the bedside lamp.

"Someone is breaking in..." Jenny cracked a whisper.

"Shhh... keep quiet," Dr. Osborne held his wife's trembling hand. "Grab your cell, call the security station. I will check it out."

"Be careful..." she fumbled for the cellphone charging on the nightstand.

"I will, just stay calm." He gently braced his feet on the creaky floorboard.

Dr. Osborne didn't even have time to stand up from the bed before three military officers burst through the bedroom door, their automatic rifles and flashlights aimed at the terrified couple.

"Dr. Johnathon Osborne?" one of the men spoke, his voice gruff. "Please take what you want, don't hurt us," the Doctor shielded his eyes from the blinding light with his hands. "Please, we have a son. Take what you want and leave."

"I asked a question; is your name Johnathon Osborne?" The man repeated, his voice void of emotion. "Don't make me ask a third time." "Y-yes, I am Dr. Osborne," he stuttered as he felt the fear swelling in his throat, a lump he could not swallow.

"You're coming with us." The gruff man nodded to his comrades, "blindfold him."

"What is the meaning of this? I have a family, please." the Doctor pleaded. The tallest of the men held out a blindfold.

"There is an easy way, or a hard way," he threatened, dangling the blindfold in his face.

"I suggest you pick the easy way, sir," the man spoke again. "If I do, will you leave my family alone?" asked Dr. Osborne.

"We have no interest in them. Only *you* have been summoned," The gruff man answered, his gun still drawn.

"I suggest you kiss your wife good-bye. It may be a long time before you see her again," the tall man tossed the blindfold on his lap. "Put it on tight."

"What do you mean?" Jenny's eyes swelled with fear, tears flowing freely. "You can't take him! We have a family!"

"You have two minutes," the third man finally spoke, checking his watch.

"Honey, I'm sorry." Dr. Osborne grabbed his wife's hand, trembling with fear. "I love you," he leaned over and kissed her softly.

"I don't understand." she whispered, trying to remain calm. "Please, tell Josh I love him. I don't know how long I will be gone,"

The Doctor fought back his emotions "Why?" she pleaded, begging for her husband to stay. "Why must he go?" she turned to the strange men.

"—because," The third man interrupted still eyeing his watch, "Your husband is the property of Aten Corp, he is needed elsewhere. They all know this day may come; it's in the contract.

"What is he talking about? What contract?" Jenny's bottom lip quivered.

"The contract I signed to work for Aten Corp, to relocate here. II knew I could be called on for special projects, but nothing like this. We've been here for five years. I thought this was our new home."

"Blindfold, now!" the gruff man ordered waiving his gun.

"I love you. Please wait for me. I will be back soon." Dr. Osborne tightened the blindfold over his eyes, "Can I please say good-bye to my son? He's in the other room."

"No," The gruff man was blunt. "We're running late. The last thing we want to do is keep Professor Aten waiting."

"The P-professor?" Dr. Osborne's voice shuddered at the name. He'd heard rumors in the lab about the facilities on the neighboring islands, talk of scientists being whisked away in the middle of the night never to be seen again. The Doctor felt the panic settling in his chest. His mind jumbled with anxiety. He tried to think of something he may have said or done... Was he being punished? His heart raced out of control... were they escorting him to his deathbed?

"Stand up; we need to get moving." The tall soldier grabbed his arm leading him out of the house with the other two following close behind.

Dr. Osborne couldn't see a thing, but he could hear the loud buzzing sound of a helicopter off in the distance. The sticky, night air hit Dr. Osborn's face the moment they left the confines of his home, bringing the surreal moment to life. This was not a dream; with every step he took the loudness of the propeller grew. After a few minutes of traversing through the island's jungle, the wet soil dampening his slippers, the loudness of the chopper became deafening. He felt the forcefulness of the soldier's hand pushing his head down as they led him up into the body of the helicopter.

"Watch your step," the soldier ordered. "I am strapping you in."
"Who is that?" an unfamiliar voice yelled from inside the vehicle,
"Is there someone else with me?" The voice sounded panicked.

"Shut up and keep your blindfold on," the gruff man snapped, locking the Doctor securely into his seat "We're ready, Cupid, lift us up."

"Copy that," Cupid responded from the cockpit.

"We're in for about an hour ride, so sit tight and shut up. There will be no answered questions," the gruff man ordered.

It was the longest hour of Dr. Osborn's life, blindfolded and scared out of his mind. *What was going on?* He tried to remain calm, but he was in the midst of a panic attack. Not that any of the soldiers would care. His chest tightened, making every breath painful, until he felt faint, and his hands still trembled. He tried controlling his breathing, focusing on the air coming in and out of his lungs, but nothing seemed to work. The sensation of impending doom engulfed him...

He'd never see his wife's beautiful smile again. Never see his son graduate high school.

All the rumors he'd heard over the years were twirling around his head. Everyone knew it; you cross the Professor, he crossed you out of existence. He knew when he signed the contract that Aten Corp played by their own rules. Declan Aten was a brilliant man not confined to any laws or ethical codes; you worked for him because you could get results.

He couldn't figure out why he was the one sitting in a helicopter guarded by three military men. What had he done? Was it because of his work? It was top secret, it was controversial, but he was under the impression that was the sole reason Aten had brought him into the company.

It felt like an eternity, but Dr. Osborne finally felt the helicopter descend. There was quite a bit of turbulence as the helicopter braced for its landing, rocking the passengers violently. The engine finally cut off, the thundering noise of the propellers slowly faded. The Doctor sat in silence, afraid to speak, afraid of what was going to happen next. "Oh, God. Where are we?" the unfamiliar voice broke the silence. "Shut up," the man with the gruff voice ordered. "I said no questions."

"You tore us from our homes in the middle of the night!" the man argued.

"He said shut up," the other soldier yelled back.

"Okay, let's get them inside," the gruff man said as he unbuckled his belt, and climbed from the helicopter

They pulled Dr. Osborne from his seat by his arm. He could smell the familiar scent of the jungle around him, his slippers sinking into the soft earth. He guessed he had been flown to a nearby island, part of a series of unchartered islands in the Caribbean Sea, all of which were purchased years ago by a young Declan Aten.

"Ouch! You're hurting me! Not, so rough…" the other blindfolded man whined from behind him.

"This one is annoying," the soldier scoffed pushing the man even harder.

Dr. Osborne didn't say a word, he kept his mouth shut. He continued to focus on his breathing, hoping to calm himself down, trying to overcome the panic racing through him. He was escorted through the dense jungle. Once the brush broke, the Doctor could feel the wet earth turn to pavement. As they led him up a few flights of stairs, he heard the locks of a door turning. They sounded mechanical, state of the art, and identical to the noise he heard every day when he entered the laboratory where he worked. He felt the cool flow of air conditioning hit his face as soon as it swung open.

"Where are we?" the blindfolded man behind him asked. "Is this another lab?"

"Do you ever shut up?" the soldier cursed. "Aten doesn't pay us enough for this crap."

"Calm down, we're almost there," the gruff man responded. "We're entering into an elevator now. We'll be going down to the sublevel. You may feel disoriented as we descend, just a warning."

Dr. Osborne heard the chime of the elevator door close behind him. The queasy feeling in his stomach began as the elevator descended into the depths of the building. The door chimed again, and the men lead them down a long hallway. They stopped suddenly. Dr. Osborne heard the clanging of keys, then a loud creak from a heavy door swinging open.

"Finally, my guests have arrived." The speaker's voice was deep, almost mocking. "A bit late, boys. You know my time is priceless. I am very displeased."

"Sorry, sir, it won't happen again. We hit some turbulence." The gruff man's normally confident voice cracked in fear.

"Of course, it won't. Now be gone, and back to your posts. This is top secret Intel we're about to discuss. If you were to overhear it, I'd have to kill you all. None of you would care for that, now would you?" "No, sir," the soldiers replied.

Dr. Osborne heard their footsteps retreating back down the hallway, the door at the far end made a small thud as it closed and locked. He and his blindfolded comrade were left alone with the man he could only presume was Professor Aten.

"Well then, now that we have some privacy, please remove your blindfolds."

Dr. Osborne fumbled nervously with the knot behind his head. His hands trembled trying to untie the blindfold. His fingers were not communicating with his brain, he couldn't seem to function. After a few seconds, the blindfold loosened and fell to the floor. His eyes blurred, the stark white florescent lights burned his eyes. It took a few moments until he was able to adjust to his new surroundings.

"Um... Hello, sir..." Dr. Osborne heard the man to his left say.

The man standing in front of them was middle aged, quite tall, and physically fit for his age. He leaned on a black glossy cane, dressed in a flawless, grey, double breasted, designer suit. He stood before them with a roguish grin. His hair was dark as night, peppered slightly with grey, pairing perfectly well with his well-trimmed beard.

The very presence of the man left Dr. Osborne speechless. "Perhaps you have heard of me; my name is Declan Aten, founder of ATEN corp. I sign your paycheck, of course."

"Y-Yes, how could we not?" the nervous man replied.

"I must apologize for such a violent intrusion into your homes," the Professor sighed. "Sometimes the needs of business precede the act of good taste. To be honest, I needed your expertise hours ago, so I sent my team to retrieve you both as fast as possible. I do hope you were able to say your goodbyes to your families, and if not... Well, I think once you see what I have in store for you both, you will soon forget about them anyway."

Forget about their families? Dr. Osborne was insulted. There was only one place in the world where he wanted to be, back at home sleeping alongside his wife.

"Dr. Johnathon Osborne, meet Dr. Phillip Hoffman. I am sure you are familiar with each other's work."

"You're Doctor Osborne?" Hoffman smiled grabbing Osborne's hand and shaking it forcefully. "It's a pleasure..."

"Yes, the feeling's mutual. I have studied your work as well," Dr. Osborne nodded, still feeling a bit uneasy with the situation but he did his best to keep his cool.

"Yes, enough with the pleasantries," Professor Aten cut the greeting short. "I promise you will have all the time in the world to exchange notes and get to know one another. I have a lot of work for you both." The Professor turned his back to the two men, facing a large computer monitoring system currently in a sleep mode.

"What sort of work?" Dr. Osborne's voice cracked. He had never been so nervous in his life. If the Professor wanted his expertise on a project it meant he wasn't being put to death. The first bit of good news he'd heard all morning.

"Good for you to ask, my friend." The Professor kept his back turned and stretched out his arms, showcasing the elaborate computer system before him, "What you see before me is our interface system. This entire building is operated through this very control room. It is state of the art in all ways, including protecting the both of you from the contents of the inner vault. But, more importantly, it's protecting the contents from your potential damaging hands. Let's be honest, you're both replaceable, the contents we're working with are not. The contents mean more than the both of your lives combined. Understood?"

"Um…okay…" Dr. Osborne didn't care to hear that. What on earth could need such elaborate protection?

"You will be doing all your research here. All facets of the laboratory and the vault itself are centralized through this hub. You are never to leave this workstation, ever, understood? You see the door leading to the right? That's your living quarters with two beds, a single shower, and a small kitchen. We will provide you food to sustain yourselves, delivered biweekly. Get comfortable folks, this is your new home."

Aten grinned.

"You are making it sound like we're prisoners here." Dr. Osborne frowned. There was no way he was living with a stranger in these small quarters, especially when he had a loving family waiting for him back at home. Not that he thought he would have much of a choice… "Is that so?" Professor Aten mocked. "Once you see what I am offering you, you will never want to leave this place. Not even for a day's embrace with your family, this I promise you. So, if I were you, I would bite your tongue."

"I would choose nothing over my family," Osborne muttered to Dr.

Hoffman in a moment of defiance.

"Shut up, you're going to get us killed." Hoffman whispered back.

"Excuse me?" Aten turned back around, his mouth pursed in anger.

"Is there an issue here?"

"Err... no, no issue at all." Hoffman stumbled.

"I told him there was nothing I would choose over my family," Osborne answered back.

"Is that right?" Aten grinned. "You're a brave man, aren't you? I don't care much for bravery, seen a lot of brave men die hiding behind that notion." Aten mused aloud.

"My family is the most important thing in the world," Osborne added again. "Nothing you can offer me would make me willingly turn my back on them."

"I will take you up on that bet," Aten grinned. "For now, shut up and listen. What I am about to show you... well... it may be a bit disturbing." Aten pulled from his pocket a small touch screen remote. He clicked it once lighting up the tablet with a series of options. Aten swiped his finger a few times on the remote until the room around him came buzzing to life. A loud and persistent hum of energy flooded the room.

The entire back wall illuminated brightly as the crystal monitor flickered to life. The screen loaded a series of applications running in the background. After a few brief moments the centralized ATEN operating system went live, the ATEN logo screensaver rotated in place.

Professor Aten couldn't hide his smile any longer. Clicking the remote once again, a live feed from another area of the facility popped up on the main screen. The feed originated in a room void of light, a lifeless black picture, with nothing of note to be seen. Aten hit a third button causing the lightless room to illuminate.

"As I said, everything in this facility is controlled here in the hub,"

Aten explained waiting patiently for the lights to power up. "It will only take but a second…"

The room in the video feed buzzed to life, the bright lights exposed a horrifying image of a mummified woman's face from its forehead to chin.

"Look at those eyes…" Hoffman's jaw dropped in bewilderment. "This… can't be…" Dr. Osborne frowned. "What are we looking at?"

The group couldn't turn their eyes away, they were looking over an ancient mummified body lying neatly on a metal operating table. It didn't take the doctors long to realize they weren't looking at a typical humanoid mummy. Strange as it may be, the corpse's eyes were still perfectly preserved. They sparkled with a vibrant emerald green, so beautiful it felt as if they were peering directly into their souls.

"They look perfectly preserved, but how?" Hoffman asked. "That's a secret. That's not all, though" Aten smirked. "Let's zoom out a bit so we can see more than just the creature's face." "Creature?" Osborne repeated Aten's unusual choice of words. "Look for yourself," Aten clicked the remote.

The image zoomed out, exposing more of the creature's body. To Hoffman and Osborne's terror, the mummy was in fact, not human at all…from its scalp grew long grotesquely withered snakes, each one with a head and beady lifeless eyes.

"My lord, have mercy on us all…." Osborne shook his head at the ungodly sight. Was he really seeing this? Could it be true? Immediately, he thought of ways it could all be some sort of hoax. Perhaps a test that Professor Aten was putting them through…

"There is more…." Aten smiled as he continued to zoom out.

The camera pulled away from the creature's ghastly face exposing more of its torso. The upper torso of the mummy looked normal, that of a female body, slender in stature, probably middle-aged. Aten pulled the camera further back exposing the entire length of its torso. Again, both of the Doctor's mouths gaped open in horror.

Aten grinned.

All sense of normality was tossed out the window. The lower half of the woman's body was void of all things human. The body had no legs; the lower extremity was snakelike, long and slender, the tip of the snake-like extremity ended much like that of a rattlesnake's.

"This is a hoax," Osborne blurted, admiring the snake-like under belly. "Why waste our time with such trickery?"

"You think I would waste my resources, a state-of-the-art facility, and your talents on a hoax?" Aten shot back. "No, this is the real deal. This is the last remaining body of the mysterious race of Gorgons. We've labeled her Medusa. Fitting, isn't it?"

"No..." Hoffman shook his head in disbelief. "Where on earth did you discover her body?"

"That answer is above your pay grade," Aten smirked. "Know that I spent more than a lifetime hunting out her existence. She is no legend; she is as real as the families you left behind."

"When can we see her?" Hoffman asked. He was practically salivating over the thought of experimenting on her body. "We have DNA, tissue samples...this is amazing! Just think of the possibilities!"

"You cannot *see* her, ever," replied Aten.

"What do you mean? How do you expect us to study her if we can't collect samples?" Osborne asked. Aten was right... if this truly was the body of a fabled Gorgon... a Greek mythological monster in the flesh, right there for him to study... he would never want to leave the lab ever again. It was a scientist's dream come true...

"Because..." Aten replied calmly. "We wouldn't want this to happen to you." Aten used the remote in his hand to reposition the camera to the right of the gorgon body. There on the floor, in a terrified state, was a man completely turned to stone. He had been petrified while crawling on all fours away from the body, terror evident on his face. A statue of a once prominent man turned to stone.

"My God...what happened to the man?" Hoffman felt his stomach sink.

"Well," Aten cleared his throat, "when we first recovered the mummified body, it was completely wrapped in linen. I called in a scientist to begin to dissect the mummy's garb to see what lies beneath. He started with the bottom, terrified at what he found, I forced him on. He meticulously removed the bandages from the creature's face. Revealing, for the first time ever to the modern world, her snakelike hair and those beautiful green eyes... the moment her gaze set upon his eyes

-even though, thousands of years deceased he immediately screamed in pain. It was a blood-curdling, agonizing howl. I remember it fondly," Aten had a sick smile. "His skin slowly stiffened, tightening with every pitiful gasp for air. It was not long before he was nothing more than a distasteful piece of room décor."

"You're kidding me...her gaze turned him to stone, even in death?" asked Osborne who did not take kindly to Aten's grotesque sense humor.

"Correct, her marvelous gaze petrifies any who looks upon it," Aten smiled. "Almost poetic, is it not?'

"This is unbelievable..." Osborne muttered to himself, his mouth still agape from the sight.

"So, do you still want to go running back to that wife and kid of yours?" Aten chuckled.

Osborne did not answer.

He didn't want to admit it, but Aten was right... How could he turn his back on this? A gorgon?

"But, how are we supposed to study her if we can't lay eyes on her in person?" asked Hoffman.

"Are we so simple minded? I thought I chose two of the brightest scientists in the world today," Aten answered. "Once I realized what I had found, I constructed this laboratory around the vault holding my precious darling. Everything in this central hub, the very room you're standing in, controls the entire facility. You have futuristic technology at your disposal. You will interact with the creature through the interface system. This allows you to manipulate the titanium mechanical arms installed inside her room. With these, you can take DNA samples, you can dissect her body; you can do anything you desire, all in the name of science."

"This is amazing!" Hoffman smiled.

"What do you want our study to focus on?" Osborne's hands shook with excitement. His fear had succumbed to the utter amazement of what lay before him.

"I want a weapon..." Aten smirked, "and you have a deadline of two years to make me a happy man. I want monthly updates, and if I decide you are falling behind...I will terminate you and bring in your replacements. Do you understand? Yes, I am asking a lot of you, but in return, you get to study something most scientists could only dream of. You're on the forefront of the scientific world. Now, enough of the pleasantries, are you both on board?"

"Sir, it would be an honor." Osborne smiled.

"Don't be confused, by termination, I do not mean your contract; I mean your lives," Aten smiled. "You have a deadline, I wouldn't waste any more time."

CHAPTER 1
ELLY'S CURSE

It wasn't often that Professor Claudio Calenstine invited children (or anyone for that matter) down into his sublevel study. So, when Elly had been summoned to his secret chamber for a personal visit, she was more than a bit nervous. Was she in trouble? Had she done something wrong? A million reasons ran through her head, but only one made any sense. After all the craziness she, and her brother, Hunter, had gotten themselves into over the last year, there was only one lingering question that still haunted Elly… Solomon's Seal…

Elly thought about that life changing moment a lot. She sat up at night replaying the events in her head, how the ancient and magical ring fastened itself to her finger, never to come off again. It was a split-second decision that would haunt her forever. Despite the suffering the ring had brought her, deep down she knew she had done the right thing. She wouldn't do anything differently given the choice. How could she? It was her courageous act that saved her good friend Remy, from a perilous fate.

Yet, the ring has been a terrible omen. Since its attachment to her finger, she had been going seemingly mad; at times she questioned her own sanity. Elly told no one about the voices, the whispers that were barely audible, sneaking up around her when no one's around. Even worse, the shadow people she caught out of the corner of her eye… were gruesome looking figures, often times deformed with maddening faces. These things…haunted her, followed her. Even in sleep she couldn't escape their presence…in fact, sleeping was ten times worse. Some nights weren't as bad as others. Sometimes she dreamt of the ghostly man who spoke to her that fateful evening when she and thering became one. He was a tall and slender apparition with kind blue eyes, silvery flowing hair. He had aided Elly in trapping the demon Moloch back within the Daupnir ring. He'd spoken to her that night, claiming he was the legendary King Solomon. It was the nights she didn't dream of the King that terrified her. Those nights were occupied by the terrifying shades, in her dreams they were more than mere glimpses, they haunted her, screaming for help, stalking her. She'd wake up gasping for air, her heart racing uncontrollably. Elly hated sleeping. She found herself spending the majority of her nights fending off sleep.

Elly hadn't told a soul about the voices, the night terrors, or the shadow-people that haunted her. She thought it was doubtful that the Professor was seeking a visit about the ring; she'd already told him everything about the night in question. How she put the ring on, how she seemed to see the world in a strange blue color, and how she spoke with the slender faced ghost with the silver-grey hair. There wasn't much else for him to know.

Elly wouldn't have to wait long to find out. She found her palms were sweaty, clammy, as she made her way down the lengthy hallway leading into the entrance of Calenstine's enormous study. She thought of her older brother, Hunter, wishing he was there by her side. Having him there would curb some of her angst. If Hunter was good for anything as an older brother, it was making her feel safe.

•　　　•　　　•

"I don't see why you're getting special treatment," Hunter had said the night before as he readied for bed. He kneeled down to feed their large Cu'Sith pet, named Trayer, a treat. The massive dog had curled up like a giant ball of green fur in the middle of their bedroom snoring loudly.

The smell of the treat awakened the dog, whose mouth salivated, leaving a pool of drool on the floor where he lay. Trayer's head perked up quickly in anticipation of his surprise. Hunter held out a very largedog treat, easily the size of his arm. Trayer was a gentle dog, who carefully snatched the giant treat from Hunter, making quick work of the tasty treat.

Even as a pup Trayer had been a monster in size. Over the summer he had matured into his full size, easily growing to the size of a large steer. Thankfully, he was mostly a lazy pet; spending his days lounging on the children's beds (he broke Elly's twice, already!).

"It's not like I asked Ms. Ellingbee to see the Professor, I'd rather spend the afternoon reading up on next year's school books." Elly was already irritated with Hunter's questions.

She normally didn't mind the extra attention from her teachers and staff. Elly was always known as the smart one, always on the honor roll, and top of her class in all categories. She fondly remembered how her parents reacted when she took first place in the spelling bee at their former school. This wasn't the type of attention she wanted, though. It felt more like she was being paged down to the principal's office. Something she knew Hunter was quite used to.

"You're crazy! Who would want to study during summer break?" Hunter shook his head in disbelief.

"Anyway," Hunter went on, "Calenstine's study is amazing. He has so many cool treasures in that mile-long hallway. Every time we go down it I find something new I didn't see before." Hunter scratched Trayer's large fluffy ear, causing the dog's right leg to thump repeatedly against their floor.

"I'd rather not deal with it," Elly sat at the edge of her bed, book in her lap. She mindlessly flipped through the pages, failing to focus on anything other than her meeting.

"So, what's it all about anyway?" asked Hunter. "Don't tell me they're punishing students for studying too hard? Because, that's all you ever do."

"What's what all about?" Elly paid half attention to Hunter's ramblings.

"You seeing the professor tomorrow for the one on one meeting?"

"I dunno...maybe he *is* giving me an award because of my perfectgrades?" Elly forced a nervous laugh, knowing it was not the reason. "You've been having a lot of bad dreams lately..." Hunter

19

added casually, not wanting to sound too worried about his little sister. Deep down, though, he was a bit worried. It wasn't like her to wake up from a dead sleep, screaming; recently it had become a nightly routine. Hunter wasn't a stranger to nightmares, either. He'd struggled with them himself, since his parents disappeared in the plane crash.

At first, the dreams would wake him up at night, too. He'd jolt awake bawling his eyes out, his pillow soaked in tears. That had changed though...with time; he'd learned to welcome the dreams. It wasn't quite as terrifying after the hundredth time, he found a bit of peace in them. Every night he went to bed knowing he would see his parents' faces one more time.

"Nightmares?" Elly frowned, unaware Hunter had any clue what she was experiencing. "Well, I don't remember what they're about so..." she lied, making light of the question, "nothing to talk about, really."

"Well, don't worry about it." Hunter smiled, trying to reassure his little sister. "I mean, the Professor hasn't seen either of us since the end of the last school year. It's been months, maybe he wants to give you some sort of academic award like you said. You did ace all your classes and passed the first year of enlightenment with flying colors." "I doubt that...," said Elly. "But, I guess I will find out in the morning."

Elly reached over to her small oak desk, clicking off her bedside lamp, enclosing the children in complete darkness. She laid her head down on her pillow and tried to rest her mind....

Please don't dream of those things tonight, she thought to herself.

• • •

"Elly, come in, please. I am so glad you could meet with me," Professor Calenstine met Elly with a fatherly smile. He sat comfortably at his large crescent shaped desk, lovingly petting his best friend, Monty, his grey-haired lap dog.

The Professor was surrounded by numerous, large, dusty books sprawled out in every direction. A steaming hot cup of tea accompanied the antique tomes.

"Please, have a seat," the Professor gestured with his bony hand. "Get comfy."

Elly obliged, taking a seat in an old squeaky leather-bound chair that sat across from him.

"It's been a few months since we last spoke, my dear," the Professor's brushy white eyebrows rose in excitement when he spoke.

"Am I in trouble?" Elly's bottom lip quivered, anticipating some sort of bad news.

"Trouble?" Calenstine let out a small chuckle, "heaven's no dear, not in the least."

"Oh..." Elly breathed a sigh of relief.

"Tea? A special blend just for you, it's called Bai Hao White Tip Oolong. Funny name I know, but it tastes a bit like peaches. I think you will find it pleasant." Calenstine slowly poured the steaming hot brew into a small tea cup.

"Two sugar cubes if I remember?" He winked playfully, dropping two cubes of sugar into the beverage. He passed it over to her, careful to not spill the steaming liquid.

"It smells amazing," Elly took a cautious sip. It tasted exactly like fresh peaches, delicious.

"I almost did not recognize you when you stepped into my office. You and your brother have both grown so much in the last few months," Calenstine closed the current book he was reading, putting it off to the side.

It was true; Elly had grown a few inches over the summer months. Her auburn hair had turned a lighter strawberry-blonde from the summer sun. Her sparse freckles seemed a bit more dominant around hercheeks and nose. She had turned twelve –a bittersweet birthday because it fell so late into the summer. All of her friends had gone with their families on summer vacation, leaving her alone with Hunter to spend the summer months. Somehow, Elly had slipped into that awkward stage where her body was quickly turning into that of a young woman's.

"My birthday was two weeks ago," Elly stirred her steaming cup of tea before taking a second sip.

"Yes, I am so sorry I missed it. I was overseas visiting with an old friend," Calenstine frowned. "I am sure you had a magical party, nonetheless?"

"No," said Elly plainly. "No one was here. I spent it with my Uncle, Margot, and my brother. That's it…we had cake and ice cream, I got a few gifts."

"I see, I am sorry to hear your friends missed out on such an important occasion," Calenstine frowned.

"It's okay," replied Elly. "I thought you called me down here because I was in some sort of trouble, like I did something wrong."

"I am sorry my dear, nothing could be further from the truth." "Good," Elly smiled.

"We are quite proud of all you and your brother have accomplished here with us at the Estate."

"Proud of us?" Elly repeated, baffled by his choice of words. She was not sure what there was to be proud of, it seemed like they got into trouble every other day for something.

"Very much so, you both have acquired many virtues that most people take years to mature into. You have shown your bravery time and time again. You came to the aid of your friends when the easiest thing to do was to run. You have sacrificed yourselves, both physically and spiritually, in order to do so. You battled a nasty feline of a monster during your first few months here. That alone is marvelous. Thanks to you two, the Estate was much safer that summer. Not even a year later you rescued your friend from a wraith, of all things, and not just any wraith, an ancient evil…there are full-blown adult Seek-ers who would have failed at such a feat; Truly remarkable, although gravely dangerous… Not quite sure what you children were thinking." Calenstine snickered.

"Oh…" Elly blushed. She was at a loss for words, unsure where the Professor was going with all this.

"Don't get me wrong," Calenstine pulled out his beloved Cobb pipe from his drawer, packing it with his favorite cherry flavored tobacco before continuing. "—many of these virtues you and your brother have shown have stemmed from mischief and disobedience. I am sure you are aware the two of you have broken numerous Estate policies." Elly squirmed a bit in her chair. It was coming. She knew it. She was going to be disciplined for something stupid her brother had talked her into. The Professor must have been playing coy, telling her she wasn't in trouble.

"But I digress," Calenstine struck a match, lighting his pipe. The sickly smell of the sulfur caused Elly to turn up her nose.

Calenstine puffed a few dark clouds of smoke from his nostrils, "Tell me of the ring," he said matter-of-factly.

"What do you mean?" asked Elly.

"Well now," Calenstine held out his fragile arm in front of him, tapping lightly with his forefinger on his wrist watch, "Let's see...If I am doing my math correctly, you have had the ring for about four and a half months. Surely, you have experienced some... how shall I say... paranormal activity?"

"I suppose..." Elly frowned, unsure of herself. She didn't know where to start, or how much to reveal; she trusted the Professor, that wasn't the issue. She wasn't sure if she was ready to admit how much stuff was truly happening.

"Err...Well... to be honest... I try to ignore it. Everyday there's stuff... like, really scary stuff; I try and push it out of my mind."

"Hmmm..." Calenstine leaned back into his chair, scratching his chin in deep thought.

"Do you remember what I told you that night?" Calenstine asked. "You know, after you and your friends rescued Remington from thewraith?"

"When you chose to become one with that ring, your life changed forever. There is no going back my dear. Pretending it's not real will only make things worse. That ring, Solomon's seal; it's a connection to a foreign world. A realm we mortals are not meant to traverse. Tell me child, what is it you have experienced? Perhaps I can help you. I have, after all, studied a great many years in the paranormal sciences." Elly took a deep breath before spilling everything out. She told

Calenstine everything she could remember: the disembodied voices, the shadow-like people following her around...Calenstine didn't say a thing, he sat back listening intently to every word she said.

Elly finished, letting out a sigh of relief. "Felt good to get all that out..."

"I see... very intriguing, glad it made you feel better," Calenstine inhaled a long drag from his pipe, slowly exhaling circular clouds of smoke from his mouth. "You are very much connected with this other realm. You are starting to blur the line of the living and the 'hereafter.' Tell me, have you seen *him* since that night you fended off Moloch?" "The ghost who said he was King Solomon?" Elly nervously sipped from her hot tea.

"Yes, you spoke of him in great detail that night."

"No, I have not *seen* him; I only see the shadows out the corner of my eyes. I dream of him though."

"I see..." Calenstine frowned. "The more you ignore these 'incidents' the more you may anger these spirits. So, do your best to acknowledge their presence, remember these entities were at one time people just like you and I. However, like people... there will be good and bad spirits. Basically, Elly, I need you to be very careful as this new power of yours matures. Do you understand me?"

"Why can't I ignore it? I don't want all this happening to me." Elly could not contain her fear. Her eyes watered from the frustration. "I have to focus on school, keep up my grades...the second year of Enlightenment courses are coming up. I don't want demons being able to talk to me...," she argued."My dear," Calenstine frowned, unknowing of how harsh and utterly terrifying his words of wisdom would sound to a twelve-year-old child. "Forgive me," he handed her a white handkerchief to dry her tears. "I only wished to advise you to be cautious. There are potential dangers with your new power, but it has been four months, and as you see, despite a few voices here and there and a couple of extra shadows following you around, you are fine. You will learn to control the ring, use it when you wish to, silence it when needed. It will become an extension of your body, mind, and spirit."

"Hunter and I never wanted any of this...we want to be normal again." Elly sobbed. She held the ring tight in her opposite hand, trying with all her might to pull it off. She knew it was impossible because she tried every night.

"Once a week we shall meet here, the two of us," Calenstine spoke softly. "I can help you, learn with you. There are techniques I can teach you that may help harness this new power of yours. We will do this together."

Elly composed herself, dried her tears. She was thankful for the Professor, albeit scared out of her mind.

CHAPTER 2
HUNTER AND THE BIGFOOT

Hunter wasn't your typical fourteen-year-old teenage boy. He wasn't sitting on a couch glued to the television set, dedicating hours and hours leveling up his favorite video game character. He wasn't out chasing girls or updating his status on the popular social network of the month. Well, he may have been that typical average fourteen-year-old if he'd been given a chance, but he wasn't. Instead, Hunter spent the last few years of his childhood saving his friends from Cyrptozoological monsters and chasing down demonic ghosts that were hell-bent on torturing his friends. Hunter wasn't even sure what the word "normal" meant anymore.

Even his school wasn't typical. Sure, he still learned about social economics and acute triangles, but he was dual enrolled in something called the Enlightenment. This Enlightenment was a collection of training classes that were to ready him for membership into the ultra-secretive, society of Monster Hunters, known as the Seekers.

Hunter spent his mornings learning how to survive in multiple hazardous climates, learning the proper medical treatment for reversing the poisonous bite of a Vampyre, and how to hunt for spiritual entities that are invisible to the naked, human eye. Not to mention a laundry list of other aspects of what his Professors called "Fringe" sciences and Hunter loved every second of it. If only he could skip the regular scholastic studies. Give him a quiz on the many varying relatives of the Bigfoot and their geological habitat over American Politics any day.

It was a hot midsummer's day, beads of sweat dripped down Hunter's forehead as he started off on his ten-minute hike through the

Belmonte Estate's southern courtyard. His goal was to reach the Forbid-den Forest's edge unseen by any adults that may be working around the courtyard. He treaded carefully, knowing that if anyone caught him sneaking into the Forest, he would surely get reprimanded, possibly even suspended from school, or worse, kicked out of the Enlightenment. That wasn't an option, it was all Hunter had anymore, the Estate, his friends, losing them would be too much to bear.

Hunter knew all too well that the forest was too dangerous for a kid his age to be rummaging about. Anyone who knew anything about the Belmonte Estate knew to stay far away from the dangers that lurk within. Despite the constant efforts to monitor the forest through diligent upkeep and utilization of their "ultra-secretive-one-of-a-kind", bio-spherical, computer system to keep its mysterious inhabitants in check, it was still probably the most dangerous place on earth.

Although it was quite scary to be ignoring the numerous *"Danger!"* and *"Private Property, Monster's About!"* signs that littered the forest's edge, Hunter knew he didn't have to venture too far into the dense forest to find what he was looking for. Heck, Hunter traveled much farther into the Forbidden Forest on multiple occasions in the past. He considered this trip a walk in the park compared to what he and his friends had done before. Hunter's only real concern was avoiding detention if he got caught.

It didn't take Hunter long to reach the forest's edge. He wasted no time slipping into the thicket of the woodlands unseen. He pushed forward carefully venturing deeper into the lush landscape. Hunter knew all too well how easy it was to get turned around in the seemingly impenetrable forest. Although he had taken this path numerous times over the summer, he had managed to get lost once. It took him over two hours of meandering about the forest before finally breaking through and back into the Estates courtyard. He'd never forget his compass again. Luckily, he hadn't run into anything unpleasant.

After about fifteen minutes of making his way through a series of thick thorn bushes, wading through high grass that reached up to his shoulder, Hunter finally reached the small clearing he was looking for. It was about thirty feet in diameter, a sharp contrast from the darkness of the thick trees and shrubbery around it.

The clearing was covered in a bedding of sweet smelling blue and yellow flowers. At the center sat one lone tree towering over all others, an ancient oak. Hunter knew it was special. It towered above all the other trees. He'd never seen a tree with such beautiful coloring either, with its dark-brown bark that swelled with a faintly glowing blood red. Its leaves bright orange and yellow.

"Finally," Hunter slung off his dirty old backpack slumping down on a small moss-covered boulder within the comfort of the large tree's shade. This was the spot, the meeting place.

Hunter remembered the first time he ever set foot in the darkness of the forest. Back then, he was a scrawny little kid with a mischievous grin and bushy unkempt hair. A lot had happened since then, and there was only one similarity about the old Hunter and the one who sat on the mossy covered rock, his mischievous grin. Over the last few months, Hunter had thankfully experienced quite a growth spurt. He rapidly shot up a few inches taller and gained a dozen or so pounds. His uncle Joe was already teasing him about watching what he ate before he started getting the "Old Gut Buster" like he had.

Hunter didn't find that amusing.

After all, Hunter turned fourteen a few months back. His growth spurt allowed him to feel a little more comfortable in his own skin. He had spent his entire life shorter than ninety-nine percent of his classmates. A physical quality that he had always hated about himself and one that made him an easy target for schoolyard bullies. Even at the Estate he couldn't hide from them, no matter where he went there would always be mean spirited kids like the vile twins, Lunette and Corbin Krueger, who'd made his first year as a Seeker in training as painful as possible.

Sitting there in the sticky wetness of the humid summer air, Hunter was not thinking about how much taller he'd gotten over summer vacation. He felt the opposite, sitting on that small mossy boulder among the enormous forest trees; he couldn't help feeling minuscule....

"Hope you're out today," Hunter spoke to the forest. He dug around in his backpack pulling out a handful of granola bars. He unwrapped one and tossed it a few feet in front of him into the grassy clearing.

"Here yea go, boy. Are you hungry?"

Nothing, he was met with the silence of the forest, a few crickets chirped, and a bird flew by, its wings fluttering.

"C'mere big boy, I know you're out there!" Hunter yelled putting his two pinky fingers in his mouth whistling as loud as possible. It echoed throughout the forest.

"Bernie?" Hunter yelled again. "Berrrrrrnie!"

Hunter unwrapped another granola bar and took a bite. He waited patiently, whistling a few more times, until he heard a rummaging from the dense forest in front of him.

"Bernie?" yelled Hunter, "Is that you?"

From the shadows came a pair of reflective green eyes. They hovered about eight feet from the ground, peering directly towards Hunter's position, he recognized them immediately.

"Bernie!" He smiled at the welcome sight.

A large, hairy hand broke through a sizeable bush, clearing the way for the creature to walk through. Out stepped a towering, ape-like creature with a hulking frame. The creature, affectionately named Bernie, had hair that was a mixture of grey and dark brown. It cautiously made its way into the clearing where it found its first granola treat near the base of the large tree. Hunter knew immediately by the color of the hair that it was his friend, Bernie the Bigfoot.

"Hey, big guy, you haven't come out the last two weeks I've been here," Hunter tossed a second granola bar to the Bigfoot.

"Sorry, I know you wanted to see Alistair, but he's not back from summer vacation, yet. Hopefully he will be back soon."

Bernie picked up the second granola bar from the muddy earth devouring it in one giant bite. Bernie hummed a low friendly noise. He gradually moved closer to Hunter, reaching out with his long hairy finger to poke Hunter on the cheek. Bernie took a seat leaning against the thick tree trunk right across from where Hunter was sitting on the boulder.

"I got a lot more where that came from," Hunter pulled out a pen from his backpack, a few notebooks, a black rock about the size of his fist, and a couple of letters, before emptying the rest of the contents (a dozen or so granola bars) from his bag in front of Bernie's.

"Aroooo?" Bernie let out a friendly noise.

"Thought you'd want a special snack. I had to sneak into the pantry in the kitchen to snag those. I hope you enjoy them."

"Arooof!" Bernie grabbed a handful of the granola bars. Being the friendly Bigfoot he was, he even offered one to Hunter.

"I can't believe the first time I met you, I thought you were going to eat me," Hunter chuckled.

"Summers here at the Estate suck," Hunter spoke to his hairy friend. "I am so glad you came out to visit today. I was getting lonely. I can't really talk to my sister about things. She's too brainy...or bratty... depending on the day." Hunter laughed at his own joke.

"—it just sucks," Hunter went on. "Everyone leaves for the summer. They get to spend time with their families, away from all the craziness here. Alistair and Olivia both left months ago, leaving me and Elly by ourselves. It's not fair; we don't have a family to go away with anymore." Hunter let out a heavy sigh.

"Wish you understood what I was saying..." Hunter tossed a nearby rock into the forest, feeling a bit defeated. He picked up the heavy black rock he had pulled from his backpack earlier and stared at it, in deep thought. The rock wasn't any normal rock. It was the birthday gift his Uncle Joe had given him a few months back. Hunter had carried it with him everywhere he went. He knew how rare and special it was. It was the rarest mineral in the world. Most people didn't even know it existed. His Uncle called it Orichalcum, and explained that the present was meant as a metaphor. The rock was the hardest mineral in the world, unbreakable; a representation of their family...unbreakable.

Hunter took that to heart.

"Oh," Hunter unfolded the envelope he had taken out of his backpack. "I got an email from Remy. I printed it out." Hunter cleared his throat and read:

Hunter and Elly,

Hey guys! I was going to write you individually, but yesterday I found out that when we actually move to the island (where my dad's gonna be working) that I won't have access to mail outside of our community. Something to do with security, I guess. Sorta sucks, because I had already handwritten both letters, and it's too late at night to mail them out now...

Anyway, not sure why they're so serious about security... My dad says he's just going to be working on a construction site on the far end of a tropical island. We don't even know for sure where this island is! Weird, right? At least its tropical, maybe it'll be like Hawaii, always wanted to go there.

All I know is my dad said we are getting picked up by a helicopter super early tomorrow morning...

Never flown in one of those before, not that I am scared or anything. So yea...I guess I live out the rest of my high school years on some dingy island going to a private school...but wait, it gets worse... Earlier today my dad tried to cheer me up about making us move away from Belmonte, right? So he tells me not to worry, because there are a few kids who have already moved there.

Yea, so that turns out to be Lunette and Corbin. Can you believe that? Awesome, right?

I guess their dad is some big wig with Aten Corp. now...working as one of the Professor Aten's right-hand men.

Anyway, my dad would kill me if he knew I was writing you guys. I know he blames you two for what happened, and that I wasn't really able to say good-bye.

But, I wanted you guys to know you're both great friends, Alistair and Liv too...I mean, you guys saved my hide from that ghost thing.

And by the way, I still have terrible nightmares about that thing. It's like there's still a bit of it in my head. I hate going to sleep. I see really bad things.

Well, I got to wrap this up… not sure when the next time I am goingto be able to write is going to be. I already know I won't have Internet access on the island. I hope this isn't the last time we ever talk…

Anyway, here's to hoping they have real toilets! I don't think I am an outhouse kinda guy…

Take Care,

-Remy

"Rotten luck," said Hunter, "Living on an island with those two jerks? I think I would rather take my chances on a wooden raft in the ocean…or out here with all the crazy monsters."

Hunter spent the rest of the afternoon with his hairy friend talking about nothing terribly important. It was nice to be able to get things off his chest without someone trying to give him advice. Bernie was proving to be one of Hunter's best friends. It wasn't long before Hunter's mind wandered off. As he sat there with Bernie beneath the giant tree, he thought of Liv. He wondered how much fun she had had over the summer. He wondered if maybe…just maybe, she missed him as much as he missed her. He doubted it, but it was a nice thought.

CHAPTER 3
A SUMMER'S END

Under the guidance of Professor Calenstine, Elly started a dream journal to share during their weekly meetings. She had written in it every day since, and up until now had managed to keep it from her nosey, older brother. She thought she was in the clear; Hunter had left for the day, probably getting into some sort of trouble. She sat at their small dining table jotting down everything she remembered from her dream the night prior.

"That's not our Seekers journal," said Hunter, who barged into the bedroom tracking muddy shoe prints onto their freshly vacuumed floor. He was met with a whirlwind of excitement from Trayer, who was awoken from his slumber by Hunter's sudden appearance. His tail wagged a mile a minute, knocking over lamps and chairs galore.

"That's a good boy, calm down now, before you break something again," Hunter scratched Trayer's ear. Trayer was in a jealous fit, sniffing every inch of Hunter in a fury. He definitely smelled another animal on him.

"You were out in the forest again," Elly ignored the question about the journal. "You know it's not safe."

"No, I wasn't," Hunter dropped off his backpack near the foot of his messy bed.

"I can tell you're lying. Whenever you go out to see Bernie, Trayer smells him all over you."

"Well, so what? Quit dodging the question, is that some sort of *love* journal? Are you writing about how much you miss Alistair or Remy?"

"Sure," said Elly with half a smile. "Probably about as much as you write about how much you miss Liv."

"Pssssh," Hunter made a quizzical "yeah-right!" sort of face. "LikeI miss her," he said in defense.

"Right, that's why you were mumbling her name last night in your sleep," Elly laughed. She knew that would shut him up, or at the least get his attention off of her dream journal.

"What? That's not funny. Don't go telling people those lies," Hunter's face went flush. "That's how rumors start."

"Rumors?" asked Elly, loving every minute of the conversation, "Everyone knows how smitten you are with her."

"Hey," Hunter shot back. "She could be smitten with me too, ya know?"

"Sure," Elly replied, sarcastically.

The dispute was interrupted by a knock at the door. It was their Uncle Joe's signature knock, the same knock he did every time he came to visit.

"Shut up, Uncle Joe is here," Hunter gave Elly one of his "serious" looks.

"Hey guys," Uncle Joe opened the door, rolling his wheelchair into their room. Joe was in his mid-thirties, confined to a wheelchair due to an injury he acquired when saving the children's lives from the Beast of Bladenboro. He had dark black hair, and a thick beard that he had let grow since the injury.

Following behind him was Patricia Ellingbee, the main caretaker for Professor Calenstine and the Estate. Patricia was a full-bodied woman, nearing her sixties; she styled her dark-red hair beneath her trademark collection of witch-like hats. Today she wore a long pointy one, with a circular brim, that happened to be bright blue.

"Children," Patricia beamed. "I am assuming we're behaving ourselves?" Her eyes centered on a series of muddy shoe prints, knocked over lamps and tables. Her eyes came to a sudden halt at the guilty looking Trayer. Who promptly hid in the corner away from her disapproving gaze.

"What did you guys do to this place?" Uncle Joe shook his head. "It looks like a bomb went off."

34

"Sorry," Hunter rushed over to the lamp, placing it back from where it fell. "Trayer got really hyper when I came back from outside...." "What about these muddy shoe prints? I am pretty sure we had one of our caretakers come up and vacuum not even an hour ago? Heavens, children...this place is a pigsty!" Patricia huffed in frustration.

"Yeah, Hunter," Elly shot her brother one of her trademark dirty looks, "what about the muddy shoe prints?"

"Err..." Hunter didn't have an excuse. "Sorry 'bout that...I guess I forgot to wipe my feet."

"Before either of you are allowed to leave this room, the place needs to be completely cleaned. I'm talking dusted, swept –I want this carpet steam cleaned," Patricia began barking orders. "I swear children...will be the death of me!"

"Yes, ma'am," they both said in unison, their heads hung low. "This is precisely the reason we came up to speak to the both of you," Uncle Joe chimed in. He wasn't nearly as angry as his counterpart. "Your living quarters are getting a little cramped with Trayer."

"Well, he is a Cu 'Sith," explained Elly. "You guys knew how big he was going to get when you gave him to us."

"Yes, I did," said Patricia plainly. "Which is precisely why I tried to talk the Professor out of giving you the pup as a house warming present. Elly, Trayer has broken your bed alone on two different occasions."

"I told Margot that I didn't need a new frame. Just give me a mattress on the floor. I don't mind sharing with Trayer," Elly argued in defense of her beloved pet.

"The point is, children," Patricia spoke up, silencing the debate. "Trayer is far too large to be housed in the Estate."

"What do you mean?" asked Hunter with a giant frown on his face. "What she means is we've built a large pen in the courtyard for Trayer to stay in," replied Patricia. "It's large, it's roomy, there's even a small barn with plenty of straw to keep him warm. You will be able to visit him as much as you want. He'll have plenty of space to run around and get exercise. It's perfect for him."

"No!" Hunter argued flatly. "He's a part of our family. We want him here with us."

"Sorry, children, this is not an option," Patricia said bluntly. "That's not fair," Elly did her best to hold back the building tears. "Children, it's not like you're losing him. He will be right out back.

He's less than five minutes away from the main courtyard. It's not like we're banishing him into the forbidden forest. We love Trayer as much as you do."

"Obviously not," said Hunter.

"Well, guys, it's not all bad news," Uncle Joe added trying to lighten the mood. "I know the two of you don't love sharing these living quarters. Especially as you both grow older, you need separate rooms." "We're finally getting separate rooms?" Hunter's tone immediately changed.

"Sort of," added Patricia. "When the Enlightenment began, all the children in the estate were to be lodged in the dormitory on the fourth and fifth levels. However, last year they were being remodeled and weren't ready in time for the school year. You both have one week before you will be moving into your new dorms. Fourth floor is for the boys, fifth for the girls. It's another reason why Trayer can't go with you. No pets allowed."

"Dorms?" asked Hunter.

"Will we have roommates?" asked Elly.

"Yes, and you will find out who you room with the day you move in," answered Patricia.

"It'll be fun, back when I was a kid I roomed with Alistair's dad," said Joe. "It's how we were able to get into so much trouble together, right Patricia?"

Patricia ignored Uncle Joe's statement.

"There will be three people per room," said Patricia steering the conversation back to business. "Make sure you will be all packed up and ready to move by this Saturday. Furthermore, start prepping for Monday, classes start back up. Summer is over, and the second year of the Enlightenment begins."

"Finally,'" said Hunter "I am sick of being holed up in this place with no friends."

"I know this summer has been boring for you," Uncle Joe frowned. "I wish I wasn't tied to this damned wheelchair. We could have had some fun adventures…"

"It's not your fault. Everyone left us," explained Hunter.

"I promise you kids, one day soon I will beat these wheels," replied Uncle Joe.

"Children, I would suggest cleaning up this mess you call a room," Patricia interrupted. "Joe, please escort me back to the foyer?"

"Sure," said Joe. He waved his niece and nephew in for a hug. "You kids behave and listen to Ms. Ellingbee. Get this place clean, okay?"

"We promise," said Elly, embracing her Uncle in a big hug. "Okay…," said Hunter following suit.

"Come now, Joe," Patricia held the bedroom door open.

Uncle Joe nodded to his niece and nephew, rolling his way out of their bedroom.

"You should really watch the things you say to the children," said Patricia pushing Uncle Joe's wheelchair.

"Listen," Joe felt his hands clench tightly, "they're good kids who have gone through emotional hell. I get that their parents died almost two years ago, but they're nowhere near getting over that turmoil. So, if that means letting them get into a little trouble here and there with their friends…"

"I am not talking about the getting-into-trouble comment," Patricia cut Joe off sensing his defensive stance.

"Oh?" Joe tilted his head in confusion.

"Trust me, I know all too well about the amount of trouble the Jakob's bloodline gets into. I did have a hand in raising you," Patricia hid a smile.

"What're you talking about then?" asked Joe.

"You need to stop apologizing for your situation. You are in that wheelchair because you saved those kid's lives. You don't need to apologize to them for that. You should think of that chair as an extension of yourself, wear it like a badge of honor."

"Are you kidding me?" Joe shot back; he felt his blood pressure surging at the unwanted advice. "A badge of honor? That's a joke, right?"

"I'm serious, enough wallowing in your own despair. If you don't think the kids notice how miserable you are, you're delirious. If you don't think they blame themselves for your condition..., then you're as blind as you are delirious. Just because you've mastered faking a smile when you speak to them does not mean they think everything is fine."

"Patricia," Joe slammed on the brakes of his wheelchair causing her to crash into the back of it forcefully.

"You can bark orders to the kids as much as you want," Joe spun around so he could look Patricia in the eyes.

"I am not that thirteen-year-old kid anymore. You have no right to pretend to know what I am going through, or how I choose to deal with my life. Those kids are my responsibility now, so keep your *advice* to yourself!" Joe spun back around, wheeling away from a speechless Patricia. "—And don't follow me!"

Joe left her behind, speeding his way down the hallway. "He'll never grow up..." Patricia shook her head.

"You need to beat those demons..." she spoke softly to herself. "Before they beat you...."

CHAPTER 4
PLATO'S MASTERPIECE

The nerve of that woman," Joe mumbled to himself wheeling his way through the Estate's sublevel library on a mission. "Telling me how to feel…" he ground his teeth in anger. Joe passed by many busy people mulling about the library, their noses buried in books. Children of all ages were studying, or leisurely reading up on the seemingly millions of texts that the library housed, but Joe was so hell-bent on his destination that he hadn't even noticed he zoomed right by Margot Merrymen, who was sitting among a group of young children.

"Joe?" Margot whispered to him, trying to catch his attention. "Damn it…" Joe slowed his chair down to a halt when he recog- nized her soft voice. He took a deep breath readying himself for the conversation. Margot could read him like a book. "Calm down big guy…" he mumbled to himself before spinning his chair around to see the beautiful young Margot making her way towards him.

Margot had a bothered look on her face, her lips pursed, her eyebrows scrunched together. Even during his fit of rage, the site of Margot seemed to calm him, at least a little. She was easily the most beautiful woman he'd ever met. Youthful and full of spirit, she was the only one who could pull him out of his slumps of self-pity, which she had done numerous times over the course of the past year. She had fair skin and jet black shoulder-length hair, and wore a swooping, long, flower printed sundress and a grey, thinly knit cardigan.

"Joe?" Margot spoke softly so as not to upset the students studying in the library.

"Margot, I must have rolled passed without seeing you. I'm sorry,"

Joe forced a smile. "Didn't mean to be rude and not say hi."

"Well, you went by so fast..." she returned his smile with a genuine one. Margot knelt down beside him to whisper into his ear. "You were mumbling something, and if I were to guess by the scowl on your face, I'd think you're pretty upset."

"No, nothing like that," Joe avoided eye contact. "Didn't mean to worry you. I have an important meeting to attend, running late, you know?"

"Are you sure? I'm not too busy if you want to talk about anything," Margot eyed the petite sliver watch on her wrist.

"Aren't you with those students?" Joe pointed to a group of nosey kids who were trying to eavesdrop on their conversation. They noticed Uncle Joe point their way and quickly buried their noses back in their books.

"Yes, today's one of my summer tutor sessions. There are always a handful of students who can't leave for the summer. I tried to get Hunter and Elly to sign up, but neither one seemed interested,"

"Elly said no to a summer study group?" Even Joe was surprised at that.

"She has been a bit...distant lately. Anyway, my students are fine; they're catching up on some reading. Today we're learning about the Yggdrasil tree and its Norse legends."

"I see... that was always one of my sister's favorites." said Joe.

"But honestly, I'm fine."

"I can't imagine how much you miss her." Margot frowned. "Well, like I said, I have an important meeting." Joe changed the subject.

"...okay then," Margot's eye's sharpened, a look Joe had gotten used to, it meant she wasn't happy with the way the conversation was going.

"I wish I could have gone with you to tell the children about the dorm room. How did they take it?" Margot was not ready to allow Joe to get away from her.

"They seemed okay with it. More upset about Trayer moving out to the courtyard."

"Ms. Ellingbee wouldn't let me off tutor duty," explained Margot.

"She came with me. It probably would have gone smoother without her, though," said Joe. "She had on her bossy pants."

"Yes, she has been very stressed out. Ever since the whole Remy incident last school year, and the Beast of Bladenboro before that... everyone is walking on eggshells around here."

"Well, you can thank Aten Corp for all that. He's been in everyone's ear, trying to steal people over to his side. It seems to be working more than I think we'd care to admit."

"It is upsetting."

"We'll do our best to combat his lies," replied Joe.

"Well, I'm off in about an hour, would you want to grab some food?" asked Margot.

"I dunno," said Joe. He ran his fingers through his beard pondering over her invitation. Things have not been the same between he and Margot after the big blow up they'd had a few months back.

"What about Sebastian, I know he doesn't like it much when we "hang'" out...."

"Sebastian knows that we are family...well...sort of a family; we share the responsibility of raising Hunter and Elly. He knows that means we are sort of...together, in a weird way, right?" Margot stumbled over the explanation.

"Together, huh," Joe liked the sound of the two of them being described as together. "I know, you know that he and I don't get along very well."

"That doesn't matter," Margot smiled. "So, in an hour, we'll meet in the cafeteria."

"Yea, I suppose," Joe reluctantly agreed.

"Okay, well I'm sure the kids are growing impatient for me to get back to them."

"Sure," Joe nodded and spun away from Margot, leaving her to her duties.

Joe was on a mission. He needed to speak with Plato. For now, he would push aside his thoughts on meeting with Margot for lunch. He had more pressing affairs to work out. It was mid-afternoon which meant that the Belmonte's friendly automaton robot, Plato, could only be in one place, the Ocelot Room. Uncle Joe would have to sneak into the hidden passage on the north end of the Library. It wouldn't be too difficult to enter using the secret lever, as the north end of the Library is off-limits to the majority of the students, and it appeared to be empty in contrast to the populated southern section.

It didn't take Joe long to reach the hidden gargoyle statue and pull its secret lever, which in turn unlocked the concealed door that led down into the depths of the Belmonte Estate's sublevel system.

●　　　●　　　●

The Ocelot room was buzzing with a bunch of computer scientists monitoring glowing computer screens, typing away like mad men. The sound of their fingers hitting each key reminded Joe of his college years sitting in a library, rushing to finish a term paper, his peers doing the same.

The Ocelot room was a large circular chamber acting as the central hub for all things that networked into the Estate's mainframe. The round walls were a series of enormous high-definition monitors that linked up twenty-four-hour reports and useful information to help the tech team keep the Estate and its grounds running efficiently. In the middle of the tech-savvy room stood the giant android, Plato, keeping everything in working order. Every few minutes one of the technicians would approach him with a series of "computer jargon" infused questions that Plato would easily answer in his emotionless computerized voice.

Plato towered over everything in the room. He was a massive machine in both height and stature built with a large broad metal frame, short, stocky legs and long, heavy arms. His looked ancient, literally the only thing in the Estate that was older than Professor Calenstine himself. It was known to a few that Plato had been built over a millennium ago although the exact date was unknown; he was the only remaining artifact from the city of Atlantis.

Uncle Joe entered to the surprise of Plato. Unable to show emotion,

Plato hurried over to greet his friend expressing his surprise through the use of his humanoid digital emotional translator; an application Plato had created himself after hundreds of years studying the "human" condition. Its sole purpose was to enable him to translate facial expressions, tone of words, and emotional cues into proper verbal responses.

"Ecstatic surprise: Sir Joseph Kendrick, it is a pleasure," Plato's robotic voice droned out.

"Plato, you old bucket of bolts," Uncle Joe was always happy to see his old friend.

"Confused notation: I was not expecting your presence for another week. Is all well?"

"Yeah, um, hey…can we speak privately? There's so many of your computer geeks around us, and this is sorta private…" Uncle Joe whispered, obviously not low enough, because one of the technicians shot him a dirty look.

"General Announcement," Plato's voice shot up a few dozen decibels. "Please take a thirty-minute lunch break. Place all monitoring systems to auto facilitate. Return to the hive at exactly thirteen hundred hours. The cafeteria's luncheon special is beef stroganoff and garlic buttered noodles accompanied with assorted rolls. Please, enjoy." The busy bodied lab techs hurried and packed up their things, wasting no time in making their way out of the room.

"The hive?" Joe asked. He'd never heard of the Ocelot Room being referred to as such.

"Informative response: The hive is the codename for all interconnected nodes within the Ocelot's computer section. The Ocelot room's connecting kiosks and computer programs create the hive; a highway of information that centralizes through me," explained Plato.

"Okay, sure, so basically you run everything, and they help you monitor," Joe pulled his wheelchair up to one of the computer nodes. "Loading facial matrix response: Data suggests you are in a worrisome state? This in turn facilitates a query of concerns for your emotional well-being. Is all satisfactory?"

"No, not really. Remember our agreement?" Joe said bluntly,

"About the operation you're ironing the kinks out of."

"Yes, in exchange for the last remaining piece of orchilium I agreed to surgically operate on your defective appendages."

"Defective appendages..." Joe shook his head, laughing. "Last we spoke we were a few months out before you felt comfortable performing the task. Still working the kinks out of whatever your secret is."

"Inquisitive Retort: Correct, most current successfully ran algorithm ratio is sitting at 68.98723% of restoring complete mobility in comparison to potential death of subject. A 12% increase compared to last inquiry. Multiple algorithms have been processed and run since the 12% increase and have failed to result in positive responses. Current Operation must be placed on hold indefinitely. Potential to safely perform operation is questionable."

"What do you mean, questionable? You told me you hit almost a 70% success rate," Joe replied back.

"There is a 70% ratio between potential success and the demise of the patient. Ratio between life and death is too great," Plato explained. "You have a high probable rate of death."

"—Wait," Joe interjected. "Why can't you wait a few more days and run some more hypothetical algorithms. We will hold off until you can find a way to increase the ratio. We're not stopping now."

"All potential equations have run numerous times. Current technology and scientific knowledge on the subject are limited. Modern technology must catch up-to-date with the hypothesis."

"Then the 70% ratio is going to have to do. You're going to go through with the operation as soon as possible."

"Rejection: Putting your physical body in such a high potential for risk of fatality is not an option."

"Listen to me, Plato," Joe spoke in a whirlwind of frustration, "The docs gave me a 30% chance of living through their spinal surgery, and of course Dr. Wong staggers those numbers a bit. Now, either you perform the operation on me, or I go their way. Back when you approached me with this *groundbreaking* idea, you were all gung-ho for it. There is no going back now. You planted this seed. It's my only hope, and I trust you a million times more than any doctor alive in this world. I don't care how amazing they are. I want you to do this."

"Tepid Clarification: Subjecting your body to the operation could potentially alter your mortal nature. Without a more positive inquiry loop, multiple possibilities of unknown side effects only complicate the risk."

"What are you talking about? Alter my mortal nature?"

"Side effects of the surgery are unknown and could completely alter your body's physiology."

"We're talking about cutting me open and operating on my spine are we not? What sort of conditions would there be? I already can't walk. If we gamble and I die...then I die. It wasn't a risk I was willing to take four months ago but, I can't live like this anymore..."

"Instructive response: Surgery is not an accurate description for the operation."

"What?" Joe furrowed his brow. "If you're not proposing to operate on me, how do you expect to fix my damned spine?"

"Nano technology. Micro-biotic organisms infused within the patients' bloodstream."

"How would that fix me?" Joe shook his head.

"Theoretical response: Micro nano bots would live within the host's bloodstream acting as extremely powerful defense mechanisms. Nano bots attack disease, eliminate harmful cells, protect against viruses, strengthen the human body against any attacks, and repair any physical impairments. Tentatively, nano bots heal and systematically repair any bodily ailments. In current situations, nano cells flow through the bloodstream eliminating the physical inadequacies within a subject's spinal cord, repairing damaged tissue and bone," Plato answered. "Nano bots efficiently eradicate hazardous cells, eliminating cancer and tumors from ever forming."

"Nano cells?" Uncle Joe's mouth fell open in awe of Plato's explanation. He knew Plato had some new-found method of fixing his crippled spine, but he never dreamed of what he had come up with. "Correct," said Plato.

"Do you have these...nano bots already created? Are they

functional?" asked Joe.

"Affirmative, current nano bots contained within own physical frame," Plato responded.

"Plato...we're doing this. The children are not to know. No one is to know, do you understand?"

"Worrisome Retort: Are you certain? Potential side effects could be ghastly," replied Plato.

"I can't live a broken man...not any longer." Joe's eyes watered. "Listen, I trust you Plato. I want you to do it. The kids are going to be going on a field assignment sometime this year. That's when we do it. You can't tell anyone, not the Professor, not Margot...and definitely not Patricia. Promise me?"

"Affirmative: The value of our friendship supersedes my scientific probabilities. If you wish to proceed with the operation I will see to it," answered Plato.

"Thank you." Uncle Joe frowned. "Now. I gotta get ready to meet Margot for a late lunch."

CHAPTER 5
NEW FRIENDS

Hunter and Elly spent the remainder of the last week of summer packing up their things and readying for their transition into the new dorms. The feeling was bittersweet; both of the kids were excited to have separate rooms, but they also had to say goodbye to their beloved Cu'Sith, Trayer, since he would no longer be sleeping in their room. Even though they could see him anytime they wanted it seemed as if they were saying goodbye forever.

Patricia had come earlier that morning with a couple of the estate's caretakers to escort the furry canine to his new home. She was nice enough to allow Hunter and Elly to walk with them as they made their way through the Estate. It proved not to be an easy task. Trayer was such a large dog it made walking him anywhere that wasn't outside almost impossible. Hunter and Elly found themselves walking behind the group picking up everything Trayer knocked down with his wagging tail. A long trail of knocked over lamps, vases and plants were left in his wake. Let's not forget about the poor souls who walked past the group having the unfortunate probability of being struck by Trayer's very hard tail…he left his fair share of bruises.

Patricia and Joe weren't lying; Trayer would have ample space out in the courtyard. His fenced in pen was enormous, within it housed a small barn filled with straw, and even a bunch of extra-large dog toys for him to play with. There was plenty of space for him to run about and do his business. It was a small slice of doggy heaven, so said Patricia.

"Maybe this isn't so bad after all," Elly was impressed. "Beats him being tied up in our small room; he can run around all day and not knock anything over."

"Yea, look at him!" Hunter pointed to Trayer, who had been let off his leash by Patricia, and was now in a full sprint around the large open yard. "I was worried you guys wanted to banish him into the forest like Bernie."

"Heavens no, child," Patricia shook her head. "Trayer is *literally* the last specimen of his kind in the entire world. When his mum passed during birth, he was the only pup to survive. We need to keep a close eye on him. Make sure he is safe and happy."

They spent the rest of the afternoon with Trayer, helping him get comfortable with his new surroundings. It was a sad day when Hunter and Elly exited the pen and locked Trayer in, saying their goodbyes. Their beloved dog hung his head low and whimpered as they walked away from the locked gate.

"He looks so sad that we're leaving him." Elly frowned.

"He will be fine," Patricia ushered the children forward. "He may have some separation anxiety now, but he will adapt to his new home. It's not like you can't come visit him as much as you'd like. Just make sure you keep your grades up.

"—And Hunter, you know well enough that Bernie is a wild animal, not a pet. Stay away from him," Patricia ordered.

"I know," Hunter hid a small, mischievous smile.

It broke the children's hearts to leave their whimpering friend behind, but they had no choice. Patricia said it was for the best and deep down, they both new Trayer needed the space to roam and get his exercise. Being stuck in a small room was not healthy for an animal his size. They spent the rest of the afternoon taking care of some loose ends before moving into their brand-new rooms. Hunter tossed all of his belongings in large black trash bags with no method of sorting. Elly found this annoying, meticulously organizing everything into plastic compartments.

"Hurry up, I've been done for over an hour," Hunter yawned. He sat peering out the bedroom window where in the far distance he could see the large pen that housed Trayer.

"That's because you're disgusting and threw everything you had into trash bags."

"So what? It's getting unpacked in a few hours once we move up to the fourth and fifth floor."

"You mixed clean clothes with your dirty, stinky socks," said Elly in disgust.

"So...my dirty clothes don't smell that bad."

A friendly tapping came from the door interrupting their debate as it slowly creaked open.

"Children," Margot's voice chimed in.

"Margot!" Elly ran over to greet her with a big hug. "We haven't seen you in days."

"I know; I'm sorry, children. I've been so busy," Margot hugged Elly as hard as she could.

"Where's Uncle Joe?" asked Hunter with two large trash bags heaved over his shoulders.

"Sorry, he is tied up with a few things. But, have no worries, I will be helping you guys move. Looks like you're all packed?"

"Yea, I have been waiting for Elly to finish for hours," Hunter poked fun at his little sister.

"Well, then let's help her, so we can get everyone situated before dinner," Margot pointed to the middle of the living room where there was a mountain of sorted out clothes. "No rest for the weary."

•   •   •

Hunter and Margot went to the fifth floor first to help Elly unpack, despite Hunter's protest and whining.

"Why does she get dropped off first?" he argued.

"Hunter, you're always to act like a gentleman. A gentleman would offer to help the lady unpack," Margot spoke sternly.

"Elly isn't a lady. She is my sister. Plus, she has way too much stuff. It's not fair." Hunter argued.

"Too bad," Elly shot back with her tongue out. "You're supposed to be a gentleman, so deal with it."

"We'll make it quick, I know you're as excited to see your room as well," Margot opened the door into Elly's room.

"At least there's a television!" Hunter pointed with excitement. "Sorry, that's not a television per say," Margot chuckled. "It's a com link, sort of like a giant phone with a screen. It will also broadcast current Belmonte news and little tidbits you may need to know throughout the school year. Go ahead, touch it to turn it on," said Margot.

"Okay…" Hunter walked over to the flat monitor and pressed his finger against the screen. It lit up quickly and Hunter saw a video feed of himself looking into the TV.

"It's a two-way communicator. When you're not conferencing with anyone else it will show you the feed into your room, see the little camera on the top of the monitor? Don't worry, the camera only records during communication. See the word "call" on the right of the touch screen? Tap that to call someone."

Hunter followed the direction. He clicked the green word "call" and a touch pad of numbers popped up on the monitor, very similar to a cellphone screen.

"You can dial any room number in the dorms, the library, the cafeteria, even the infirmary from here. Basically, if you need to get a hold of someone in the Estate, this is how you would do it."

"Wow, that's so cool!" Elly had never seen anything like it before. "I'd prefer cable…" Hunter grumbled.

"No time for television shows, you two will be studying and readying yourself for the Enlightenment."

It took about an hour and a half for Margot and the children to unpack. Margot left Elly behind to get comfortable and wait for her roommates while she escorted Hunter down to the next floor down.

•   •   •

Hunter was excited to finally have a room away from his little sister, although he was a bit nervous about whom he'd be rooming with. He voiced his concern to Margot during the quick walk down to the fourth floor where his dorm would be located.

"What if I get stuck with some jerk?" asked Hunter waiting patiently for the elevator door to chime open.

"Who do you know in the Estate who is a jerk?" asked Margot. "Lunette and Corbin were total jerks."

"Well they're not here anymore; they left with their father for Aten Corp. So, unless there were other kids in the Enlightenment that were *jerks* you shouldn't have too much to worry about."

"Well, we didn't get to know all the kids in the class. It was a pretty big group," Hunter replied as the elevator door chimed opened. "There could still be some jerks though."

"Well, living in the dorm is a very important step in growing up," Margot held the elevator door open for Hunter. "This is going to be your first real taste of independence. You should be excited!"

"I guess I am..."

"Anyway, don't worry about any *jerks*, I doubt Ms. Ellingbee would room you with someone who would cause any trouble." Margot led Hunter down the long hallway and turned to the third door on the left-hand side.

"This is it?" asked Hunter.

"Sure is," Margot motioned with her finger to stay quiet. "Do you hear that? Sounds like someone has already moved in," Margot knocked, slowly opening the door.

"Good afternoon, boys," Margot smiled at two young boys sitting in the middle of the room with bags of clothes spread out in a heap of a mess.

"Alistair!" Hunter blurted out.

"Hunter? You're our third roomie? Awesome!" Alistair jumped up from the mess and gave Hunter an enthusiastic high five.

"I was hoping you'd be one of my roomies," said Hunter, who had never smiled so hard in his life. The loneliness of the summer was almost too much for him to bear. He hadn't fully realized how much he truly missed his friends until this very moment.

"Wow, you grew, like, three inches since school ended, nice!" Alistair took a second look at his friend with amazement.

"Everyone keeps telling me that," Hunter snickered. "I was so bored when everyone left; I guess I didn't have anything else to do but grow."

Even Margot chuckled at that response.

Alistair was a few inches shorter than Hunter, which was bizarre; a few months before he had been the taller of the two by about a half an inch. Other than a few slight changes, Alistair remained the same tech-savvy, energetic boy Hunter had become best friends with. Alistair had let his hair grow out over the summer, and now his long swooping blonde hair fell over the frame of his glasses causing him to continually brush them away from his eyes. Hunter thought it made Alistair look older, and smarter, not that Alistair needed to look anymore brainy. The kid was a technological prodigy. He never went anywhere without his brand-new laptop that he kept safe in a khaki colored messenger bag slung across his shoulder.

"What's in the bag?" asked Hunter.

"Oh," Alistair swung the bag around to the front. He unhooked the front flap and showed Hunter a silver laptop computer. "My mom bought me this as a gift for making it through the first year of the Enlightenment! It's amazing, has a twelve-hour battery life, and it connects to the internet anywhere." Alistair spoke with excitement.

"And who is your friend?" Margot interrupted the boy's reunion. A tall, muscular teen sat quietly in the middle of the room surround- ed by the half-opened luggage. He was a few years older than Hunter and Alistair. He was a handsome young man with dark, tan skin and jet-black, spiky hair. He stood up and waved with a friendly grin.

"My name's Tully," his voice was surprisingly deep.

"Hunter, meet Tully," Alistair introduced the two. "He's really cool. I have been unpacking with him for the last hour. He's in tenth grade!"

"You call this unpacking?" Margot barely stopped herself from laughing.

"How come I don't recognize you from year one?" asked Hunter.

"My cousin and I had to go with her parents on some field work. We got permission from Professor Calenstine."

"So you missed the entire first year?" Hunter seemed baffled.

"Well, my aunt and uncle taught us what they could. Ms. Ellingbee sent us packages every two weeks with stuff we had to catch up on. So, we learned a bit."

"Last year was crazy," Hunter replied.

"Yeah, sounds like I missed a lot. Alistair was telling me about Bernie, how cool is that?"

"Very cool," Alistair added.

"I have been taking good care of him while you've been gone," Hunter whispered to Alistair glancing at Margot.

"Thanks, I've been saving up lots of granola bars over the summer for him," he whispered back.

"What were you doing overseas? Capturing a werewolf or something?" asked Hunter.

"I wish. Nothing that cool!" Tully went back to going through his clothes. "We were looking for some sort of ancient stone. Our parents wouldn't tell us much."

"Not any stone," Alistair interrupted. He pulled out his laptop and began typing into a search engine and handed the laptop over to Hunter. The website showed a picture of a brilliant looking pearl stone. "They were looking for the fabled Cintamani stone!"

"Never heard of it," Hunter was not impressed. It looked like a piece of fancy jewelry his grandmother would've worn. "Why is it important?"

"Well," Tully spoke up, "they say that whoever holds the stone is granted wishes. It can heal the sick, purify water, and deliver gold and riches. At least, that's what my aunt and uncle told me. We had no luck though; they've been searching for it for years."

"I guess that *would* be pretty cool," replied Hunter. "I'd wish for super powers, or something awesome like that. Maybe super-human strength? Oh, invisibility!"

"I'd want to be the smartest person on Earth," Alistair interjected.

"I'd read minds," answered Tully. "Never fail a pop quiz," he laughed.

Immediately, Hunter thought Tully was the coolest kid in school. "Okay, boys, we can chat about fantasy wishes while we unpack. I think you guys need some help. This room is a mess," Margot began organizing the countless bags strewn across the floor.

It took a few hours to get the room set up, but surprisingly, Margot didn't have to deal with too much stalling or whining from the boys. They worked hard as they talked about what would be the coolest super power to wish for. They settled on the power of persuasion, which Margot thought was quite carefully thought out for boys their age, keeping her giggles to herself over how in depth the conversation was. Once the boys were unpacked they had a chance to step back and check the room out. It was nothing fancy, completely identical to Elly's room. They had the three-tiered bunk beds, a com-monitor, one small bathroom and a kitchen area. Despite its lack of size, the boys were excited to have their own space.

"Not too shabby," Tully jumped up to the third bunk. "Anybody mind if I call tops?"

"Go right ahead, I hate heights," replied Hunter, who took the bottom bunk.

"How's Liv?" Hunter peeked out from under Alistair's bed. "Dunno, I haven't seen her since we left the Estate. She went off with her mom on the West Coast for the summer. My parents took me on a road trip. It was awesome. We stayed at a bunch of different camp sites; saw some cool tourist's spots."

"What about you, Hunter? What did you do over the summer?" asked Tully from the top bunk.

"Nothin', I was stuck here all summer. It was boring."

"You didn't go back home or go on a vacation anywhere with your parents?"

"My parents died last year." Hunter said bluntly. "Oh...sorry...."

"His uncle Joe and Margot take care of him and his sister, Elly,"

Alistair answered trying to save the conversation from getting any more awkward.

"I'm really sorry. I didn't know," Tully frowned.

"It's fine," said Hunter. He sat up on his bed and watched as Margot waited for his sister to answer the com link. The screen made an annoying chirping noise every time it rang.

"Hello? Did we answer it?" Elly's smiling face popped up on the com link.

"Elly, did your roomies show up?" asked Margot. "Yeah, they're both here!" Elly sounded excited.

"Come visit us down here in the boys' room. It's number 412."
"Okay, we're coming," Elly clicked the com link.

"You excited to see my cousin?" Alistair whispered to Hunter with a sly smile.

"Maybe," Hunter turned a shade redder. "I wonder if she changed a lot?"

"Dunno, feels like it's been forever since we were all together."
"I'm excited to meet them," answered Tully, who jumped out of bed and grabbed a soccer ball from his bag. He began kicking it up in the air, bouncing it off his feet, knees, and head... "I feel so left out missing the first year. I don't know anyone here."

"That's where we come in," said Alistair.

"Yeah, we'll catch you up to speed." Hunter looked on as Tully effortlessly kept the ball from falling to the ground. "Wow...you're pretty good at soccer."

The boys chatted for about fifteen minutes before the knock at their door. Margot answered it; Elly entered the room followed by two girls. "Elly, Liv!" Alistair jumped off his bed and ran over to the girls pulling them both into a bear hug.

Hunter also smiled, but did his best to act cool. The second Liv walked into the room he turned red in the face, which didn't go unnoticed by Elly. Liv looked older, Hunter wondered if she would think the same of him. He hoped so; he didn't want to be the shy, young kid he was before the summer. Maybe she would even notice that he grew a few inches.

Liv was a thin, stylish girl with stunning, long blonde hair that fell softly to her shoulders. Hunter was surprised to see that she had one lengthy purple streak dyed into it. Her beautiful, dark-blue eyes hadn't changed; they were as easy as ever to get lost in. Seeing her walk into the room made Hunter feel doubtful she felt the same. She was so much more sophisticated than him. If she wasn't out of his league before...she was now. He felt completely intimidated by her presence.

Hunter swallowed hard, mustering up the courage to make his way over to the girls.

"Elly, Liv, this is our new roomie, Tully," Alistair introduced their friend to the group.

"It's actually Olivia," Liv corrected with a friendly smile. "Olivia?" Hunter asked a bit confused. He knew Liv hated being called by her full name.

"Liv is too childish. I prefer Olivia now," she corrected.

"What, I don't get a hug?" A shorter girl with dark tan skin poked her head into the room with a bright smile.

"Guys, meet Symphanie," Elly waved the energetic young lady into the room.

"Err, hi?" Alistair wasn't sure how to answer the question about the hug.

Symphanie was a bit older than Elly, fourteen to be exact. She admitted to being a bit of a diva, loved fashion, makeup, and the attention of boys. Symphanie had made the girls wait ten minutes so she could properly re-curl her stylish, black hair and touch up her makeup. "Don't I get a hug? Your glasses are cute," Symphanie smiled at Alistair with her arms spread wide open waiting for a hug. "Sort of going for that hipster, coffee-house look, right?"

"Um, sure…?" Alistair wasn't certain he was going for any sort of look. He reluctantly leaned forward and gave her an awkward hug.

"Sorry about my little cousin. I think she has a crush on you," Tully chuckled.

"Boys with blonde hair are my fave," Symphanie winked before walking towards Hunter.

"So, you're Elly's big brother? She was telling me all about you. Super excited to meet you," she extended her hand and formally shook Hunter's.

"Hopefully it was all good stuff?" Hunter joked.

"A little bit from column A, a little bit from column B," Symphanie laughed.

"So what's this about not being called Liv anymore?" asked Alistair.

"I don't like the name. My name is Olivia," she answered bluntly. "Oh, well okay then." Alistair didn't mean to offend Olivia with the question, but he felt he had.

"How was your summer?" Hunter asked, changing the subject. "Pretty boring," she replied.

Olivia the normally sweet, sincere, and outgoing person, seemed distant to Hunter and the group.

"Don't lie," Elly added with excitement. "Tell them about the necklace."

Sure enough, Olivia had a silver heart shaped necklace dangling from her neck.

"Oh, it's nothing," Olivia turned red.

"She met a boy named Marcus. His picture is in the locket. He's so cute!"

"Elly," Olivia couldn't help but smile.

"What? They asked. You shouldn't be shy about dating a cute guy like that!" said Elly.

"Yeah, he is cute," replied Symphanie.

"A boyfriend?" Hunter whispered to himself. He felt his stomach sink a bit. How could that be? He thought that, despite his nervousness, there was something between him and Olivia. He always doubted it, but deep down, he had thought there was.

"Yeah, he's in a band and everything. It sucks having to leave home and move back here. It's so far away from him. We spent every day together over the summer..."Olivia explained, holding the locket in her hand.

"Marcus, huh?" Alistair didn't seem too impressed with the guy.

"Yes, but I don't think you guys would like him," Olivia added. "Why not? He a jerk or something?" asked Hunter, trying to hide his jealousy.

"No, not at all, he's into music and stuff. Not into bizarre creatures and ghosts."

"What's that supposed to mean?" asked Alistair taken aback by her words.

"I mean, you know..." Olivia stammered. "He isn't into the stuff we are forced to do here."

"We're not forced," Alistair shot back.

"Children," Margot stepped in, sensing the tension in the room. "I am sure we're all happy that Olivia met a boy over the summer. But, school is starting up tomorrow, so let's get back to our rooms and settle in."

The girls were escorted out by Margot leaving the boys to mull over the awkward conversation.

"So, yeah, what was up with my cousin?" Alistair frowned.

"What do you mean?" asked Tully. "Seems like she's bummed that she'll be missing her boyfriend. I had to leave my girlfriend for a year when I went overseas...it sucked. We wound up breaking up because of the distance. It's not fun."

"She's totally different; acting like her boyfriend is cooler than us because he's into music? We're Seekers; it's what we do!" explained Alistair.

"I can't believe she has a boyfriend..." Hunter fell onto his bed, sulking.

"Why does that matter?" asked Tully. "Crushing on her?"

"Those two have been googly-eyeing each other since before last school year even started," Alistair explained.

"Isn't she way older than you?" asked Tully, "No offense, but she looks more like my age, sixteen or seventeen."

"No she's our age, a year older is all," sighed Hunter.

"Take it from me," Tully kicked the soccer ball over to Hunter and onto his bed, "they won't last. They probably won't see each other ever again. She's gonna be depressed for a while, but if she likes you at all, be patient, you'll have a chance."

"You think?" asked Hunter, who despite feeling weird discussing the matter with his friends, felt thankful for the advice. He placed the ball on the floor and trapped it beneath his foot.

"Never had a girlfriend before?" asked Tully. "Err...no..." Hunter put his head down.

"I have had a few, so no worries. Listen to me, okay? I will have your back," Tully signaled for Hunter to kick the ball back over.

"Sure...I guess...," said Hunter, not too sure how to take his offering.

"And you, my friend," Tully smiled at Alistair, "watch out for my little cousin; she crushes hard."

"What's that supposed to mean?" This time it was Alistair, who turned red.

"I have known Symphanie since she started kindergarten a few grades below me. She always has a crush. You're definitely the new one."

"Awesome," said Alistair digging his nose deeper into his laptop trying to avoid the conversation.

"Not your type?" Tully chuckled. "Umm...I don't know...."

"You never had a girlfriend either?" asked Tully. "No."

"Neither of you have ever even kissed a girl?" Tully was a bit shocked.

"Have you?" asked Hunter.

"Well, yeah, man. C'mon, you guys aren't ten or eleven anymore."

"Well, we have been sort of busy fighting crazy winged cats and wraiths," Alistair explained.

"I will give ya that," Tully patted Alistair on the back.

"Well, I think this is going to be a fun year," Tully smiled. "Hopefully it gets better," said Hunter laying his head down on his pillow.

"So...anyone else think that Margot is cute?" asked Tully.

CHAPTER 6
FIRST DAY OF ENLIGHTENING

Good morning, children!" Professor Pike beamed brightly in front of a dusty old chalkboard, eagerly waiting for the bell to sound off for the start of the new school year. Professor Pike wore her usual attire, a thick, grey, cable-knit sweater accompanied by a freshly pressed pair of black slacks. Her hair was done as it always was, tightly held up in a bun by her trusty number two pencils. The children learned quickly, during their first year, that Professor Pike was not the teacher to toy with. She ran her classroom like a business, anything other than professionalism and a hard work ethic would not be tolerated.

"Good morning," the class replied in a broken chatter.

"I hope we all had a safe summer. I also hope we kept our oath and spoke nothing of our *secret* lives to anyone outside of the Estate. Of course, if you did, you wouldn't be sitting here with us today."

Alvan, a freckle faced kid raised his hand. "Yes, Alvan?"

"What do you mean we wouldn't be here?"

"Yeah, how would you know if someone said something?" asked Alistair.

"Alistair, I didn't see your hand raised. You know the rules," Professor Pike shot him a disappointed look.

"Ugh...sorry..." Alistair had forgotten the main rule in Pike's room, never speak out of turn.

"To answer your question, Alvan, no one can keep a secret from the Grimoire. The book is all knowing. It would have already written you out of its pages, blacklisting you from finishing the Enlightenment."

"The Grimoire would know?" Hunter whispered over to Alistair while Professor Pike had her back turned, writing the day's activities on the chalkboard.

"Indeed, Hunter," The Professor snapped. "Did you forget your manners over the summer as well, Hunter?"

Hunter's face turned beat red.

"Yes, the Grimoire is all knowing. The minute you set foot back on the Estate the Grimoire accepts or denies you on the Enlightenment roster. Of course, only Calenstine is privy to such information. The Grimoire rarely shows itself to anyone else."

"Before I go any further, there are a few introductions that we need to address," Pike smiled at the two new students sitting at the head of the class. "For those of you wondering about our new friends, I would like to introduce to you the Galindos, cousins Tully and Symphanie."

The class chattered a few broken hellos.

"Tully, Symphanie, would you please stand up and say hello to your peers," Professor Pike waved the two up to the front of the class. "Uh…hey," Tully awkwardly made his way up and stood next to the Professor.

"Hi guys, I'm Symphanie!" Symphanie loved the attention.

"Tully, why don't you tell the class how you spent the first year of the Enlightenment?" Professor Pike asked.

"Well, Symphanie and I were basically stuck in a desert all year trying not to sweat to death. It was pretty boring…."

"Yeah," Symphanie added. "Our parents led an expedition overseas, but we were never allowed to know where exactly we went. It was hot though…" Symphanie added. "Lots of sand, I got an awesome tan."

"And your parents' home schooled you, correct?" Professor Pike added.

"Yeah, we had to sit in these hot tents to get away from the sand storms. It was terrible. Worst of all, there were no bathrooms. We had to go out in the sand super far from camp." Symphanie had a disgusted look on her face.

"I am sorry to hear that," Professor Pike seemed pleased. "But, that's exactly the type of living conditions we Seekers must get used to. At some point in your lives you will find yourself traveling to an exotic location where the comfort of modern society may not exist. It's a good lesson to learn. Now, despite the fact that your parents did their best to keep up with your studies, you will be a bit behind on your Enlightenment knowledge. I encourage your classmates to help you along the way as we begin our second year. You may take your seats."

"Yes, Ma'am" Tully nodded.

"As you will remember," Professor Pike went on, "last year I taught the Intro to Enlightenment class. This year we will be switching it up a bit. So class, I'd like to welcome you all to Field Work 101." Professor Pike grabbed a stack of thick papers labeled 'Class Itinerary' and began passing them out row by row. "This class is designed to prepare you for your annual fieldwork. Yes, you heard correctly," Professor Pike did not pause to respond to the sudden intrigued chatter among the students, and instead shot off one of her trademark evil glares…

"May I continue?" Pike said sternly. "Thank you, being a part of the Enlightenment includes actual fieldwork. All future members of the Seekers must conduct so many allocated hours in the field, and document their experience in their Seeker journals. So, class, what does this mean for you?"

Alistair raised his hand as high as he could, waving it back and forth.

"Alistair, I hope your summer went by without incident," Professor Pike nodded. "Glad to see you've returned to us safely after the mischief you and your friends got into last school year…."

Alistair frowned. He wasn't expecting the snarky comment.

"Cat got your tongue?" Pike asked. "Go on, don't be shy. Please, do answer. What does this introduction class mean for you?"

"Well…uh, we actually get to go out on cases, right?" Alistair's eager smile had crumbled into a nervous frown. He hadn't been in class for an hour yet and already he was getting lectured.

"Well, you would be correct," replied Professor Pike. "It's true; we can train you for years about all the knowledge in the world regarding mythical creatures and magical relics through our text books. However, nothing can beat actual experience learned in the field by your elders. Of course, you're just kids, so we will keep the fieldwork to acceptable tasks; noteworthy, yes, but not too dangerous.

"No need to worry about flying down to the jungles of South America or venturing through the hostile Gobi Desert seeking out the deadly Mongolian Death Worm. Although Symphanie, there's a good chance you may go somewhere that does not include modern plumbing," Pike chuckled. "We will be sending groups off at different times through the year. The goal will be to partner up a group of students with a couple of elders to ensure everyone spends their time out in the field." "Why can't we travel to South America?" Alistair interjected. "I would love to find a Mongolian Death worm! I watched an episode of Myth Hunters with Johnathon Gates where he found evidence they may exist! There was this track in the sand dunes and—"

"Alistair!" Professor Pike slammed her ruler against the desk. She immediately wrote his name on the chalkboard with a dreaded "check mark" next to it. "Do not speak without raising your hand. Interrupting me is a quick way to get detention. You've been warned, check one."

"Sorry…." Alistair sank into his chair.

"Ahem… as I was saying…" Professor Pike cleared her throat, "for the first year, you should expect to accompany the Seekers on a more trivial expedition. After all, your safety is our number one concern."

"Awesome, because trivial matters sound super fun!" Alistair whispered to Hunter.

Hunter hid his laughter within his sleeve; he didn't want the Professor's attention focusing on him. He preferred allowing Alistair to get into all the trouble. Plus, Hunter was okay with keeping the fieldwork to trivial matters. In the last two years he'd seen enough adventure. Dealing with cryptid monsters and evil spiritual beings were starting to take their toll. Perhaps a quiet and unadventurous school year was something he and his little sister needed. He could focus more on important things…like Olivia.

Olivia had sat in the back of the class, doodling in her notebook as the teacher carried on with the lecture, going over in detail prior second year expeditions. Hunter couldn't help but wonder what she was thinking…probably writing a love letter to "Marcus". Hunter didn't understand why, but he hated the guy. He'd never been so jealous in his life....

He kept telling himself that there was no reason to be upset. It wasn't like they were a couple, they were just close friends. He didn't even know if she liked him or not. Despite all the confusion, he still didn't understand why she had changed so much in three months. Purple hair, darker clothes, wanting to be called by her full name... He settled on the only reason he could grasp..."girls are weird" and tried putting the thought out of his mind.

"Hunter!" Professor Pike slammed her ruler down on his desk. Hunter jolted, almost falling out of his seat from the sudden THWACK of the ruler.

"Errr...umm...sorry Professor Pike..." Hunter was caught red handed.

"Stop daydreaming and answer the question."

"Um, could you repeat it?" asked Hunter. He could feel the blood rushing to his face, how embarrassing...

"Have you not been paying attention at all?" Pike shook her head in disproval. She walked over to the chalk board and scribbled Hunter's name beneath Alistair's. "Two check marks mean detention after school, so shape up, boys."

"Sorry," Hunter curled his lip in frustration.

"I asked you to come to the front of the class with your Seekers Journal. Just like your sister did a minute ago, if you were paying attention, you'd have known that."

"My journal?" Hunter felt the sweat beading on his forehead. He hated that thing, and specifically ignored it over the summer. Who assigns summer break homework, anyway? Hunter thought it was ridiculous.

"Yes, Hunter." Professor Pike said sharply. "The one you are to keep updated with everything Seeker related. Knowing of your adventures last year I am assuming yours is filled with important information you learned, much like your sister's was."

Hunter peered over to his sister who smiled back contently. He knew exactly what she was thinking, "I *told you to keep up with your journal, stupid."*

Professor Pike frowned and turned towards the chalk board. "I suppose I should begin writing that second check mark."

"No, I got it in here somewhere..." Hunter shuffled through his bag. He was sure he threw it in last night while getting ready for class. "Hey, you kept it up to date, right?" Tully whispered, noticing the fear in Hunter's face. "It's a pretty big deal. It's like half our grade..." "No, I hate the thing...pretty sure I'm getting detention." Hunter sighed.

Elly sat back with contempt, watching her brother struggle to find his journal. She wouldn't have been surprised if he'd left it in the dorm. She'd tried to tell him to keep it up to date, but he always replied with some snarky comment.

"Journals are for little girls. I am not keeping some lame diary," he'd say with a boyish smile.

Elly hated his excuses, always cracking some stupid joke. She knew if their parents were still alive there was no way he'd get out of not keeping up with his homework.

Despite Hunter's lack of interest with the Seekers Journal, Elly used it every day; she loved it. Sometimes she'd even use it to go into more detail about her nightmares than she did in her dream journal that she shared with Professor Calenstine. She wrote pages and pages of info on wraiths and the spiritual world after their run-in with Moloch. Professor Pike gave her an "A" for her thoroughness. Not that she was surprised.

Hunter finally found his Seekers Journal and, like a dead man walking, began his slow journey to the front of the classroom.

Elly felt a bit bad for him, but she knew it was his fault. He shouldn't slack off so much. These were not their normal studies, this was the Enlightenment. He should know how important it was, how much it would mean to their parents.

Hunter walked up to Professor Pike, handing over his journal. He hung his head low, staring at his feet, preparing for the mother of all lectures. Professor Pike quickly thumbed through the journal.

"This is it?" Professor Pike dropped the journal onto her desk with an echoing thud.

"Well...there was a lot going on. I mean...we were fighting a wraith..." Hunter argued.

"All the more reason for you to take notes! It helps you to prepare yourself for the next time you have a run-in with one. If you did your job as a Seeker you would have had all the info you needed. I am very disappointed, Hunter. You will never make it as a Seeker unless you start taking things seriously. Your parents would be disappointed. I taught them both, and they took their studies to heart."

The mention of Hunter's parents hit him hard. Initially he was sad to hear Professor Pike tell him his parents would be disappointed. That sadness quickly changed to anger.

Did she seriously just use his dead parents to scold him in front of class? Hunter's blood boiled, he wanted nothing more than to put that old hag in her place. He saved his friends life! He was a hero! He was not some stupid kid who deserved detention!

Professor Pike could see the anger in his face and a smile grew on hers, like she was welcoming the dispute.

"You seem upset?" The Professor's mouth pursed tightly. "Is there something you wish to say?"

"Yeah," Hunter blurted out. He was so mad his hands were shaking. But before he could say anything, the freckle faced student, Alvan, blurted something about his sister.

"Professor, something is wrong with Elly..." he said in a panic. Elly had suddenly grown pale. Her face was white, forehead dripping with beads of sweat. She could hear her classmates talking about her, but everything seemed muffled, like her head was underwater and they were screaming for her to come up for air. Her head started spinning, making it hard to concentrate on anything other than not falling out of her chair.

Elly felt the pain splintering through her head, almost making her sick to her stomach, and now her finger that wore Solomon's Seal suddenly burned like white hot coals, scorching her finger.

Elly stood up abruptly, holding on to the desk for leverage. She winced in pain, "Help me..." she mumbled.

"Elly, dear?" Professor Pike hurried over. "Darling, are you okay?

You look sick."

"Something…is…wrong." It hurt when she spoke. Every word seemed like it vibrated inside her head, rattling her brain. Elly couldn't focus; she lost her balance falling hard to her knees, then passed out on the cold classroom floor.

Elly was still conscious…or at least she thought she was. She tried to focus on Professor Pike's voice, but everything was blurry. A thick, blue fog seeped up from the floor, covering the entire room. Was she hallucinating? She had seen this before, the day she put on Solomon's ring… and more recently in her bizarre dreams. It was like she was slipping away from reality and into some foreign world covered in the blue mist.

Elly could faintly hear Professor Pike's voice asking her if she could stand, but it was now almost completely inaudible. Soon everything went completely mute. The classroom was completely engulfed with the blue haze. She felt weightless, like she was floating in the middle of a storm cloud, with faint outlines of the real world barely visible. Elly could still make out the blurry faint lines of her friends huddling around her, their bodies almost transparent. They looked like ghosts, shades of their former selves; it sent chills down Elly back. Whatever this place was, she did not like it.

She looked all over the room for anyone, anything that might give her some answers. There, in the distance, she could make out one lone figure. It was a dark hooded shadow, tall and thin. Was it Solomon? He had spoken to her once, aided her in capturing the evil Moloch.

"Elly…" the voice called her name, clear and vivid.

But, Elly couldn't reply. She was too weak to even move, floating aimlessly in this bizarre cloud-like mist.

"It's too soon," the voice echoed into her mind. "You are not strong enough yet. Bear through the nightmares, learn the secrets. You are still too attached to your physical being…soon…" the voice echoed through her mind.

Elly's surroundings suddenly went black. It was like someone had flipped a switch turning off all the ambient light, leaving her alone in complete darkness.

Elly found herself back in her classroom. Her head was still spinning, Professor Pike and Margot stood over her.

"Elly, you're awake!" Margot smiled. "Are you okay?" "My head...," Elly winced. "Did I pass out?"

"You were unconscious for a while there, dear," Professor Pike held a cold damp towel to her forehead. "We were about to stretcher you to the infirmary."

"Glad you came back to us," Margot squeezed her hand tightly.

"I don't need to go to the doctor. I'm okay." Elly tried to sit up but found it much harder than she expected.

"Okay? Honey, you passed out," Professor Pike replied. "Lie there and rest."

"No, I need to see Professor Calenstine...he needs to know..." Elly waved off the cold compress.

"Elly," Margot frowned. "We can speak with Calenstine as soon as we get you taken care of."

"Class, please, remain calm. Hunter, please help Margot escort your sister to the infirmary." Pike smiled, trying to ease the pain written all over Hunter's face. "She is going to be alright, no worries."

"Okay," Hunter replied. A million thoughts ran through his head. After the untimely death of their parents, anything sent him into worry mode. He'd almost lost his sister a few times since moving into the Estate. Seeing her unconscious was too much to bear. He had thought the worst, he thought she had died.

"I am going to grab a wheelchair; we'll wheel back into the Estate, okay?" Margot returned with a rickety old wheel chair.

"Okay..." Hunter said again.

"Just help me, nice and easy now." Margot and Hunter lifted Elly up onto the chair.

• • •

"Well, your vitals are strong," Dr. Wong scribbled notes on a large clipboard. Dr. Wong was no stranger to the children. She had been the amazing surgeon who saved Uncle Joe's life after the brutal attack by the Beast of Bladenboro. Normally, her talents found her in the operating room, but she had taken a liking to the Jakobs family. Dr. Wong insisted she be the one to check Elly out.

Dr. Wong was in her late thirties, extremely successful in her field, and dubbed a prodigy by her peers. She was an attractive woman, had a petite frame, and a beautiful smile. Today she wore her black hair pulled tightly back, in favor of makeup, her reading glasses sat at the tip of her nose.

"How's your head now?" Dr. Wong held up a small flashlight that shone brightly into Elly's eyes. "Still throbbing..." Elly winced.

"You were in class, felt dizzy and fainted. Any other symptoms?" asked Dr. Wong.

"No, the room got really hazy."

"Well, I can prescribe some meds to help with the headache. Your blood pressure is elevated, but after that sort of ordeal it's to be expected. I will want to keep a watch on it; we need to bring it down before we can let you go."

"She's okay then?" asked Hunter who sat nervously in the corner chair.

"Yes, she looks to be healthy, minus the headache and fainting. Hopefully, this is an isolated incident. However, if it continues, we will have to run some more tests, but everything seems to check out. Healthy as any ordinary 12-year-old girl I've ever met."

"Ordinary?" Hunter mumbled the words to himself. There wasn't much ordinary about him and his little sister. Even living at a place where a kid's parents moonlighted as monster hunters, teachers kept vampyres for pets, and the two of them still seemed like the least ordinary people in the entire estate.

"Elly?" Uncle Joe barged through the infirmary doors wheeling himself at the highest possible speed towards her bedside. "Uncle Joe," Elly smiled.

"I got here as fast as I could," Uncle Joe grabbed his nieces hand and held it tight.

"Yes, he wouldn't even wait for us," Patricia entered the room breathing heavily, trying to catch her breath. She was followed by the automatic wheelchair of Professor Calenstine.

"Your uncle was worried sick," Calenstine carefully maneuvered his chair through the door. "I dare say he won the race, even with my sophisticated, state-of-the-art chair, the power of his love was no match." Calenstine chuckled.

"I'm sorry," Uncle Joe didn't find the joke all that funny. His niece was in the infirmary after all. "I couldn't get here fast enough."

"Margot, what happened?" asked Joe. "Well, she got dizzy and fainted in class."

"She has a bit of a headache now. We will be giving her some pain relievers to get her comfortable," Dr. Wong smiled, brushing away the few stray strands of hair that fell onto her forehead. "Joe, you are looking healthy."

"Thanks, Margot keeps me in check pretty well," Joe smiled to Elly, half ignoring the doctor's comment. "These two keep me running around like crazy. My arms get a really good workout wheeling myself around all day."

"He does his exercises daily," Margot replied, not finding the humor in his remark.

"Well that's good, we need to strengthen that spine of yours," Dr. Wong added. "I haven't seen you recently for a checkup. Have we thought about the option for surgery?"

"Yep," said Joe purposely not making eye contact with the doctor.

"So...does that mean you'll let me operate?" "Nope," Joe said bluntly.

"Oh...?" Dr. Wong frowned, unsure how to take his blunt answers. "Joe," Patricia's voice sounded stern, "mind your manners. She is trying to help you."

"Sorry, I understand that. But, this is about Elly," Joe turned to Calenstine. "She's okay right? Weird that you came all the way to the infirmary when she didn't have any serious injuries... Is something going on that I don't know about?"

"Oh, heavens no," Calenstine wheeled up to the bed. He winked playfully at Elly. "Then again, when has anything *not* been going on in the Estate?" Calenstine chuckled.

"What's that supposed to mean?" Joe shook his head. He wasn't in the mood for riddles, even from the Professor. He wanted straight answers to ensure Elly was all right.

"That means that things are never what they seem," Calenstine held Elly's other hand, the one that provided a home to Solomon's Seal. It felt warm to his touch, just as he thought. "But I assure you my old friend," Calenstine offered a friendly nod to Joe. "Your niece is fine, no need for anything more than a few aspirin to rid her of the headache."

"Are...are you sure?" Margot interjected. "I saw her on the floor passed out. It was really scary." "It was creepy," Hunter added.

"Dr. Wong, we appreciate your expertise. However, you will not find anything wrong with Elly. Margot, often things we don't understand may seem scary and foreign to us, but Elly will be fine. I ask that you trust me. Joe, I would ask the same of you. If you wouldn't mind, I would like to speak with Hunter and Elly alone. Patricia could you escort the group out for me, please."

"Of course," said Patricia. "Let's wait out in the waiting room for them to finish up."

"Okay..." said Joe squeezing his niece's hand tightly before leaving. "Love you."

"Love you too," Elly smiled back.

The group made their way out of the room. Hunter joined Calenstine at her bedside.

"Hunter," Calenstine maneuvered his wheelchair over to him. "How much do you know about the changes going on with your sister?"

"What do you mean?" Hunter frowned. He wasn't sure where Calenstine was coming from.

"He doesn't know much," Elly spoke slowly trying to minimize the throbbing in her head. "Only about my nightmares."

"You see, when Elly put that ring on her finger her life was altered. More importantly her soul was opened up to a world you and I could only dream about."

"Another world?" Hunter looked at his little sister, confused. She still looked pale and sickly. Despite how much the two argued as siblings, it tore him up to see her in pain.

"Figuratively speaking, yes. Those nightmares are not nightmares. It's her soul separating from her physical body and entering into the 'hereafter' realm."

"What is that?"

"The hereafter is a world much like our own, but on a different level of consciousness. It's the layer of the universe that is home to our spirits, our souls. For obvious reasons, we know very little of it. Elly here, when she put the ring around her finger, was granted the ability to slip into what we call her ethereal form. She can detach her spirit, her soul, from her physical body. These nightmares and this little incident were her body and her soul separating."

"Her soul left her body?" Hunter's eyes widened.

"Sort of," Calenstine explained. "She is still learning how to manipulate her new powers. It sounds like she was not completely out of her body when she had this attack. The sensations and stimulation of both worlds on her senses were too much for her, she went into what I would call sensory overload. This caused her to pass out."

"Elly…" Hunter didn't know what to say. "Could she see our parents in the hereafter?"

"I am not sure…" Calenstine replied honestly. "Doubtful…."

"I don't like going there, Hunter. I never want to go to that place ever again."

"This is why I am telling your brother about the situation. We need someone in the know, so he can help you and not overreact. We also must keep this a secret. There are people who would find your talents very useful. I am afraid they would hound you for your powers. Is this understood?"

"Yes," they both nodded.

"Elly, I know you said you don't want to go back to that place. Unfortunately, you have no choice. It *will* happen again. However, much like riding a bike, you will get better at it. The first time you rode a bike, were you scared?"

"Yeah…I guess." "Did you fall?" "Yes."

"Did falling hurt?" asked Calenstine with a hint of a smile. "I had a cement burn on my knee."

"Think of this last experience like that cement burn. Next time you will know what to expect. Don't be afraid and don't fight the sensation. Hunter will keep you safe."

"How do I do that?"

"You will be her anchor," Calenstine answered. "You must continue to speak to her. It is very important. Elly, when you leave your physical body and become stronger at venturing into the other realm you must always try to keep your focus on Hunter's voice. Is that understood? He will guide you back to your body. Because we don't know how this experience works…we must remain safe. Never travel too far. I am afraid your soulless body could be in danger. You could get lost, or worse."

"It sounds so scary…." Elly frowned

"Remember though," Calenstine raised his finger into the air signaling he had something important to say. "King Solomon wore the ring. He was a mortal. He used it for good. It is safe when used prop-erly. We practice caution until we learn more. Understood?" "Yes, we do," replied Hunter.

"Now, let's get you out of this bed. The headache will go away soon enough. It's still early in the day, and you have your scholastic classes in about an hour."

"Oh man…" Hunter whined.

"Elly, you have my blessings to relax for the rest of the day. Hunter, you're responsible for bringing her back any missed assignments."

"Yes sir…," said Hunter.

CHAPTER 7
SCHOOL DAYS

The first month of classes went off without a hitch. Elly still had the nightmares, but nothing close to the episode she had during the first day of school. They were relatively tame, allowing her to keep up with her school work. She looked forward to her weekly visits with Professor Calenstine and sharing with him her dream journal and all the dark details. The conversations with him helped put her mind at ease, and she no longer feared falling asleep every night. For that,

Elly was thankful, but she got the feeling that Calenstine was a bit disappointed with the lack of progress in the subconscious dreams.

As the weeks went by, Hunter and Alistair became close friends with Tully. Being older and extremely athletic, Tully was their complete opposite. He was one of the "cool" kids, popular with everyone. Hunter swore Tully had the attention of all the girls in both school buildings. Wherever he went, girls stared. All it took was a simple hello, and the girls giggled and whispered to one another.

"Tully is so dreamy."

"I love his perfect dimples; do you think he'd go out with me?" Hunter and Alistair were quickly looking up to him.

"Do all girls fall in love with you when you say hi to them?" asked Alistair. The three of them passed by a small gathering of ninth grade girls outside of the Friedrich School of Higher learning, they whispered and pointed towards their group. Tully smiled at the girls, flashing his bright whites as the boys made their way down the steps and back towards the main Estate.

"What do you mean?" Tully played off the awkward question

pretending that he hadn't noticed all the girls swooning after him.

"He means all you have to do is smile and girls go crazy. They get all embarrassed and red in the face," Hunter laughed, more so in amazement than anything humor related.

"No way!" Tully deflected the statement. "Those girls were staring at you guys."

"Yeah, right!" said Hunter.

"What do you mean, yeah, right?" Tully was surprised by the exasperated tone of his friend.

"Girls don't like us like that," Hunter answered. "We're not popular like that."

"Are you kidding me?" Tully shook his head.

"He's right, girls don't like us, and we're totally not popular. We spent the majority of the first year being bullied," replied Alistair.

"Who's the bully," Tully stopped walking. "Want me to put these punks in their place?"

"No, they left last year. Their parents quit the Seekers to work with Aten corp."

"What? That's crazy!" Tully shook his head. "Idiots...." "Good riddance, I say," said Alistair.

"Listen, don't count yourselves out," Tully added. "You're more popular than you think."

"I think we'd know if people liked us," argued Hunter. "No, really," Tully answered back.

The group finally made it to the top of the small hill that overlooked their destination. At the heart of the Estate's courtyard sat the elegant botanical gardens. Olivia and Elly loved the flowers that blossomed year-round in the controlled environment. During the summer, the garden was completely open, allowing flora to flourish in their natural habitat. During the colder seasons the Estate constructs a giant bio dome. It was late in the summer and the garden was budding with elegant and mystical plants. Bright orange flowers that smelled of butterscotch, thorny pink vines that produced a venomous sap that paralyzes...the Botanical gardens could be a dangerous place if one did not heed the warning signs posted throughout the complex.

Although sticking to the main passageways was safe enough.

"You guys are sort of like heroes around here," Tully continued on. "The kids know all about the crazy things you guys have done. If anything, they're probably just a little shy around you."

"You think so?" asked Alistair. The group wasted no time walking down the passageway deep into the garden.

"Are you kidding me? You guys fought off the Beast of Bladenboro! I have had at least four kids tell me that story already. Not too many people know what happened at the end of last year though, other than that kid went missing and you guys found 'em. They know you guys did something crazy, though. People are still talking about it."

"Everyone looks at us like we're the crazy ones," said Hunter. The group made it to the back entrance of the garden to the spot where they always met up with the girls after school. There was a small clearing with a fountain in the middle of the paved passage.

"Well, I think they know you guys have been through a lot. Maybe it's a little strange for them, like...you know they don't want to say the wrong thing."

"Doubt it," said Hunter. "The majority of the kids in the Enlightenment believed Corbin and his sister when they started up those rumors about my parents being double agents...everyone hated Elly and I forever for it."

"Oh...no one told me that," Tully frowned.

"It's whatever," Hunter blew off the topic. "We proved them wrong, and no one seems to bring it up anymore. I guess it's gotten better."

"So, changing the subject...have you spoken with Olivia, yet?" Tully dropped his gym bag, unzipped it and took out his soccer ball kicking it over to Hunter, who caught it beneath his foot.

"About what?" Hunter tried to emulate Tully's soccer skills by bouncing the ball from his knee to his head in one fluid motion. He wasn't very good at it. "How do you do that?" Hunter completely missed the header, the ball bouncing away from him and back towards Tully.

"Practiced for years," Tully kicked the ball up into the air from the ground and caught it on the back of his neck, resting it between his head and his shoulder blades. "Before my dad moved me away from my high school, I was the only freshmen on the high school Varsity team. I wanted to play pro...."

"You're that good?" asked Alistair, poking his nose up from his laptop.

"Well, my coaches said I was pretty good," Tully made light of the subject. "But, once I found out what my dad really did...I mean, wow...hunting monsters? Seeking out magical relics? Kinda makes sports seem pointless. There is so much of the world we don't know about...started making me wonder. Ya know? Like what's really out there? How much stuff is hidden from us?"

"Yeah, it's so cool, huh?" Alistair smiled. "That's why I love Johnathon Gates' TV show, Myth Hunters."

"Anyway, we're off the Olivia subject," Tully spun the soccer ball on his index finger, showing off his athletic skills. "You know what I mean. Have you talked to her about her new boyfriend, that Marcus kid?"

"No," Hunter said bluntly. "What would I say? She hasn't said much to me at all since she came back. We used to be good friends, now it's like she tries to avoid me."

"Well, who knows? Maybe she thinks you're avoiding her because she has a boyfriend? My dad always tells me relationships are a two way street."

"I'm not though," Hunter replied feeling helpless over the situation. "Plus, we don't have a relationship."

"I dunno," Alistair added. "You don't say much to her anymore. She may think that you're the one avoiding her."

"Well..." Hunter wasn't sure how to respond. "I guess maybe. I don't really know how to talk to her anymore. I mean, I'm always so nervous around her."

"Hunter," Tully patted him on the shoulder, "girls are complicated man. Just be yourself and pretend like Marcus doesn't exist."

"That sounds easier said than done."

"Well, the other choice is to spend the rest of the next five years being awkward around her."

"Yeah…" Hunter took a seat on a park bench. "Quiet, here they come," Alistair pointed.

There she was…the object of Hunter's affection, the awe-inspiring Olivia. She stood in-between Elly and their new friend Symphanie. Olivia smiled brightly, discussing what Hunter could only presume was some juicy tidbit about her new boyfriend, Marcus. He felt jealousy bubble within him, but he knew it wasn't fair to be upset. He looked at Tully who nodded to him sympathetically. He swallowed the feeling down. "Be her friend…," he told himself.

"You got this, man," said Tully.

"Hey, ladies," Tully waved to the girls. He passed the soccer ball over to his little cousin who caught it easily beneath her right foot.

"We should play a friendly game, boys versus girls," Symphanie kicked the ball up into the air and headed it back to Tully, who caught it with his knee.

"Wow, you're pretty good too!" Alistair finally closed his laptop. "Must run in the family?"

"Yep, both our parents played together as kids. They taught us." "Symphanie played on the girls team in middle school, top scorer," said Tully with a proud smile.

"Hey, Olivia!" Hunter waived. He was surprised to see that Olivia looked shocked. Perhaps she did think he was treating her different than before. That bothered Hunter, he'd hoped it wasn't true…nothing could be further than the truth.

"Oh, hello," Olivia smiled back. "Were you guys waiting long? I had to stay after class and speak to Professor Wyndham about our essay on nocturnal cryptids."

"It's due next week," Elly added. She gave Hunter a glaring stare as a reminder.

"I know." Hunter rolled his eyes. "After getting in trouble with Professor Pike about my journal, I've been turning in all my assignments on time."

"Good," said Elly, "because now that we're not rooming together,

Ican't remind you constantly."

"I'm doing the Beast of Bladenboro," said Hunter. "Sort of an obvious choice I guess...."

"It stinks that no one can do the same cryptid," Elly whined, "I wanted to do the Beast too."

"There's loads of cryptids to choose from," Alistair slipped his laptop into his backpack carefully. "Lochness Monster, Agowago, the Adjule, werewolves, the shape-shifting Philippine Aswang, Thunderbirds...man, I could list dozens more."

"I decided on the Mothman," said Olivia.

"Mothman?" Hunter hadn't heard of the particular creature.

"Yea, there were a handful of books written about it and even a movie made about it. Half man half moth, giant wings. Seems interesting, except it hasn't been seen for years now...probably a hoax."

"Cool..." said Hunter trying to figure out what to say next. He was nervous with Olivia. Over thought everything...

"So what are we doing today? I'm all caught up on my homework," Tully checked his watch after the awkward silence. "We got all day to waste with our regular classes being canceled."

"Gotta love half days," Symphanie took a seat next to Alistair. "So Alistair, did you hear that the Estate is throwing us a dance this year? I'm excited."

"Err. They are?" Alistair blushed.

"You guys didn't hear?" asked Elly, shocked that the boys hadn't seen the flyers posted all over the dorms.

"No, who is running it?" Hunter assumed the majority of the flyers were posted throughout the girls floor. He hadn't seen anything down their hallway.

"The scholastic program, it will be held at the Friedrich Building of Higher Intelligence. The good news is that it's not just Enlightenment students, it's anybody. All grades too." Olivia answered. "The three of us signed on to help set it up."

"Guess what kind of dance it is?" asked Symphanie smiling as if she was holding some juicy tidbit of information that Alistair would be dying to know about.

"I dunno…the kind where people dance?" Alistair joked.

"Sadie Hawkins," Elly answered. "Where the girls ask the boys to the dance. It's going to be in October, near Halloween. We're going to mix the two themes up. Awesome, huh?"

"Yeah, really awesome." Alistair looked over to the guys mocking the girls excitement. "Just the way I want to spend my Saturday night, dancing to lame music."

"C'mon, it'll be fun," said Elly, ignoring his sarcasm.

"I already know who I'm going to ask," said Symphanie with a sly smile.

"Oh, yeah?" said Tully who was unable to hide his heartfelt chuckle. "I wonder who that could be?"

"You'll have to wait and see." Symphanie spoke in a sing-song tone.

Tully nudged Alistair's arm with his elbow. Alistair didn't find the humor. He felt weird.

"Anyway, the dance isn't for a few months. What about today?" asked Tully. "Summer is coming to an end. This could be one of the last few days where we can enjoy the nice weather."

"Hunter, we're supposed to wait here after class for Uncle Joe and Margot. Remember?" asked Elly. "They needed to tell us something."

"Yeah, hopefully it won't take too long."

"Our parents wanted us here, too," said Alistair, referring to his father Benjamin, and Olivia's dad, Abram Winters.

"Weird not having our parents back yet," Tully added. "They didn't come back with you?" asked Olivia.

"No, they had to stay at the site. We flew back to the states by ourselves. Professor Calenstine didn't want us missing two years of the Enlightenment."

"Oh, I assumed they came back with you," said Hunter.

"Nope, but with the dorms back up they said it was fine to come back."

"Wonder what our parents want to meet about?" asked Alistair.The kids waited a bit before any the parents showed up at the gardens. They killed time by listening to Tully's stories about playing soccer at his old high school and all about their summer vacations. Unfortunately, for Hunter, that meant listening to Olivia talk up her new boyfriend, Marcus, about how amazing and cute he is.

"I love his long dark hair," Elly added, "...so dreamy."

"He is very cute," said Symphanie with a half-smile. "I prefer blondes though."

"You never told us," Elly's eyes got big with excitement, "did you guys kiss?"

"You gotta be kidding me..." Hunter whispered to Tully in frustration. Of all the things Hunter did not want to hear about....

"Keep your cool, it is okay," replied Tully.

Olivia didn't answer; instead she blushed timidly with a sly smile slowly spreading across her face. As much as she wanted to hide it, she could not.

"Of course, they have," Symphanie laughed. "They spent every day together over the summer; they were probably making out for half of that."

"Tell us the details," Elly sqealed. She grabbed and shook both of Olivia's hands excitedly. "Did he kiss you first? Did you make the move? Was it romantic, like in the movies?"

"Err...guys..." Alistair tried to warn the girls.

"Quiet, Alistair," Elly shot back, "I want to hear all the details!"

"No, seriously, turn around..." Tully pointed behind Olivia and Elly.

Two grown men stood a few feet away from the gossiping girls. Olivia did not have to turn around to realize it was her father Abram Winters who stood behind her. She could feel his fatherly gaze burning a hole into the back of her head.

"Hello, kids..." Abram Winters nodded to the group with a serious look. He did not look happy.

Abram was in his early forties and built thick, like an ox. He was average in height with dark sun-tanned skin. His thick black hair waspulled back neatly into a pony tail with just a hint of grey at his roots. Abram was an intimidating man, with muscles that bulged through his tight black shirt.

He stood alongside Alistair's father Benjamin Jenson, who, from an appearance standard, looked like Abram's polar opposite. Ben was taller than Abram but a little lanky in size. His soft, sandy-brown hair was styled neatly, as always. Ben's most dominant feature was his jovial smile that seemed to lighten the mood, no matter the occasion.

"Jeez, Abram," Ben chuckled. "You can't even say hello to the kids without scaring them to death."

"What are you talking about?" Abram shook his head in frustration. He had no intention to intimidate the kids, but he was extremely disappointed with the topic of conversation he had overheard. Abram was not the type of man who forced a smile on his face.

"It's okay, guys! Don't let the stern look on Abe's face worry you. It's hard to tell, but he's actually smiling right now!" Ben managed to get a few chuckles from the kids. Not Olivia, though. She stood with her head hung low, trying to swallow her embarrassment.

"Funny," Abram added. "Real funny."

"Still waiting for Joe and Margot?" Ben asked peering around the garden for the others.

"They're coming up now," said Tully pointing behind the adults. "Olivia, how was class?" asked Abram. Olivia purposely averted her eyes.

"Fine," she answered.

"That's it? Just fine?" Abram cocked his head curiously. He was not very keen with her limited response.

"Yes, just fine," Olivia pursed her lips. Everyone could feel the tension between the two, it was unsettling.

"Okay, umm…hey, look!" Ben attempted to break the tension by waving to his best friend Joe who was now merely a few yards away. "Sorry guys," Margot smiled at the group. "Hope you weren't wait-ing long."

"We just got here ourselves," replied Ben.

"We will talk more about your attitude later," Abram whispered to Olivia while the other adults greeted one another.

Olivia's embarrassment quickly subsided. Now she was flushed with anger.

Hunter was completely shocked at the interaction between the two. He knew that Olivia had some issues with her dad, but he hadn't realized how bad it had gotten over the summer. What had happened that strained their relationship so badly? Maybe her dad hated Marcus as much as he did. Hunter relished that thought at first, but it was obviously causing Olivia pain, and that just wasn't cool. He felt bad for her, wishing there was something he could say or do to take the anger away from her.

"What's up, guys? What's with all the long faces?" Joe rolled up with his wheelchair.

"Everything is fine, isn't that right kids?" said Abram in a gruff voice that was more of a statement than a question. "Yeah, sure," Olivia mumbled.

"Okay..." said Uncle Joe. It was evident to him that he was missing something but he chose not to press the matter any further. "Well, we wanted to gather the group for a big announcement."

"It's exciting news!" Margot chimed in, trying to add some enthusiasm to the morose looking group.

"I know I am super stoked," said Ben with a wide smile.

"So, what's the news?" asked Tully. "You've got our attention."

"Well, you learned a few weeks ago about the second-year field work assignment, right?"

"Yeah!" Alistair's excitement was paramount. He stood up from the bench in anticipation. "We're going somewhere awesome, right? The Himalayas? Loch Ness? How cool would it be to be the first people to find real evidence of Nessie?"

"Well, we're glad you're so enthused," Margot was taken aback by Alistair's positive energy. "But before we discuss where the mission is located, we need to discuss who is going. Traditionally, you follow your guardians and their team on an excursion. However, with Joe unable to travel in his current condition, my duties here at the Estate, and Tully and Symphanie's parents still overseas, we have come up with a plan that Professor Calenstine has approved."

"Basically, we get to take the entire lot of you with us!" Ben gave his son an exhuberant high five.

"The six of you will be traveling with Ben and me on our next investigation," Abram said.

"How awesome is *that*?" Alistair turned to face Tully and Hunter. "I thought for sure we'd be broken up."

"Sucks you can't go with us, Uncle Joe," said Elly. "I wanted to do the fieldwork with you."

"I know guys." Joe said bitterly. "I can't really rummage around a forest or hike up mountains stuck in this wheelchair. There is nowhere else I'd rather be than heading out with the two of you into the field." "It's okay, Uncle Joe," said Hunter, "at least we'll be with our friends."

"So where are we going?" asked Alistair.

"Well, sorry to disappoint you, bud," answered Ben. "But, the Himiofferlayas are out of the question."

"So is Lock Ness..." Abram added. "Awww, man...!" Alistair frowned.

"How's Mid-Michigan sound?" said Ben with a hearty chuckle. "Seriously?" Alistair sounded defeated.

"What kind of cool stuff ever happens in Michigan?" Hunter was not impressed with the option.

"Well, the last two months there have been a series of strange sightings. Locals are seeing a tall slender figure out in the rural areas that they claim has long horns coming out from its oddly shaped head, and it can walk up right or run on all fours like a deer. Pretty freaky sounding, huh? Not to mention, lots of the local livestock is disappearing, or being found mutilated."

"Seriously?" asked Elly. "That sounds gross." "Sounds sorta scary," replied Symphanie."Yeah, I thought we were supposed to go on a safe trip?" asked Elly.

"Well, none of this is proven," Abram added. "Ninety percent of the cases we go on end up being debunked. People's imaginations tend to run wild. It's probably a rogue wolf or fox that's attacking livestock, or some other local predatory animal. Due to the lack of evidence, we're pretty sure it will be a run of the mill case. But, because of the popularity of the sightings and the closeness of the case, it's a perfect fit."

"So, what do they think it is?" asked Tully.

"Locals are claiming it's a Wendigo," replied Uncle Joe.

"A Wendigo?" Alistair flipped open his laptop and began searching information on the monster. "Never heard of that one before...." "Well, we won't spoil it for you," Margot added. She was impressed with Alistair's excitement. "I am sure you can find a world of info in our library on the creature, more so than what the internet has to offer." "Yeah, you're probably right," Alistair replied back typing in a frenzy. "But this is a bit quicker, we can weed out what is probably false info, at least get an idea." "Well then," Margot chuckled.

"So when are we going?" asked Olivia, purposely posing the question to Alistair's dad in favor of her own.

"Soon, we don't have an exact date yet, still waiting for Calenstine to approve the case. Soon as we know, we'll set the dates up with you kids. Until then, focus on your studies and keep your journals up," Ben answered eyeing his watch.

"It's getting late, isn't it?" Abram nodded.

"Yeah, we need to get back," Ben leaned in to give his son a hug. "Oh, man. This is so exciting!" Tully was peering over Alistair's shoulder checking out the mass of images that came to life after searching the term "Wendigo". "There's a bunch of different looking ones." "Don't believe everything on the internet," said Joe. "Margot is right; you will have better luck researching in the library. But remember, this case hasn't been approved, yet."

"Right, right," said Alistair, only half paying attention. He continued to click on link after link of different artists renditions of what a Wendigo may look like.

"Well I think they will be occupied for the rest of the afternoon," said Joe, spinning his chair around to face the other adults.

"We need to get back to work; Calenstine will be waiting for us." Abram looked over to his daughter who purposely had her back turned away from him, talking with her friends.

"Say goodbye and let's head out?" asked Ben.

"No," said Abram bluntly. "She's fine, let's go." Abram turned away from the chattering kids and made his way back to the estate. "Do you know what's going on with them?" Margot whispered to Joe.

"I have an idea," answered Joe. "But it's none of our business."

CHAPTER 8
SEBASTIAN BELL

"Darling, where were you?" Sebastian eyed his watch, keeping a close eye on the time. She was late, again. This time he was livid, he had spent the last fifteen minutes pacing between the living room and the kitchen waiting for his fiancé, Margot, to make it home. "What are you talking about?" Margot had just walked into their fifth level apartment and set her purse down on the counter. She looked exhausted, dark bags had formed under her eyes, her hair was a mess, and her regular cool demeanor seemed tense and distant.

"We were supposed to meet for lunch. I waited at the blasted cafeteria for over an hour." Sebastian's face was a mixture of fear and anger. "I was worried! I thought something had happened."

"I'm sorry, honey," Margot pulled her hair back tightly and tied it off into a ponytail. It had been a long day and all she wanted to do was relax; light some candles, maybe draw a bath…anything other than fighting with Sebastian. Margot approached him and affectionately placed her hand on Sebastian's shoulder. She kissed him softly on the forehead. "What a day! The Professor has Patricia running around like a mad woman, so of course, that means I am too."

"Even so," Sebastian pulled away her. "You couldn't even call me? Where's your head at?"

"I said I was sorry." Margot frowned, taken aback by the sudden outburst. Unfortunately, this was not an isolated incident. The last few months had been a strain for the couple, mainly due to Sebastian's quick temper. He seemed to get aggravated over every little thing she did, or didn't do.

"You know how demanding the school year is for Patricia and I, what's the big deal?"

"It's called respect," Sebastian shot back. "I am your fiancé; I think I deserve to know why I was stood up, again!"

"What do you mean, again?" Margot shook her head in frustration. Every week it was something, a forgotten phone call, a late night at work, lunch with Joe... She was beyond sick of the attitude, the constant belittling.

"Oh please," Sebastian threw up his arms in protest. "How soon you forget? Two weeks ago you ditched our dinner plans for Joe and the kids."

"Oh great, here we go again." Margot felt the stress rise in her body. A sharp pain shot between her eyes.

"What's that supposed to mean?" Sebastian slammed his fist down on the kitchen countertop with a loud thud.

"Real mature!" Margot jumped from the sudden noise. "I'm tired of this, you're acting crazy. You don't need to know where I am every second of every day. I have my duties to do, and that takes precedence over anything else."

"Oh, so your little errands for Patricia mean more than our engagement?" Sebastian took a deep breath trying to calm down. He immediately regretted losing his temper and slamming his fists.

"My career has always been important; you knew that going into this relationship." Margot shot back, now the angered one.

"Look, it's just..." Sebastian swallowed hard. "I'm worried about your safety," he spoke softer. It was easy for him to confuse anger with fear. He knew of the threats on Margot's life due to his previous actions. He was forbidden to tell her of the dangers. She assumed he was constantly in a jealous rage, which he knew deep down had hints of truth to it. Life hadn't been the same since Joe and the kids became part of their lives. It was something he was willing to work through. But it wasn't all jealousy; there was a real danger at play as well.

"What are you talking about? You're just deflecting," Margot grabbed her purse. "There is nothing dangerous in the Estate, it's not like I'm out hunting with the Seekers."

"It's not that." Sebastian's normally calm grey eyes watered.

"Then what?" Margot stopped shy of their apartment door. "Nothing…" Sebastian wanted so bad to come clean. "I can't say…."

"Yeah, right," Margot shook her head. She was sick of the games. "Enjoy the apartment, I am going to Patricia's and getting my own room. I'll pack up my stuff this weekend."

"Wait, what?" Sebastian suddenly felt his world collapse around him.

"We need space, this relationship is a mess. Every other day we are at each other's throats." Margot turned her back to Sebastian and gripped the doorknob. She hid her swollen tearful eyes from his.

"Please, don't…" Sebastian ran over to his fiancé and pulled her close, forcing her eyes to look into his. "I know you can't understand where I am coming from. Darling, it is rooted in love, I promise you. It's not what you think. Please, don't leave."

"No," Margot sobbed. Her feelings came crashing through her emotional walls. "If we continue to keep doing the same things…" Margot choked on her words, forcing them through her tears proved harder than she imagined. Thinking the words and saying them were completely different. "If we keep doing this, we're done…for good."

"But-" Sebastian was cut short.

"I'm leaving, and I *am* moving out. We need to re-evaluate our relationship." Margot spun the door handle making her swift exit and leaving Sebastian alone in their former room.

"What did I do?" he muttered to himself. Sebastian felt hopeless. He wanted to chase after her, but what good would that do? He was forbidden to tell her the truth. He couldn't come clean about his past or it would jeopardize his future at the Estate, even if she forgave him, Calenstine would cast him out.

So what now? Should he just sit there alone and sulk?

Sebastian wandered into the bathroom, drowning himself in a whirlwind of emotions. He ran the water from the faucet, cupping the cold liquid in his palms. He splashed his face, allowing the cold water to wash away the salty tears that stained his cheeks. Crying would do nothing, only proving to himself how weak he had become. He'd taken responsibility for his actions, now he needed to take back control.

"I did it all for us," Sebastian spoke to his mirrored reflection, there he found a stranger staring back. Who was this man staring back at him? This weak, sad excuse for a man...

He even changed physically, allowing the turmoil in his life to eat away at him like a cancer. His normally stylish, blonde hair was a disheveled mess, his smooth baby face had been taken over with days of stubble, and his eyes were sad and heavy, thickened with heavy bags beneath them.

He clenched his fist, pursing his mouth in frustration, "How pathetic."

He yelled as loud as he possibly could, screaming at the mirror like a madman. He hammered his right fist repeatedly against the solid glass mirror. The first hit struck the middle of the mirror, causing a spider-web of cracks splintering across the face The second and third hits brought the mirror to the floor throwing hundreds of sharp, jagged fragments out in a crash.

Sebastian grabbed his throbbing fist, his eyes wide and maddened. A piercing hot pain shot through his hand, blood spewing from the open wounds mixing with the broken shards beneath him.

"Dammit...!" Sebastian fell back exhausted onto the bathroom floor. He gripped his bloody hand tightly out in front of him and stared at the mayhem, his mangled hand, the broken mirror mixed in the thick pool of his own blood, surrounded in chaos.

"Idiot!" Sebastian fought back the tears. He was losing it, or had he already lost it? He'd never felt so lost in his life, so confused.

Suddenly his phone rang from in the kitchen. Was it Margot?

"Oh, god..." Sebastian moaned in pain. He would need to clean up the bathroom before she came back. Embarrassing, how would Margot react to him losing a fight to a mirror?

The phone continued to ring.

It had to be Margot...who else would be calling?

Sebastian wrapped up his bloody hand with a towel, careful to not leave a trail of blood across their apartment floor. Foolish, where had his faith gone? He should have known she would come back. People argue...it happens.

Sebastian eagerly picked up the phone expecting to hear her voice at the other end.

"Hello?" Sebastian answered the phone somberly.

"Sebastian, old friend." It was not Margot's soft feminine voice. Instead, it was a voice void of human characteristics, robotic in nature, masked using a machine to disguise the caller's true voice.

"Who is this?" Sebastian's heart sunk to the pit of his stomach.

"Tsk, tsk," mocked the voice. "Seems like ever since you left the Order of Shadows, your meaningless little life has been crashing down around you. Sad really. Professor Aten always thought you had promise. We had big things in line for you."

"Who is this, damn it? What do you want from me?"

"We want nothing from you," the voice answered. "Only to remind you that traitors suffer pain worse than death. Even if the one you love, her name is Margot, correct? Even if she leaves you, we know how to make you suffer. Your hands will be stained with her blood. She may break your heart, but we will stop hers from ever beating again. If I was you, I would have chased her down...it might be the last time you ever see her."

"How did you know that? How did you know she just left?"

"We know all, you fool. You should know that, you were one of us. How soon one forgets how far our eyes and ears reach... We're everywhere, just waiting for the perfect time to strike, hiding away never to be seen, we are the shadows, the darkness where you cannot see."

The phone clicked off and there was silence once again. "Jesus..." Sebastian looked around the room in fear.

How did they know? Was the room bugged? Were they compromised by the Shadows? Sebastian looked around for anything that seemed out of place. He checked the walls and ceilings for anything out of the ordinary, even perhaps a pin sized hole hiding a camera. Or maybe a microphone hidden in a picture frame was where they had hidden a mic. He ran rampant through the apartment looking for anything. By the time he was done, he had torn every room apart. Ripped up every picture frame, tore off every cushion from the couches and pillows in their bedroom... How did they know?

He found nothing, the room was clean. He had to have missed it. "Wait a minute!" Sebastian realized it may not be the room. He began patting down his shirt and pants...nothing. He kicked off his shoes and took them off, feeling down each one's seems. He knew the mics could be extremely small. Again nothing...

Feeling defeated he fell onto the floor, his hand throbbing in pain. He needed medical assistance, he was sure he required stitches. He couldn't worry about that, he needed to warn Calenstine...things were escalating. He had to warn Margot before it was too late. Sebastian reached over with his good hand and grabbed his Italian leather, dress shoes he had been wearing. He noticed a strange slit in the bottom of the inside heel. Sebastian stuck his finger into the small incision and felt something hard, small and plastic like.

"Rat bastards!" Sebastian swore as he pulled a mic from the sole of his shoe.

CHAPTER 9
AN UNHEARD PLEA

Sebastian could not wait to speak with Professor Calenstine. Time was of the essence, and his fiancé's life hung in the balance. The threat was all too real, he needed help, fast. Sebastian knew he couldn't be too careful, so he stripped out of his clothes, grabbing a fresh pair of shorts and a tee shirt. Before putting them on, he inspected them closely for any type of bug or microphone, feeling up and down every inch, inspecting every seam for anything out of the ordinary.

He still didn't feel safe. Maybe he was being paranoid, but for a good reason. He didn't want to give the Order of Shadows any more info.

An idea slowly formed and he darted towards the bathroom, side stepping all the broken glass. He turned the bathtub knobs, filling up the tub with warm water. Wearing the clothes, he submerged his entire body underwater, carefully keeping his bandage dry. If he missed any bugs in his clothes, he hoped drowning them in water would short circuit any mics. He opted to go barefoot, the less he wore, the less chance of anything getting by him.

It was late in the evening and he had no idea where Calenstine would be. He only had one choice; he had to speak with Patricia.

•　　•　　•

Patricia endured a long hard day at the Estate; running the business end of things was a monumental task, especially with Professor Calenstine out on a business trip. This meant extra-long days at the office, larges piles of paperwork, and a countless number of mishaps she was in charge of correcting. If only there was two of her to divvy up her duties. Between the second year of the Enlightenment, the scholastic board meetings, and all this nonsense with Aten Corp threatening the Estate…she felt ready to tear out her hair in frustration. Calenstine couldn't get back soon enough.

Despite the stress, Patricia loved her job, of that there was no question. As long as she was able to unwind after a long hard day, she was okay. She needed that time though, to recharge her batteries, relax, get lost in a good book, and forget about her professional problems. She found her escape with a tall glass of dark-red wine, a scented bubble bath, and a steamy romance novel by her favorite author. Once she got submerged in the hot soapy water everything would be better, her worries would melt away.

Patricia wasted no time running her bath water and added a generous amount of lavender scented bath salts. While her tub was filling up she poured her tall glass of wine in the kitchen and grabbed her book off the bedroom nightstand. By the time she returned to the bathroom the mirrors were steamed over, the bathroom felt like a sauna.

Heavenly…

Patricia had no distractions so she could literally sit and soak in her bath for hours. She carefully put her toes into the hot soapy water first, inching in ankle deep, allowing her skin to get used to the heat of the water. A knock came from her apartment door before she could sink into the soapy water.

"What the heck?" the noise startled Patricia and she dropped her wine glass into the bath. "C'mon!" she grumbled, the blood-red wine mixing into the soapy waters. There went her relaxing night, she thought in dismay.

Patricia uncorked the bathtub allowing the ruined bath water to drain out. She angrily grabbed her robe, tying it tightly around her waist.

"This better be the mother of all emergencies," she cursed to herself.

Patricia peeked through the small peephole on her apartment

door. There she saw a disheveled Sebastian pacing back and forth frantical-ly. She could tell he was agitated; it looked like he had hurt his hand. It was wrapped up in a blood soaked white towel. She unlocked the deadbolt (leaving the chain lock in place) and swung the door open just enough to speak to her unwelcome guest.

"Sebastian, it's late. What on Earth do you want?"

"Patricia," Sebastian spoke in hurried breaths, pain written across his face. "I need to speak with Calenstine, it's an emergency."

"You cannot," Patricia said bluntly. "What did you do to your hand? What's wrong?"

"I must!" Sebastian threatened, eyes wide with madness. With his good hand he forced the door open, but the chain lock kept him at bay. "C'mon, let me in!"

"Sebastian! Don't make me call security! What is wrong with you? You're acting mad!"

"It's Margot!" Sebastian's eyes welled with tears. "What? What happened?"

"I can't tell you! But, it's serious, which is why I need to speak to Calenstine," Sebastian took a deep breath attempting to calm himself. "For heaven's sake," Patricia unlocked the chain. "Your hand is bleeding through that towel!"

"It can wait, Margot is in trouble. Calenstine will know what to do."

"First tell me what's happening," Patricia ordered.

"I said I can't!" Sebastian yelled in a fury. "What part of that do you not get?"

"Listen, the Professor left earlier in the week for a meeting, he is not available," Patricia ran the sink water in her kitchen and pulled Sebastian over to the counter top. "Let me at least clean your wound while we figure this out. How is Margot in danger?" Patricia asked as she pulled off the blood soaked towel.

"Ouch!" Sebastian winced. Patricia held his hand underneath the water cleaning away the dried blood. "Someone is after her..." he muttered.

"Jesus..." Patricia concentrated on the wound. Multiple

lacerations scarred his fist, small shards of the mirror was still embedded in his skin. "We need to pull these out. Let me get something."

"Yes, fine, but you're not listening. Someone is after her," replied Sebastian.

"Explain," Patricia yelled from the other room. "But, don't take your hand out of the running water."

"Calenstine has prohibited me from telling anyone anything." "Okay..." Patricia came back with tweezers and a large bottle of peroxide. "This will hurt a bit."

"Is there any way we can contact him?" Sebastian closed his shut his eyes tightly waiting for the pain.

Patricia dried Sebastian's wet hand with a washcloth, pouring a good amount of peroxide over his wounds. Sebastian gasped. With her tweezers she went to work, pulling out the embedded glass.

"Christ, it hurts..."

"What did you do?" asked Patricia.

"Margot and I got into a fight. I punched a mirror. I acted like a brute...embarrassing, I know..."

"Smart," Patricia pulled a rather large shard out of one of the numerous wounds.

"Listen, the Estate is not as safe as you think. Margot is in trouble and I need to warn her, but I must speak with Calenstine first."

"Let me re-wrap your wound and then I'll call security. They can monitor Margot to make sure she is safe. Then, we have to get to the infirmary to get your hand checked out by a real doctor."

"Security may not be enough. We need to get her out of the Estate, somewhere safe."

"You know we can't do that," Patricia frowned. "The Estate is by far the most secure place for her. We can watch her here, keep her guarded. Who is after her anyway? What exactly has she gotten herself mixed up in?"

"She didn't do anything wrong. Someone is going to try and hurt her, to punish me."

"Who and why?"

"I can't say..." Sebastian shook his head in frustration. "That's why I need Calenstine!"

"You can't say, or you won't. If you want my help, I need the truth."

"I can't because I don't know who. But, I know they threatened me with her death. I won't tell you why, because Calenstine has forbidden me to."

"Someone wants her dead...?" Patricia suddenly felt the weight of the issue.

"I need you to help me Patricia, before it's too late...."

CHAPTER 10
THE YGGDRASIL TREE

Wednesday was Elly's favorite day of the week. Wednesdays meant Botany class with Professor Latimer, Elly's favorite Enlightenment subject. Elly was a bit disappointed with the first month of the classes, they were basically just a series of lectures and pop quizzes to review what they had gone over the first year. This didn't make for the most exciting lesson plans, but Elly aced all her tests and felt the need to constantly rub it in Hunter's face. She never passed up an opportunity to prove to Hunter how much smarter she was than he.

This just gave Hunter another reason for him to hate Botany.

Hunter did not find the class about cryptid flora all that fascinating, but he had learned the hard way to respect it. He was still recovering from an almost deadly error the year prior. He had mixed up the difference between a blood-sucking Romanian Blood Moon and a Western Lilly Drake during a pop-quiz; seven stitches later left him with some cool looking scars on his right forearm.

However, this week was a little different. Even Hunter was excited to attend Latimer's lecture. Last year the Professor had promised the class would take a field tri deep into the Demeter Station to see firsthand the mysterious Yggdrasil Tree.

Originally Hunter could care less, "Who cares about some old tree… real cool…" he mocked his little sister just days before. It wasn't until Alistair started doing some research on the Tree that Hunter became excited (although, he would never admit it to Elly).

"It's this ancient tree that stems back to Norse mythology. We're talking Vikings, Gods and spirits, different realms…man it's awesome. Also, it's supposed to contain magic…."

98

"Sounds cool, why is it so important?" asked Tully.

"Who knows," Alistair flipped his laptop over so Hunter and Tully could see a series of drawings of the mythical tree. "I am sure it holds loads of secrets."

"Wonder what sort of magic it contains?" asked Hunter staring in awe at the cool hand sketched drawings of the giant tree. One in particular showed a dragon wrapped around the base of the tree.

They weren't able make the field trip at the end of the last school year as promised (due to the Moloch attack) so Professor Latimer was making good on his promise this year.

"I have a feeling we've only scratched the surface on its true power," Alistair said with a wide smile.

The class was asked to wait outside the Demeter Station's entrance instead of their normal classroom inside the Francis Drake building. The Demeter station was a huge oval shaped building that sat far off towards the back of the Estate's grounds. Half the station was nestled deeply into the thick forest, so the kids really didn't know how far back the building actually went.

"Children, it looks like you all made it," Professor Mortimer Latimer yelled over the loud motor of a small golf cart being driven by their Legendary Creatures Professor, Dr. James Lannin.

"Good morning!" Elly and a few of the more excited students greeted the Professors.

Mortimer Latimer was in his late sixties with thin sandy brown hair, and a thick bushy mustache. When he wasn't teaching the children about the curious and sometimes deadly cyrptoid flora, he was spending his days (and most nights) inside the Demeter Station running tests and peering down microscopes. He actually led a large team of botanists, hundreds of the most brilliant minds in the world today, and monitored and maintained the enormous infrastructure.

"Dr. Lannin, why are you here?" asked Tully who was excited to see his favorite Professor show up.

"Well, to be honest, I have never seen the Yggdrasil tree myself. Morty doesn't open up the inner chamber to the tree very often, and I couldn't miss out. I think it's been almost twenty years?"

"About that long," Latimer smiled, stepping out of the cart. "Not since the last Enlightenment. The last few people, outside of me and a few trusted colleagues, to see the tree were your guardians. The rule is simple, if the entire class passes the first-year exam, I open the door. Thankfully, Dr. Lannin is a well-respected Professor and I enjoy his company. He should feel special for being allowed to see the tree and all its glory."

"Couldn't be more excited!" Dr. Lannin shifted the golf cart into park. He was wearing his usual attire, thick khaki pants and a blue polo shirt. Dr. Lannin was of Asian descent with thick black hair that he kept buzzed short.

"Well, it's a bit of a hike towards the middle of the station, so I hope everyone wore comfortable shoes." Latimer swiped his identification key at the Demeter station's only entrance.

"How large is this place?" asked Symphanie, who, up until now, had never seen the station up close and personal.

"Well, let me put it in terms you can understand," Lannin held the large heavy door open for the children to enter. "It will take us about forty-five minutes to walk to the center of the building, and that's just the surface level. The Demeter Station has many sublevels, each one regulated to different climates controlled by the main floor, specifically to house our many species of fauna and flora. It's a giant sublevel in the bio dome that stretches out for miles and miles beneath us and around us. Tropical, arctic, arid, each climate equipped with its own ecosystems, rivers, lakes... It's truly awesome what Professor Calenstine has been able to create here at the Estate.

"You control all of that, here on the top level of the Demeter Station?" asked Alistair.

"With help from Plato and the Ocelot room, yes. We also control certain parts of the forest around the estate. A few years back we found out that we could monitor and control different parts of the forest with our technological advances. We were able to protect certain crypto-zoological animals by housing them in the forest, far away from civilization. Remember, only a few government agencies even know we exist," Dr. Latimer winked.

"It's been an amazing program," Dr. Lannin added. "Partnering with Morty, we are able to keep track of the Cryptids through microchips, keeping them comfortable through regulating their habitats thanks to small localized biospheres we've installed in certain parts of the forest. For instance, we have a pack of Florida Skunk Apes that live in a specifically controlled section of the forest that we've domed off. This enables us to keep a warm, humid climate for them to thrive in, even during the winter months."

"That's insane...!" Tully was dumbfounded by the sheer size of the operation.

"There have been some issues...but we are working on them," Dr. Lannin admitted. "Even with the domes up, certain cryptids escape, run amok. Itch away at their microchips, get them torn off in territorial fights, etc."

"Like Bernie," said Alistair. "Exactly," Lannin smiled.

"Keep up, children. We've got some ways to go!" Dr. Latimer ushered the group on.

There was a decent number of children in the Enlightenment group, and the hallway was fairly narrow. Most of the surface level of the Demeter station was a level one tropical forest ecosystem, meaning there were no real dangerous plants living within it. The other half of the top floor was dedicated to the laboratories and computer systems running the multi layered station.

To the left of the kids was a thick glass wall into the tropical climate. Bright flowers budded in the simulated sunlight that peeked through the thick towering canopy of trees. The lush green landscape was thick with vegetation and a myriad of wildlife. The group saw colorful birds bathing in a small stream emptying out into a giant lake that butted right up against the glass. Insects flew and landed on the glass, some were the size of Hunter's head, with creepy eyes staring at him. At one point the tropical forest began to have a storm. Thick drops of rain pelted the long flat leaves and shrubs."It's raining in there?" asked Olivia with wide eyes.

"It's a self-sustaining ecosystem, cut off from the outside world. They all operate this way; it's how they can provide the habitat for the wildlife as well. It's also why the Demeter Station is so large in scale. What you see to your left is by far the smallest landscape we have. When you travel deep beneath the main floor, we house sprawling landscapes, three times the size of this."

The children marched on, deeper into the center of the Station. They finally reached their destination, the long hallway they were following suddenly stopped at heavy mechanical door.

"Behind this door is the Yggdrasil Tree. Here, the Demeter Station opens back up to the outside. The station is built like a giant donut and we just walked our way to the center. The Yggdrasil Tree was originally housed inside the Station, but after a few decades with the proper treatment it grew exponentially. We were forced to open the ceiling up so the tree could continue to grow. Similarly, as it grew, so did its roots below us. They broke into the multi-layers of different ecosystems below us. It was a mess; we had no idea how large the tree would get... But the roots didn't seem to be affected by the different climates. It just kept growing...."

"How big is it?" asked Hunter.

"It's big," smiled Dr. Latimer. He swiped his identification card one more time, unlocking the heavy door to the inner circle of the station. "I'm so excited!" Dr. Lannin held the door as the children made their way through.

Just as Latimer said, the door led back outside into a large oval shaped area. It was roughly the size of Hunter's old middle school's football field. At the openings center stood the enormous tree. Despite it being early afternoon, the bright sun did not reach them; instead they stood in almost complete darkness from the shade of the large tree. Thankfully there were spotlights out in the field, illuminating the area.

"Holy crap!" Alistair's jaw dropped at the awe-inspiring sight. Nothing could prepare the children for what they saw. The trunk itself took up the majority of the outside opening. There were maybe ten yards between the walls of the building and the base of the tree trunk. It was wider than most houses Hunter had ever seen.

"I can barely tell where the tree ends on either side..." Elly peered in both directions trying to see where the tree wrapped into a circle.

"Don't look up," said Tully.

"Wow!" Elly cranked her head as far back as her neck would allow. The tree literally literally taller than the kids could see. It was like looking at a sky completely made of huge thick branches and leaves, it covered every inch of the opening.

"Big, right?" Latimer smiled. "The tree branches over the majority of the diameter of the Demeter Station. So, has anyone ever heard of Sequoia Sempervirens?"

"Sequey, what-a-verns?" Alistair raised his brow. "California Redwoods?" Latimer chuckled.

"Oh, yeah! I have," answered Olivia. "They're huge trees. Super tall."

"They are thought to be the tallest trees in the world. They can reach up to 350 feet tall. They tend to be much smaller in diameter than the beast you see in front of you. Also, the Yggdrasil easily surpasses 600 feet tall, so the Redwoods dwarf in comparison to the specimen in front of you. Needless to say, the Yggdrasil is not a Redwood. It actually closely resembles an Ash Tree."

"It's so beautiful…" Symphanie reached out and touched the large trunk.

"Where did it come from?" asked Hunter.

"Great question," Dr. Lannin chimed in. "First, let's discuss the folklore behind the magical tree. It was thought to be the sole connection for all nine of the different realms in Norse mythology. The branches are said to reach the heavens, its roots connecting to the other eight realms. It was thought to be a Holy tree. Modern society labeled the Yggdrasil Tree as mere fantasy, a silly anecdote from an ancient religion. That is until a few hundred years ago when Professor Calenstine traveled to the far reaches of the world and found the small withering tree, saving it from extinction."

"Hey," Latimer chuckled. "I thought I was teaching the class?"

"Sorry," Lannin added, still awe-struck at the sight. "I am just so fascinated with this tree…."

"Well, you're right. Rumor has it that the only reason why Calenstine was able to find it was due to the Grimoire speaking to him one night. It gave him a map and told him what to look for. He uprooted the tree and restored it here. Since then, it has grown to what it is now."

"How big was it when he found it?" asked Elly.

"No bigger than the average tree you would see outside. It was sickly though, withered and sad." Latimer explained.

"My predecessor dedicated his entire life to nurturing it back to its glory. Now it is my main objective; my sole purpose as an honorary Seeker, to keep the Yggdrasil alive and healthy."

"Looks like you're doing a good job," said Tully.

"Well, thankfully it has had a couple of centuries to restore itself."

"I can't believe how beautiful it is," Olivia whispered to Elly. "Are you feeling okay?"

"Yeah…" Elly's face had gone pale. She lied, not wanting to draw attention to herself, she felt sick to her stomach, dizzy…

"You don't look so good," Symphanie hurried over to her side. "Soon as we stepped out here, I just felt weird."

"Professor Latimer, Elly isn't looking good," Olivia yelled over to her teacher a few yards away.

"Oh no," Hunter turned towards the girls. Fear set in his eyes, he recognized the symptoms.

"What's wrong?" asked Alistair.

"It's happening again." Hunter ran over to the girls. "I'm okay," Elly shrugged Olivia off.

"Elly, you need to sit down and breathe. Concentrate on my voice." Hunter grabbed his sister's hands. "Do not pass out!"

"This feels different…" Elly pulled away from Hunter, stumbling towards the trunk of the giant tree.

"Children, what's going on?" Dr. Lannin rushed over.

"It's okay, I know what to do," Hunter held out his arms to keep the crowding people at bay. "Let her be, Calenstine's orders…."

"Don't lose me Hunter…." Elly whispered. She reached out to regain her balance. The moment her hand touched the Yggdrasil tree a burning white light shot through her head and she fell.

• • •

Elly wasn't sure what happened, she had never experienced the transition from the physical realm into the "thereafter" so violently before. The last time was a slow and painful process that left her convulsing on the classroom floor. This time it felt like she was shot out of her body, forcefully injecting her spirit into this bizarre place.

It looked different too. Normally, the "thereafter" accompanied her with thick blue mist that made it difficult to see more than a few feet from her face, now there was only a hint of the eerie mist settling around her feet. She was surprised to be alone; she was used to seeing the faint outline of her classmates. This time there was nothing left of the physical realm except for one thing...she awoke on her side, facing the large trunk of the Yggdrasil Tree.

Elly slowly stood up using the bulky base of the tree for support. Gathering her bearings, she immediately felt better. The dizziness diminished, her mind cleared. Yet, her body felt a bit weird, like she was lighter than normal. It was a surreal sensation; like she could float instead of walk... It took her a minute to realize she was still at the Demeter Station. The Yggdrasil Tree looked different, though. It had a dark red, power source surging through its bark, beating to a rhythm, much like that of a heartbeat. It was faintly glowing, almost mesmerizing. Elly caught herself staring at it, trying to make sense of what would cause it. It looked so...beautiful.

"Where did everybody go?" Elly peered around the circular opening. Being alone frightened her, especially in such a strange place. Something was wrong, the last time she went under she could still faintly hear her friends; she could still see their physical outlines, shades of their bodies. Calenstine warned her to keep close to her brother's voice, not to travel too far into the void... She hadn't traveled at all...and yet, no voices, no shades...

"Hunter, can you hear me?" Elly yelled into the nothingness.

She slowly backed away from the Yggdrasil. She heard a rustling from overhead, her heart began to race. Was something watching her? "What was that?" she turned, but there was nothing. She searched the base of the Yggdrasil with her eyes. "Is someone there?"

From the thick trunk of the tree, hidden in camouflage, two large yellow eyes blinked, staring her down. Elly gasped in horror at the bizarre sight. A low hissing noise came from the creature, it didn't sound friendly...

Elly didn't want to wait and find out; she made a run for it. Judging from the size of its eyes, she thought it was probably huge and hungry. She took off without warning, sprinting with all her might. She only made it a few steps before she felt a gush of forceful wind blast overhead. It was so powerful that it blasted her hair into her face, blinding her temporarily. The creature leapt from its perched position, landing violently in front of her, blocking her escape.

Elly nervously brushed the hair from her face. The creature stood a few feet away from her. She could feel it's hot breath on her face accompanied by the smell of rotting earth. She froze in fear...

It was an enormous lizard, huge, easily the size of a school bus.

Elly thought she was staring down a living breathing dragon.

A *dragon*?! Elly swallowed the lump in her throat. She opened her mouth to say something, yet no words came to mind. She was completely frozen, petrified by fear, and even if she could muster a sentence... what could she possible say to a dragon?

The creature was long and skinny with a snake-like torso and four short stubby legs, it was three toed with long, black, razor sharp nails. Its black body was covered with thick armor like scales. The dragon appeared to be aggravated, poised to attack. Its head was huge, bobbing slightly up and down, with two giant, yellow eyes still staring her down. As eerie as its eyes were, nothing frightened Elly more than the long, killer-looking snout resembling that of a crocodile. If drag-ons could grin, Elly was sure that it was, its snout smirked open, lips curled up just enough to show off the multiple layers of serrated teeth. Elly shrieked again at the sight, covering her face with her hands.

She dropped to the ground and curled up into a ball, waiting for the creature to pounce.

"You see me?" The creature spoke in a deep thunderous voice, amazed that Elly was reacting to its presence.

"Y-You…err…speak?" Elly could barely form words; she barely man ageda squeaky response. Her knees trembled in fear. All it would take was one wrong move, saying one wrong thing, and this Dragon could rip her limb from limb in a millisecond.

"You understand me, as well?" The dragon's yellow eye's widened even larger than before. The reptile cocked its head trying to make sense of the situation.

"Yes…you're a talking dragon?" Elly swallowed hard. "Please don't eat me!"

"Eat you?" The beast let out a loud chuckle that made Elly's body shake. "I have spent an infinite lifetime finding sustenance from this tree's delicious roots. I have no taste for flesh, child. Unless it came from that devilish flying rat who sits atop of the tree. That wretched bird, always taunting me. I would swallow it whole."

"Excuse me? What bird," asked Elly.

"Cute, don't play coy with me, young girl. It's obvious; the bird put you up to this, didn't he? Some sort of spell, a shade perhaps?" The dragon moved in closer to Elly sniffing her up and down.

"I haven't seen any bird." Elly held still as the dragon sniffed away.

His hot breath blasting in her face, it smelled of dirt and earth.

"You smell of Gaia's soil!" The dragon jumped back a safe distance from Elly. "Whose doing is this!? What foul game do you play?"

"No game, I swear it. I think it's my ring! I think it brought me to this realm." Elly held out her hand showing the dragon Solomon's Seal.

"The ring?" the creature approached once again, carefully inspecting her hand, sniffing the metal band on her finger. "It does smell of the arcane…"

"I mean no harm, my name is Elly. I am lost and I need to find a way back home."

"So, you are from Gaia, then?" asked the dragon. "Is Gaia, Earth?"

"Hmmm," the dragon pondered the question. "Perhaps it is. You are frightened? I apologize for my abrupt entrance. I thought you were a joke being played on me by the blasted bird. Always scheming...."

"Sorry, we don't have dragons where I come from," Elly breathed a sigh of relief; at least the creature seemed friendly.

"Dragon? I am no filthy Dragon, I am a Wyrm. Vastly different, I assure you. Dragons are bloodthirsty maniacs. Do I look bloodthirsty?" "Well, you did at first..." Elly offered a half smile to try and ease the tension.

"I suppose my intentions were to startle you. My name is Nidhogg," the Wyrm lowered its head in a nonthreatening position.

"Hi, Nidhogg. I'm confused, is this the "thereafter" or am I somewhere else?"

"I have never heard of this "thereafter". This is my home, though. I have lived here for an eternity beside this tree. I have seen it grow as high as the heavens, and wither away into almost nothing. Outside of the tree and its roots, I am afraid my eyes have never seen. So, forgive me if I know naught of this "thereafter" world you speak of."

"But, you said I smell of Gaia," Elly frowned. "Do you know of my world then?"

"Yes, this tree is thought to exist in many realms, including yours. You smell strongly of it. We call it Gaia, the realm of soil and flesh. I am intrigued by your presence here, a strange combination of energy and matter. For all known purposes, you should not exist in this realm. Yet, here we are sharing words."

"Who are your people? Are there many Wyrms like yourself? Should I be worried?"

"No, no worries," Nidhogg chuckled, "The world you see is not the same world in which I exist. Confusing I know...." Nidhogg thought deeply as to how he could explain it to the young child. "Think of it this way, this world is shaped by those who enter it, although I exist in all of its renditions, so do the few others who call this place home. There are not many of us: the bird high above, who even now, after an infinite amount of time, I still have no clue as to why he exists. Myself, who feeds off the tree's magical roots, and the spinners of fate, called the Norns. They preserve more secrets than the Yggdrasil has leaves."
"No offense...but, when you try to explain things, my head hurts."

Elly did her best to decipher the riddled information. "This is what you called, the collective conscious of humankind?"

"Sort of, it is simply your rendition of it. Everyone's is different; it is shaped by your life experiences. It is both different and exactly the same compared to everyone else's. There are not tangible truths to my physical world, save for the Tree, simply because we currently exist on a plane where the physical world is nonexistent."

"Okay..." Elly was lost. She decided it wasn't worth the effort figuring out the Wyrm's conundrums. All she really needed was a way home.

Nidhogg saw the confusion expressed on her young face. "As I said, you are not able to come to terms with your current surroundings. Perhaps when you're older it may make more sense. Then again, probably not."

"Okay, so let's skip this existence stuff you keep going on about," Elly took a seat next to the base of the tree. "Can you get me home?"

"I have never come across one like you in all my years. To answer your question, I can't even understand how you came here; let alone how to figure out a safe passage back."

"Great...so, I am stuck?" She rubbed her index fingers against her temples in frustration. Her head was pounding...

"Well, not so fast. At one point, many of your kinds shades came through my home, seeking guidance through the tree. So, I know a little about your kind. The Norns' know far more."

"Well, I can't stay here; I have a family, friends...I need to get back to them. Should I go talk to these Norns?"

"As good a plan as any," Nidhogg peered over to the far edge of the Yggdrasil tree. "This is the northern side, it is my home. High atop the branches is where the devilish bird lays his claim. He will be of no help. He is a trickster, an evil mind wanting nothing more than to mock and ridicule all things. Stay clear of him. Then the Norns' call the southern side of the tree home. Follow the base of the tree until you reach the other side, they should show themselves."

"Thank you, Nidhogg," Elly nodded. She stood up and began her journey around the large base of the tree.

Nidhogg smiled, nodding, as Elly made her way forth. Nidhogg effortlessly leapt high into the air, landing with a loud thud against the Yggdrasil's thick bark. "I bid you farewell, and good luck on your journey!" Nidhogg faded into the Yggdrasil tree, its scales blending in perfectly with the bark.

Elly turned around to wave goodbye, but he was already gone. "Hope these Norns are nice..." Elly whispered to herself as she made the lonely journey through this strange foreign world.

CHAPTER 11
UNIVERSAL SECRETS

As Elly made the long walk around Yggdrasil Tree she felt eerily alone. She realized wherever, or whatever, this place was, it was completely void of any and all noise. No wind rustling through the leaves high above her, no bugs buzzing by her ears, no birds chirping in the distance… no sound.

She didn't like it one bit. She wished Nidhogg (and his long-winded bantering) had accompanied her on the journey. She would have welcomed the company. Anything was better than the muted landscape. The silence made her skin crawl, to the point that she no longer felt comfortable walking the length of the tree's diameter. She decided to break out into a full sprint until she found the southernmost side of the tree where the Norns lived. She wanted to get back home as soon as possible and the longer she stayed the more danger she was in. She needed to get back to her physical body before it was too late.

Elly ran as fast as her legs would carry her, she never let up, she pushed and pushed. Normally she could go a solid ten minutes without getting winded, but this tree was huge. It was like running around the perimeter of a football field that was as long as it was wide. She ran a solid half hour before taking note of the time. She was impressed with herself, she never faltered once. Her legs never burned, her feet never cramped, she never even gasped for air…. She could have gone on running forever and never felt a thing. Then she realized what was going on. It made sense; she was no longer confined to her physical body. Of course she wasn't getting winded; there were no physical limitations in the spiritual realm.

She kept the pace for a while longer until she saw something come into view. Two dark figures stood on the horizon waving her forward. They must be the Norns, with new-found excitement she sped up.

Then she saw them.

The sight of them stopped Elly dead in her tracks.

It was *them*... They looked exactly like she remembered. Her parents...

Elly's mouth dropped open, her legs trembled uncontrollably. The sudden pain of her parents' death came flooding back to her all at once. She had tried so hard to bury that pain deep down inside her, to ignore it and move on with her life. It was like someone opened her emotional flood gates, all the pain and agony she swallowed down just came pouring out. The emotions hit her so hard she could no longer stand, the pain crippled her. She fell to her hands and knees. The agonizing sadness was too much for her to bear.

Her mother and father only stood a few yards away. They wore dark robes, hoods down exposing their warm and gentle faces. It was really them...her parents.

"Mom...?" Elly's voice cracked in a broken, shattered shriek. "Dad...?" Tears poured from her eyes. Her face flushed with emotions, beet red.

They were so close, but yet, they seemed so far away. Her brain urged her on, to continue forward. She pleaded with her legs to find the strength to stand up and run towards them, but they weren't listening. Her body wouldn't cooperate. She wanted nothing more in the world than to fall into her parents' warm embrace. She tried to crawl towards them.

Elly continued to sob freely, tears streaming down her salt stained cheeks. Her legs felt like boulders, her hands felt like they were chained to the earth. With all her strength she reached up with her trembling hand towards her mother...

Was this real? Were they really her parents? Why couldn't she move...? What was holding her back? Was this some sick cruel joke?

Her mind was racing...

"Darling," her mother reached her hand out to embrace her

daughter. They were only a few inches away from touching. It was her voice. Her mother's soft sweet voice, the same voice that sang her to sleep at night, that read to her before bed.

"My princess, we've missed you so much!" Her father smiled, wiping away a single tear.

"You can't touch em', you know?" A third figure came into view from the corner of Elly's eye.

"Please...," she begged, turning her head to see the robed body. This one was much shorter than her parents, its hood pulled up, disguising its face.

"It's not me stopping you," the hooded figure answered calmly.

Elly recognized the voice. "Hunter?"

The figure dropped the hood exposing Hunter's young expressionless face, his normal dark brown eyes were gone, and he had no pupils, his entire eye was pure black.

"Hunter!" Elly yelled, "Its mom and dad! Look! Help me!"

"No," Hunter said bluntly. "You know that's not true. They're dead, gone forever. These are just shades of who they were. Your own memories of them pulled from your subconscious and projected in front of your very eyes."

"What? No, they are real, just look..." Elly turned back to her parents. There they stood smiling back at her. Her mother's hand still stretched out waiting for her embrace.

"You're smarter than this," said Hunter. "Before you can know the truth, you must see past your own desires. You must come to terms with your reality."

"You're not my brother." Elly frowned. It was obvious the emotionless figure in front of her was not Hunter, rather, some sort of fraud, mocking her for amusement.

"I am Hunter, and I am not," the figure who looked like Hunter replied.

"Enough with the riddles!" Elly yelled. The crippling sorrow was subsiding; her tears began to dry, quickly replaced with raw and unadulterated anger. Her fists shook in angst.

"Good, now we are getting somewhere," Hunter lifted his hood back over his face. "So, if I am not truly Hunter-"

"No," Elly interrupted. "They...they *are* my parents." Elly ignored the figure posing as Hunter. She turned her back to him, her eyes fixed upon her mothers. She was going to grab her mother's hand if it was the last thing she did. She continued her futile attempt to crawl closer. But the truth sank in. She knew...there was no point in lying to herself...even if she didn't want to accept it.

These people in front of her were not her parents. Just like Hunter who stood behind her wasn't truly her brother. How stupid was she? Thinking for a second it was true...that they were her actual parents. Elly felt ashamed, she felt embarrassed. She was being forced to play some sort of sick game.

Elly decided enough was enough, she didn't have it in her to fight anymore, so she gave up. Instead of fighting the immense weight holding down her hands and legs, she let them weight her down. She fell onto her stomach face first, lacking any and all desire to move. Tears once again rolled down her cheeks. In that moment she didn't care about anything...

Elly's suffering was so severe, so overwhelming that She didn't care if she ever stood up again. If she could, she would just dig herself deep into the dirt and hide away from the world, forever.

Her fake parents took notice. They lifted their hoods hiding their faces from her view.

"You must conquer the pain," the figure that had taken Hunter's identity spoke calmly.

"I can't..." Elly wept. "It hurts so badly."

"It is okay to feel pain, pain is what makes you real, makes you human. Cherish the good. Allow the love to flood over your heart. But, if you cannot float in the ocean of despair, you will surely drown in the waters of life. The blessings of the Yggdrasil Tree have shown you the way, but it is up to you to fight."

"The tree did this?" Elly lifted her face from the earth, wiping away the dirt from her cheeks.

"It has been beckoning you for months. It sensed your powers, even from different realms. It has never shown interest in a living human, you are the first. You are special, different, the seal upon your finger, it has unlocked your potential. This allowed the tree to beckon you. Yggdrasil felt your pain, your suffering. It knows you locked up all your anguish, bestowing it into the darkest depths of your spirit. If you were not cleansed of this agony, it would overcome you. It would kill you sooner than later."

"You...you are the three Norns?" Elly was still weak, but she managed to sit up.

"We are the keepers of time, the spinners of fate, caretakers of Yggdrasil, the foreseers of all." The shortest of the three Norns dropped her hood once again, exposing a pale, white, wrinkly old woman's face. The other two figures followed suit, dropping their hoods as well. Each figure looked identical; all three were old women with frizzy white hair and long crooked noses.

"We are the past, the present, the future. We are everything and nothing combined."

"More riddles..." Elly sighed, trying to collect herself. She felt exhausted from the emotional experience, her heart still racing. "So, what does that actually mean? What do you do?"

"We have bountiful duties; we are both the spinners of fate, as well as caretakers for the all-powerful Yggdrasil."

"Why did the tree make me go through this? It brought back so much hurt. I just wanted to die...to give up."

"That is impossible; in your current state you are neither alive nor dead. You equally exist and do not exist. Here, there is no time; it is both the beginning and the end and all that lies in between. It is here where records of your lives spin in a million different existences. In every version, every reality, every realm, every world in the universe, every god worshipped, every society constructed, there is one simple connection, Yggdrasil. His roots connect them all. He exists somewhere, everywhere, past, present, future, thereafter, Gaia, Asgard, Roman Gods, Native American, purgatory, heaven, hell, hades, Shan-gri-La... All creations from the human mind, all born from the fruits of the Yggdrasil, all exist and do not exist equally, depending on the perspective of the soul."

"Okay…" Elly shook her head in confusion. "So, why me?"
"Yggdrasil hoped to save you from a dark future, which we, as the Spinners of fate, have spun an infinite amount of times. Without

Yggdrasil's assistance, all roads led you down a dark and lonely life." "You're telling me you can read the future?"

"Yes and no. We spin many different futures, some real, some never come to be. What we found more often than not with you, was a tragic ending. Far too soon, a young death, premature."

"Yes and no?" asked Elly. "You're telling me I am going to die soon?"

"Fate is not the end all be all," one of her former parent impostors spoke up. "This is why the fabric of fate is thread and not concrete. We spin an ever-changing past, present, and future, it never ends. An infinite number of possibilities."

"So, what are you trying to tell me? I am doomed to live a tragic life?"

"Your life is already tragic. However, even with an infinite amount of possibilities, an alarming rate of your thread ends prematurely. Too much despair poisons your spirit. You are both lucky and unlucky to have found the ring. The probability for you to have been the one to slip on the ring was nearly impossible. We spun a billion different threads, all of which led to your brother harnessing its power, not you. Yet, here you are, with the ring. Your brother is/was strong enough emotionally to handle the weight of your parents' death; he fends off the pain head on. You are not strong enough; you swallow the pain and hide. You have a broken soul.…"

"The moment you slipped the ring onto your finger, your thread changed both in density and thickness. We'd only ever seen such a thing once, but never so abruptly. The ring somehow connected you with the Yggdrasil. It is Yggdrasil who has been speaking to you in your dreams. It has been calling you, pushing you through the many different realms of existence into its own world. By happenstance, you came to visit him in *your* world, Gaia. The moment you touched his physical presence, he was able to connect with your spirit and pull your forth. Much easier than calling for you from your subconscious."

"Okay…" said Elly. " That's why it felt different than the other times. He ripped me from my body?"

"Yes," one of the women nodded. "Not slowly pulled."

"Well, I definitely feel unlucky. I never wanted this dumb ring…!" Elly shook her head. "How was I lucky?"

"As we said, your threads spun an almost certain fate of a young death. You were destined to wallow in despair and anguish. Depression would swallow you whole. When the time came, and you wore the ring, Yggdrasil had to intervene. You are now too important to allow such a meaningless end to come to fruition."

"No, I don't believe tha., I am fine!" Elly argued back.

"Believe what you wish, it does not change things."

"I want to speak with Yggdrasil," said Elly. "I want answers." "Yggdrasil does not speak. He exists, lives, has needs and wants, but he is a tree, he cannot speak to you, not with words. We are a part of his essence, created by him, so we sense his desires. You are connected but not in the same way. You may ask questions, and we may answer, we may not."

"What exactly is this place then? Why is there Yggdrasil here and in my world, too? Why does he care if I die young? Why not just let me live like anyone else?"

"Yggdrasil is one of the very few omnipotent beings born through the Universal hands of fate. No one knows how he came to lay his roots, but he exists in every world. This realm claims home to his pure essence, his original form. He was here even before your planet was born. He is timeless."

"Err…okay...what does he do?"

"He acts as the anchor to all divine energy. Your people call it the soul, or spiritual consciousness. It has many other names as well. More importantly he gives birth to your Mortal Gods, as well as others."

"*He* gives birth?" Elly's eyes opened. "To…mortal…Gods?" "He, she, Yggdrasil is both," the Norn replied.

"What do you mean births Gods? Like the God, who I go to church and pray to?"

"There are a few omnipotent beings whose origins are masked in the mysteries of the Universe, even we as spinners cannot explain. Yggdrasil is one. However, your world is riddled with many other Gods as well, not all of which are related to the omnipotent hierarchy of Yggdrasil. However, there is one overseer who shares the same origins of Yggdrasil who lays claim to Gaia. The multitudes of your other Gods were not born from the Universe's womb like Yggdrasil and the Overseer. These lesser Gods were born from the mind of Humanity. When this occurs, a magical fruit looms on the Yggdrasil tree branches. The fruit grows and ripens and gathers strength from its followers on Gaia. Once it matures enough, it drops to the earth, and a Mortal God is born. Ra the sun god, Odin, and Zeus are popular examples you may relate to."

"Yeah, I learned about them in school. They were real?"

"Mortal Gods are born from the mind of man to make sense of the world. Yes. They live in the spiritual realm you know as the "thereafter". Powerful beings that have the ability to interact with Gaia across the realms. They lose their influence and control once their people cease to pray and sacrifice in their name."

"Wow! This is crazy. Am I the only one who knows this stuff?" asked Elly.

"One other, you know of him as King Solomon, the man who created the ring you bear."

"Okay, so..." Elly was pondering all the information, her mind racing. "Moloch, the demon who tried to kill me, he was a mortal God?" "Gaia's mortal Gods are born from the human mind, strengthened through prayer and sacrifices. Moloch has no relation to Yggdrasil. He is a powerful spirit born from the human physical experience, not the mind. Moloch was born from the emotional residue left behind when one very evil man's physical presence expired. This man's spirit was so vile, so evil and spiteful that it created the first demon on Earth. Your friend, King Solomon was tricked by the demon, and unknowingly empowered the creature. Solomon believed Moloch as one of the mortal Gods, and the two struck a demon's covenant. Moloch gave the King supernatural powers of alchemy in exchange for his peoples' prayer and sacrifice. Moloch grew with monstrous power, almost garnering the same influence as an omnipotent being. Thankfully, King Solomon learned of his true evils with the help of Yggdrasil. Solomon then created two rings to capture the creature: one granting him the power to enter Moloch's world to draw him out of hiding, and the second to capture his essence, trapping him for an eternity."

"That sounds so scary!" Elly let out a deep breath. "I miss being a normal kid."

"Ignorance is not empowering," the Norns all said in unison. "You are learning of the mysteries of existence, the secrets of life, and you complain? Many humans would give their soul for this knowledge. That demon, Moloch, was just re-released into your world. You and your friends saved the fate of humanity when you were able to recapture it. Thankfully, the demon was weak when he reemerged. Without prayer and sacrifices, the demon was nowhere near the height of its power."

"She is just a child," Nidhogg growled from afar, exposing his hiding place by the base of the tree. "You can't expect a child to comprehend this. She asked me the same questions, and I chose to leave her at peace. I assumed you three would do the same. Obviously, you know nothing of the limitations of the mortal mind."

"Yggdrasil wished her to know the truth," one of the Norns retorted.

"Nidhogg?" Elly smiled.

"I am sorry to have followed you." Nidhogg leapt from the tree taking a seat next to Elly. "I wanted to make sure you made it home safely, and that the Bird did not interfere."

"This is not your territory," the Norns scorned the Wyrm. "Without me, your precious Yggdrasil would die out. So, cut me some slack. I am just here to aid the girl."

"He is right," one of the Norns whispered. "We will grant you access, only while our guest exists in this world. It is possible the Bird could influence her against the Yggdrasil. Keep him at bay, Wyrm."

"That's why I followed her, he won't show up if I am nearby."
"You keep the Yggdrasil alive?" asked Elly.

"Well, to be fair, it's mutually beneficial. I eat and drink from his roots, and my compost keeps his soil fresh." "Ugh, your poop? That's gross," Elly frowned. "You asked," Nidhogg gave a toothy smile.

"It is true. Nidhogg is a magical creature; born with the Tree, much like we were. He feeds off the tree and sustains it as well."

"Sorry, this is all very interesting, but what do I need to do? I need to get home. How do I pass this test?" asked Elly.

"You already passed the test," one of the wrinkled old women replied with a smile.

"I did?"

"I believe the appearance of your parents was the test," added Nidhogg.

"Yes, the Wyrm is correct. The Yggdrasil wanted to flush your spirit clean from the thick darkness that possessed it. You hid your pain well from the world. What you did not know, was all the metaphysical damage it was doing to your body," explained one of the Norns.

"You were a ticking time bomb," Nidhogg explained. "Pain is nothing to bottle up and hide. Release it little by little. It was the reason you were doomed to a young death."

"He is correct," the Norns nodded. "The Universe is in the midst of an expansive war. A new threat is climbing to dominance in your world. There is a mortal whose hatred and self-interest outweighs the entirety of Gaia's spiritual influence. You and your friends find yourself in the midst of that struggle; much like Solomon had found himself. Yggdrasil needs you spiritually sound and ready to go to war to eliminate his presence. This is why he called you here; you bear the seal, you are now too important to allow your despair to end you."

"What does that mean?" asked Elly. "Outweighs the world's spiritual influence? And War? I can't go to war. I am just a kid!"

"This specific mortal's celestial essence is powerfully evil. He alone is offsetting Gaia's balance between good and evil. Depending on how future events pan out, this mortal's spiritual residue could bear a new deity, one much stronger than Moloch," answered one of the Norns. "We have spun his thread time and time again…the future looks bleak."

"This one mortal could offset the entire Universe's balance? No mortally born being can ever be allowed to eclipse that of any of our omnipotent beings," Nidhogg added.

"Correct," said the Norns.

"You must stay safe, Elly," said Nidhogg. "You must return," said the Norns in unison. "Wait, I still have questions," said Elly.

"I am sorry, but it is goodbye, for now," said the Norns. All three of the old women snapped their bony fingers.

A vibrant white flash blinded Elly. She felt her energy being sucked through the universe. She felt her body tense up, her bones felt like they were being ripped from her body. Her eyes shot open and she gasped for air.

Elly awoke in a dark room. She lay in a stiff bed; mechanical noises came from the side, where a series of monitors and wires were attached to her. It took her a minute, but there was enough moonlight shining into the room that she recognized where she was, back home, at the Estate, in the infirmary.

Elly sat up and swung her legs over the side of the bed. She needed to find Calenstine… She took one step down but she was still too weak. She fell, sprawled out on the cold hospital tile floor.

"Elly!" Dr. Wong came rushing into her room. "Please, don't move, you need rest." She helped Elly back up into her bed.

"I need Calenstine…" Elly mumbled. "Help me…" Her eye lids felt heavy, and soon, she was back asleep….

CHAPTER 12
HEMLOCK, MICHIGAN ONE MONTH AGO

I never knew how huge these woods were," Whitney poked the fire with a large stick, making sure it was not going to die out on her and her friends. "Thank god you know your way around this forest, because I would get lost in a heartbeat."

"Spent my whole life up here," Brandon handed his girlfriend a marshmallow to roast on the open fire. "Nice to be able to come from college and escape the big city, I love the outdoors. We're a good five miles out from the closest town. It's no wonder no one's bothered us out here."

"Yeah, thanks for inviting us," Brandon's best friend Timmy blew on his marshmallow, which had just been engulfed in flames. "I have not been camping since I was like ten."

"It's a great couples retreat," Timmy's girlfriend Fran sprayed a thick layer of bug spray over her exposed skin. "Just hate the bugs... I will *never* get used to them"

"You're such a city slicker," Timmy joked with a sly smile. He squished his roasted marshmallow between two graham crackers and handed it over to Fran. "S'mores minus the chocolate, just the way you like it."

"It's kinda creepy out here so far away from everything," said Whitney keeping a close eye on her marshmallow so it didn't end up burnt and charred like Timmy's.

"That's because most people have never gone *real* camping. We drove two hours on a dirt road to this campsite. We're the only campers for a reason. It's small and very isolated. Only die-hard campers take the trip here. No running water, no working bathrooms, no chargers, just us, nature, and the lake," explained Brandon. "My dad took me and my brothers here every summer. There were only a few times we ever ran into anyone else sharing the grounds. People don't like leaving their tablets and televisions behind. Here, we get real unadulterated nature. Us versus the wild, the way camping should be."

"Yeah, when I was a kid, we always had a camper; we would go to the sites with working showers. I can't say I enjoy using the woods as the bathroom," Timmy laughed.

"Agreed," said Fran taking a careful bite of her S'more so none of the gooey marshmallow got on her face. "As fun as the last two nights have been, I will be excited to start the drive back home tomorrow. I want nothing more than to soak in a hot bubble bath."

"It's getting late; we should get to our tents. We want to be up early so we can hike back to our vehicle and get back at a civilized hour," Brandon stood up dusting the dirt off his denim. "All good things come to an end, I suppose."

"I'm going to miss it here," said Whitney staring up at the beautiful starry sky. She had never seen so many stars in her life, it was so beautiful, so majestic, and it made her feel so small, so insignificant, staring up at the expansive universe. The big city lights blurred the majority of the sky away, she was lucky to see the big dipper out of her dorm room window. Whitney wasn't quite ready to call it a night, but she knew morning would come sooner than she'd like. "Never knew how beautiful northern Michigan was."

"We'll do this again next summer?" asked Timmy. He stood up shaking all the graham cracker crumbs off his hoodie.

"We can do it every year," said Brandon pouring out his bottled water onto the fire pit. "It will be our annual getaway." The fire crackled loudly before dying out, smoke barreling skyward.

"I'd love it," Fran let out a loud yawn. "It's just so serene...after a semester like we just had this getaway was needed."

The group picked up their things and made their way into their small two-person tents.

Brandon and Whitney settled into their sleeping bags with only the light of their flashlight as a guide. "I'll tell you what," said Whitney, "I'm with Fran; I can't wait to get home and run a hot bath though. Not sure if I enjoyed the bathing in the lake part of the trip," she laughed. "Yeah, thankfully it's just a quick ten-minute hike back to the Blazer. I'll need a good night's rest. I am pretty exhausted," Brandon yawned.

"Do you think Timmy and Fran had fun?" Whitney zipped up her sleeping bag.

"Definitely, Timmy was stoked when we went fishing yesterday afternoon, and he caught that trout. You should have seen his face."

"Well, that's good. Let's turn out the flashlight. I'm about to pass out."

"Love you," said Brandon. He flipped the flashlight off.

It was a quiet and peaceful night until Brandon was woken by a thunderous rumbling noise. It was loud but seemed distant. Was it a plane? He turned over to see if Whitney had awoken, but she was still out. He sat up and flicked the flashlight back on; making sure it was away from her face. He had no clue how she could sleep through the noise. The tent was literally vibrating from whatever was going on outside. It was steadily getting louder. Brandon thought it was weird, the last two days the group hadn't seen or heard anything other than the natural wildlife. He decided to go investigate; quietly, he stepped out of the tent where he saw Timmy already out exploring.

"Shhh, Fran's still sleeping," whispered Timmy loud enough to be heard over the thunderous noise.

"What is it?" asked Brandon looking up to the sky. He saw nothing but the sparkling stars.

"Sounds like a low plane, but I can't see much over the trees. It's getting louder though."

The noise changed, something large was breaking through the trees not too far from them. Crackling and loud explosions of splintering trees echoed through the forest.

"Crap, get down!" Timmy yelled as a medium-sized plane passed over the campgrounds clearing. It was flying so low it crashed through the treetops, raining down branches and leaves on the group. "Jesus!" Timmy cursed, "That was low!"

"Are you okay?" Brandon stood back up after narrowly dodging a large tree branch. By this point, the two girls exited from their tents in a panic.

"What happened?" Whitney yelled.

"A plane, it crashed through the tops of the trees!" Brandon pointed towards the direction of where the plane was heading. Without warning an even larger crash thundered throughout the forest, it sounded like it hit a large body of water.

"That sounded like the lake. We need to go help! They could drown, there may be survivors!" Brandon ran to the tent and slipped on his sneakers.

"Hurry, Tim, c'mon! You girls stay put, see if you can get a signal out here and call authorities, or the Depart men of Natural Resources, or anyone! I know it's been spotty out here, but just keep trying."

"Okay, yeah, but be careful!" said Fran who frantically began dialing her cellphone that was almost completely drained of its battery life, she was surprised it had lasted this long.

"Of course!" said Timmy sprinting after Brandon.

Timmy and Brandon raced through the forest with their flashlights leading the way. There was debris from the tree tops everywhere, large branches riddled all over the forest bed from the plane crashing through.

"It was a decent-sized plane," said Brandon breathing hard as he stepped over random debris. "Was it a passenger plane? I couldn't tell."

"Me neither, definitely wasn't big enough to fit too many people though. I don't think it was an airliner. Who flies out this way anyway? Maybe it was a corporate plane, cargo or something like that."

The two men broke through the forest and stepped onto the beachfront of the large lake. There, about halfway out into the lake, sat the quickly sinking plane. The nose of the aircraft was completely sub-merged; about a third of the back end of the plane was still above the surface of the water, but it was sinking fast. Brandon and Timmy both shined their flashlights towards the area, but the lights were too small, they were not strong enough to light up the crash site. Thankfully, the night sky was brightened by a full moon which gave them a decent amount of visibility.

"Do you see anyone in the water? Any survivors?" asked Brandon peering out into the lake.

"No, but look...the side of the plane...it looks like something is..." Timmy pointed towards the center of the exposed plane.

A low thumping noise could be heard echoing over the lake top. "Sounds like someone is trying to bang their way out," said Brandon, listening carefully.

Suddenly, two long, slender arms burst through the planes siding. Whatever it was broke through and began ripping the exterior of the aircraft to pieces, creating its own exit from the quickly submerging aircraft. The guys could barely make out what was happening in the darkness of the night. But they could see something crawling its way out of the newly made exit.

"What the heck," Brandon squinted his eyes. "What are we seeing?

What is that thing? Did it just rip its way through the plane?" "I have no idea..." Timmy's mouth was agape.

Finally, the figure broke all the way through the siding. A strange being with a long, slender body and an awkwardly shaped head, slowly crawled its way out from the hole. The boys had a hard time making out what exactly it was they were looking at, as the moon provided poor lighting. They could tell whatever it was, wanted nothing to do with the lake water. It feverishly crawled its way up to the top of the plane trying to escape the ever rising water.

"Is that a person?" asked Brandon.

"It has to be, right?" Timmy swallowed down the lump in his throat.

He didn't sound very convincing, even to himself.

"Hey, are you okay?" Brandon yelled to the figure frantically trying to get away from the rising lake water. "Swim ashore! We'll help you!"

As soon as Brandon yelled for it, the figure shot completely upright, it moved quickly, its head jerking in fast birdlike motions, definitely not human. Standing tall on its legs it spun around quickly towards their direction. Its head shot up against the back drop of the full moon allowing for the first time a perfect view of the figure's face. It was not human. Its oblong shaped skull sprouted two large, antler-like horns.

The image struck pure horror into the boy's minds.

The creature howled in an eerie blood-curdling shriek. Looking towards them, the creature pounced about ten feet into the air and crashed hard, belly flopping into the lake.

"Crap, that thing had horns!" yelled Brandon grabbing Timmy's shirt. "It's coming for us; we need to get back to the girls and into the Blazer!"

Timmy stared in horror at the sight of the creature coming towards them.

"Timmy, c'mon man, run!" Brandon slapped his friend as hard as he could on the face.

"Okay…okay!" Timmy shook his head. The two men sprinted back towards their camp ground.

"I don't think that thing is a very good swimmer!" Timmy yelled up to his friend.

"Good, let's hope that gives us enough time to get to the Blazer!"

●　　　●　　　●

"I can't get a signal, we're too far away from anything," said Fran trying for the umpteenth time to dial through to authorities.

"I'm not having any luck either," said Whitney, who had just given up and pocketed her phone. She began tearing down her tent and packing up their things. "We need to get to the Blazer as soon as the boys get back so we can get closer to town and call the crash in. God, I hope everyone is all right…!"

"I hope they found some survivors…," said Fran following suit, she packed up their stuff.

"Use your phone's flashlight app, so we can see better. My battery is about to die," said Whitney.

"It won't last long. It's basically dead...."

"Run!" Brandon burst through the thick trees towards the camp. He was yelling frantically to the girls.

"What?" The sudden commotion caused Fran to drop her sleeping bag.

"Something is chasing us!" yelled Timmy not too far behind him. "Brandon, stop!" Whitney yelled. "This is not funny!"

"This isn't a joke..." Brandon dropped to his hands and knees, hunched over he breathed in deep gasps attempting to catch his breath. "There was a plane..." Timmy wiped the sweat from his brow. "The plane was sinking fast. Something big broke through the side... it had horns."

"No time to explain! It's coming after us...we gotta get to the Blazer, now!" Brandon stood back up.

"I don't hear anything, maybe the animal got scared off?" asked Fran.

"It wasn't an animal!" Timmy was now yelling.

A loud hellacious shrieking noise echoed throughout the forest. It literally sent chills down Whitney's spine. "Jesus, what was that!?"

"Oh God!" Fran felt tears brimming in her eyes.

"It's after us. Run, now!" Timmy grabbed Fran's hand. Now, both couples began running through the forest towards the Blazer.

"We can't slow down," Brandon yelled, "follow me. I know the way. Hopefully, we can outrun the thing."

Brandon led the group through the dark moonlit forest. They ran as fast as possible, not allowing any one of them to slow down. Every few minutes they heard the shrieking howl of the creature. There was no way Brandon was leaving anyone behind. What did the creature want? Was it hunting them? Brandon couldn't shake the image of its head. He kept picturing the moonlit silhouette of the creature and its antlers... It wasn't human."There it is!" The forest finally broke onto a small dirt road. "Quick, get in!" Brandon ordered.

The group ran towards the Blazer. They rushed into the vehicle, slamming the doors closed. Brandon's hands trembled uncontrollably with the keys as he attempted to start the vehicle up. He inserted the key into the ignition, turning the engine over. Before he could shift the blazer into drive a large creature burst through the forest right in front of the jeep.

It had cut them off.

The group screamed frantically at the grotesque sight.

There the creature stood in front of them, howling, with wild animalistic eyes that were glowing brightly from the headlights shining on it. The creature towered over the car, easily twelve feet, tall and lanky. Its oblong shaped head looked like a goat or a horse of some sort, with yellowish fangs protruding from the top of its jaws. It let out another shrieking howl exposing an overly long, thin tongue. It was grotesque and its legs were covered in short dark brown hair, its feet hooved.

Brandon quickly turned on his brights hoping to blind the creature. The flash exposed its yellowish human-like upper torso that was matted with muddy coarse hair. It squealed painfully from the light and threw up its arms to block the light. Its grotesque giant hands were now exposed, and they were huge, with long slender fingers that seemed disproportionate with the rest of its body. At the end of each finger were thick black nails, perfect to rip through the flesh of whatever victim it had set out to hunt.

"Floor it!" said Timmy.

Brandon shifted the car to drive and forcefully hit the gas. The Creature did not move, still momentarily blinded. Brandon knew he had to hurt the creature, kill it, or at least stop it from giving chase. He had no idea how fast that thing could run in an open road, but he didn't want to find out.

There was not that much space between them and the creature, but it would have to do. Brandon had floored it and turned the wheel to-wards the creature, clipping it with his Blazer as it stood dazed. The creature hit hard on, its body folding onto the Blazer's hood. Its large, long hand struck the vehicle in a haphazard attempt to fight back. It struck the hood, leaving four deep cuts where its nails pierced right through the frame. The creature made a loud thud as it hit and rolled off onto earth.

"Get out of here!" Timmy peered through the back window, hoping the creature would not get back to its feet.

"Did you see its hands!?" Fran was hyperventilating from the commotion.

"It's okay. We're getting out of here." "Oh God..." Timmy frowned.

"What is it?" Brandon yelled from the driver's seat.

The road was dark as the group fled, but Timmy watched as the creature stood back up.

"Go as fast as possible. It's chasing us!"

CHAPTER 13
BACK TO REALITY

Ally hadn't felt normal for days after her spirit was ripped from her physical body. Patricia Ellingbee made her stay in the recovery ward over the weekend to make sure all her vitals stayed normal (despite Dr. Wong's assurance that she was fine to go home later on the night of the incident). Thankfully, Elly had many visitors throughout the week making her stay not as boring as it could have been. Hunter and her friends met with her every day after class to keep her company. Despite Ms. Ellingbee's direct orders to rest and relax, Elly made Hunter promise to smuggle in all of her homework so she could keep up to date on all the classroom activities. With no television or radio in the infirmary, the days were a drag, so, Elly slept them away. She opted to stay up early into the morning hours where she could study in peace while the rest of the estate slept.

It was late Saturday night, early Sunday morning; Elly was cozying up with her Seekers journal writing the night away. She was distracted by the infirmary's door creaking open.

"It's three in the morning, why are you awake?" Calenstine powered his electric wheelchair into her room. "I thought I was going to have to disturb your sleep."

"Professor?" Elly clapped her text book closed with a thud. "I have been asking for you all week!"

"I know, dear, I am sorry I was not on the premises during your last episode."

"I have so much to tell you!" Elly went on for over an hour explaining to Calenstine everything that happened. She explained about touching the Yggdrasil tree, how she woke up in the other realm, how it felt different from the other times she slipped away into the ethereal form, about Nidhogg the wyrm, the Norns, how the tree was calling for her, how the Yggdrasil needed to cleanse her spirit of the darkness she was harboring within it.

Calenstine was, for the first time ever, speechless. Elly spoke very carefully; she explained how the tree was beckoning her. How the Norns spoke of a single earthly presence who could, as they explained, "transform," into a powerful godlike demon in death and offset the natural universal balance.

"Elly..." Calenstine's bony fingers ran through the top of his head. His eyes could not hide the worrisome nature of his soul. "I cannot explain how groundbreaking your journey into the ethereal realm has been. You are literally rewriting our understanding of the human experience... you traveled past the afterlife, deeper into the unknown than I never even dreamed could have existed."

"I don't understand all of it," Elly fiddled with Solomon's ring on her finger. "But, I know they were really worried about this guy who is completely evil."

"We know this man." Calenstine directed his chair over to her bedside window, peering out into the starry, night sky.

"Is it the Aten guy?" Elly already knew the answer. All any of the adults ever spoke about anymore was how Aten Corp was recruiting all of Calenstine's people, and how no one understood how terrible of a person he truly was. Elly had met him before, he crashed the Enlightenment... she remembered his voice and how it sent shivers down her back.

"I am afraid so," Calenstine did not look back to her. "I must ask you to carry a heavy burden on your soul. I apologize, if what you say is true, and the Yggdrasil tree needed to purge your essence of all negativity, this may add to it. However, we must not let fear and panic take over our Estate. I would ask of you to keep your knowledge hidden. If anyone asks about what happened, please refrain from going into too much detail. No one is to know about the foretold evil. It is detrimental to keeping our Estate secure and safe."

"To be honest, I don't think anyone would believe me...sounds like a silly fairy tale."

"Well, remember," Calenstine finally turned around and offered her a warm smile. "You're not out in the cities anymore. You're here in the Estate where we specialize in these things, especially when it involves the stuff that most people don't believe in."

Elly got a few hours of sleep after the Professor left, signing the paperwork to allow Elly to be released once she got a few hours of shut eye. She had awoken around noon on that Sunday, eager to get back to her dorm room and a normal life. Symphanie and Olivia were studying in their dorm and met their friend with warm hugs.

"It's about time they let you out," Olivia poured her a hot cup of mint cocoa.

"It's been weird not having you in the dorm all week," said Symphanie who was sitting at their dinner table doodling Alistair's name in her Seekers journal.

"It felt like a month," Elly jumped onto the small sofa, kicking her legs up on the arm rest. "This is what I am talking about, that hospital bed was for the birds."

"We heard Calenstine met with you last night?" asked Olivia who joined Symphanie at the table and resumed penning a letter she had started working on.

"Wow, news travels fast," Elly chuckled. "Yeah, I guess he has been gone on a business trip for the last week."

"Well, it's been a pretty boring week without you. Plus, Margot stopped in this morning to let us know. She wanted to make sure we kept a close eye on you." Olivia took a sip from her own steaming cup of cocoa.

"So no more passing out, okay?" Symphanie added. A light rapping came from their door.

"Who could that be?" Elly jumped off the sofa and slowly pulled the creaky door open to peek through.

"Let us in!" Hunter whispered loudly, pushing the door open. "What are you guys doing here," Symphanie couldn't hide her excitement at seeing Alistair following Tully and Hunter hastily into the room.

"We snuck in," Hunter motioned with his finger to his lips to keep everyone quiet.

"You guys are going to get in so much trouble. You know boys aren't allowed on the girls floor," Elly reprimanded the boys.

"Nice to see you're back," Hunter rolled his eyes.

"It's okay," Tully opened their fridge and grabbed an apple, taking a huge bite out of it. "We've been sneaking in almost every day," he swallowed

"Yea, we are basically pros at sneaking in," Tully tossed Alistair an apple.

"We got some exciting news," Alistair placed his laptop on the dinner table and logged in.

"What's going on?" asked Elly.

"Have the seat next to me," Symphanie pulled out a chair for Alistair to take a seat. She slyly closed her journal so he couldn't see his doodled name.

"Remember when our parents told us we may be going to Michigan to search for the Wendigo creature? Well my dad set me up with this website the Seekers use to monitor news reports and post about sightings," Alistair explained in-between giant bites of his apple. "...sorry we skipped lunch"

"This better be worth it, you guys could get expelled for this!" Elly pursed her lips in anger.

"Well, if we get caught in here, we're all expelled." Hunter corrected.

"See, look at this, capturing anything on video is extremely rare...!"

Alistair clicked play on a video file on his computer. The video was shot on a shaky cellphone camera in the back seat of a vehicle. There was a lot of noise, people talking all at once about some sort of creature following them. The man holding the cellphone was filming out the back window. It was dark and there wasn't much to see. After about a minute of the video something suddenly smashed into the back window causing the glass to splinter into a million web-like fractions.

"Did you see it!?" Alistair's eyes lit up.

"I saw the back window get smashed, but not from what...,"

answered Symphanie looking closely at the video.

"I will freeze it, you can see it when it makes contact," Alistair manually rewound the video and paused it on a specific frame.

"What is that thing?" Olivia frowned at the sight.

The image showed a blurry creature's face. It was goat-like with long horns sticking out from its skull. The head itself was very blurry, but the two eyes were glowing brightly, like two floodlights illuminating the darkness around it.

"It's so blurry..." Elly waived it off. "It's probably photo-shopped."

"No way, these kids were chased for miles by this thing. As soon as they got to town they wrote up a police report. This was about two months ago. Ever sense then, look at all these strange sightings about a walking goat man with glowing eyes." Alistair clicked off the webpage to a series of windows all showcasing reports of a creature terrorizing Mid-Michigan. "I think it's real."

"Well, if that's the thing your parents want us to hunt, it looks way too dangerous," Elly responded. "These field trips are supposed to be novice cases. We're just kids; they are not going to have us out in the wilderness hunting a blood thirsty goat monster."

"It's not a goat monster, it's a Wendigo," Alistair corrected.

"And they would if they felt as you did," Tully answered. "If they think it's a hoax, we're game."

"Yep," said Hunter. "I talked to Alistair's dad about it. He's excited, but he thinks someone is hoaxing the entire thing. Said there was supposedly a plane crash in the woods where the kids claim the creature came from. But the local authorities said they searched all over for the crash and it wasn't there. They also got in contact with local airlines; nothing was flying, to their knowledge."

"So why are you excited?" asked Elly. "Sounds even more like a hoax if you ask me."

"Did you see the video!?" Alistair was baffled by Elly's lack of interest.

"Hoax," said Olivia, siding with Elly.

"I agree with you, Ally," said Symphanie in a cute, playful voice.

"Ally?" Tully chuckled.

Hunter noticed Olivia was mostly ignoring the conversations of the group. She looked pretty sitting at the table writing, but he noticed she seemed troubled. He was happy they were on talking terms again; it had taken a while before he realized he had been treating her differently.

"Working on a paper?" Hunter offered a friendly smile.

"Oh?" Olivia looked up, she hadn't seen him approach. "No, nothing like that," she said as she quickly covered up the notebook.

"Oh, I'm sorry. I didn't mean to intrude..." Hunter frowned, backing away.

"No, you're not. I'm sorry. It's just...." "What's wrong?" asked Hunter.

"You probably couldn't care less, but Marcus hasn't replied to any of my letters. It's been a month and a half...."

"Oh," Hunter's heart sank a bit. Not exactly the topic of conversation he'd hoped for. But, she'd never really talked to him about Marcus before. This was a first.

"Well, I'm sure there is a reason," Hunter didn't really know what to say. He didn't like seeing her sad.

"Yeah, like he met some new girl at school."

"No, I doubt that. He'd be crazy to do that..." Hunter hadn't really thought before he spoke, he immediately turned red in the face. "Err... you know what I mean."

"I guess," Olivia couldn't help but half smile. She always thought Hunter was a sweet friend.

"Look, we live in a mansion in the middle of a forest no one knows exists. We have one guy run mail through once a week. He has to travel all the way out into the nearest city to get all of our residents' mail. I'm sure it gets backed up. I know he's replied, you just haven't gotten it yet. Just be patient."

"Yeah, that does make sense." Olivia stood up and gave Hunter a hug. "You always know what to say...thank you."

"So guys!" Symphanie broke up the moment with a loud banging noise. She stood up on her chair tapping a spoon onto her hot cocoa mug. "We all know the dance is right around the corner," she smiled brightly, blushing.

"Yeah, if right around the corner means four months away," Tully raised his eyebrows at Alistair, who was equally as red in the face.

"Well, it's coming up soon," Symphanie waived off her older cousin. "*Anyway*, as we all know we are having a Sadie-Hawkins dance, and I wanted to be the first one to lock down my date!"

"Here we go," Elly snickered.

"Ally, I was hoping you would make me the happiest girl in the world and be my date!"

"Oh…" Alistair was embarrassed, his face was beet red. "I mean, yeah, sure?"

"Yes, awesome! We're going to have a blast! We'll be the cutest couple there!" Symphanie ran over to Alistair and gave him a big hug.

"Alistair, you're such a ladies man," Tully chuckled. "But, I think we have to cut your romantic embrace short. We need to get back to our dorms before they realize we're missing."

So the boys made a sneaky escape back into the hallway and back to their own dorm. The girls had a lot to discuss and spent the remainder of the day catching up on all the gossip Elly had missed while in the infirmary.

CHAPTER 14
A SECRET SEEKERS MEETING

Deep beneath the Estate is a hidden, ancient catacomb. Few know of its existence, and those that do, are sworn to protect the secre- tive lair from outside eyes. Buried hundreds of feet deep in the earth, the creepy lair is void of all-natural light and any and all forms of technology. Nothing modern exists in the catacomb, nor is allowed. Here is the main gathering chamber where all the secret meetings are held for the Seekers Society.

The round room is lit by twelve large torches evenly spaced around the oval perimeter. In the middle of the chamber sits a large stone table, carved right out from the stone floor where the group gathers to discuss any news related to new sightings of creatures, and to decide what to do in each situation. At the center of this table sits an ornate, blazing-hot altar casting dancing shadows against the cold chamber walls.

"Welcome Seekers," Calenstine poured out the contents of a small leather bag into his boney hands. A small mound of finely grained powder mounded in his palm. He tossed the substance into the altars flame causing a beautiful eruption of fire exploding before the group. The blaze turned bright blue, shooting as high as the cave's domed ceiling.

"I thank you all for making this meeting on such short notice," Calenstine spoke slowly, peering intently at the blue flame.

The founder of the Seekers stood amongst his loyal companions. They all wore black, communal, Seekers robes, hoods up with their society's sigil sewn on the right breast of the garment. Calenstine was the only member to wear a dark red robe. He was also the only member whose face was completely exposed, his hood down. Calenstine seemed troubled which solidified the importance of the situation at hand. "Much has happened in the last year. Dark times continue to approach us. It is important we tread lightly and remain on the same page."

"It's been quite some time since you've held a summit," Alistair's father spoke up from the hooded group. Benjamin dropped his hood, a worried look drawn across his face. "The Estate is in a panic. People are getting scared...many are taking Aten's offers to work for his corporation. We lose numbers every month."

"Yes, it is true my friend," Calenstine fought back a frown. "Tension is at an all-time high. In little over a year, we have had monsters breaking loose in our home, and demons running amuck within our walls torturing our children. We have been breached by the enemy, and turncoats infiltrate our numbers. Aten Corp was serious when they said they would bring the war to our front door. They have more than just a personal vendetta against me. It is no secret, Declan Aten and I have long running feud. However, he knows how successful I have been in finding many of our world's relics and creatures. He wants to run the Estate into the ground, to eliminate our presence in the world. He wants my specimens, my treasures, everything we have worked so hard for. He wants power... He wants...weapons...."

"He can try," said Abram, also dropping his hood. His face was stern, eyes resolute. "I'd like to see him step foot here, one more time."

"Don't underestimate him," Calenstine shook his head. "He is evil, his humanity died long ago. Let us hope he never shows up at our doorstep again. He grows in power every day. Recent events point towards his ungodly hands."

"Has something changed?" Margot removed her hood.

"Yes, bizarre events have been happening all over the world. The recent number of cryptid sightings, in the U.S. alone, has tripled in the last year. In nearly every state there has been some sort of paranormal sighting, recorded monster attack, or some other cryptid behavior. Social media is popping up with videos, weekly. Most notably, our team of digital, forensic scientists think that the majority of them are not faked. Although…they are working around the clock trying to dismiss the videos as fakes."

"Why the sudden spark in sightings?" Joe dropped his hood, hanging onto every word the Professor spoke.

"It is unknown," answered Calenstine. "Some of these new sightings are unique cryptids we are just learning about. I fear something is afoot, but we have no Intel as of yet. But where there is smoke, there is fire.…"

"It's Aten corp, isn't it?" asked Benjamin.

"Perhaps," said Calenstine. "This is why we are here today. This meeting has been called to address the threat of Aten Corp. We must continue our duties as usual. We cannot allow their presence to manipulate the Estate in any way. If you catch wind of any moles within our walls, please contact me immediately. When we are out in the field, we must be diligent. We will continue on with the Enlightenment as usual. Abram, Benjamin, I have approved your assignment request to take the following students to investigate the recent Michigan sightings of the proposed Wendigo: Hunter, Elly, Alistair, and Olivia will be under your care during the visit. Also, Tully and Symphany's parents are still overseas on their mission to find the elusive Cintamani stone. Therefore, I will ask you take them along as well, guide them as your own. You will have a large group, please be aware of your surroundings and the children's whereabouts at all times."

"That is excellent, thank you, sir," Abram nodded.

"I do not know what will come from the recent sightings," Calenstine spoke sternly. "The Wendigo is a magical cryptid, and as far as we know, is nothing more than a fictional beast derived from Native American lore. There has been zero evidence in our field that it is a real creature. If it appears the sightings and evidence are tangible, return home with the children and we will suit up a new team."

"I highly doubt we are dealing with a real life Wendigo," said Benjamin with a sly smile. "It's going to be a case of mistaken identity. If we walk into the path of a *real* Wendigo it would be a game changer.

It's probably a large bear or something."

"I hope you're correct," Calenstine nodded. "If it is something else, then we have a whole new issue to deal with...."

"We can leave in one week, will that be acceptable?" asked Abram. "Yes, I will have Patricia partnered with the Friedrich building and their teachers," Calenstine replied. "For the rest of you, please partner with Patricia Ellingbee when it comes to your children's fieldwork. She will be your go to person to communicate between both schools and to keep everything in compliance. You can see me with ideas for investigations. After the recent events involving demons here in the castle, I will not allow any investigations dealing with spirits or hauntings. As always, for the safety of our children and time restraints, all investigations must remain within the continental United States. Remember; keep the field assignments simple, nothing too intense for their first scouting."

"Professor," Joe added raising his hand. "May I speak on what we talked about earlier?"

"Of course," Calenstine smiled and nodded.

"Thank you," Joe nervously cleared his throat. "Well...as you all know, I have been struggling with this... condition of mine. So, I have come to a decision. It wasn't an easy one...and I can only pray it's the right one," Joe's voice trembled with nerves. He peered at the group, his eyes landing on Margot's.

"When my niece and nephew go off on their field work with Ben and Abram, I have decided to go ahead with surgery to repair my legs. It's risky, the potential outcome is a bit dire, but it is a decision that I have made."

"Joe!" Margot beamed. "I am so proud of you. Dr. Wong and I have been discussing the operation for months. She really thinks she could fix you up."

"Margot I am sorry, but I will not be allowing Dr. Wong to operate," Joe replied. He dropped his eyes to the floor. He didn't care to see the confused and soon to be disappointed look on her face.

"Wait, what?" Margot frowned. "You just said...."

"Joe came to me a few nights ago with an alternate plan," Calenstine interjected. "We must remember his bravery the night he saved Hunter and Elly from the Beast of Bladenboro. Since that moment, he has been cursed to a life in a wheelchair. He sacrificed his legs for the children's safety. We all owe him our gratitude and support for his unmatched heroics. With that being said, I ask us to be supportive as he will be undertaking a very…ummm, controversial operation."

"Controversial?" Margot shook her head in disbelief. "What are you talking about?"

"Plato approached me a few months back," Joe answered. "He says he can fix me up without surgery. He will be utilizing these things called nanobots, some sort of fancy technology he created. These little machines will go into my bloodstream, and they'll live within my body, acting as a million little surgeons fixing my spine."

"You're joking!" Margot blurted out, her face red with anger. "You won't let a world renowned spinal surgeon touch you, but you will let a giant robot use these…these…nanobots?"

"Margot," Joe held his head down, kept his voice soft, "Please… understand…!"

"No, no!" Margot yelled. "We are in this together. We're raising those kids. You didn't even talk to me. This is serious, who knows what could happen."

"Margot," Calenstine interjected once again. "We understand the situation. I would ask to keep personal affairs outside of the summit. Joe has given a lot to the Seekers and even more to his niece and nephew. I have spoken with Plato myself to learn more about the operation. Joe believes it is his best option. I must ask all of you to please, back him up."

"You really think these nano-things will work?" asked Ben.

"I don't know. But, I trust in Plato more than going into a high risk surgery," said Joe.

"What is the risk?" asked Ben

"Not sure, there is no way to know how the nanobots will react once they enter my body. Plato is fairly sure-"

"Not totally sure?" Margot asked as tears streamed down over her cheeks.

"Yes, not sure." replied Joe. "Listen, I can't live my life missing out on Hunter and Elly's Enlightenment. I can't even go out on their first field work assignment, I can't dance with Elly, and I can't throw a football with Hunter. This damned wheelchair is going to kill me if I don't try this. The surgery with Wong is not an option for me, it's personal, but it's just not. I don't plan on dying, people. I plan on walking out of that infirmary on my own two feet."

"Or in a coffin..." Margot pushed aside one of her fellow robed Seekers and stormed out of the chamber. "Margot...," Joe sighed heavily.

"Do not chase her," Calenstine put his hand on Joe's shoulder. "But..." Joe let out a sigh.

"There is nothing you can say to make things better. You made your choice. She must find a way to deal with it," said Calenstine.

CHAPTER 15
MYSTERIOUS LETTER

Margot was furious. She stormed through the hallway keeping her head low so as not to attract attention to her emotional state. She wiped away the tears that raced down her flushed cheeks, failing to compose herself. She was embarrassed, mad at herself for losing her emotions at the Seekers meeting.

She couldn't believe Joe dropped that sort of information on her in front of such a large group. He didn't even discuss it with her... selfish as always. Did he not understand? She was a part of his life now, whether he liked it or not. Together they had to raise Hunter and Elly, and that meant at least to her that these sorts of life altering decisions were to be made together, and at the very least talked about. "Stubborn jerk," Margot cursed under her breath turning down the hall towards her room. All she wanted to do was get home, and take a hot bath. Get as far away from everyone as possible.

Unfortunately, Sebastian had other plans. He stood outside her apartment door patiently waiting. He saw her turn the corner, her head low, walking a mile a minute. He noticed the redness in her face, that she was upset. Had something happened? Was she attacked? A thousand thoughts flooded Sebastian's mind, all worse than the last. Or maybe she was upset because of their split? It made sense to him, Patricia was keeping an eye out for Margot, and no one could have attacked her without someone knowing. Yes, there was no other reason, she wanted him back.

"Ahem, hello, love..." Sebastian stood with flowers in hand, a wide charming smile across his face.

"Sebastian, what are you doing here?" Margot turned away from him, wiping away the remaining tears."I have been waiting for you, we need to talk..." Sebastian held out the flowers. "You've been crying? Love, please this whole thing hurts me too. Let's talk about it. I have missed you so much!"

"I am not crying over us," Margot blurted out in anger.

"Oh..." Sebastian frowned. "But I..." he stammered, confused by her outburst.

"Look, there are a lot of things going on in my life. Believe it or not, everything does not have to center around you."

"I didn't mean to-" Sebastian let out a frustrated sigh.

"—I have had a long day. All I want to do is be alone," Margot cut him off.

"I have been waiting here for over an hour," Sebastian put out his arm, blocking off the doorway. "I love you dear, I want to make things right."

"Sebastian..." Margot was past impatient. "Right now is not the time."

"We need to talk," Sebastian begged. "You can't keep ignoring me."

"I will get a hold of you when I am free, okay? I am sorry you're hurt about what is going on. But, at this point in my life I need to be alone. I need to figure some things out." Margot brushed passed Sebastian's arm, opened her apartment door and walked in.

"Okay..." Sebastian's head hung low.

"Just..." Margot shook her head. She hated hurting Sebastian. "Give me a few days, okay?"

"Yeah," Sebastian kept his eyes down at his own feet. He couldn't muster the strength to look her in the eyes. "Of course...a few days...."

"Thank you..." Margot closed the door, locking it.

Margot never thought accepting the guardianship for Hunter and Elly would make her life so stressful. Everything seemed to be crumbling all around her, although she knew this had little to do with Hunter and Elly. She loved her time with them. They needed her.

Margot went straight for the kitchen pouring a tall glass of wine, immediately taking a seat on her sofa and taking in a long sip from her drink. She needed to clear her head, to put Sebastian and Joe out of her mind.

A knock at the door interrupted her retreat. She hadn't even gotten through half of her first glass before someone was bothering her. She downed the rest of her wine in one long gulp. If she had to get up, at least now she had the excuse to grab a refill.

"This better not be either of them..." Margot grumbled, peeking through the peep-hole but seeing no one.

She turned towards the kitchen, accidentally kicking something with her foot. It was a letter, slipped under her doorway.

"Weird..." Probably just another attempt by Sebastian to apologize and win her back... "You just don't know when to give up, do you?"

Margot picked up the envelope making her way back to the kitchen. She fixed herself a second glass, debating over whether or not she was even going to open the letter. Perhaps she would just toss it, better to not get worked up over something that was sure to say something she wasn't ready to deal with, yet.

She returned to her cozy spot on the sofa, setting the letter on her lap. She looked closer at it, but didn't recognize the handwriting. Maybe it wasn't from Sebastian.

But who would slip a letter beneath her door?

Margot slipped her finger into the envelope, tearing it open. Inside was a letter written on a thick piece of parchment, folded in half. Unfolding it caused a copious amount bright green powder to fall out onto her lap and all over her hands.

"Seriously?" Margot threw up her arms. The substance was everywhere. She brushed her pants off with her hands creating a small dust cloud. "What is this crap?" she sneezed, her nose stung from inhaling the substance. It had a strong aroma, almost sickly sweet, like someone was melting a pot of salted caramel.

The letter didn't say much. Just one sentence: "You can thank your fiancé."

Margot crumbled up the envelope, tossing it in her kitchen trash. The powder had gotten all over her, stickier then she thought it would be, she undressed and drew a bath in hopes to clean herself off. "Real funny," Margot frowned.

Who would play a stupid joke like that? A perfect end to a crummy day...

CHAPTER 16
PACKING

I am so excited!" Hunter was hurling clothes into his luggage with reckless abandonment. "We are actually going out into the field for some real life monster hunting!"

Hunter and the boys were in their dorm room readying for their field trip. It looked like a tornado had hit their room spilling over there dressers and tossing out their clothes all over the floor.

"Hunter, fold those. You'll fit more in your luggage if you don't wad them up like a ball," Uncle Joe shook his head at the mess. "It's not a race."

"Hunter doesn't care," said Elly who sat with the other girls, Olivia and Symphanie, at the dinner table. The girls were already packed and enjoying a sweet snack of coffee cakes and pastries as they made fun of the boys idea of getting ready. "Look at this place, it's a pigsty! There are clothes everywhere, gross!"

"It was clean before we started packing," said Alistair who tested out his compass before packing it into his hiking gear.

"Boys are messy," said Symphanie. She watched contently as Alistair packed up his bag. "Do you need help packing, Allie?"

"Allie?" asked Tully with a chuckle beneath his breath.

"That's my pet name for Alistair," said Symphanie. "He's my little Allie bear."

"Allie Bear?" Joe and Tully roared with laughter.

"Uh...no, I think I'm okay," Alistair blushed but offered Symphanie a nervous smile. He liked Symphanie, he was a bit amazed someone like her found him to be "cool" so to speak, but he wasn't all for getting teased by the guys.

147

"Man, she is really smitten with you," Tully whispered. He playfully elbowed Alistair on the arm.

Alistair did his best to ignore Tully and continued packing.

"Did Margot show up to help you girls pack?" Joe asked as he tossed Hunter a couple of sweaters to pack. "It gets cold in Michigan this time of year. Pack warm."

"No, she never showed," replied Olivia. "We did it ourselves," said Elly.

"I see," replied Joe with a bit of a worried look on his bearded face. "Everything okay, Uncle Joe?" asked Elly.

"Yeah, it's fine, Elly," Joe made light of the question. "Hunter, make sure you pack up your journal and all the homework you have to keep up with too."

"What?" Hunter whined. "We have to do homework on the road?" "Well, duh," said Elly mocking her brother. "Why wouldn't we?" "Because, we're hunting monsters," Hunter argued.

"There's a lot of down time. You will have plenty of opportunity to keep up with both your scholastic work and your Enlightenment assignments," said Joe.

"Lame..." Hunter sulked at the thought of a mountain of homework.

"I wish I could go with you guys." Joe helped Hunter fold his messy ball of clothes jam packed in his luggage.

"Did you go out on an assignment when you were in the Enlightenment?" asked Tully.

"Sure did," Joe smiled. "Hunter and Elly's mother and I went to Wisconsin to hunt down a famous cryptid, the Beast of Bray Road."

"Beast of Bray Road?" asked Symphanie. "What is that?" "Wisconsin's resident werewolf," Joe smiled fondly as he reminisced. "It was your mother Kim, myself, Abram and Ben. We went with our guardians for a week trip. It was a blast. First time on an adventure, I remember how excited we three boys were. Kim was a bit more hesitant, she was a lot cooler headed then Ben and I. A lot like you are Elly. She loved her books...," Joe frowned as he spoke about his long-lost sister.

"What did you find?" asked Alistair wide eyed.

"Well, we spent three nights out in the nearby forest searching the grounds, looking for clues, anything really. We didn't find much. Walked away with a potential footprint that was inconclusive, probably a local pack of wolves. I remember we found a few strands of hair that was unidentifiable, so that was sort of cool. As of today, though, the Beast of Bray Road is just a myth. No hard evidence."

"That sounds like a boring investigation," said Hunter who had to use all his strength and body weight to zip up his overflowing luggage. "Well, ninety-five percent of all cases end that way. Don't think going out on an investigation is all action and adventure. It's not. If it was easy to hunt cryptids then there wouldn't be any cryptids, they'd just be documented animals," explained Uncle Joe.

"I guess that makes sense," Hunter couldn't help but frown a bit. "Get used to it, boys, being a Seeker is not all action, it's a lot of camping out in a tent and waiting," Joe chuckled.

"I think we're finished," said Tully who had just finished packing up his bag.

"We got everything we need, right?" asked Joe.

"Yep, water bottle, sweaters, hiking boots, rain jackets…," Alistair listed off.

"Good then," Joe nodded. "I think you're ready to set off."

"Hi guys," Margot knocked on the dorm door and stuck her head in. She looked exhausted; her skin a shade of yellow and she had heavy bags under her eyes. Margot walked into the room and took a seat next to the girls at the table; she winced in pain as she took a seat.

"Margot!" Elly jumped down from her chair and gave Margot a hug.

"Oh, careful please. I am in a lot of pain today," Margot returned the hug with one arm around Elly.

"Pain?" Joe questioned. He rolled himself over to Margot. "What's wrong?"

"Just give me a second," Margot insisted. She took some aspirin from her purse and swallowed a them down. "Children, please excuseJoe and I for a second. Elly, Olivia, Symphanie, I am sorry I missed helping you pack this morning. I had a hard time getting motivated." "It's okay, you look sick. You should probably rest," said Olivia.

Joe followed Margot out into the hallway where she held her right arm in pain. Her face strained in discomfort.

"What's going on?" asked Joe. "Why are you holding your arm like that?"

"I am not feeling well is all," Margot waived off his concern. "That's not why I came to talk. I came here to try and stop you from doing this asinine little stunt you and Plato are talking about."

"Listen, I'm sorry I didn't talk to you about this one on one. I knew you would react this way." Joe frowned. His intentions were never to hurt Margot.

"Then why? Why do it?" asked Margot. "It just sounds so crazy. Think about Hunter and Elly…think about me."

"I have to do it. I can't live like this anymore. I don't trust the surgery with Wong. I don't want to live my life alone confined to this wheeled prison," Joe's voice cracked.

"You're not a broken man!" Margot reached out and held Joe's hand. "You understand that, right?"

"You don't have to live the way I do. What good am I? What do I have to offer?"

"You are the only thing keeping Hunter and Elly going. You are their guardian now." Margot squeezed his hand tightly.

"I can't even do that right." Joe shook his head in frustration. "You're an amazing and loving person. I don't know anyone who would have sacrificed themselves like you did. You should wear that wheelchair like a badge of honor. You saved their lives, Joe. A selfless act… You're a hero!"

"No…," Joe shook his head, holding it low and away from Margot's eyes.

Margot frowned. She could not understand why Joe felt so worthless. She gently lifted his face by putting her hand beneath his chin; softly, she wiped away a single tear that rolled down his face. He looked so sad. It broke her heart to see such sadness in his eyes.

"I never meant to upset you, or get you mixed in with my problems. I know you have Sebastian to think about." Joe frowned; he knew he was a mess.

Margot wanted his pain to go away, to see him happy again. He deserved so much more than all the pain he'd been going through. She sat there staring into his soft brown eyes. She had been fighting back these feelings for a while now...she never wanted to admit it before. So many things had changed in the last few days though, and she couldn't hide her feelings anymore. As much as she would never admit it to anyone, Joe did play a big role in her wanting to leave Sebastian. She even tried to talk herself out of it...but at this moment she knew...

Margot watched as another tear fell down his cheek. She wiped it away. Slowly she leaned forward hoping he would return her embrace.

Burning pain shot through Margot's entire right shoulder causing her to wince.

"Margot?" Joe grabbed her quickly before she fell onto the floor.

"What happened? Are you okay?"

"My shoulder...it's so stiff I can't move it." She cursed in pain. "It's that painful?" asked Joe.

"It's okay, it comes and goes," Margot frowned. She could feel the stiffness already loosening up. "It's been like that all morning. I think I slept on it wrong. I am sorry..." Margot let out a deep sigh. She was visibly embarrassed.

"Sorry for what?"

"For...I dunno... Everything is so confusing right now. Sebastian and I... well, we called off the engagement."

"You did *what*?" Joe held back a smile. It was hard, but he did his best not to show how happy he was. "I am sorry to hear that."

"I know you two didn't get along," Margot offered a smile. "Well, I mean..." Joe turned red.

"It's okay, things are complicated. I am a mess, emotionally and physically."

"Is there anything I can do?" asked Joe.

"No, I think I just need to soak in a hot bath, maybe it will loosen up the sore muscles. Just please promise me one thing…"

"What's that?" asked Joe.

"This thing you're doing with Plato…?" "I promise, Margot, I will be okay."

Margot leaned in and gave Joe a hug. "I will see you tomorrow when the kids leave for their trip?"

"Tomorrow it is," said Joe with a faint smile.

•　　•　　•

Hunter and the boys were awoken early the next morning by Uncle Joe. They had a long road trip ahead of them and an early start was a must. Hunter yawned and pleaded with his Uncle for just a few more minutes of sleep.

"C'mon Hunter, we're wasting time, the girls are waiting for us already," Joe pulled the covers off of Hunter forcing him to wake up. "Ugh! C'mon, ten more minutes," Hunter pulled the blanket back over his head.

"C'mon, Hunter," Tully smirked knowing the perfect way to get Hunter motivated. "Olivia is waiting for us."

"What's that?" Uncle Joe laughed. "Olivia, huh? Hunter's got the hots for Olivia?"

"C'mon guys, that's not funny," Hunter shot up from the bed giving Tully his patented death stare, his face red from embarrassment.

"C'mon, we got a Wendigo to hunt down," said Alistair already waiting by their door with his bags and equipment slung across his shoulder.

It only took Hunter a few minutes to get dressed and readied for the big trip. The group quickly made their way down to the main foyer where the entrance of the Estate's manor sat. There Margot sat outside with the girls waiting for Ben and Abram to show up with the sport utility vehicles.

"Good morning, guys," Margot forced a smile as the group approached.

The boys exchanged pleasantries with Margot and the girls.

Symphanie immediately ran up to Alistair asking him questions about what sort of stuff he had packed for the trip. She was fully aware how much Alistair loved his technical gadgets.

Olivia, on the other hand, seemed distant. While everyone else talked about the trip, Olivia strayed away, peering out into the woods, holding in her hand a single letter. Hunter could tell by the sorrowful look on her face that something was upsetting her. He wanted so badly to find out what it was, but at the same time he didn't want to overstep his boundaries.

"Margot," Joe wheeled his way next to her. "Hope you're feeling better today."

"A little," Margot half smiled. Truth was her shoulder and arm had gotten worse overnight. The stiffness now extended all the way down to her elbow and up into her neck, making it almost impossible to move at all. A steamy shower and a hot press had thankfully relieved some of the pain and she regained a bit of her range of motion, but it was once again stiffening.

Two black jeeps pulled up to the group from around the back of the estate. They were sharp vehicles, and Alistair ventured they had never even seen the road yet due to their pristine condition. He thought they looked brand spanking new. Benjamin and Abram both exited the vehicles and made their way towards the group.

"Your guides are here!" Benjamin showed off the two brand new jeeps as if he was a model in a game show by waving his arms in the air. "You can thank Professor Calenstine for these two lovely vehicles, fully equipped with state of the art Seekers technology to help aid in all aspects of investigation. These bad boys are cool!"

"Yes, Ben," Abram shook his head. He was already borderline annoyed with Ben's antics, "...they will be sufficient for our trip. Children, let's not waste any more time. We need to hit the road as soon as possible. Boys, you're with Ben, and ladies, you're with me."

"Awesome, I can't wait to see all the cool gadgets inside," Alistair high fived his dad.

"I can't ride with Allie Bear?" asked Symphanie with a frown. "Allie Bear?" asked Ben, his eyes wide with intrigue.

"Don't ask..." Alistair whispered to his dad, once again feeling embarrassed.

"No," Abram said bluntly. "Boys with Ben, girls with me." "You're riding shotgun, Allie bear" Benjamin snickered. "Hunter and Tully, you're in back," he held the doors open for the boys to hop in and get comfortable.

"Olivia, you'll be up front with me," Abram opened the door for his daughter.

"I'd rather sit in back with my friends," Olivia ignored his gesture and opened the back door for herself and sat next to Symphanie and Elly.

"Okay then," Abram sighed shaking his head. "Of course you'd prefer that," he said and shut the passenger door making his way around to the driver's seat.

"We've got a long drive ahead of us, kids, so try and get comfortable," Abram turned the key in the ignition allowing the Jeep to roar to life.

"Why aren't you sitting up with your dad?" whispered Elly. "Because," Olivia replied simply.

"Okay...you two are fighting again, huh?" asked Elly.

"You don't know my dad. You guys only see how he acts here at the Estate. I wish I could have stayed home with my mom and not come back here," said Olivia, trying to hide her bitterness. She made sure to talk low enough for her father not to hear.

"Oh," Elly hadn't been expecting that response. She wasn't quite sure what to say to her friend. She noticed the letter Olivia held in her hand and thought it might make for a good change of topic. "Is that a letter from Marcus? He finally wrote back! How exciting!"

"Yeah, you've been expecting his letter for like ever!" Symphanie beamed with excitement.

"What did it say?" Symphanie asked with a genuine smile. "I want to hear all the lovey-dovey details."

Olivia frowned, her eyes swelling up with tears. She had spent the entire morning trying to avoid these invading questions. She knew the moment she was forced to talk about it she would lose control of her emotions.

"Uh oh…" Elly put a supportive arm around Olivia. She could see the tears budding in her eyes.

"He sent it weeks ago," Olivia wiped away a trickling tear, "my dumb dad just forgot to give it to me."

"Oh, no…" Symphanie frowned.

"So…he dumped me," Olivia said matter-of-factly, trying to not show her emotions. "He said it wouldn't work out, but if I wanted to see him next summer to get a hold of him… he said he was seeing this other girl from his homeroom. Can you believe that?" Olivia took a deep breath trying to calm her nerves. The last thing she wanted was her annoying dad to ask her what was wrong.

"What a jerk!" said Symphanie scowling. "He's not good enough for you anyway!"

"Yeah, he's obviously a total loser if he actually said that," Elly added. "*That* is why boys suck."

"If I could have stayed home we'd still be together," Olivia replied, almost in a defensive nature. "It's all because of my dumb dad and all this Seeker stuff," Olivia whispered, making sure her dad could not hear her anger. "I begged my mom to let me stay with her. But no…."

"You really would want to stay home and not be here with us?" asked Elly a bit dumbfounded.

"Sorry, I know it seems mean, but I hate it here." Olivia frowned. "I wish you guys could come live with me and my mom. We could have our normal lives back, go to a regular school, and not have to worry about monsters attacking us at night, or ghosts possessing us. Living with my dad…it's terrible."

"That would not make my life normal, Olivia," Elly was a bit hurt by her friend's words. "You have a mother to go home to. You have a dad to be mad at for whatever reason you make up. Hunter and I have no one. A normal school is not normal to us anymore. Being here, with our friends, our Uncle and Margot…is our new normal."

"I didn't mean to…," Olivia began backtracking. "But, I am not making up anything. I have my reasons."

"Whatever," Elly cut her off.

"Girls, everything okay back there?" Abram turned down the radio station and asked.

"Yes, dad," answered Olivia, annoyed with his question and with Elly for her comment.

"Okay then," Abram turned his tunes back up. "Get comfy, it's a full day's drive."

CHAPTER 17
THE OPERATION

Poe sat in the stark, white hospital waiting room alone with his thoughts. Today was the big day; in just a few minutes he was going to put his life in the hands of Plato.

Was he crazy? Sure, maybe a little, but he made peace with this notion; to him living his life without his legs weighed a bit more heavily on the crazy scale.

Joe had weighed his options for over a year before settling. He knew what he was getting into, about how the procedures worked. He was going to allow Plato to introduce microscopic robots into his body in hopes of repairing his damaged spine. Saying it aloud to himself he realized it was just a little crazier then he cared to admit. He broke it down in his head, "Just add some high-tech micro-organisms into my blood, so they can swim around my body and fix everything wrong with me like little worker bots, in hopes I can walk again. Nothing weird about that!"

Who was he kidding? It sounded like a cheesy plot to a sci-fi, horror movie.

"What's the worst that could happen?" Joe said to himself in jest right before he forcefully closed the curtains on the window. "Oh, just death…or maybe something worse."

There was a gentle knock at the door that interrupted his musings. "Come in," Joe yelled from across the room.

"Hi," Margot popped her head into the room offering a sympathetic but forced smile. "I brought some friends. We all wanted to show our support. Do you mind?"

"No, not at all. Plato hasn't even arrived yet, so bring them in, I could use the company."

Margot waved the group in. First was Patricia with a tall bouquet of colorful flowers, followed by Professor Calenstine who had get well balloons tied to his automatic wheelchair, and to Joe's surprise, Sebastian.

"What's he doing here?" Joe whispered to Margot who had just given him a supportive hug.

"He said he wanted to show his support," Margot whispered back. "He's trying, so be nice."

"You better come out of this okay," Patricia's eyes were stern. "You have two beautiful children to raise now. You can walk away still... it's not too late you know."

"Patricia..." Professor Calenstine shook his head signaling her to stop. "This is his choice. We are here to show support, not to change his mind."

"I know, I understand, Professor," Patricia frowned. "I just...we all care about you, Joe; we don't want to see you get hurt."

"I know," Joe smiled. "But what you all fail to realize is how hurt I am every second of every day, in this wheelchair. I must do this...."
"We respect your decision," Sebastian walked up next to Margot and put his arm around her waist.

Margot smiled at Sebastian's gesture but slowly moved away from him.

"I'm sure you do," Joe said and rolled his eyes.

"You're brave," Sebastian added awkwardly putting his rejected hand into his pocket. "I know we have had our differences, but I ran when that winged cat thing attacked in the auditorium. You stayed and fought, you saved those kids' lives... You're a better man than me, I see that now," Sebastian extended his other hand to shake Joe's out of a sign of respect. "I just wanted to tell you that."

"You mean that?" Joe raised his eye brow, "or is this some trick to look like a good guy in front of Margot?"

"Joe!" Margot frowned. She couldn't believe he would say that out loud in front of everyone.

"No, it's okay, Margot. I understand your skepticism, Joe. I wouldfeel the same. A lot has changed for both of us. Either way, I wish you a speedy recovery. I will leave you all alone now," Sebastian nodded. He dropped his hand and turned away with a heavy sigh, exiting the waiting room.

"Joe, you could've at least shook his hand," Patricia frowned.

"We don't really get along, Patricia, it's fine. He won't be crying himself to sleep over it."

"Joe," Calenstine smiled brightly from his own wheelchair. "If there is one thing we share in common, it is our hatred for these blasted wheels we're confined to. I count you a lucky man having the option to rise above them. I miss my legs more than almost anything in this world. I have no fear that you will come walking out of those doors. I will have a celebratory cigar waiting for both of us when that time comes."

"Thank you, sir." Joe smiled. If there was one person in the world who he could believe wholeheartedly it was Professor Calenstine. If Calenstine said something, he knew it was true.

"Patricia, Professor, could you give Joe and I some alone time before he goes in with Plato?" asked Margot.

"Of course, dear," Patricia reached in and gave Joe a heartfelt hug and whispered into his ear, "I know I'm a bit bossy at times, but you better come back to us!" She pinched Joe's cheek affectionately.

"I plan on it," said Joe with a smile.

Margot leaned in to give Patricia a hug, offering her a whispering of advice "We all see the way you two look at each other...better let him know now how you feel, just in case there isn't another chance. We only get one chance in this life at happiness."

Margot frowned and began to tear up a bit at Patricia's words. "Come now, Patricia, let us leave them be," Calenstine waved her over to the exit door.

"Again, good luck, my dear," Patricia smiled before she exited with Calenstine.

"You okay? What did Patricia say to upset you? You look like you're about to cry." Joe said, wheeling himself over to her side. Hegrabbed her hand and held it. "I'm going to be fine, you know?"

Margot did not say anything. She stared into Joe's dark brown eyes, lost in a sea of "what ifs". There were so many emotions running through her head. Focusing on anything was impossible, when the only thing she felt was despair. Her head went dizzy and she suddenly felt sick to her stomach.

Margot hadn't stopped to think this may be the last time she'd see Joe alive. She had thought about the possibility but never allowed it to be real. Patricia's advice scared her; she had been so wrapped up in her own world. Everything was real now. Joe really could die while she sat there in the hospital waiting room. She never gave herself time to think about losing him and was never honest with him.

There was no thinking, Margot grabbed Joe by the back of his head and gently pulled him forward. Her soft lips touched his for the first time. Margot felt her lower lip tremble at their first touch. Her heart raced in her chest. She had wanted to kiss him long ago, but she never could, it never felt right... She was confused, scared, and she was supposed to be with Sebastian, but she had all these deep feelings for someone else and she would never admit it. Margot felt the warmth of a single tear trickle down her cheek as she pulled away slowly.

"I don't want you to do this," Margot spoke softly.

"Margot..." Joe replied, but there were no words that followed. He wiped away her tear with his thumb.

"You go in there with Plato.... You might not come out," Margot could not fight the strength of the ever-growing fear plastered on her face.

The operating door opened and the massive automaton, Plato, entered into the small waiting room. Margot and Joe quickly pulled away from eachother.

"Master Joe," Plato's robotic voice said. "We are ready. Now is the time."

"I..." Joe couldn't turn away from Margot's eyes. He didn't want to, either. He wanted to sit there with her, to hold her and tell her everything was going to be okay, better even.

"I have to go," Joe muttered before turning his wheelchair around and making his way towards Plato.

"Inquisitive Inquiry: Is everything satisfactory?" asked Plato holding open the two large swinging doors into the operating room.

"Yeah, Plato... it's just..." Joe stopped momentarily and spun his wheelchair towards Margot. "Will you be waiting for me when I wake up?" Margot was sobbing quietly into her hands.

"Yes, of course," Margot replied softly.

Joe wheeled himself away from the sounds of her tears and through the thick double doors. It was one of the hardest things he'd ever done.

Joe followed Plato down a long hallway with multiple operating rooms until they reached their room.

"Could you help lift me onto the bed," Joe asked. "Legs still don't work, ya know?"

"Emotional Inquiry: Sensory facial manipulation matrix suggested sadness and tension between yourself and Ms. Margot," Plato reached his large thick metal arm out for Joe to grab on to. Joe used Plato's arm to shuffle himself onto the bed, using it as a railing. "Are you having doubts?"

"You could say that," said Joe plainly.

"It is not too late to terminate the plans," said Plato.

"Yes... it is too late to terminate the plans," Joe added shuffling himself onto the operating table.

"So, I need you to do something for me..." Joe, although he would not admit it, was scared beyond belief. His stomach was in knots and he had a prescient lump in the back of his throat. "In my room on the nightstand is a letter written to Hunter and Elly, you know... just in case I won't get to see them again. I wanted to tell Margot about it... but I think she'd worry even more. Could you just... you know, if I don't..." Joe stumbled over his words nervously. "If I *die*, Plato...tell the Professor to please give them the letter."

"Of course, Master Joe," Plato responded. "You are perspiring badly, heart rate elevated. You are nervous. We will use a mild sedative to calm your nerves before we begin administration of the serum."

"Yea, give me some good stuff, because I am sort of freaking out over here..."

"You will find comfort soon," Plato said, "I have paged my assistant, she should be here any moment."

"Assistant?" Joe asked. "We didn't talk about an assistant."

The operating room door opened and the young Dr. Julie Wong walked in wearing full operating scrubs.

"Doctor?" Joe asked a bit perplexed by her sudden appearance.

"I am only here to oversee the operation and act as a right hand to Plato. He approved me being here. I hope that's alright," Wong smiled.

"Master Joe: I apologize, an assistant is a necessity."

"I will take care of you, Joe, and I promise not to operate on you," Dr. Wong laughed. "Plato is just too big. Look at his hands? They're the size of boulders, you would have had to inject yourself with the

I.V. and it's no secret how scared you are of needles."

"I just didn't want anyone around if..." Joe flinched with discomfort as Dr. Wong poked him with the I.V. needle.

"If you flat-line on the table? I am the best person to bring you back. Plato is not a doctor, he can't even grip the defibrillator pads. You need me here as a "just in case scenario". You're in good hands, Joe, I promise."

"If you say so..." Joe cracked a nervous smile.

"It's normal to be nervous before an operation. That's why we are going to add the sedative to your I.V. It will help you relax."

"Am I going under for the surgery?" asked Joe.

"Correction:" Plato responded, "there is no surgery. You will remain awake. We will ask questions once the nanobot serum is injected into your bloodstream to monitor your physical reactions."

"We need to know what you're feeling. Plato assured me the process should be pain free," Dr. Wong held Joe's hand. "You're gonna be okay. Just let the sedatives take effect."

"Awesome..." Joe closed his eyes and sighed. Joe tried to concentrate on his breathing.

Breathe in.

Breathe out....

Joe tried to clear his mind. He thought he would be fixated on the idea of death...but he wasn't. Every time he'd try to clear out his thoughts there was always one thing that crept back up through his subconscious. It was Margot... He had wanted for so long to kiss her. Leaving her like that broke his heart. She really did care for him.

"Good, your heart rate's getting back to normal and your blood pressure is stabilizing." Dr. Wong added, "The sedative is kicking in."
"We will be injecting the nanobot serum momentarily," Plato add- ed.

"Joe," Dr. Wong tapped his shoulder. "I want to show you something."

Joe opened his eyes to see a syringe filled with bright blue liquid held by Dr. Wong.

"That looks like poison," Joe said with a nervous chuckle. "Correction: That liquid consists of the nanobots created within me," Plato interjected.

"Joe," Dr. Wong smiled. "You're going to feel a pinch as I inject the needle and potentially some burning through your arm as the liquid is pushed through."

"Okay, Doc, just do it." Joe turned away from the needle as it punctured his skin.

"Wow!" Joe grunted in pain. "That burns like hell...."

"I am going slowly with the injection, it's going to take a full minute to inject the entire dose."

"Informative announcement: Master Joe, you have over five million nanobots currently coursing through your bloodstream."

"That's pretty freaky!" Joe began sweating profusely. "Wow, I feel so hot...."

"Must be a side effect, just breath slowly, almost finished." Dr. Wong finished injecting the liquid into Joe's blood stream.

"Master Joe, how are you feeling?" asked Plato.

"I am burning up and my arm is stiff...it's extremely painful," Joe winced.

"His heart rates rising, so is his B.P." Dr. Wong said, "This isn't good...."

"I.. Can't..." Joe began gasping for air, his face turned blue.

Suddenly Joe's body began convulsing violently on the operating table.

"Plato, hold him down!" Dr. Wong yelled, "He's going to-"

Joes body went limp and the heart monitor flat-lined.

"We need to resuscitate!" Wong rushed to grab the defibrillator

"Vitals crashed," Plato said.

"I know!" Wong yelled. "Move out of the way!"

"Clear!" Wong pressed the defibrillator pads against Joe's chest hoping the volts would kick his heart back into gear. Joe's body shot up violently from the voltage but the heart monitor continued to flat line. "C'mon... clear!" She tried again to no avail.

"It's not working! He's not coming back..." Dr. Wong stared at Plato lost for words.

Plato stood hovering over his friend's lifeless body trying to assess the situation.

"Plato!" Dr. Wong yelled.

"Dr. Wong: I cannot find a proper expression to relay communications."

"Jesus, Plato!" Dr. Wong shook her head, her eyes tearing up. "I have to call the time of death."

CHAPTER 18
FIELD WORK

Two SUV's, driven by Benjamin and Abram, pulled into a rundown motel parking lot. The weather had turned dreary, a constant driz- zle of autumn rain spattered on their windows and a thick blanket of grey clouds buried the moon in the sky. It had been a long trip, over a full day of straight driving with a quick three-hour pit stop for the adults to catch a quick bit of shut eye. Everyone felt cramped, their legs burned, boredom set in half a day ago.

"All right, boys, let's stretch it out!" Benjamin shifted the vehicle into park. "We finally made it!"

The boys had fallen asleep in the back a few hours before and were awoken by Benjamin's enthusiasm.

"We're finally here?" Tully yawned, rubbing his eyes. He opened up the car door and welcomed the fresh air into his lungs with a deep breath.

"That was the longest ride ever!" Alistair stepped out from behind Hunter on the opposite side of the car. They both stretched out their arms and legs, ignoring the light sprinkle.

"I felt so cramped...next time can we fly?" Hunter asked.

"If we fly we wouldn't have our awesome decked out SUV with our entire monster hunting toys," Ben pointed to Abram's vehicle that had just found a parking spot a few spaces down from them. "There are the others, let's meet up. You kids can stay in the car if you don't want to get wet out here in this drizzle."

"No thanks!" Hunter answered, quickly sprinting towardsAbram's car. "No more cars for me, I'd prefer to sleep out here in the rain if we have a choice."

"Fair enough," Ben chuckled. He opened the door for the girls, all of whom looked equally as worn out from the ride. "Hi, ladies," Ben smiled as the girls exited the car. "Hey," Elly said with a bit of an edge.

"The ride was that fun, huh?" Benjamin looked at Abram who had just exited the vehicle with a quizzical look.

"They were pretty quiet throughout the whole drive," Abram shrugged his shoulders, completely ignorant of the situation.

"I could cut the tension with a knife in that back seat, what happened?" asked Benjamin.

"I don't know, they didn't talk too much with me," Abram pointed to the motel's entrance. "Looks like we check in there," he said as he walked towards the building.

"What do you mean they didn't talk to you much? It was almost an entire day's drive!"

"I dunno," Abram said only half paying attention to Benjamin. "Don't care, we're here safe, that's all that matters."

"You don't care?" Benjamin questioned, a bit put off by his lackadaisical response. "Is everything okay with you and Olivia?"

"I said, I don't know!" Abram turned around quickly and shouted. "Drop it," he ordered.

The kids who had huddled around were startled by the sudden outburst. Olivia just shook her head and stormed off from the group, embarrassed by her dad's actions.

"Nice, Abe," Benjamin replied. "What is going on with you, man?"
"I am sorry. I didn't mean to lose my temper." Abram could not fight back a persistent frown.

"You've been wound up lately, man. We've all noticed it. You need to talk?"

"Olivia is just acting different lately. It's like she won't even look at me, let alone have a real conversation with me. So, I just gave up trying. When she is ready to let me know what's wrong she will tell me. I just don't get her...you know? I'm in over my head with her."

"She's a teenager, I am not entirely sure you're supposed to get her," Benjamin answered back with a charming smile. He put his armaround Abram and walked with him towards the entrance. "Let's get our rooms and we can talk about it over a six pack, deal?"

"Yeah," said Abram letting out a frustrated sigh.

"If you think you are confused with Olivia, I am pretty sure little Alistair has his first girlfriend." Ben chuckled as the two adults entered into the motel lobby. "Can you believe that?"

The kids stood out by the two SUV's waiting patiently for the adults to come back, despite the dour weather, they appreciated the open space and fresh air. They chatted about the trip, and about the Wendigo they were hunting, but despite the friendly banter all Hunter could think about was Olivia. She had left the group, embarrassed by her dad and the way he had spoken to Benjamin. She had made her way towards the opposite side of the parking lot where she sat alone.

"What's up with Olivia?" asked Hunter breaking up the conversation. "She just stormed off after her dad yelled at Alistair's dad. She's being distant again."

"Don't ask," Elly answered with an attitude.

"Marcus dumped her," Symphanie frowned. "Then, she and Elly got into a fight in the first ten minutes of the car ride. They didn't speak the entire ride…made for a fun trip, not!"

"Symphanie!" Elly snapped. "Stop gossiping!" she stormed off in the opposite direction of Olivia.

"Hunter, you go check on Olivia, I will go check on your sister," Tully pointed to Olivia who was sitting on the curb underneath the motel's awning. "Alistair, you stay here with your little lady," Tully winked. "We need to get these girls being friends again, or our trip is going to suck."

"Dumb girl drama," Alistair tried to play it cool, despite his ears turning bright red.

"Yeah, okay," Hunter swallowed his nerves and made his way over to Olivia.

Hunter felt bad for feeling so happy over her misery. Olivia was no longer dating that guy, which meant, maybe, just maybe, he had a chance. But, it was obvious how hurt she was over the breakup. The look on her face as she sat underneath the parking lot spotlight far outweighed the little bit of excitement Hunter was feeling. Olivia looked miserable, broken, sitting there with her elbows on her knees, head down, staring at the cement.

"Olivia?" Hunter tried to call out, his voice cracked nervously. She hadn't even heard him. He cleared his throat, gathered his bearings and made his way to her.

"She's just a girl, just a friend, no need to get all nervous..." he murmured, giving himself a quick pep-talk.

"Hey," he said as he stepped up beside her. "Hey..." Olivia frowned.

"I heard the news..." Hunter took a seat next to her. "...sucks...." "Sucks" Hunter rolled his eyes. That's all he could muster, and he wasn't happy with his response.

"Just play it cool," he told himself.

"Figures..." Olivia bit the bottom of her lip. "That was the worst car ride ever. Who told you?"

"Symphanie," Hunter swallowed the nervous lump in his throat.

"Oh," Olivia appeared to be deep in thought. "I got into a fight with your sister. Our first real fight, she's pretty upset with me."

"Well, fighting with Elly is an easy thing to do, trust me." Hunter offered a small chuckle to try and ease the tension.

"Yeah," Olivia cracked a half smile. "I understand why she got upset with me, but I don't think she totally gets what I'm going through." "What are you going through?" asked Hunter. "Did you like that guy that much?"

"I did..." Olivia answered honestly. "He was so cute and popular. But, I saw this coming when I didn't get any letters for such a long time."

"Oh..." Hunter was hoping for a different answer. Cute and popular? He was neither of those things.

"So...is there more than that going on?" asked Hunter.

"There's a lot more. Ever since my Uncle Dominick said that terrible thing last Thanksgiving, I just, I can't even look at my dad thesame."

"You mean about the murder thing?" asked Hunter who

remembered exactly what Olivia was referencing. Her uncle, Dominick, a former Seekers member who had left the society to form his own paranormal hunting group, had made some slanderous accusations towards her father in front of the entire estate. Her uncle had claimed her father murdered his unborn child and wife…

"Yes…" Olivia slipped her cold wet hand into Hunter's and held it tightly.

"Oh…" Hunter's heart pounded in his chest. She was holding his hand.

"I don't know what to think," warm tears began to flood down her cheeks.

"Well, did you ever-?" But before Hunter could finish Olivia interrupted.

"Ask him?" Olivia shook her head, no. "How do you ask your dad if he killed someone?"

"I guess… I don't know…" answered Hunter truthfully.

"I did sort of ask my mom about it over the summer. I asked her why Uncle Dominick hated him so much. She got all upset and wouldn't answer me. I just don't get it."

"I am sorry." Hunter took off his jacket and placed it around Olivia's shoulder. "You're shivering."

"Thank you," Olivia smiled. It had been a long trip and she was exhausted. She placed her head on Hunter's shoulder and sighed. "I just want to forget about all this craziness."

Olivia and Hunter sat there, they didn't speak again, and Hunter didn't think they needed to. He held her hand and let her be. He knew she was going through a crazy time, she was miserable and confused, but he couldn't help but feel on top of the world. He was there for her; he only hoped he was helping her cope.

"Excuse me," Abram cleared his throat. Hunter and Olivia had not noticed the group walk up behind them.

"Oh, Mr. Winters…" Hunter pulled his hand away from Olivia'squickly, as if they were caught doing something dreadfully wrong. "Did we interrupt?" Tully winked at Hunter behind the adults' backs.

"No," Olivia shot Tully a dirty look. Hunter couldn't help but crack a smile.

"You kids as hungry as the rest of these guys?" Benjamin asked pointing to Alistair, Tully, Elly, and Symphanie.

"Yeah, I'm starved," answered Hunter. Olivia remained silent.

"Alright," replied Abram. "There's a diner across the road. We'll grab a bite to eat then call it a night. It was a long trip and we will need a good night's rest. We have another early morning tomorrow."

The parents led the children across the street into an old, rundown, twenty-four hour diner that sat right off the interstate. The building had aged roughly over the years, the darkened parking lot made it look quite creepy as they approached across the busy road. But it appeared to be lively, even as late into the night as it was. All Hunter could think about was the creepy horror movies he and his father would watch on late night weekends. This little diner would be a perfect location to film a crazy, chainsaw wielding, masked murder plot.

Hunter was the first to enter the dimly lit eatery where, thankfully, a young attractive woman greeted him with a bright smile instead of a crazed, axe swinging psychopath. The waitress's name badge read Libby with the dot above the "i" accented with a small red heart. Libby was the diners head waitress, despite wearing the diners bland wardrobe consisting of a ugly puke colored green apron and khaki pants, Libby somehow managed to radiate with energy. She was of medium height with dark brown hair pulled back into a pony tail. Libby had beautiful soft features, most notable her friendly and welcoming smile. "Welcome to the Midnight Diner, follow me and I will set everyone up," Libby waved the ragtag group over to the opposite end of the diner.

"Follow the young lady," Abram ordered the kids.

"Ahh, stale coffee and the smell of delicious sizzling bacon. Get used to these greasy truck stop diners, kids. They're a staple of the Seekers road life," Ben inhaled deeply, taking in the diner's stale aroma. "I feel home again."

"I love bacon!" Alistair smiled. "Can I order pancakes too?"

"Whatever you want," Benjamin motioned for Alistair to follow the waitress. "When we're on the road, Calenstine pays for everything."

"Will a booth be okay?" Libby wiped down the table with a white cloth and put down the menus.

"Yes, this will be fine, thank you." Abram took off his jacket and laid it out on the back of the booth. He took the far seat near the rain battered window.

Libby couldn't help but notice his tight Henley t-shirt that showed off his manly physique.

"A man who takes care of himself," the waitress smiled at Abram. "You're a rare breed in these parts."

"Excuse me?" Abram was not expecting the flirtatious response.

"Strong man like you probably brought a healthy appetite, I'd recommend the gyros, we're sorta famous for them in these parts," Libby winked as she poured him a tall glass of water.

"Oh yeah?" Ben took his seat staring at Abram in a teasing manner "Gyros, huh?"

"My name is Libby, I will be your waitress for the night. You guys look exhausted, long trip?"

"It's a pleasure to meet you," Benjamin nodded. He kicked Abram under the table, who was ignoring the waitress and looking through the menu.

"Ouch, why would you kick me?" Abram shot Benjamin a dirty look.

"Seriously?" Ben whispered, nodding his head towards Libby.

"What?" Abram asked. He was completely oblivious. "Oh, um... yes it was quite the trip. We've been driving for over twenty hours, so excuse us if we're a bit zombie-like."

"What brings you to little old Hemlock, not much around here," Libby asked. "To be honest, we're one of those paranormal groups. We came out here to check out the recent Wendigo sightings in the area. Heard of it?"

"Oh yeah," Libby answered. "We've had a few of your kind swinging through here."

"Is that so?" asked Abram, his interested piqued.

"Yeah, in fact, just last night two guys close to your age came through here. They asked all sorts of questions about that thing, sorta rude folks though. Didn't even tip."

"Well, there are lots of groups like us nowadays. That reality television sort of created a frenzy of small time hunters. Most of them don't know a Ahool from a Adjule," Benjamin mocked.

"Never heard of either," Libby chuckled.

"Sorry for my friend, he's a bit touchy on the subject of what we do.

Do you remember their names?" asked Abram.

"No, but they wore matching jackets. MFPA was written on them,"

Libby thought for a second, "Yep, definitely MFPA."

"No way," Alistair whispered to Hunter.

"Great, just what we needed," Benjamin sighed. "You know them?" asked Libby. "Unfortunately," Ben replied.

"Well, if you see them two jokers, tell them their cards bounced.

They owe me twenty-five bucks," said Libby.

"Jerks," said Hunter under his breath.

"MFPA? Who are they?" asked Tully in a whisper.

"The Monsters and Find Protection Agency. We'll explain later," Elly whispered back.

"Anyway, you guys look ravenous," Libby finished pouring the last glass of water. "Why don't I let you folks read over the menu? Can I pour the two of you some coffee?"

"Please, that would be nice," Abram offered a smile. Libby walked away towards the kitchen.

"Mr. Winters," Tully gave him a thumbs up. "I think the waitress likes you."

Olivia sighed, trying to ignore the conversation, she felt very uncomfortable knowing her Uncle was nearby and the last thing she wanted to deal with was her dad flirting with some young girl.

"What?" Abram waived off the notion. "You're just a kid; you don't know what you're talking about. I'm probably twice her age."

Olivia let out a small chuckle at the first smart thing she'd heard her dad say in ages.

"Abe, are you serious?" Ben laughed. "She just told you you're buff and hot. She totally digs you."

"Really?" Abram frowned, unsure how to respond.

"She's cute too," Ben winked as he took a drink of his water. "She's coming back, act cool kids," Ben joked. "Don't embarrass
Uncle Abe."

"Uncle Abe?" Abram shot a death stare over to Benjamin.

"Well, have we decided what we're having tonight?" Libby dropped off the two steaming cups of coffee to the adults. She awaited their response with a pen and pad in her hand.

"Abram is going to listen to your advice and go with the gyros," Ben smiled.

"I am?" Abram was now the one to kick Ben under the table. "Ouch!" Ben blurted out. "Are you not going to listen to the young lady?"

"I promise, you'll love them," Libby smiled.

"Well, if you promise," Abram returned her smile, albeit a bit forced and awkwardly.

"Oh god…" Olivia shook her head.

"I think myself and the kids will go for your all you can eat pancakes and bacon, sound good kids?" asked Ben.

"Heck yes, I bet I can out eat everyone," said Alistair.

Symphanie chuckled at his enthusiasm. "You're so adorable," she said aloud without even realizing it.

"Adorable?" Ben tried to hide his laugh. He didn't want to embarrass his son but all this lovey-dovey stuff was new to him. He still couldn't believe his little boy was dating.

"You're on," said Tully to Alistair's challenge. "I have never been hungrier in my life! I will double whatever you eat."

"Pancakes it is," Ben nodded.

"All right, let me go and place the order. I will be back as soon as possible with your food," Libby finished writing down the orders before disappearing into the kitchen.

The group was exhausted, and despite the growling in their

stomachs, the only thing that sounded better than a heaping plate of pancakes and bacon was a warm and cozy bed. It didn't take too long before the young Libby returned with their food. They devoured their meal, with a surprising win by the smaller and skinnier Alistair, out eating Tully by three entire pancakes. Olivia hardly touched any of her food despite her dad's direct order to finish her plate.

"How were the gyros?" Libby asked as she freshened up his cup of coffee.

"Surprisingly, they were delicious," Abram thanked her for the coffee refill.

"I told you, see, you should listen to a lady every once in a while," Libby slid the bill over to Abram.

"Please let me know if there's anything else," Libby smiled before walking off to her next table.

"What's the damage?" asked Ben rubbing his belly as if he'd eaten far too much.

"Well…" Abram turned a shade redder than normal.

"Let me see that," Ben quickly snatched the bill from Abram. There on the bottom of the bill was Libby's name written inside of a heart with her number scribbled below it.

"Abram, you sly dog!" Benjamin almost shouted.

"What is it?" asked Tully in excitement. "She gave him her number, didn't she?"

"You bet!" Ben chuckled.

"Give that to me, you're both embarrassing," Abram snatched the bill back.

"No, you're embarrassing!" Olivia interrupted. She stormed out ofthe booth and out of the diner.

"I better go get her," Abram sighed.

"How about I take the girls and meet up with her," Benjamin suggested. "You get the boys all set up…?"

"Yeah…sure," Abram shook his head.

With that the groups split up to call it a night.

CHAPTER 19
GOODBYE'S AREN'T FOREVER

I can't believe this happened," Patricia spoke through her tears.

She sobbed uncontrollably while standing over the lifeless body of Joe. Calenstine sat next to her in his wheelchair holding Patricia's hand as she wept openly. He had no more tears to shed, living a life as long as the Professor had made him distant from such things. He'd buried more friends than most people would ever make in an entire lifetime.

It wasn't that Calenstine was a cold hearted person, anyone who had ever known him knew better. Calenstine had made his peace with death a long time ago. A big piece of him was jealous that Joe had met his eternal rest.

"Nothing hurts more than the loss of a loved one," Calenstine squeezed her hand tightly while he peered through the door and out into the waiting room where the shattered and broken Margot wept freely as well, her head buried in her hands, waiting for her turn to say goodbye.

A half hour earlier Dr. Wong excused Plato back to his librarian duty and exited the surgical room making her way into the waiting room where Joe's friends and family had gathered to await the outcome of the operation. She had just pronounced him dead a few moments earlier with Plato as the witness for all records.

Plato did not acknowledge the doctor, instead the automaton left through the back exit to avoid Joe's friends and family. Plato, despite his constant updates to his human emotional response program, and unbeknownst to anyone, could not comprehend the concept of his good friend Joe passing away under his care. The situation was wreaking havoc on Plato's internal algorithms, he was experiencing real life emotional pain for the first time internally, the only thing Plato could do to combat the inner response was to hide away from people, so he wandered off into the estate to seek solitude until he could figure out what was happening to him.

Dr. Wong, on the other hand, did not have the option to run away and hide from the situation. Rather, she now stood in front Joe's friends and family searching for the words, eyes filling up with tears. She found none; she had none, for the first time ever no words would come, only a deep sadness.

This was not Dr. Wong's first time delivering the news of the loss of a loved one to a broken family. As much as she hated doing it, it was a part of her job, and one she took seriously. This time was entirely different for her. Under any other circumstances she had perfected a calm and honest approach with the families. This was the doctor's first time speaking to friends and fellow colleagues about someone she had cared about as well. It was not easy...

Dr. Wong had opened her mouth to deliver the news, but instead stumbled over her words.

Not that any words were needed...her eyes told everything.

Margot shrieked the simple word "no" over and over; she fell to the floor in a heap.

"I'm... I'm sorry..." Dr. Wong finally said. "Joe did not make it."

Calenstine took it upon himself to take the group in, one at a time, to say their goodbyes, offering everyone words of consolation as they said goodbye. If anyone knew what to say at a time like this, it was the Professor. Although, deep down he knew the truth about losing a loved one, no words can ease the pain...

Patricia finished up with her goodbyes and Calenstine escorted her back out into the waiting room. "Margot, dear, you're the last one to say your goodbyes..." Calenstine offered his hand for her to take.

"I..." Margot's bloodshot eyes stared at Calenstine. She didn't want to face the lifeless body of Joe, she didn't have the strength. "No, I can't..." She shook her head sobbing.

"Margot, darling..." Calenstine drove his wheelchair over to herside and took her by the hand. "It's okay to be scared, to be lost. But, if you don't find the courage to walk into that room and say goodbye you will never get a second chance. No one is forcing you, but I think we both know how important it is."

Margot nodded and walked with Calenstine across the threshold. There, a few feet away from her, was Joe's lifeless body laid out on a cold, white, operating table. Someone had placed a white blanket across his body. His lifeless face was bare for the world to see. It was too much, her legs shook as she approached, falling to her knees, she had to use the bed to keep herself up. She found his hand and held it.

"You don't have to say anything." Calenstine frowned. "Take as much time as needed; we will be waiting for you outside." Calenstine wheeled himself out, closing the door behind him.

Margot sat there on the cold, hard, hospital room floor with Joe's hand held in hers.

She kept waiting for him to wake up, that there was some sort of weird mistake, that Dr. Wong missed something. She knew it silly to think that but… he couldn't be dead!

Margot sat there for what felt like hours crying into Joe's bed sheet.

CHAPTER 20
ONE MIRACLE AT A TIME

The human body is a magical and remarkable thing, especially one with super intelligent microorganisms cruising through its veins. Joe's body lay alone in the stark white room waiting for Calen- stine to send the orders to move his body from the operating room to the morgue. He was pronounced dead just a few hours prior. For all intended medical purposes, Joe's body was void of life. Dr. Wong was unable to find a heartbeat; there was nothing else she could do to revive him. Everything pointed to the end of Joe's life; his story was written and finished.

What Dr. Wong did not know was that, despite Joe's physical body expiring, the nanobot microorganisms were fast at work repairing the damages they caused resulting in his death. As Joe's friends and family came in one at a time to say their goodbyes the nanobots were focusing their attention on repairing his heart, and after hours of death, all alone in that lonely stark white room, Joe's heart began beating once again.

But all was not better; a beating heart did not mean life was surging through his body. Joe had been dead for hours and the human brain can only go four minutes without oxygen before permanent damage begins to set in. The nanobots still had much to do before Joe could be considered "alive". The nanobots turned their attentions to repairing the damage to Joe's brain. Millions of the organisms swarmed his cranium doing the unthinkable…repairing dead brain tissue.

Plato's controversial method was working, even in death. The organisms were repairing Joe's body and healing him every step of the way. They were able to repair his heart and start it beating once again.

He was now breathing on his own once again, his lungs taking in freshair. The nanobots were also able to do the impossible and restore his brain tissues back to working condition. There was one last part of his broken body for them to fix… his spine.

The lifeless body of Joe jolted awake, his body tensed, muscles spasming, he couldn't even cry out in pain if he'd wanted to. Burning fire shot through his body as life coursed through his veins. Joe opened his eyes for the first time gasping desperately to fill his lungs with air. He was riding a wave of adrenaline, his mind not catching up with his newly awakened body, he attempted to roll off the table, falling face first onto the cold operating room floor.

His head was spinning, his body throbbing, he felt his stomach tighten as he purged bile, painfully curling up in a ball on the cold floor.

He'd never experienced anything like this before; then again, he'd never been dead and brought back to life either. It felt like everything he had learned, a lifetime of knowledge and experience, all his former emotions and feelings, everything that made him who he was prior to his death came surging back into his conscious.

His chest felt like it was being crushed by a herd of elephants. His lungs burned like a raging fire was spreading uncontrollably. Every breath felt like a beautiful, painful miracle. It was like he was breathing for the first time. Tears streamed down his cheeks.

Where was he? What happened?

Joe could not remember a thing…all he could think about was how amazing the air in his lungs felt and how desperately thirsty he was. He needed water, he felt like he would die if he didn't get water

Instinct found Joe crawling on his hands and knees to the nearest sink. Mustering all his strength he lifted himself up to the fountain. He fumbled with the handle until the cool water came pouring out of the faucet.

He cupped his shaky hands, bringing the cool water to his lips. Water had never tasted so sweet, so delicious. He gulped down as much as possible until the fogginess of his head slowly began to clear.

Joe fell back to the floor. He positioned himself so that he was staring back at the operating table where he had fallen from.

He remembered bits and pieces now…

He remembered the operation, Plato and Dr. Wong… But, why would they leave him alone? What happened?

Something was not right…they had left him alone in a dark room. There were no monitors keeping track of his vitals, no one around checking up on him… Had he died!?

He definitely felt like death.

Joe opened his mouth, but the mere attempt of talking made his head spin.

That's when he noticed the red, exit sign that lead out to the waiting room. It was the only light source that spilled into the darkness around him.

That's also when he also realized he had just used his legs to crawl over to the sink!

Joe looked down towards his bare feet, staring at his toes. Would it work? Could he actually…?

Joe tried to wiggle his big toe, and watched wide eyed as it wiggled on command.

His big toe wiggled!? It wiggled!

Joe gasped out a deep and rough sounding laugh…he hadn't quite got his voice back, but he didn't need words. Tears of joy burst from his eyes.

He slowly moved his legs into an Indian sitting style, rubbing them up and down rejoicing with every inch of feeling.

Joe took a deep breath and mustered up every little bit of strength he had to stand up, but his legs were just too weak to carry his weight. He tumbled forward, falling through the door leading out towards the exit. He spilled out onto the waiting room floor where Calenstine and Margot had sat discussing the best way to inform Hunter and Eliza their uncle had passed away.

"Joe!" Margot gasped in horror.

"My God…" Calenstine whispered to himself.

A dead man just crashed through the morgue, crashing on the floor,only to look up to him with a wide smile on his face.

"My… toes… moved… Joe whispered before falling back into unconsciousness.

CHAPTER 21
INVESTIGATION WENDIGO

Abram had woken up early, showered, and left his snoring counterpart, Ben, behind in their small two bed motel room. Abram had never been the type to sleep in, he required only six hours of sleep on the dot. Any more or less would throw him off his personal regimen. He knew the kids would be exhausted from the prior day's drive and didn't mind allowing them to catch up on sleep, it would allow him to get some work done. He'd also been on enough investigations with Ben to know he'd sleep until noon if he let him. A little alone time to catch up was exactly what Abram needed.

Abram liked discipline, it was in his blood. He needed order in his life to function, it kept him at peace, even when he felt certain parts of his life were out of his control, like his daughter hating him, at least he could control this. He woke up every day at six in the morning, did a series of pushups, sit ups, curl ups, and, when time allowed, he'd run three miles as well. It was no wonder he'd managed to stay in such great shape despite his middle age. Once he'd finished his routine, he'd jump into a hot shower and get ready for his day. Waking up out on the road was no exception for Abram, and so he went on with his morning ritual, all the while never causing Ben to stir.

He checked his watch, it was close to seven.

Abram grabbed his briefcase and took a seat at the small dining table near the one window in their rustic motel room. *Never too early for research,* Abram thought to himself. He began thumbing through all the info Benjamin had dug up on the Wendigo before they left the estate, which was quite a bit. If there really was a Wendigo running around, it kept itself busy. After catching up with all the info, marking on a local map where all the sightings occurred, and studying the locallay out, Abram took this time to plan out their day. There was a natural order to an investigation; it wasn't all long hikes in the woods, setting up trail cams and night vision cameras. There was a lot of prep that had to occur.

Phase One: The Locals.

Abram knew they needed to gather more intel. They needed to speak to people closer to the encounters, the ones who actually witnessed and took the videos. Where better to start than the diner? Abram had already made his mind up before he'd dropped his notes back into his briefcase and headed for the door.

Abram flipped the collar up on his jacket as he moved across the parking lot with his head down against the misty rain.He thought of her…

Would she still be working? It had been a long trip for his crew before they made it to the diner, It was close to two am before they had even parked their cars. If she was pulling third shift, she may still be on the tail end of it. Abram pulled out his wallet and took out the receipt that Libby had handed him. He stared at her name with the heart circled around it.

Libby.

Abram would be lying to himself if he said he hadn't gone to bed thinking about her youthful smile. Abram had been divorced for years. He wasn't worried about romance in his life; a relationship just didn't fit into his lifestyle. The last few years all he'd thought about was readying himself for his daughter's Enlightenment.

Being a Seeker is what defined Abram as a man, he knew this. He also knew it was the reason his marriage was doomed to fail the minute he'd placed the ring on her finger. Abram always put his job first; it was ingrained into his very being. He would always be a Seeker first, a father second. Although, recently he had been trying much harder to put being a father first, despite often failing…

Hell, his daughter had hardly spoken to him in two months!

Abram wasn't good at being a dad, at least that's what he told him-self. It was his excuse, some people were born to be a parent and oth-ers had to work very hard at it. It did not come natural to him, at all.

Not like hunting, that was the gift he was born with. Abram was a master hunter. It was all he'd ever known, his passion in life. The entire estate knew he was Calenstine's best Seeker. It was a badge Abram wore proudly.

So why couldn't he get Libby out of his mind? He'd just met this woman, and she seemed far too young for him.

Abram took a deep breath and entered the dinner where the smell of stale coffee danced around his nose. It was busier in the morning than it was late last night. Dozens of people lined up at the counter, enjoying their steaming cup of coffee, eating their myriad of breakfast platters, reading the newspaper.

She wasn't there. No friendly smile to greet him with a good morning.

Abram guessed it was better that way. He'd make his rounds, and ask a few of the patrons if they'd heard the rumors before retreating back into his hotel room. He'd have to wake Benjamin up, rustle up the children and they'd hit the road to do some exploring.

"Good mornin', sunshine," Libby's joyful voice startled him. She had managed to sneak up behind him. "I didn't think I'd see you in here so early."

"Oh, Libby," Abram could feel his ears warming up, an embarrassing side effect. He'd hoped he'd grow out of it when he was a young teen, he never did. However, it wasn't often that Abram felt nervous in his adulthood. The feeling was foreign to Abram, for a second, he thought he enjoyed it, made him feel young again.

"You're up so early," Libby winked. "Let me pour you a hot cup of coffee, I am sure you need it."

"That would be great, thank you!" Abram replied.

"Follow me," Libby waved towards an empty stool near the end of the counter and poured him a cup of coffee. "I am about to get off my shift. It's been a long night. I hate thirds," she fought back a yawn. She looked exhausted, a long night of coffee refills, and poor tips.

"Understandable," Abram took a gentle sip from his steaming coffee. Its warmth felt good going down his throat.

"So, I won't be taking care of you this morning, but I will make sure Martha takes extra good care of you." Libby smiled. "She basically owns this joint."

"Actually," Abram slowly put his coffee cup onto the saucer, careful not to spill the hot beverage. "The coffee will be enough. I was hoping you might want to join me for a cup. I had a few questions about the sightings; I thought you might be of help."

"Is that so?" Libby cracked a half smile. "I think I can hang out for a few. My babysitter likes the over time."

"Oh, you have kids?" Abram replied.

"Two boys," Libby smiled. "Twins actually, they're a handful for a single mother, let me tell you. Wyatt and Cassidy, my little cowboys."

"Those are wonderful names," Abram found himself smiling like an idiot, he wasn't even sure why. "Umm, the blonde teen that stormed off last night was mine," Abram gave a nervous smile. "Olivia," he said trying to hide the tension that seemed to roll off his tongue at the mention of her name. "That was a bit embarrassing. I guess I am not the dad of the year in her eyes."

"Well, you're here with her, and just being there, even when they don't think they want you around, is all that will matter in the end. My boys don't even know their father's name, up and split before they were born," Libby put her hand on Abrams shoulder. "Let me clock out and I *will* have that cup of coffee with you."

"Great," Abram nodded.

She walked off into the back room.

Abram couldn't help but question what the heck he was doing. What was the point of flirting with the young woman? In one week he would be back on the road to the middle of nowhere. He lived in a secret Mansion hidden in an even more secretive forest. Only the highest of government officials knew the Seekers even existed… It's not like he could ever take her out on a real date.

"Sorry for the wait," Libby came back. She had tossed off the grotesque apron in favor of a lightweight jacket. She had also let her hairdown from the bun she originally had it tied up in. It made her look more relaxed, even prettier than before. "You must be lucky; I don't usually hang around after work with tall dark handsome strangers from out of town."

Abram chuckled, "So, why I am so lucky?"

"You have kind eyes, they say it's the window to the soul, ya know. Eyes don't lie," She tore off the edge of a sugar packet and poured it slowly into her coffee. "Plus, you're cute."

"Oh," Abram cleared his throat. "Ha, well, I just had a few questions, about the sightings. I promise I won't take up too much of your time." He could feel the blood rushing to his ears.

"Okay," she smiled between sips of her sugar and cream filled coffee. "Perk of working at a diner is hearing all sorts of stories."

"Okay, so have you seen the videos?" Abram asked. He took out his tablet and pulled up the first queued video.

"Everyone in this town has," Libby waved the video off, having seen it hundreds of times. "It's the biggest thing since the fake crop circles we had a few years back. Some dumb high school kids had looked it up on the internet and found out how to do it; had the town in an uproar for months. Bunch of weirdo's from the cities came flooding into our town staring at the sky for months until the kids were caught red handed. I guess we like our mysteries. I think it's probably some prank again."

"The video is compelling evidence. Also, rumors say lots of livestock being slaughtered around these parts?" asked Abram.

"From what I hear, mostly near the Wanigas State Forest. The farmers there have been finding their livestock mutilated. Our little town butts right up against that forest. Perfect place for a creature to hide I guess. If, you know…if you believe in that stuff."

"Do you?" asked Abram.

"Who knows," Libby chuckled. "I find it romantic to think that there are things out in this world left to find and explore. I would hate to think we've learned about everything out there, makes life sound so boring. But, as for this… What is it called again?"

"Wendigo," Abram answered.

"Right, some sort of half human, half goat thing…seems a little too cartoony to me. Probably a bear or something, or like I said earlier, dumb kids being kids."

"What about the original case of the kids being chased in the woods?"

"Frightening, but authorities went out to their campsite a few days later. They even checked out the lake for the plane. Nothing… Tall tales I am sure…who knows what those kids were doing out in those woods."

"Interesting," Abram frowned.

"So, let me get this straight. You do this for a living?" Libby couldn't help but chuckle when she asked the question.

"Yes," Abram answered matter-of-factly. "I travel around the world hunting creatures thought to be myth, finding ancient relics thought to possess magical qualities. I do this in the name of science. Normally, not with my daughter," Abram broke the seriousness with a small smile.

"—and someone pays you? Sounds like you're living the dream!" Libby replied. "Who on earth do you work for?"

"Sorry, *that* I can't say," Abram took a long sip from his coffee.

"Oooh," Libby couldn't hold back a sly half smile, "mysterious…!"

"Yes, just a bit."

"Well make sure you swing back through the diner and let me know what you find out. I am curious to know if there really is some bizarre creature terrorizing the cows of Hemlock."

"Thank you for your time," Abram stood up and nodded. "We will be staying across the street for the time being."

"So you will stop in and see me?" asked Libby who now joined Abram in standing as she buttoned up her wool coat and wrapped a scarf around her neck.

"Perhaps," Abram left a five dollar bill on the table to pay for the coffee. "That would be nice."

"All right then," Libby blushed beneath her scarf. "Good luck."

•   •   •

"You're awake?" Abram was surprised to see Benjamin up with the kids getting ready for the day.

"Alistair woke me up," Benjamin yawned.

"Sorry," Alistair shrugged. "I couldn't sleep, too anxious for the hunt. I feel like it's Christmas morning!"

"My little Ally, so excited," Symphanie slipped her hand into Alistair's.

"Err…" Alistair looked over to Hunter who rolled his eyes at the public display of affection.

"Get used to it, pal," Tully slapped Alistair on the back. "My cousin's a little clingy."

"Hey!" Symphanie yelled.

"Okay, guys, calm down." Abram threw up his hand. "No funny business. We have a lot of ground to cover on this trip."

"Speaking of funny business," Ben shot Abram a wide smile. "Where were you this morning?"

"I was doing research while your lazy butt slept in," Abram said ignoring the inquisition.

"Maybe you should follow your own rules," Olivia mumbled to herself.

"So you're saying you didn't head over to the diner to talk with Libby?" asked Ben who was packing up his backpack.

"Well, she had some local info…" Abram sighed. "We're not here to discuss Libby; we have a serious cryptid to hunt."

"Did you learn anything?" asked Elly, who had her Seekers journal out ready to take notes.

"Yes, lots of rumors spreading around the town. As we know from our maps, this small town sits up against quite a large state forest. Most of the sightings and cattle mutilations appear to be near there. There has been one caught on video, it's grainy, and the lighting isoff, but it shows a rather large creature running off into the woods. A farmer heard a ruckus and came out to investigate; they found a cow with its head bashed in."

"What could do that?" asked Ben.

"Local law enforcement agencies are blaming a bear, but...." Abram didn't seem impressed with the concept.

"So, we really think we're dealing with a real life Wendigo?" asked Hunter.

"We're hunting a cryptid, and locals are *calling* it a Wendigo. They claim the creature is long and slender, able to walk upright or run on all fours, and has a horse-like face with long pointy antlers. For all intended purposes, they describe what many people claim a Wendigo would look like," Abram explained.

"Yes!" Alistair high-fived Tully, "This is so exciting! A real Wendigo!"

"Don't get too hung up on this Wendigo thing," Benjamin added. "We're here to be unbiased and find the truth, not to find what we want to see. Ninety percent of investigations are misidentified animals."

"Your dad's right," Abram nodded. "We follow Occam's razor." "Whose razor?" asked Hunter?

"Occam's," Elly answered back, "it means when there is a simple answer, it's probably the truth."

"What do you mean?" asked Tully.

"Ugh..." Elly seemed annoyed. "Didn't anyone pay attention in science class?"

"I did," said Olivia. "Basically, it means if you lost your shoes, Tully, it makes more sense that you left them in gym class, rather than an alien snuck into your room and stole them."

"Oh..." said Tully. "So...it's probably some sick deformed bear? Not a Wendigo?"

"The problem with the Wendigo solution," answered Abram, "is that we as Seekers have been following sightings of cryptids for over a millennium. We have countless records of creatures, some found, some still elusive, but we know about them. We've captured multiple different Big Foot species, we relocated the Loch Ness Monster to our Crooked Lake...."

"—What! We have Nessie in our backyard!" Alistair almost exploded from happiness.

"Yes," Abram acted like it was common sense and moved forward with what he was saying. "But we have never heard of a Wendigo sighting actually having any truth to it. It derives from old Native American spiritual lore. Perhaps it's a different cryptid? We need more intel."

"It is a prime location for a Big Foot," answered Benjamin.

"So where do we go first?" asked Hunter. "Do we stake out the woods?"

"No," answered Abram. "We meet up with an old friend."

CHAPTER 22
RECOVERY

Poe dreamt of a glorious magical tree, a tree that transcended life as he knew it; its branches reaching deep into the dark blue sky, past the fluffy white clouds, sprouting its colorful leaves into the darkness that is the cosmos. Its roots buried deep beyond the physical earth, connecting his subconscious mind to an infinite number of other realities. Each reality sprouting the same glorious tree, each reality harboring mirrored images of the one before it, yet subtly different. A collage of spiraling alternate versions of Joe flowing through space/time until they all crashed as one simple Joe at the base of the tree. He was all of these lives; all of these alternate Joes rolled into one. There, tucked away in some small crevice of the universe, Joe stood before the tree that sat at the center of them all. Joe was speechless, but even more bizarre was that sitting at the base of this magnificent tree was his niece, Elly. She was there, smiling brightly, petting a long and slender dragon. Her eyes lit up as she noticed her Uncle standing before her, a warm smile stretched across her face.

"You're not dead yet, silly" Elly pointed to the top of the tree. Joe suddenly felt his body getting sucked out from whatever the place was. His body was sent flying through the cosmos at light speed. Everything around him blurred until…

Poof! A warm bright light engulfed his being.

Joe awoke gasping for air for the second time in less than twenty four hours.

"Master Joe," Plato's inert metallic frame buzzed to life. He had set his physical body to standby, conserving his energy in order to be fully powered when Master Joe awoke. Plato had not moved from his friend's side since Calenstine beckoned him back to the surgical room. "Worrisome Response: Are you conscious?"

"My head..." Joe whispered, the sound of his voice echoed through his head causing him great pain.

"Unfathomable Statement: Master Joe, you perished during the injection of the serum. I witnessed your death, recorded the memory. You should not be talking. You should not be alive."

"Is that so, big guy?" Joe cringed as he sat up. "Feels like I died... that's for sure." His body ached, every muscle stiff, he could barely move his arms and legs.

"He's right," Dr. Wong entered the room scribbling on a clipboard. "Glad you're awake. You broke a lot of hearts today. You were dead for over four hours. Congratulations, Joe, you're a medical anomaly now," Dr. Wong smiled brightly. "You know, you should be brain dead right now. I don't know what those nanobot things are doing in your body, but it is *not* natural."

"Glad to see you, too," Joe held his head, attempting to make the throbbing subside.

"Please, don't take my concern as a lack of relief. We all stood beside you, we cried, said our goodbyes. We mourned your loss, Joe. Then you rose from the dead like some terrible clichéd zombie movie. You understand how crazy that is? Modern medicine has no explanation."

"Margot...is she here?" Joe could only imagine how angry she'd be with him, putting her through so much emotional distress.

"She is outside waiting. When I am done here, I will bring her in. She's worried sick, you know? She was a wreck...thought she'd lost you."

"How pissed is she?" Joe asked with half a smile.

"Joe..." Dr. Wong shook her head in disbelief. "You *died*, d-e-a-d, dead. I'm talking demised, perished. Call it whatever you want, but your heart stopped, brain dead for over four hours. No one is angry... You sitting here is a miracle. Do you understand that? Everyone is ecstatic you're alive."

"Well that's good to hear. But, not to sound too dire or anything, but there's no such things as miracles doc, sorry to disappoint," Joe answered. "I just got lucky with these nano things."

"Is that so?" Dr. Wong grinned. "Have you not noticed?"

"Notice what?" Joe asked. All he "noticed" was the tremendous pounding of his head.

"This," Dr. Wong stabbed Joe's leg with the butt end of her pen.
"Ouch!" Joe winced. "My god..." his eyes lit up.

He felt it... the slight poke from the pen, he felt the dull pain. Joe remembered now, it was hazy, but it came flooding back to him. He had fallen to the floor, crawled into the other room. He'd used his legs... he could move his legs!

"Like I said," Dr. Wong checked Joe's vitals "...a miracle."

"My God..." Joe's eyes filled with warm tears. "It worked...it really worked..."

"Let me bring Margot in, I am sure you're both dying to see each other."

"Thank you," Joe wiped away the tears, feeling embarrassed.
"Master Joe," Plato spoke. "I would like to inform you, I have been tweaking my human emotional response algorithms to further develop proper emotional response during social activities."

"Yeah?" Joe couldn't shake the overjoyed smile on his face. He kept poking his legs, rejoicing with every sensation he felt. "You've been trying to be more human for as long as I have known you."

"When you died..." Plato responded, "I believe I felt something."
"You did?" Joe's excitement doubled. "Plato, that's great! That's a huge breakthrough! Is that...even possible?"

"I did not believe so. My kind was created to act as servants, never to develop a conscious or act outside any of their verbal demands. When Professor Calenstine restored my body, he also reprogrammed my logistics, enabling the act of free will. Professor Calenstine urged the study and observation of the human condition. Since then I have spent countless hours attempting to become more humanlike, writing and rewriting my internal code to simulate human emotion, but never to actually feel."

"And you're saying you felt something?"

"Possibly, with your death a darkness came over my streamline of internal thought processes. I found myself replaying recorded events that we shared."

"Plato, that's great! I can walk, you can feel..." Joe smiled. "Master Joe, it was terrible." Plato added. "Did Master Calenstine curse me with this human emotion?" "What do you mean?" asked Joe.

"I believe the feeling was guilt. Your heart stopped beating due to a direct correlation of my actions. Feelings of responsibility flooded my emotional filters. Automatons are not meant to think, or reflect on actions. Before Calenstine reprogrammed me, we were only allowed to perform direct verbal tasks, answer queries, run logistics, etc. The pain on your colleague's faces as they said goodbye to your lifeless body weighed heavily. Realization set in: there would be no more communication between Master Joe and myself. Strong urges to turn off my artificial intelligence system, and go dark. A sensation of fleeing was dominant. Master Joe, I wanted to escape the feeling your death was causing me."

"Plato..." Margot had just walked in, her eyes red and very swollen, burning from a long night of confusing tears. She reached out and touched his large metal hand.

"Margot..." Joe wasn't sure what to say. He felt terrible, he was the reason why she looked like she'd had been to hell in back. Exhaustion was set on her face, deep black bags hung below her swollen eyes; her skin sickly pale.

"To be human is to feel all sorts of scary emotions," Margot looked up at Plato. "Fear, heart ache, depression... Sometimes it feels easier to run away than to face them head on. But, those feelings you're just now starting to realize... those are what's going to make you human. Welcome to the club...."

"Margot, thank you," said Plato. "Allow me to exit the premise. I was told you'd want to be alone."

Joe gave a nervous chuckle. "Thanks, big guy." Plato exited the room leaving the two alone.

"I hate you..." Margot's voice cracked, she spoke softly. Her eyes locked onto Joe's. She shook her head in defeat as she fell into his embrace. "If you ever do something like that again…."

"I am so sorry…" Joe brushed her hair back away from her face, placing his lips gently on her forehead. "You don't really hate me, right?"

"Shut up…!" Margot pulled him closer, kissing him deeply. Tears once again flowed down her cheeks.

"Ahem!" A voice broke their embrace.

Margot pulled away from Joe. There stood an angered Sebastian, a scowl of pure hatred stretched across his face.

"It all makes sense now, doesn't it?" Sebastian snorted, tightening his fists in anger. "The truth finally rears its ugly head! He is why you pulled yourself away from me. I knew it all along… You cheater, you lowly, selfish, cheater!"

"Sebastian, now is not the time." Margot's cheeks flushed red.

"You should leave," Joe pointed to the exit, his mouth pursed tightly in anger.

"There is never time, Margot!" Sebastian threw up his arms in disbelief. He was ready to hit someone, anything. "Here I come, to show support to your so called 'friend', to wish this home-wrecker a speedy recovery, only to catch my fiancé cheating on me with him! Marvelous, kudos! You two are quite an act! I always knew I was better than you Margot, you stupid, immature child!"

"I am not your fiancé anymore, Sebastian!" Margot yelled. "We are no longer a couple!"

"Margot, calm down…" Joe tried to stand, still weak; he felt his knees give way under his weight.

"No!" Margot waved her finger feverishly at Sebastian. "You are not the man I fell in love with. Listen to those hateful words you're saying! You grew dark and angry. You talked about taking me away, marrying me and moving us out of the country!" Margot was livid.

"To get away from all this craziness. To start a family!" Sebastian yelled back, face boiling with anger.

"This is my family! I have lived here for five years, it's my life. You never asked me even once what I wanted!" Margot grabbed her arm in pain. "—Ouch!" She fell to her knees. "Oh my God…something is wrong..." she cried out.

"Margot!" Sebastian ran over to her. His anger turned to fear. He was spewing out hateful words he knew he'd regret later. The look on Margot's face struck fear into his heart. She was in pain and lots of it by the grimace on her face.

"Cool it, I got her," Joe had already made it to her side. "What's wrong?" asked Sebastian.

"I can't move my arm..." Margot gritted her teeth. "Roll up her sleeve," Sebastian ordered.

"Chill out," Joe carefully pulled back her sleeve. "What on earth?" his mouth fell open at the sight.

"What? What's wrong?" Sebastian peered over Joe's shoulder. "We need to call Calenstine, now!" Joe ordered. "Go, get him!" "Okay, okay!" Sebastian stood up, rushing out of the room. "What's wrong with it?" Margot breathed heavily, trying to focus on anything other than the deepening pain.

"You're arm..." Joe calmed himself, trying to figure out how to explain the disturbing sight.

"Yeah, it hurts I know, what about it? Is there a rash or something?" Margot rocked back and forth.

"It's... turned to stone...."

"My God, what?" Horror flooded Margot's face. "Stone?"

CHAPTER 23
MIPARANORMAL

"Where are we going?" Alistair buckled up, getting ready for what he hoped was a big adventure hunting the elusive Wen- digo. He'd never been so excited for a field trip in his whole life. This definitely topped the field trips to the local museum or train station his old middle school would have sent him on. Nothing sounded more fun than spending the next few days out in the elements with his best friends and his dad, capturing a cryptid monster. This is what it meant to be a Seeker!

"Are we going to the forest where the sightings happened?" asked Hunter. "Because I didn't grab my camping gear from the motel, I need to snag it before we leave."

"No," answered Ben. "Not yet at least. We have some more work to do before we can even think about an overnight investigation."

"Where are he headed then?" Tully sighed with boredom. Another pit stop to somewhere uninteresting is not what the boys wanted to hear. "So far all we've done on this case is eat pancakes. We could have done that back at the Estate."

"Remember the first lesson of being a Seeker?" asked Ben with a sharp smile. "It's boring, a lot of paper work, even more research. You need to learn this right now; our life is not always glamorous and filled with action. When I said it's not all fun and games, I meant it. You have to have all your ducks in a row, talk to the locals, meet your contacts, sift through fact and fiction, scout the area out, know exactly what you're dealing with. Very little of the time is spent out in the field hunting. Most of the time, there isn't even a hunt to be had. So, stop whining and suck it up, because we got work to do."

"Okay, we get it," Alistair frowned. He was not impressed with his dad's lecture. "If it's not that fun to be a Seeker, why bother? I don't want to grow up to be some guy who flips through books without ever getting a chance to capture a monster."

"Because," Ben said with a heartfelt chuckle, he couldn't help but remember he was the same way when he was Alistair's age. "We make a difference in the world; it's not all monsters and cryptids. There is real evil out there, and we do our best to keep it at bay. You boys are caught up in the thrill of the hunt, and it *is* thrilling when you find evidence of an elusive creature. You just have to understand, for every ten leads we get, we may get one with a hint of truth to it. That's when you get your so-called *monster hunt*. And when that time comes, a world of possibilities begins to open up. When we first found out that the elusive Bigfoot was real, it was a huge deal. Can you imagine being the first person in the world to come face to face with a creature the majority of society thinks is a hoax?"

"Bernie is pretty awesome, even without me being the first to see him," said Alistair.

"Now, the reason why we chose this Wendigo creature for your first investigation is because the chance that we uncover a real Wendigo is slim. There's a better chance for some random guy stumbling on a pink unicorn in the middle of Times Square during broad daylight. All of our current knowledge in cryptozoology tells us Wendigo are nothing more than ancient lore. No truth to their existence has ever turned up, anywhere in the world."

"So you chose a case you knew was a hoax?" asked Tully with disbelief. "Boring...."

"Not a hoax per say. Anyway, we never know for sure until we scope it out, but yes, it was a safe bet that the dangers for this case would be minimal. We don't want to take you kids out into the desert hunting down the Mongolian Deathworm, you'd be toast. Your safety is still our number one concern. However, you still get to learn everything that goes into an investigation, the research and all the other fun stuff. We're training you kids to stay alive out in the field. That's the end goal. We lose too many Seekers out there; it's a dangerous game we play."

"Man...no Wendigo?" Alistair whined. "That sucks!"

"Did you listen to anything I just said? And watch your mouth," Ben snapped at his son's choice of language. "Your mother would have your hide if you spoke like that in front of her."

"Sorry, it's just we thought we were actually going to go out on a *real* hunt," Alistair frowned.

"You are on a real hunt," Ben explained shaking his head in frustration.

"How so," asked Hunter. "Seems like just a bunch of reading and talking to strangers."

"It's a real hunt because the local's fears are real. There is some decent evidence out there, video and stills of something in the woods. It's our duty as Seekers to make sure there isn't a creature out there. Hopefully we can put the good folks of this town fears to rest with some explanation as to what's going on. We're not just here for the cyrptids, but to help the people too. Maybe it's not a Wendigo, but maybe it's some other cryptid, we won't know until we fully investigate. Probably a bear, though. It's always a bear...."

"Okay, okay..." Alistair rolled his eyes.

"You realize we've taken down the Beast of Bladenboro and that Moloch demon already, right?" said Hunter giving a high five to Alistair in the back seat, trying to cheer his buddy up. "We're pretty good at this Seeker thing already. No need to baby us, we can handle a Wendigo. A Deathworm sounds awesome, we could totally capture one of those! Let's skip this fake Wendigo and go for the Deathworm."

"Seriously?" said Ben bluntly, his voice stern. "Do you remember your broken arm, Hunter? What about your friend who was possessed and almost killed by Moloch? Do you remember when Elly was shot with the dart and almost died from blood poisoning because you two went out sneaking around at night? What about your uncle? Remember how he lost the use of his legs from the Beast's attack? If you don't realize sooner, rather than later, that this is a dangerous game, you're going to die. We do not mess around with the unknown, understood?"

"Okay, we get it, sorry." Hunter immediately regretted high fiving Alistair.

"There is no need to be sorry," said Ben. "Just be careful and stop looking for trouble."

"Okay, okay..." said Alistair feeling the urgent tone of his father.

He did not want to push it any further.

"If you don't think we've lost Seekers to the hunt, you're dead wrong," Ben went on. "We have lost plenty and some of them were close friends. Hell, your parents Hunter... They were victims of the Seekers life. What we do is very real; this isn't some movie or lame children's book where everything ends happy. When you go into the unknown and stare down monsters for a living, people get hurt. People die. This little trip is us teaching *you* the proper ways to stay alive. So start taking notes...!"

"Okay, we get it!" said Alistair growing tired of the lecture. "Information is your best friend. That's why your teachers stress the Seekers journals. We all use them, saved my life more than once." The rest of the car ride was a bit uncomfortable; a thick cloud of tension halted almost all conversation between the boys. Alistair's father was normally a light hearted, fun loving, wise-cracking dad, but even he was tired of the boys' poor attitude. Hunter had never seen him more serious than during that lecture. It was a bit scary.

"We're here," Ben flipped on the turn signal and pulled onto an old road filled with small store fronts on both sides. They passed a local shoe store, coffee barista, even an old homemade toy shop specializing in wooden train sets.

Hunter was surprised at the sight of old shops. They seemed like they'd been frozen in time, they reminded him of something he'd seen in the old black and white movies he and his dad would watch on cozy weekends away from school. Hunter had never seen a small strip of local stores like this, he and his sister grew up in the city where corporate coffee shops sprang up every three blocks and a giant mega mall was where everyone shopped. Even the road was paved different,replacing the cement he'd been accustomed to seeing with carefully laid red bricks.

Ben parked on the street near a sign that read "Hemlock Olde Towne Preserve".

"Looks like Abram and the girls are waiting for us already," Ben pointed out the driver side window.

"What is this place?" asked Tully. "Looks like somewhere my *great* grandparents would have lived."

"This is the first road ever built in the small town's history. They've protected it; the majority of the businesses here have been around for generations. It's a cool little throwback to the town's origins," Ben explained exiting the car. A few miles south and you start seeing fast food chains and corporate America at its finest... I love this small town feel."

"How do you know so much about this little town?" asked Tully stepping out into the cold fall air.

"The internet, duh," Ben joked, trying to ease the boys' mood. "C'mon that's where we're going," he pointed to a tiny store on the corner of the street. A small hand painted sign that read MI Paranormal hung in the front door.

"You found it," Abram exited his vehicle.

"Yeah, looks like a ghost town. The photos online made it look like it would be booming with people," Ben replied.

"It's a tourist spot, dies out, come the cold weather. Businesses here make all their money in the summer. Most close down come first snowfall." Abram nodded to one shop that already had their seasonal closing sign posted. Abram tightened a thick scarf around his neck to keep the chilly air at bay. "Feels like it could snow any minute. Got to love Michigan weather...."

"That's the place, MI Paranormal, local group of paranormal investigators," Ben explained to the kids.

"A local paranormal group?" asked Alistair, his interest once again piquing.

"I didn't know those existed outside of cable television," said Hunter.

"You'd be surprised," Abram wasted no time crossing the street towards the store.

"How was the trip?" Tully asked his younger cousin, Symphanie, who had just walked up next to Alistair, snuggling up against his arm to keep warm.

"It was weird, maybe I can ride back with you guys," Symphanie rolled her eyes.

"Why was it weird?" asked Hunter.

"Just a lot of tension with Olivia and her dad, not fun."

"Oh..." Hunter watched as Olivia finally exited the vehicle.

"You don't want to ride with us, either," said Alistair who was now growing more comfortable with his newfound girlfriend's public displays of affection.

"Why's that?" asked Elly, who was only half paying attention. Her nose was deep in her journal writing down notes about the small town. "We got lectured the entire time about staying out of trouble,"

Alistair huffed.

"You should probably listen to your dad," Elly replied bluntly. "Sounds like he is giving you good advice."

"Whatever," Hunter shook his head with disapproval. "Whatever to you," Elly replied with a disgusted look. "You should go check on Olivia," Tully elbowed Hunter.

"I wouldn't," said Elly. "She's not herself lately, a bit rude."

"Elly, why don't you tell me what sort of notes you're taking?" Tully put his arm around Elly and started walking towards the store front. "Oh umm..." Elly wasn't expecting the sudden interest. "Well, I find it strange that there is a local Paranormal group in such a small town, don't you?" Elly began asking a series of questions about the case to Tully who nodded enthusiastically to each.

"Oh yeah, interesting, I never thought of that!" Tully turned and gave Hunter a thumbs up.

"Hopefully she doesn't bore you to death on the walk..." Hunter chuckled to himself.

Olivia had just met up with Hunter, who had stayed behind the group. "You didn't have to wait." Her face was emotionless.

"Well, you looked a bit lonely. Thought you'd need a friend?" "Who needs friends," Olivia frowned.

"Still fighting with my sister?"

"More like ignoring one another," Olivia sighed. "I think she hates me, now."

"You're her best friend," said Hunter. "She is just a stubborn brat.

Tomorrow she will probably forget all about it." "Yeah, Maybe...."

"Look at this place..." Hunter held the MI Paranormal door open for Olivia to enter. The group had already gathered around the place, scoping out all the weirdness. "Looks creepy!"

"Uh...yeah..." Olivia hadn't expected to enter into such weirdness. The little shop was filled with strange things, littered with posters that said things like: "I Believe" or "They're Out There", loaded with movie posters of cheesy alien movies and creepy ghost flicks. There were all sorts of jars filled with weird specimens of animals and lizards. It reminded her of the weirder parts of the Estate, the places the kids weren't supposed to go, but always found while sneaking around.

"Hello!" Ben yelled out in the small store.

"Anybody here?" Abram scoped the area. He picked up a book about Native American Ghosts and thumbed through it.

"Kids, see that?" Ben pointed to the checkout counter. "See that little logo etched into the counter?"

"Where?" Alistair ran up to his dad to see the mark etched into the wood surface.

"Look familiar?" asked Abram. "That's our sigil," replied Elly.

"Yep, Solomon's Seal with the two-headed snake within it," answered Ben.

"What is it doing there?" asked Tully. "I thought we were a secret society?"

"That we are," replied Abram. "That means they have connections with us. When you see one of these stamps, that means they have some sort of relationship with us and they can be trusted. Professor Calenstine is the only one who approves these."

Alistair's eyes suddenly grew with excitement. "This place seems familiar, like I have seen it somewhere before."

"Well unless you have been sneaking out of your room at night and traveling to Mid-Michigan, I don't think you've been here before,"

Ben chuckled.

"Why, hello there!" An attractive black woman stepped out from the back of the store with a warm smile. She was in her mid-thirties, her hair braided and tied back neatly into a pony tail. She carried with her a steaming cup of hot cocoa that she carefully sipped from. She affectionately rubbed her pregnant belly as she introduced herself. "My name is Reeta Lirette, welcome to our little shop."

"Hello," the group replied.

"I dig the layout," Ben smiled pointing at one of the UFO posters. "I'm glad, my husband and I are obviously quite interested in the unknown," Reeta placed her cup down on the counter, careful so as to not spill it. "What brings you in? We don't get many visitors."

"My name's Ben, this is Abram. This ragtag group of kids behind us is on a field trip for school," Ben pointed to each kid with a brief introduction. "Hunter, Elly, Olivia, Tully, Symphanie, and the handsome fellow in the back is my son, Alistair."

"A pleasure to meet you all," Reeta smiled awkwardly. "You said you brought a group of kids on a field trip to a local paranormal shop? That's... different."

"Well, we hear you have connections," Ben nodded.

"I apologize, connections?" Reeta's brow furled at the choice of words.

"Yeah, we were just adoring your little shop when we saw this," Ben tapped on the etched sigil with the two headed snake.

"Oh..." Reeta replied. "Nick, dear," Reeta yelled to the back. "I think you have some guests."

A Caucasian man in his late thirties stepped through the backthreshold. His name was Nick Lirette. Much like his wife, he met the group with a soft smile and his own half-drunk cup of cocoa. His dark brown eyes were hidden behind black, round rimmed glasses; his sandy brown hair was tucked underneath a matching black fedora, a personal style he'd kept up since his college days.

"Good evening," Nick spoke politely to the group. "Name's Nick, but everyone around here calls me L.J. I heard we had guests, but I didn't realize we had a full house." L.J. wrapped his arm around his wife's shoulders.

"Yes, and they were inquiring about your 'connections'. I thought you'd be inclined to visit for a bit while I go pour our younger guests some of our hot cocoa, deal?"

"Connections?" L.J. frowned briefly unsure of what his wife was getting at.

"Name's Ben, and my partner is Abram," Ben smiled tapping on the logo once again.

"Oh Lord!" L.J.'s eyes got wide. "You're Seekers!?"

"First, why is this logo etched onto your table?" Abram spoke bluntly.

"Abram, no need for interrogations, these people are our friends," Ben shot Abraham a dirty look. "Excuse my large friend, he is always grumpy."

"I am careful, just like we should train our kids to be," Abram exchanged dirty looks with Ben.

"Oh, umm…" L.J. stammered over his words trying to remember all the important details of his story. "Well, about five years ago an elderly man came through here with Johnathon Gates, you know, the star of Myth Hunters? This was before he was a big star on cable television, but that's beside the point," L.J. began talking with excitement. "Anyway, he came strolling in here with this older gentleman in a wheelchair, and I am talking really old. He looked ancient, but he was so excited about our shop. He seemed like a kid in a candy store, he knew so much about everything we had, the Grassman, the famous hauntings around here, he just knew everything! So, anyway, they were asking us all sorts of questions on the Michigan Grassman, it's sort of our specialty. Where were the sightings, how long had it been going on, all sorts of questions," L.J. pointed towards the back of the store that was dedicated to all things "Grassman", newspaper clips, blown up photos and the likes.

"Michigan Grassman?" Hunter asked.

"I've heard of it before," said Alistair, trying to remember how he'd heard of the creature.

"Yes, children, the mysterious Michigan Grassman," Reeta came back with a serving tray of coffee mugs filled to the brim with steaming hot cocoa and marshmallows.

"Reeta, my wife and I, we met at a statewide Grassman convention about seven years ago. We fell in love at once, a perfect fit," explained L.J.

"Thank you, it smells so good!" Elly passed out the cocoa to the group.

"There have been accounts of the Grassman in these parts for generations. Gates introduced us to Professor Calenstine and we aided them on an investigation for the creature. A few years later Gates came back and filmed one of his episodes following the Grassman, we were even on the episode!"

"I knew I recognized you and this shop!" Alistair said with a wide smile. "I love Myth Hunters. I remember that episode."

"We like to think of it more as a command center than a shop, but we do sell novelty stuff," Reeta winked holding up a plush Grassman doll.

"We were able to find some strands of hair out in the forest that summer. Gates and the Professor were so happy with our research they made us honorary Seeker aids. Of course, I didn't know what they were talking about. That's when Gates pulled out his traveling knife and etched that sigil into our desk. To be honest, I was pretty upset that he just whipped out that knife like that and scratched up our service desk."

"Well, to be fair," Reeta chuckled, "we'd never heard of this Seekers group. It's not like you can Google anything about you guys. Trust me; we did our research, nothing."

"As it should be," replied Abram.

"Well, to be honest we still don't know too much, other than we are grateful and forever in the Professor's debt. A few years ago we had some money problems, we were going to lose our store here," Reeta added affectionately squeezing her husband's hand.

"I got pretty sick. Lost my day job, it was rough," L.J. explained. "But one day we got a letter slipped under our front door. It was signed, Professor Calenstine, it was a check. More than we could have ever imagined. More than enough to pay off our loan on the store, and to live off comfortably, for a while. Then they kept coming… every month. 'Keep following your dreams, pursue the truth, and the Seekers will guide you' is all that was ever written on the letters that came with the checks. We met this man once, and he has taken care of us ever since. He paid for all my medical bills too."

"We are not sure how to thank him," Reeta wiped away a single tear.

"Wow, that's so amazing," Olivia cracked her first real smile of the day.

"I see, then I should shake both your hands," Abram extended his firm grip to the married couple. "I apologize for my abrasiveness, but in this field we are trained not to be too trusting. We have our enemies."

"Enemies in monster hunting?" asked L.J. "You have no idea," Abram nodded.

"Words cannot express how grateful we are to meet you both," Reeta came from behind the counter offering two mighty hugs to the men. "We're naming our baby boy after your Professor, Calenstine Lirette. I don't know where we would be without your kindness."

"Well, we will make sure we let him know," Ben said with a smile. "I am sure he will be elated with the news."

"So, what brings you folks back to little old Hemlock? Not much here, Grassman sightings have dropped off in recent years."

"Have you folks been following the news on the supposed Wendigo haunting the local woods?" Ben pulled from his satchel a local newspaper headlining a grainy black and white photo of the creature in a thicket of woods.

"Yes, of course. It has the entire town in a frenzy," L.J. frowned. "Why the grim look?" asked Abram.

"Well, when it comes to the paranormal, I am sure I don't have to tell you guys this, but, the most outlandish ones usually *are* hoaxes. I mean, look at what people are saying. A long slender humanoid body with the head of a demonized horse with antlers, eyes that illuminate… just seems fishy."

"So you're saying the local paranormal group isn't investigating?" Ben was a bit surprised.

"Well, we went out to where the first few sightings happened. We know the forest well; we have done many weekend hunts for the Grassman in the same area. But, we didn't really come up with anything. We even scoped out the area where the original story came from, with the kids being chased out of the woods by a monster."

"Wait, we don't know about that story," Abram thumbed through his Seekers journal to check if he missed something.

"Yeah, it's not out in the news. Only a few locals know about it," Reeta added.

"So what happened?" Ben pulled out his weathered Seekers journal.

"Well, a group of city kids went into the woods for camping, they went real deep into the forest too. Anyway, they claim a plane crashed into Pickerel Lake, they went to see if they could find any survivors when some monster burst out of the plane and chased them through the woods. They claim they narrowly escaped in their vehicle."

"A plane?" Abram mused aloud.

"Yep, a monster coming out of a plane," L.J. added. "All sorts of fishy stuff."

"So you two investigated that area?" asked Ben.

"Well, we are familiar with the lake, decent size. We went out there and camped for a few days, took a small raft out into the lake to see if we could find any debris in the water. Parts get fairly deep but we figured if a plane crashed into it we could tell. We didn't see much at all. If a plane crashed in that lake, it doesn't look like it's there anymore." "Could you show us on a map how to find the lake?" asked Abram. "Sure, there's a small trail that just a few miles off from where the kids said they'd camped, and it's about a twenty minute hike from the camp to the lake. Maybe you can find something we missed."

L.J. took out a local map, unfolded it and drew a line where the trail begins off the main road. "Follow this and you will run into their camp. Looks like a storm hit because there is some damage to the trees in that area, so it sticks out like a sore thumb."

"Awesome, a lead!" Alistair elbowed Hunter with excitement. "Reeta, L.J., this is valuable information, we can't thank you enough." Abram folded up the map and placed it securely in his Seekers journal.

"Children," Ben turned and smiled, "tomorrow we hunt!"

CHAPTER 24
CHOICES

It was a long ride back to the motel but the boys didn't mind, they spent the trip fantasizing over how amazing the hunt would be. This is what they had wanted all along, they didn't want all you can eat pancakes, or a musty old motel room, they wanted action and adventure. That is until Ben asked one simple question, "So what happens if you get separated and the creature is staring you down one on one, its blood thirsty fangs ready to rip the flesh from your bones?"

The boys' excitement fizzled, as the reality of the situation began to settle in.

"You heard L.J., he said that the creature supposedly ripped itself out of the back end of an aircraft. Just think of what it could do to any of us if it had a chance," Ben explained.

"That wouldn't happen; you guys are with us to keep us safe, right?" asked Alistair.

"That's the thing when you go into the unknown," Ben explained. "Sure, we are going to do everything we can to keep you from harm. Starting with the basics, eliminate you from the threat."

"What's that mean?" asked Tully.

"It means if we go in that forest and find reason to believe the creature is real, you kids won't be finishing the investigation with us. Too dangerous, because if it did catch any of you...well, you get the idea."

"So, what? We go back home to the Estate?" asked Tully.

"No, you would be sitting in the motel waiting for us to finish up. With a creature as violent as a Wendigo is claimed to be, Abram and I are to tag and bag it."

"Tag and bag it?" Hunter repeated.

"Yep, remember that dart that stuck Elly when Dominick was try-ing to shoot down the Beast of Bladenboro?" "Yeah, don't remind me," answered Hunter.

"Well, Abram and I have our tranq rifles with extra doses. We will put that puppy to sleep. If we snag it, we will contact Belmonte and they will send over a helicopter to pick the beast up. We will keep it at the Estate where it can't hurt anyone, but it will live in a safe environment where we can study it in a natural habitat."

"Back at the Estate? Where we live? That doesn't sound safe at all!" Tully was shocked at the response. He knew they had creatures hidden around the grounds, but a Wendigo?

"Don't worry, you kids have no idea the sort of stuff we have at the Estate. That's why we tell you kids to stay out of the forest. There are a lot of roaming creatures that would find you all an easy little snack." "Sheesh! We didn't know it was that dangerous!" Alistair frowned. "What do you mean? You're best friends with a Bigfoot, of course it's dangerous," Ben joked.

"Yeah, Bernie is friendly though."

"The stink ape that attacked us wasn't though," added Hunter. "What other sorts of creatures live in the forest? What keeps them from attacking us at the Estate?" Tully flipped open his Seekers journal to jot down the notes.

"All sorts of creatures, honestly. I couldn't tell you even if I knew them all, we're sworn to secrecy. To answer your second question, we have engineered the forest into a sort of zoo for cryptids. Certain creatures are confined to certain locations of the forest. That way we can monitor their living environments through the Estate. Think of like, a giant bio dome, you know... without the dome."

"That doesn't make sense." Tully shook his head in confusion. "A zoo?"

"Well, not a zoo for visitors, but in the concept that we raise and care for these creatures. We keep them safe, you know, that sort of stuff. All you really need to know is that the Estate is state of the art, nowhere on earth can compare to the technology we have at our disposal. We are able to keep the creatures at bay through medical tagsthat will not allow them to cross over their sectioned out areas of the forest. So, if we tag and bag us a terrifying Wendigo, you kids will never see it ever again. How deep into the forest we place a creature depends on their hostility level. This Wendigo guy seems to have a bad attitude; he will be placed fairly far out into the forest, miles and miles away from the estate."

"That's good," Hunter said with a half-smile.

"So do you think the Wendigo is real after speaking to those guys?" asked Tully.

"You heard L.J. and Reeta, they scoped out the area, they saw nothing of the sort. No plane, no debris, sounds like it's just a bunch of rumors running rampant. That's why Abram and I decided it was okay for you kids to come along."

"Lame..." Hunter frowned. "At least we won't have to worry about getting eaten!"

The boys chuckled. The closer the investigation got, the more the boys were changing their minds on the matter of the Wendigo hunt. Perhaps the Wendigo not being real may be a good thing.

•   •   •

"Finally back to the motel," Abram pulled the vehicle into the parking lot. "Hope you girls are tired. We got an early morning tomorrow. We have to be up at five a.m. to meet up with L.J. and Reeta."

"It's only eight!" Symphanie frowned. "I'm not tired at all." "Well, the rest of the night is yours to relax. We don't have cable or television at the Estate, maybe you kids want to catch up on some television or something. Ben and I will be going over a game plan for tomorrow that will probably take up the rest of our night. Just make sure you go to bed at a decent hour."

"Where are they anyway?" asked Elly stepping out of the SUV stretching out her legs.

"They had to make a pit stop, they will be here shortly. Let's get into our room, we can order a pizza or something, sound good?"

askedAbram.

"Pizza!" Symphanie yelled in excitement.

"Haven't had pizza since we moved to the Estate!" Elly replied with excitement.

"C'mon Olivia, let's get inside where it's warm," Abram held the car door open for his daughter.

"I'm coming, don't rush me!" Olivia replied adding snootiness to her voice.

Abram grabbed his daughter by the arm as she stepped off, "Olivia, I am getting tired of your bad attitude." His face was bright red, beyond the boiling point. "You will respect me. I am your father!"

Abram had finally snapped, after days of snotty replies and the blatant ignoring of his wishes, his daughter had gone too far. "I don't know where my sweet daughter went, but this new snotty jerk of a daughter I have is *not* alright!"

"Go to hell, dad! You're terrible!" Olivia pulled away from her dad's grip and ran off behind the motel.

"Olivia, stop!" Abram demanded, to no avail. "Leave me alone!" Olivia burst into tears. "Christ…" Abram sighed.

"Kids, take the keys and stay inside your room. I will order us dinner as soon as I get her back." Abram handed the keys over to Elly, who had the fear of death in her eyes.

"Olivia! Come back!" Abram ran after his daughter towards the small wooded area behind the motel.

"Yikes…" Symphanie peered over to Elly with an uncomfortable look on her face.

"Umm…yeah…" Elly sentthe look back to her. "Let's get inside where it's warm."

Abram cursed under his breath and ran behind the motel into the little woodland that sat behind the establishment. Olivia had run into a small clearing, Abram could only imagine his daughter's face, eyes bursting with tears because her father grabbed her in a fit of anger in front of her friends, yelled and scolded her due to his own frustrations… he felt like a failure… an idiot.

"Olivia! Please stop!" Abram yelled into the trees. There was no response. He rifled through some thick shrubs until he saw her sitting on a small bench with her back towards him, her head buried in her hands, sobbing. She had broken through the small thicket of trees and into a parking lot of the small supermarket that sat behind the motel.

"Olivia..." Abram spoke softly.

"Just leave me alone," Olivia shot back, her voice riddled with anger.

"Listen... it's freezing out here, let's go back and talk." "No, I never want to speak to you again!"

Abram let out a deep sigh....

"I am sorry for grabbing you like that... speaking to you like that in front of your friends."

"Whatever, you don't mean that," Olivia gasped through her sobs. All her frustration came to a boiling point, the last time she cried this hard was when her parents sat her down for the divorce talk.

"I am sorry. I am not the best father. I..." Abram sighed, scratching the bridge of his nose with his thumb and forefinger in distress. Opening up about his feelings to anyone was not something Abram ever did, let alone towards his daughter. "I always needed your mother's help in that department. I am a failure at being your dad. I know that. I just... I don't know what you want... you know?" Abram felt a foreign feeling of warm tears budding in his eyes.

"What?" Olivia peered up to her father for the first time. She saw the sadness in his eyes. He hadn't even cried when her parents split. She had never seen her dad shed a tear.

"I am trying. I really am. I always had your mother when you were a little girl, it was easier then. Now you have boyfriends; you're talking back to me...."

"This is all your fault, you're cruel and mean," Olivia shot back.

Her sadness now mixed heavily with anger."Tell me what I did, all this anger? Is it because of that boy you were seeing?"

"No!" Olivia blurted out. "You don't know anything about that. It's none of your business."

"Okay... okay..." Abram soothed.

The two sat there for what seemed like forever. Neither said a word.

Abram wished there was some magical statement he could make to better things but there wasn't. Instead he sat there in the cold night air, rubbing his temples, wondering how everything had gotten so bad between him and his little girl.

"What happened between you and Uncle Dominick?" Olivia finally muttered.

"What?" Abram's mouth fell open.

"You act like I wasn't there when he said that terrible thing." Abram took in a deep breath.

"He called you–"

"–I know what he called me." Abram cut off his daughter. "You don't believe that, right?"

"I don't know what he meant." Olivia wiped away a tear. "Why would he say that? I even asked mom and she ignored me, got all weird about it...murderer?"

Abram shuddered at the term.

"I made a mistake," Abram stood up, pacing in front of his daughter. His normally cool demeanor was gone. He was disheveled and emotional.

"Dominick was never a member of the Seekers, but he was allowed to be on my team. He was my number two; we worked a lot of investigations before it happened." Abram cleared his throat, his voice softer than normal, and the edginess of his masculinity gone.

"He had met this girl on one of our trips together; this was a few years back before the incident. They fell in love; she was one of our sources in a local case here in the states. Our last case together... The three of us, with a few others, flew out to Tibet. Searching out some recent sightings of the Jo-Bran so-called "man eater of Tibet". You probably know if it more commonly as the Yeti. Anyway," Abram shook his head in sorrow as he continued on with the story.

"It was going to be an extremely difficult expedition. We would be traversing the Himalaya region, lots of mountains. During the trip, which spanned two months, Dominick and Cheryl...her name was Cheryl... had found out she was six weeks pregnant. He proposed at the summit, gave her this ring he purchased at a small market we had hit a few days prior. He was so happy, so excited about the news. All three of us were seasoned mountain climbers, everyone knew the risk."

"What happened?" Olivia listened intently. "A slip..." Abram said easily.

"A slip?" asked Olivia.

"I lead the team. We had Sherpas with us too."

"Sherpas?" asked Olivia getting caught up in Abram's seemingly cryptic words.

"Indigenous people of the region who aid climbers. We weren't climbing to the top. We had our scouted out the area... dangerous still, but..." Abram fumbled over his words. Only two people had ever heard this story before; Dominick who lived the experience with him, and his ex-wife.

"What was this slip?" asked Olivia.

"Nothing special," answered Abram. "We were tied together. Cheryl lost her footing and slid. She went over the ridge, dangling over a deep crevasse. Dominick descended to try to pull her up. I followed as fast as possible. He then lost his footing... he held on, but he was losing his grip...."

"Oh...?"

"By the time I got to him, he was holding on by one hand. I grabbed him, but I was holding up two people. I didn't have a firm position... there wasn't a choice."

Abram felt his hands shaking.

"She yelled up to me to cut her loose. I could save Dominick... she knew two people was too much weight.

"I waited still... I tried to pull them up together. The Sherpas were trying to get down to us... if we had a bit more time...maybe we could have..." Abram squeezed his trembling hands. "My foot slipped and I was about to go down with them. We have these safety release triggers... I got Dominick up far enough to reach down and pull hers... I had to pull it... we all would have went over."

"Dad..." Olivia ran up to her father and held him tightly.

"She fell. It was so slow. She just, disappeared into that crevasse,"

Abram choked on his tears.

"He thinks you murdered her?" Olivia couldn't comprehend.

"He blames me. If I would have held on longer for the Sherpas to reach us, that's what he says. We haven't really spoken since. He blames me, blames the Estate, and blames Calenstine. He lost everything."

"But you're no murderer," Olivia argued.

"It doesn't matter what I am," Abram held his head low.

"My boyfriend," Olivia spoke softly, "Well, my ex-boyfriend..." she corrected herself. "He really hurt me."

"Oh, Liv, honey," Abram reached over and hugged his daughter. "Being young means having your heart broken, and probably breaking a few yourself. I know you're upset right now, but it gets better, trust me."

Abram held his daughter for the first time in years. Together they wept underneath the autumn stars.

CHAPTER 25
ADVENTURING 101

"Got everything packed up?" Benjamin tossed the last of his bags into the SUV.

"Should be good," Abram shut the rear door of his vehicle.

"You pack your diving gear?" asked Ben. "Just in case we want to scope out that lake."

"First thing this morning," answered Abram with a hint of a smile. "Looking forward to getting the gear on. It's been too long since I've done a dive."

"So, what exactly happened last night? When the boys and I pulled up you were gone. Elly and Symphanie said you and Olivia got into a heated argument."

"Yes," answered Abram, checking the air in each of his tires.

"Yes?" prodded Benjamin.

"Yes, we got into a bit of a dispute."

"I mean, is everything all right? They said she ran into the woods behind the motel."

"We shared our feelings. We are much better now," Abram nodded. "YOU shared feelings?" Ben's mouth dropped playfully.

"She asked me about something very personal. Something that had been bothering her, and well... I think it helped us both."

"Fair enough," Benjamin patted Abram on the back. "All right, guys!" Benjamin yelled. "Get the girls and let's rock!"

Ben turned to Abram, "Glad you guys worked it out." "Yeah, thanks." Abram replied with a faint smile.

"Yes!" Alistair pumped his fist in excitement. He had been helping his father and Abram pack, overly excited about the investigation.

"You hear that? We're ready to go," Alistair high-fived Tully who returned his excitement with a small yawn.

"Cool," Tully was not fond of the early morning. "I miss my bed though."

"C'mon, guys, saddle up, it's about a two hour drive to where we're going," Abram ordered.

The teams gathered into the vehicles and buckled up for another long car ride. First stop was meeting up with L.J. and Reeta at the MI Paranormal shop. When they pulled up next to the shop, L.J. and his wife were already waiting in their car to guide them to the entrance to the Wanigas Forest. The team took a turn down an old country road about fifteen minutes before they stopped in front of a sign that said "Wanigas State Forest, Pickerel Lake Entrance".

"Well, this is as far as we go," L.J. shook Abram's hand. "Just follow the sign there into the woods. It will be a rough ride, dirt road the entire way. You will find a camping ground about a half hour in, the lake's a bit of a hike east of the grounds. There's a few different camping grounds in this location, all reachable only by foot as the road dead ends. Here..." L.J. opened his car door and pulled out a map of the forest, he circled two camp grounds. "You may need this. The circled camp site on the lake's edge is where you'll want to set up camp. The one a bit east of it was the camp ground where the kids stayed. As you can see from the map, if they followed the plane west towards the lake, they would have been real close to your campground. So, anything you need to find should be right around there."

"This is a big help," Abram folded up the map, placing it in his pack. "We can't thank you enough."

"It's our pleasure," replied Reeta.

"Okay, I think we have everything we need, we'll make sure to tell the Professor about little Calenstine," Ben smiled.

"We wish we could come with you, but Reeta is due in a few months," L.J. put his arm around his wife.

"I don't think the baby would enjoy camping out in this cold weather," she laughed.

"Well, we got a lot to do before nightfall, so thank you again," Abram nodded. He gathered the girls back into his SUV. Ben followed suit.

"Be safe, guys," L.J. waved as the SUVs turned into the small dirt road and towards Pickerel Lake.

"To be honest," L.J. held his wife close to them as they watched them drive off. "I hope they don't find anything close to a real Wendigo out there..."

•　　•　　•

"This is the place," Abram pulled his SUV to a stop. The dirt road they followed finally came to an end.

"This is a campground?" Elly looked out the car window with a frown. It wasn't much of anything at all, just the end of the dirt road surrounded by a daunting forest.

"No, the campground is still a hike away, see the trail over there?" Abram pointed to a small clearing in the brush. "Only the die-hard campers come out this far. We'll be looking for a clearing in the woods due west from here. According to the map there are a few other campgrounds within hiking distance, none accessible by vehicle though, so lace up your hiking boots."

"Looks like we made it," Ben stepped out of his vehicle stretching out his arms and legs. "Wow, chilly out here. You're going to have a cold dive later."

"Yep," Abram replied with a nod. "I'll be okay, been in worse." "Children, I know we just spent a few hours on a bumpy car ride, but it's time to gear up, we got some woods to hike through," Ben popped the back end of the SUV open and began unloading the bags. "So grab your stuff."

"Getting excited yet?" Abram asked Olivia who was strapping her hiking pack across her back.

"A little," she answered with a smile.

The group took ten minutes gathering their supplies, double checking everything, and making sure all their equipment was functional.

Olivia made her way over to Elly who was struggling to snap her hiking pack around her chest. "Let me help," Olivia clipped the strap tightly for her friend. "Is that too tight?"

"Oh, no... thanks," said Elly with a half-smile.

"Listen I..." Olivia frowned searching for the right words. "I'm sorry if I have been a jerk."

"Oh?" Elly held her head low.

"It's just-" Olivia began to explain, but Elly was quick to cut her off.

"—Me too," Elly reached out and gave Olivia a big hug. "I'm sorry too. Let's never fight again."

The two girls hugged, both feeling so much better now that they had apologized.

"You two are so cute! I want some!" Symphanie ran up to the girls, joining the embrace.

"I think they made up," Tully pointed to the hug fest going on near Abram's vehicle.

"You think?" Hunter laughed.

"Good, I was getting tired of Symphanie telling me about all the gossip," Alistair chuckled. "C'mon lets pack up."

The group triple checked all their gear before making their way into the thick Wanigas State Forest. It was mid-day, and the cold autumn weather made the hike difficult.

"It's freezing and we've been hiking for almost an hour," Hunter whined. "My toes are freezing!"

"Just a bit further," Benjamin answered back as he and Abram led the group through the forest.

"Beautiful out here, isn't it?" asked Symphanie, sneaking up alongside Alistair.

"Yeah, kind of. Pretty cool to get away from the Estate and out into the wild," Alistair answered. "I mean, I miss my laptop, but this is pretty cool too."

"Sort of romantic, too." Symphanie smiled.

"Err... sure?" Alistair looked over to Tully who answered with another thumbs up.

"Could be, little cuz," Tully caught up to the couple. "If it wasn't for the huge group of us rummaging around the forest with you," Tully slapped Alistair on the back as an "atta-boy" signal.

They marched on a bit further until Abram broke into a small clearing near the lake front.

"Finally!" Abram shouted back to the group. "I see the lake, we're here!"

"Nice," Benjamin ran up to his partner. "Hurry up, kids, we can make camp and catch a bit of a break."

The group settled into the small clearing at the front of the lake. It wasn't large, but it would hold their tents and equipment just fine. The lake was much larger than Hunter had expected, he could barely see across to the other side.

"What's the plan? We set up camp, then what?" Tully dropped his hiking pack and unloaded a small tent.

"We got some day light still," Abram checked his watch. "I am going to be getting into my wet suit and scoping out the lake. If L.J. was right, this is the clearing where the kids saw the plane sinking into the lake. So, I am going in to see what I can find."

"That's a big lake," said Hunter. "How are you going to find anything?"

"It's a plane," Abram answered. "We know if the testimony of the kids is real, that the plane dropped right out in front of us. Even if the lake gets pretty deep, a plane is going to stick out like a sore thumb. With any luck, I can find the plane and scope it out underwater."

"They said the authorities already looked for the plane though," Alistair added.

"One of the first things you learn as a Seeker," Abram unpacked his wet suit. "Double check everything. I wouldn't be surprised if the authorities rowed out on a boat and that was that. I doubt they dove in and really checked. If we see a plane, or the remnants of a plane, then we may be onto something here."

"Let's hope!" said Tully.

"You gear up, the kids and I will get the camp ready," said Ben.

Abram got his gear together and waded his way into the extremely cold lake water. He swam out a ways before beginning his dive. Benjamin and the kids took their time setting up the series of tents and getting a strong fire going at the center of the camp.

"All right, we got the tents up, fire is strong, and we've got freshly charged batteries for our cameras and gear. If everything works out, we're ready for a real investigation," Ben held out his hands near the fire.

"How cold will it get tonight?"

"Not freezing, that's all we need to worry about," answered Ben. "So what exactly are we looking for?" asked Elly.

"Yeah, do we just sit around and wait for Mr. Winters to finish his dive?" asked Symphanie.

"Well, the plane is important. If the authorities missed it, and we find it, then there is some credibility to the kids' story. If there is no plane... Well...then it's doubtful. We'd look around the forest, try to find any evidence, and see what turns up."

"Needle in a haystack," said Olivia. "Usually," Ben smiled.

"I am going to look around, see if there is anything out of place," Alistair stood up from the fire pit. "Better than sitting around here being bored and maybe we can find something that will help."

"Well, if a plane went down in these woods, there should definitely be some evidence somewhere around here. We just don't know which way the plane was coming in," Ben explained. "So sure, go have some fun. Be careful though, there are bears and wolves around. So don't go too far out.

"Look over there though," Hunter pointed down the lake front. "What?" asked Elly.

"The grass and sand looks different from the rest, sort of smashed down," Hunter explained.

"Good eyes, Hunter," Ben grabbed a camera. "We always film our investigations. I will be in charge of the camera. Let's go."

Ben led the group of kids towards the side of the bank.

"Looks like there was a camp here recently," Ben filmed some random trash left behind.

"Check this out..." Hunter kneeled down on the sandy beach. There was a faint broken tire track that led into the grass. "Something with wheels was here."

"What do you mean?" Ben hurried over.

"Look, tracks!" Alistair peered over Hunter's shoulders.

"What's that mean?" asked Olivia. "How could they get a vehicle way back here? There is no road."

"You can see where whatever it was pushed down the grass and crushed the bushes," Ben filmed the strange clearing.

"You think they dropped it here?" asked Elly.

"What do you mean dropped?" Hunter frowned at the thought. "I dunno, like from a large plane or something."

"Why would they want to drop a car in a forest where they couldn't drive through?" asked Tully.

"I wonder...," Ben scratched his chin, looking out into the lake. "What?" asked the kids?

"Maybe not a car, but perhaps a crane of sorts? I mean, if they pulled the plane out from the lake they would need something big to pull it up, depending on the size of the plane."

"Is that even possible?" asked Symphanie.

"Well, it depends on who wanted the plane out of the lake. A helicopter could have dropped off a crane, if the plane wasn't too far out into the lake they could have pulled it to the shoreline, here," he explained. "Abig enough helicopter could have lifted the plane out of the forest. It's possible, however, not likely."

"Hey guys, why are you not at the camp?" Abram walked towards the group. He was still in his wet suit.

"Just investigating, what did you find down there?" asked Ben. "Did you find the plane?" asked Elly, eyes wide with excitement. "It's a murky lake. Not too visible down there, definitely no plane though."

"Hmm..." Ben frowned.

"Not anymore at least," Abram held out a piece of grey metal.

"What's that?" Ben zoomed the camera in on their findings.

"I found a few of these on the lake bottom, shards of metal, debris of what I believe was a crashed plane," Abram handed it to his daughter.

"You think there was a plane crash, then?" asked Olivia. "Check this out," Hunter pointed to the disturbed lake edge.

"Interesting, someone was doing some sort of work on this bank," Abram knelt down picking up some litter. "At the very least, a recent camp."

"So what went on here?" asked Alistair. "A cover up?" asked Ben, musing aloud.

"Well, here's what we have been told: A plane crashed into these woods, hitting the lake, campers close by ran to aid the plane but before it sank, supposedly, a creature that may or may not be a Wendigo, burst through and gave chase. If a plane was transporting a creature like that, then-" Abram raised his eyebrows towards Ben.

"Whoever that plane belonged to needed to cover their tracks," Ben ran his hands through his hair. "It makes sense; we're talking Aten, aren't we?"

"Why does it have to be Aten?" asked Symphanie.

"We know it wasn't a Belmonte plane that crashed. Aten is up to some seriously bad stuff, who knows what they were trying to do or where they found a creature that would even resemble a Wendigo," Benjamin started pacing.

"This is just a theory, we don't know anything yet," Abram added.

"Well, what do we have here?" a deep voice interrupted.

"Don't move!" another voice yelled.

Behind the group, with their weapons drawn, were two well-armed military men.

"Who the hell are *you* guys?" Ben dropped his camera, raising his hands over his head.

"Hands up, no sudden movements!" one of the masked men yelled.

"Calm down, boys," a man walked up from between the two soldiers. He wore similar military garb, but his gun was strapped along his shoulder. He stepped out and pulled his face mask back to reveal his scarred face.

"Dominick?" Abram clenched his fist. "What are you doing here?"
"I am doing my job, cleaning up another mess," Dominick waved someone up. Another man came up, standing alongside Dominick unmasked.

"Funny how we keep meeting," Gerald Krueger smirked. "Things just got interesting, didn't they?"

CHAPTER 26
TURN FOR THE WORSE

Gerald Krueger, father of the despicable twins, Corbin and Lunette, stood before the group with a sly smile. How lucky had he been?

Out in the middle of a nowhere forest and the Kendrick kids fall right into his lap. He enjoyed this, taking in the chance to revel in the moment he cracked his knuckles. Gerald hadn't changed since his last days at the estate, still as pompous as ever. He was in his mid-forties, a balding man, his hair thinner now than Hunter remembered from just a few months prior. He'd put on some weight too, but despite that, he looked quite formidable in the military outfit, Hunter was not happy to see him.

"Well, what do we have here?" Gerald mocked, his eyes honed in on Hunter and Elly. "This must be my lucky day. I think I'm getting an early bonus this year."

"Awesome, two traitors leading a group of armed men," Ben held out his arms in front of the children, doing what little he could do to separate the kids from the men.

"We have children with us, Dominick, lower the weapons. You're frightening them," Abram scowled, his eyes sharp, readying for anything.

"Yeah, right," Gerald chuckled. "You think we care about your precious children? In fact, two of them come with a pretty little price on their heads. I think we should cash in, what do you say, Dominick, old friend? I've been wanting a new addition to my luxury island home. Splitting the bounty fifty-fifty would be more than enough for us to splurge a bit. I'm thinking maybe an in ground pool in the back for the kids, maybe a hot tub for the wife and I? What do you say?"

Dominick remained silent, but couldn't help it when a disgustedlook came over his face.

"What's that supposed to mean?" Abram gritted his teeth. "A bounty on their heads?"

"Well-" Gerald's sly tongue began to explain.

"—Enough, Gerald," Dominick put up his hand, signaling for Gerald to shut up. "Soldiers, drop your weapons. We're here for the creature, not for any children. We hunt monsters, not people."

"What?" Gerald threw up his hands in disgust. His face bright red with anger, he stormed over to Dominick in a fit. Gerald began poking Dominick's shoulder as hard as he could as he spoke, "What are you doing? You know what Professor Aten would give us if we brought back those two brats!? This is my call, not yours! He's had a hit out on those little jerks ever since Sebastian weaseled out!"

"What!?" Ben's mouth dropped. "What does Sebastian have to do with this?"

"Gerald, you need to stand down," Dominick forcefully grabbed Gerald's finger, twisting it backwards. Gerald howled in pain, falling to his knees. Dominick bent down directly in front of Gerald's face, nose to nose and whispered calmly, "You touch me again with that finger, I break it off."

"Okay... okay," Gerald whined.

"What is he talking about, Dominick?" asked Abram. "What's this about Sebastian, and this bounty?"

"Nothing you need to worry about," Dominick shot back. "We're here hunting an animal. We have our duties. It has nothing to do with any of you. So get out of here while you still can."

"Gerald, speak up!" Abram yelled. "What's this bounty? What's this about Sebastian?"

Gerald cracked another crooked smile holding his finger in pain. Gerald opened his mouth to answer once again, but before he could mutter a single word....

CRACK!!! Dominick struck Gerald with a hard straight jab directly at the base of his nose.

Gerald's nose burst open with a splatter of blood across his face.

Hefell to the ground once again holding his face, blood pouring between his fingers. "What the hell!?" he whimpered.

"I told you to shut up," Dominick shook his hand to alleviate the pain from the strike. "Aten put me in charge of the group. So follow orders!"

"Nice shot," Ben smirked, thoroughly enjoying the blow. "Listen," Dominick walked up to the group, purposely calming his voice. "Let's not pretend, there is no love lost between us. If you don't leave here, I have no issue acting accordingly. I may even enjoy it a little. All I need is a reason."

"Is that a threat?" Abram's eyes burned wild with fury. He clenched his fist ready to strike his younger cousin, if given the chance.

"Stop it!" Olivia shouted from behind. "Both of you just shut up!" She burst through Ben's arms, face flushed with tears.

"My dad tried to save your fiancé!" Olivia blurted out in anger.

"Olivia!" Abram yelled. "This is not your concern! Get behind Ben, now!"

"It is my concern!" she shot back. "You tried! You held on as long as you could. Why doesn't he see that?"

"Abram, tell your daughter to stand down," the anger in Dominick began to swirl, the blood rushed to his face, his ears turning red.

"No, he told me everything that happened! He raced down to grab you both. She asked him to unclip her, it was her choice! She knew what would happen if he held on any longer!! He's lived with you hating him every day, and it kills him! You're supposed to be adults!" "Abram, shut your girl up!" Dominick pulled a pistol from his side holster and fired three shots into the air.

"Jesus! Kids get down!" Ben dropped to his knees, covering his ears pulling the kids down with him.

Everyone dropped immediately, searching for cover. Except for one, Olivia stood resolute staring down her Uncle Dominick, her eyes unwavering.

"Your dad killed them! He had a choice!" Dominick's lip curled in disgust."

Dominick, cool it!" Abram cautiously stood back up. "Olivia, get behind Benjamin, now!"

"No," Olivia yelled back. "This ends now!"

"Stubborn brat's going to get everyone killed," Gerald smiled beneath the bloody hands covering his swollen face.

"Dammit, listen to me, Olivia!" Abram demanded.

Ben grabbed Olivia and forced her back behind him with the rest of the children.

"I gave you a chance to get out of here," Dominick shook with anger. His gun trembled in his hand.

"Dom, don't do anything crazy, I know you're a good guy. We had a lot of good memories when we were younger," Ben spoke calmly, slowly enunciating his words. "Kids get back, get far back," he whispered behind him.

"That's right, let the anger in! Just shoot them all!" Gerald stood up, tilting his head back to stop the blood from dripping any more onto his shirt. "Get it done with, they're the enemy!"

"One last warning, Gerald!" Dominick took a deep breath, trying to calm himself.

"This is getting way out of hand!" Ben held out his hand slowly, motioning for Dominick to lower his weapon.

"Boss, what do you want us to do?" one of the military men asked from behind the commotion, gun poised, ready to mow down the group if needed.

"Just stand down, I will handle this," Dominick ordered.

"Dominick, drop your weapon and we'll walk out of here and back to our vehicles," Ben spoke slowly. "You made your point; this is your hunt, not ours. We don't even know what we're hunting. It's all yours. We just came to scope the place out, no big deal."

"We're going to die," Symphanie whispered to Alistair, her eyes red with tears. Her entire body shook in fear.

"Just stay calm," Alistair held her hand tight. "I will protect you... promise."

"What did he mean about Sebastian?" Hunter whispered to Elly.

Elly did not reply. She was white as a ghost, frozen in fear, eyes locked on the pistol Dominick had just fired.

"Did you just hear that?" one of the military men turned quickly, startled by a noise from the thicket of the forest.

"What?" asked Gerald. "Hear what?"

"None of you heard that?" The man asked again, looking towards the forest's edge.

"What's the problem, soldier?" Dominick turned to his men.

"I heard something over in the brush, something moved. Twigs snapped, something rustling through the forest...."

"Check it out, report back quickly," Dominick ordered turning back to Abram's group.

The soldier drew his weapon once again to ready himself. He walked towards the forests edge peering into its darkness, looking for anything out of the ordinary.

"Probably just a squirrel," the second man joked, following his partner. "Keep cool, stay calm."

"Let's hope it's just a squirrel," the soldier replied.

"I really wish they would have told us what we're out here hunting," the soldier whispered back.

The two men scoped around the nearby forest finding nothing of importance other than a small white tail rabbit darting out from a nearby bush.

"Anything?" asked Gerald, holding his chin up high to prevent the blood from flowing.

"No, just some stupid rabbit," the man turned back towards the group.

"Let us walk away," Abram nodded to Dominick. "You can have your hunt, the rabbit is all yours."

"Funny," Dominick's mouth pursed in annoyance. His back was turned from his men, so he hadn't seen it. But he saw the look of horror in the young eyes of Symphanie as she let out an ear splitting, blood curdling scream.

She was the first one to see it perched atop one of the nearby trees.

Two large eyes appeared from the darkness of the foliage. Bright as the stars in the night sky, yet hauntingly mad, sending the fear of death through Symphanie's body.

The creature was so fast... from the top of the nearest tree it dropped. A grotesque looking creature, it hit the earth swiftly, almost making no noise at all. It was tall, long, with lanky arms and legs. Its skin was as pale as the moon, looking like death warmed over. Its eyes blinding, like bright flood lights staring down its prey. Hunter's mouth dropped open in utter fear. The thing looked like an abomination, evil incarnate. Hunter had seen some wild things in the last two years, but this vile creature made the Beast of Bladenboro look like a kitten in comparison.

Elly turned pale and fell unconscious into Benjamin's arms from the ghastly sight. Olivia and Symphanie averted their eyes, both clinging to Hunter and Alistair.

"We're all going to get eaten!" Symphanie cried.

"Quiet, get down," Benjamin whispered to the kids, trying to keep the calm.

It was hard to tell at first what Hunter and Alistair were witnessing. The creature moved so fast, so fluid, it seemed unreal, unnatural. It pounced from the tree top down onto the unsuspecting soldier, soundless. If it wasn't for Symphanie's scream, and the sudden terror stricken cries from the soldier being attacked, no one would have seen a thing.

The initial blow was crippling, the entire creature's weight crushed the man into the earth, knocking the breath out of him. There was no escape for the soldier; he was completely disabled from fending off the brutal onslaught. The creature was tall, twice the size of the man in its grips, almost completely hiding the man from the children's vision. It violently attacked in a haze of swipes and scratches with its long sharp nails. The creature snarled and howled as it ripped into the soldier's flesh. Dominick pulled his gun and fired a warning shot high into the air, hoping to startle the beast.

The loud noise rang out into the woods. It worked, causing the creature to stop its fatal onslaught, momentarily. It averted its attention from its prey towards the group. Its soulless shining eyes staring them down, blood splattered across its long, slender face. The monster's skull was grotesque, unnatural, like something caught in-between the living and a rotting corpse. Its head was oblong shaped, resembling a horse with a long snout and nose. Wicked looking antlers, sharp and already blood stained, protruded from the top of its head.

"The Wendigo!" Gerald squealed with excitement. "It's beautiful! Look at it, look at it!" He pointed; a sick smile growing from ear to ear.

"Children get away, hide!" Ben demanded. "Don't watch this!"

"Beautiful? It's killing your man!" Abram couldn't believe what he was hearing. How could he say such evil things? Gerald was a sick man, he'd always been a selfish man while in the Seekers, but he wasn't mad, he was not a murderer... Something had changed him since he set foot in Aten Corp.

"Kill it!" Dominick holstered his pistol and swung his rifle from his shoulder. He locked the stock of the barrel against his armpit and aimed for a kill shot. He lined up his sights; the bullet would tear through the creature's chest, a direct hit through its heart. Before Dominick could pull the kill trigger, Gerald grabbed the muzzle and pulled it down towards the earth.

"He's killing our man!" Dominick grabbed Gerald by the scruff of his jacket and tossed him to the ground. "Are you mad!?"

"We must keep him alive, tranqs only!" Gerald ordered.

The second soldier dodged for cover after the initial attack. He'd been so close to his partner that the creature hit him with a glancing blow during the frenzied attack. It took him a second to gather his bearings before realizing what was happening. Shocked at the ongoing madness, the soldier froze in fear at the sight of the Wendigo ripping into his friend, tearing him into pieces.

"Soldier!" Dominick's voice knocked the soldier back into reality. He had to act fast if he wanted to save his friend. He had one chance and he had to make it count. The soldier pulled his pistol from his hip, aimed as best he could with his trembling hands, shouting, "Get off him!" He fired off a shot, grazing the creature in the shoulder. Dark thick blood sprayed from the open wound, and the creature merely flinched. Angered, the Wendigo turned its blood stained face towards its new attacker. Its eyes beamed brighter than the sun on a hot summer's day, blinding the soldier. He raised his hand to block the piercing brightness, leaving himself open for a critical blow.

The Wendigo pounced from the downed soldier, head-butting its new attacker square in the chest. The blow was brutal, so powerful it knocked the unsuspecting soldier back five feet in the air, crashing his limp body up against the trunk of a large oak tree. Intense pain shot through the man's body, his chest cavity fractured from the blow. He gasped for air in short breaths; his ribs felt broken, vision blurred and hazy. It felt like he'd been hit by a semi-truck.

The creature stood unyielding, staring down its newest victim, eyes wild with madness. The Wendigo did not go for the kill, but instead it turned its attention away from the wounded soldier, leaving the man in a broken, bloody heap. The Wendigo snarled, rolling its oblong shaped-head around its shoulders cracking its neck with a series of sickening pops, settling its sights back on the first victim, ignoring the panicked group a few yards ahead of it.

"It's killing them!" Elly cried. She tried to look away from the violent sight, but no matter where she averted her eyes, she could not escape the screams and howls. "Somebody save him, please!" she cried.

"We need to get these kids out of here," Ben yelled to Abram. "Yes, get them out of here," Abram ordered. "Head back to the camp, grab one of our rifles, then head back to the vehicles."

"Kids, focus on me," Ben gathered the kids in a small circle, huddling together. "We've got to get back to the camp, now. We need to move quietly so as not to garner any attention from that thing."

"We can't just leave my dad!" Olivia protested.

"Listen to Ben, get out of here. It's too dangerous!" Abram ordered.

"I will be fine, been in worse situations."

"He's right," explained Ben. "C'mon, the camp is just a few yards away; we can still see what's going on."

"C'mon, Olivia, it will be okay, we won't leave your dad behind," Hunter grabbed her hand and pushed her forward with the group.

"Swap to your tranqs, we must take him alive!" Gerald ordered the soldier who was lying in a bloody heap. "Get back up, do your job, you worthless fool!"

"You're the damned fool!" Dominick had had enough, his eyes wild with anger. Without warning, he grabbed Gerald by his shoulder and spun him around so that they were face to face. Without saying a word, he cracked Gerald across the jaw with a solid right hook.

Gerald made a muffled grunt before falling to the ground like a sack of rocks, motionless. It was a knockout blow that left Gerald sprawled out on the muddy earth.

The Wendigo was hunched over the first downed soldier who had finally fallen silent. The Wendigo's eyes shot back towards the second injured soldier, its mouth dripping with the fresh blood from its first victim.

In a fleeting attempt to escape, the soldier managed to crawl his way to the base of a tree, holding his chest. He took shallow, slow breaths, trying to regain his composure and not pass out from the pain. The creature charged with its head down, ready to tackle the soldier once again. Its sharp antlers aimed to skewer the soldier where he sat, easily a fatal blow.

Dominick quickly raised his weapon and took a shot from the hip, having no time to aim. It went wide, causing a small eruption in the earth a few feet in front of the charging Wendigo. It was enough to stop the creature in its tracks.

"Damn!" Dominick cursed. He aimed and took another shot but the Wendigo was too fast, this time the bullet hit a tree causing the trunk to splinter. The Wendigo charged onward towards the soldier, reaching out with its long boney hand it grabbed the wounded soldier by his leg and tossed his body onto its shoulders. The Wendigo growled at Dominick, almost daring him to give chase. It turned back towards the thick of the forest and disappeared into the undergrowth.

"I need to follow it!" Dominick reloaded his rifle before taking offafter the creature.

"Don't be a fool, you can't take that thing on alone," Abram grabbed his younger cousin by the shoulder, stopping him in his tracks.

"I just lost a man to that thing, I won't lose another!" "Then let me go with you."

•   •   •

"We can't just leave my dad!" Olivia wiped away her tears. She held Hunter's hand tighter than she'd ever held anyone's. They were in the midst of a mad dash back to camp, away from the Wendigo's attack.

"We won't, I promise." Hunter said. He stopped a few feet behind the rest of the group. "We will go back and get him, I promise. Even if that means we have to go back ourselves."

"Thank you," Olivia sniffled. "That thing…it was…." A sickening howl from the Wendigo made Olivia jump. "Oh my god!" she cried.

Hunter and Olivia turned back to see the Wendigo grab the downed man and retreat while Abram grabbed Dominick by the arm, halting his chase.

"Look, it's running away from them. C'mon we need to catch up," Hunter led the way back to the group.

Hunter and Olivia joined the panicked group at the campsite.

"Tully, hand me that rifle over there, careful with it," Ben pointed to Abram's equipment stack near his tent.

"What did we miss?" Hunter ran up next to Alistair.

"We're just getting the important stuff, and then we're hiking back to the vehicle."

"I am so scared, I just want to get back home," Symphanie still trembled in fear. "Did you hear it growling?"

"Everything is going to be fine, kids," Ben's face was more serious than ever.

"We can't leave my dad," said Olivia once again. "I am not going without him."

"Your dad wanted you safe. We're heading back to the vehicle, and we will wait for him there."

"She's right, we can't leave him," Hunter added.

"This is not up for debate," Ben slammed down the pack he was filling. "This is dangerous, that creature tore that guy to shreds! He is dead! Do you understand? DEAD!"

"Guy's!" Tully interrupted. "Mr. Jenson's right. Olivia, your dad can take care of himself."

"Look though," Olivia pointed back towards where the attack took place. "The creature fled."

"What is he arguing about?" Ben's eyes were squinted, barely able to make out the two men. Ben pulled a radio that was clipped to his belt. "Abram, you there?"

"Ben, the creature fled," Abram's voice cracked over the walkie-talkie.

"We'll wait here at camp, then we'll head back together," Ben clicked over.

"Negative," Abram added.

"What do you mean, negative? We need to get out of here. We are not equipped for such a violent cryptid."

"I will be going on with Dominick to save his man," Abram shot back.

"No," Olivia's eyes swelled back up with tears.

"I do not think your daughter will ever forgive you if you go into that forest," Ben spoke over the radio.

"Put her on," Abram replied.

Ben handed Olivia over the radio.

"Dad?" Olivia clicked the button as she spoke. "Honey," Abram's voice crackled.

"Dad, don't do it. Don't follow that thing, please!"

"Honey, listen to me," Abram replied. "I need to do this, I owe it to Dominick. You understand, right? If he goes out there alone...."

"But, he hates you! He blames you for-" Olivia began to choke over her tears.

"This is my chance to set things right, or at least try to, " Dominick sounded somber. "I have stared down many evil looking creatures, honey, more than you'd care to know. Together, Dominick and I can capture any cryptid."

"But...," Olivia didn't have any words.

"We will meet up with you in exactly two hours, back at the SUVs.

Be ready, once we come back, we need to get out of here a.s.a.p."

"Okay, please be careful," Olivia frowned as she handed the radio back over to Ben.

"We good now?" asked Ben over the radio.

"Almost," Dominick clicked back over. "We're going to follow the Wendigo in, but we can't leave this fool lying out in the open in case it tracks back around. Gerald is easy prey. Can you swing back here and grab him?"

"Copy, I will grab him and carry him back to the vehicles."

CHAPTER 27
THICKER THAN WATER

"What's the point?" Dominick curled his lip when he spoke. He kept his rifle aimed and ready for anything. His eyes continued to scan the forest looking for any tracks or signs of a large creature moving nearby, bent twigs, crushed leaves, the Wendigo was large and proved easy to track.

"Point of what?" Abram responded with a defiant tone.

"Enough with the act," Dominick stopped, he took a long deep breath before turning around to face his older cousin, his eyes locked on Abram's. "You think coming out here to help me rescue my man is going to make up for killing her?"

"I didn't kill anyone," Abram did not avert his eyes. "You let go," Dominick retorted.

"I listened to Cheryl's advice. She wanted me to save you," Abram replied, his mouth now pursed, attempting to hold back the anger about to spill out from it.

"You could have saved us both," Dominick gritted his teeth, he found himself gripping the handle of his rifle with sweaty palms.

"If I hadn't we'd all be dead!"

"Would we?" Dominick broke the stare, hiding the one single tear dripping down his battle hardened face. He took another deep breath to collect himself. A small pool of fresh blood puddled on a patch of fallen leaves. He wiped away the single tear, smearing it into his thick stubble of a two day old beard. He dropped to one knee for a closer inspection.

"Are we on the trail?" asked Abram.

"Yes, but, he's bleeding out," Dominick fingered a small droplet of the soldiers blood. "I don't think the Wendigo took him far. He must have some sort of nest around here...a feeding ground perhaps? We need to get him some medical attention, and quick."

"Let's keep moving," Abram pointed towards a broken branch. "Trail picks up here."

The two men pressed on with few shared words. The hostility boiled, the tension thick, but both men knew the soldier's life rested in their teamwork, they pushed their issues aside and moved forward. Night fully set in, the illumination of the moon gave little visibility through the darkness of the forest. This made the journey dangerous, as Abram and Dominick had only their flashlights to rely on to guide them towards the creature, which left them easy prey if the creature decided to add to its body count.

"Wait," Dominick held up his palm signaling for Abram to hold. "What?" Abram whispered. "See something?"

"No, but wait..." Dominick took in a deep breath.

"Oh god," the ungodly smell of sulfur and rotting meat hit Abram's nose.

"Shhh!" Dominick put his finger to his lips. "Did you hear that moan?"

"He's close!" Abram drew his rifle.

"Here! Through here," Dominick broke through a thick bush and into a small clearing where the soldier sat hunched over, breathing heavily.

"Where is it?" Abram followed suit. "Check your man, I will cover you!"

Dominick kneeled over his soldier, checking his pulse. "Breathing is shallow, faint pulse...."

"Here," Abram lowered his rifle and swung his pack off his shoulder and tossed it over to Dominick. "First aid, patch up what you can." "I know what I'm doing," Dominick caught the bag and quickly rifled through it.

"Then make it quick, clean out and dress those wounds!" Abram peered around the clearing's edge, using his flashlight to scope out any signs of the creature. "If your man was an intended late night snack for the Wendigo, it won't be gone for long."

"You think?" Dominick mocked. He carefully laid out his medical supplies and began cleaning the many wounds to prevent infection. There was no time to stitch the wounds now, he'd clean them out as much as possible and dress them quickly. It was going to be a long walk back carrying the soldier, and time was of the essence.

"It hurts…" The soldier came to, "Hard to breathe…."

"You have some severe damage to your chest and ribs, we need to get you to a hospital, now," Dominick grabbed the soldier by his chin, forcing him to look at his face. "You need to stay alert, help us keep an eye out—"

"Dominick!" Abram shouted. He pulled his rifle towards the right of the two men, squeezing the trigger. Shots echoed through the forest, the bullets shredding through the foliage, the missed shots exploding splinters of bark everywhere.

A pale, grey figure exploded from west of the clearing. It was the Wendigo in full sprint, head down, antlers ready to impale Dominick, making him the third victim.

Dominick reacted quickly and spun his body, with his rifle cocked out in front of him, taking the majority of the blow, breaking it in half. The force of the beast drove him back, crashing into a thick bush.

"Dammit!" Abram tried to line up a shot, but the bush and the frantic commotion made it impossible, too risky.

The Wendigo slashed and clawed at Dominick who fought diligently for his life, using both ends of his snapped rifle to fend off as many of the blows as possible. He was lucky to have something between him and the wild creature hell bent on tearing him limb from limb. He did his best to block and dodge the blows, but he was lucky to defend himself a handful of times, grunting in pain with every swipe that made it through his defense. The Wendigo snarled, hot sticky saliva from its horse like snout dripped onto Dominic's face. Its sharp nails tore through his clothes like butter, his skin splitting open, and somehow he managed to push the pain back, swallowing it. He could not give into the pain, not if he wanted to survive the attack. He'd been lucky so far, the wounds weren't cutting deep, but he could feel his arms burning with fatigue. He wasn't going to be able to fend off the beast's blows for too much longer.

"This ends now," Abram strapped his rifle across his shoulder, there was no way he was going to pull a safe shot with the two engaged in physical combat. Instead, he pulled a bowie knife from his belt and readied himself. "I can play dirty too," Abram gripped the blade tightly, readying himself for an attack.

The creature focused on breaking through Dominick's defenses, trying to strike a fatal blow. Its evil, bright-yellow eyes were maddened, staring down its prey. The Wendigo was too powerful for Dominick to continue to fight, he was growing weaker and the beast sensed it.

"You're one ugly son of a—" Abram thrust his bowie knife forward tip first, attempting to time his blow with the Wendigo's attacks. He was aiming to puncture through the creature's chest cavity and pierce its heart. The Wendigo saw the blow coming and spun towards Abram just in time to knock the blade away, causing a large open slash down the creature's forearm, the blood poured out from the beast. It was thick and black, almost tar-like, splattering all over Dominick's chest and face. The Wendigo let out an ear splitting howl, so loud that it caused Abram to drop to his knees covering his ears, bloody bowie knife and all.

"Kill it," Dominic spit the creature's blood from his mouth. He was covered in lacerations from head to toe. He was bleeding heavily, but was conscious and of sound mind, and he didn't appreciate being showered with the creature's blood.

Abram nodded. He stood up gripping the knife, circling the Wendigo who held its bleeding arm. It was hurting, and for the first time showed a sign of weakness.

Let's play," Abram yelled at the beast, attempting to provoke it. "You and me, big boy!"

Dominick pulled his pistol from its side holster and took his time while the Wendigo was distracted to line up his shot. He cracked a half of a smile when he pulled the trigger.

A thunderous gunshot rang out through the moonlit forest.

The Wendigo howled once again, this time it was a direct shot. The bullet penetrated through its back and exited its right shoulder. It stumbled a few paces before falling face first onto the blood-soaked earth. "Finally," Dominick took a deep breath. He winced in pain as he sat himself upright.

"Nice shot," Abram bent over to inspect the damage. "I thought I was going to have to take it out with just the knife."

"You killed it?" the soldier from across the clearing moaned in a half-conscious statement.

"We need to get him back, but first we got to clean you up. You both need medical assistance," Abram walked over to the soldier where the medical supply bag had been left so he could dress Dominick's wounds.

"Make sure it's dead; put a bullet in its brain," Dominick wheezed. Abram stood over the fallen beast. He let his eyes look the creature up and down, the sight was unnerving. The creature was a menacing sight alive; in death… its gruesome nature was even more noticeable. Its long lanky body was sprawled out awkwardly on the earth; the bottom of its torso covered with coarse goat-like hair with hoven feet.

The hairline broke near the creature's midsection where it gave way to decrepit, pale skin that looked and smelled like rotted flesh.

"God, is this thing ugly," Abram kicked the creature's goat-like leg to see if it would move. It did not.

"Just shoot it already," Dominick couldn't help but muster a small chuckle.

Abram pulled his rifle from his shoulder and aimed his shot up. "It doesn't look like its anything from this planet. Alien, or some cross between the living and the dead; something right out of a horror movie; never seen anything like this before."

"Not sure where it came from," Dominick pulled himself upright, leaning against a tree trunk. "I get orders and follow them. Learned a long time ago, working with Aten, it was best to not ask too many questions."

"Wish we could have saved you," Abram frowned. There was no hesitation when he pulled the trigger, but instead of the expected kickback, the trigger simply clicked.

"Dammit!" Abram pulled the rifle quickly.

"Out of bullets? Such a rookie mistake for a veteran like you," Dominick chuckled even louder this time.

"Funny," Abram shot him a dirty look.

"Here, use my pistol, I got plenty of rounds left," he tossed the firearm over to Abram who caught it one handed. "Just give it back, my dad gave me that. Sort of a family thing."

"I'll take good care of it," Abram turned back towards the prone Wendigo ready to pull the trigger. Abram took his eyes off the creature momentarily to check the pistol. He hadn't seen the Wendigo's hind leg violently kick upright as hard as it could. The hooved foot went directly into Abrams hip, crushing his remote radio into pieces and causing him to crumble into a heap of pain.

"No!" Dominick yelled. "Shoot it, shoot it!"

The Wendigo sprang back to its feet, still bleeding the thick, oozing blood from its back and shoulder. It snarled loudly at the downed Abram, almost daring him to stand back up and fight. Even if Abram wanted to, he couldn't, the pain from the blow engulfed him. The Wendigo snarled one last time before escaping back into the woods.

"Crap, it's getting away!" Abram stumbled back to his feet. He was hurt bad, barely able to put any weight on the right side of his body. Angered, he fired off round after round into the forest where the creature had disappeared into the foliage.

"Drop your weapon!" Dominick yelled, "You're just wasting my ammunition."

"Dammit, it's heading back to the camp!" Abram cursed.

"We definitely got the short end of that encounter," Dominick continued to spit the thick Wendigo blood from his mouth. "God, the thing bled all over me, even in my mouth."

"Quit your complaining, we need to get moving. Three injured men aren't going to move that fast." Abram walked over to the downed soldier who had been in and out of consciousness.

"It...got...away?" the soldier cringed with every word.

"We hurt it," Abram lifted the soldier to his feet. "We're gonna have to hold each other up; we're all pretty roughed up."

"This isn't gonna be easy," the soldier somehow managed to smile through his swollen face. "I'm just...thankful you...came back for me."

"What's your name, soldier?" Abram asked.

"Brian," the soldier spit up blood onto his uniform, his face stained with drying blood and pale.

"We need to grab your boss; he almost lost his life getting you back."

"Yeah, right," Dominick groaned in pain as he stood himself up with the help of the trunk of the old oak tree. "Been worse."

"It went back towards the camp," Abram pointed. "Let's hurry."

CHAPTER 28
GERALD KRUEGER

"Wake up," Ben slapped Gerald snapping him back to reality. "Err...what happened?" Gerald rubbed his swollen jaw, wincing in pain.

"I think you made Dominick mad," Hunter chuckled.

"What did you say, you little brat?" Gerald slowly got to his feet. "He said my Uncle knocked you out with one hit," Olivia's face burned with anger, "you old creep!"

"Watch it, brat!" Gerald raised his hand to strike Olivia, but Ben grabbed his arm preventing the blow.

"Hey!" Ben spun Gerald around. Forcing Gerald's head into a firm side headlock, Ben swiftly shifted his weight into his hips, swinging Gerald over his body, slamming him into the ground. It was a vicious throw, all of Ben's weight and momentum crushed into Gerald's sternum. Ben pulled his forearm forward, burying it deep underneath Gerald's chin, blocking off his air.

"Whoa, nice Judo throw!" Tully's eyes went wide with amazement. "If you think—" Ben's face was maddening, eyes wild with anger "—that I am going to allow you to touch any of our kids, you're crazy. I could choke you out right here, your last breath, ever! Understand?"

Gerald gasped for air, unable to speak. "UNDERSTAND?" Ben pulled the choke tighter.

Gerald managed to slightly nod his head despite not being able to breathe.

Ben released his hold.

Gerald gasped for air, coughing uncontrollably, curling up into a ball on the muddy earth grasping at his neck and chest.

"Mr. Jenkins, where did you learn that?" Symphanie shared her older cousin's amazement.

"Man, you could fight in mixed martial arts!" Tully looked over at Alistair with pride. "That's your dad? Awesome!"

Alistair was just as amazed over his dad's sudden hand to hand fighting skills as anyone; he'd never witnessed his father in an altercation.

"Later," Ben shrugged off the kid's comments. He grabbed Gerald by the scruff of his collar, stood him up and slammed him up against a nearby tree. "Have you learned your lesson, willing to play nice?"

"Y…yes, sir," Gerald gasped out, still trying to catch his breath. "We came back to save your worthless life. We didn't feel right leaving you out here for that creature to come back and snack on. You should be thanking us."

"Yeah…right," Gerald's voice was hoarse from the choke hold. "I said, thank us!" Ben slammed Gerald back up against the tree.

"Thank you, thank you," Gerald's eyes went wide with fear. "Please, don't hurt me!"

"Wow, what a guy," Hunter frowned.

"No wonder Corbin and Lunette are such jerks, look at their pathetic father," Elly suddenly felt bad for the twins. She could only imagine living with Gerald as a father figure; he seemed like a dishonest weasel of a man.

"Everyone in the family is a jerk," Alistair grabbed Symphanie by the hand and walked away from the sight of his dad beating up a grown man. "I don't wanna see any more of this."

"Here's how it's going to work," Ben loosened his grip from around Gerald's collar, causing the man to drop to his knees. "We're heading back to the vehicles. You're coming with us, so you can live to tell Aten how royally you messed up. It's about an hour's hike back and we've gathered the supplies we need from our campground. You will keep your mouth shut during the hike and keep pace. Once we get to the SUVs we'll sit tight for your soldier, Dominick, and Abram to come back. Understood?"

Gerald nodded, swallowing his pride.

"Good," Ben held out his hand to help Gerald back up to his feet. Gerald knocked it away, scoffing at the gesture he stood up on his own accord.

"Fine, we'll stay enemies. Never cared for traitors anyway," Ben pointed towards a small trail heading towards the camp. "C'mon kids, we've got to move."

The group moved forward past the camp, following the small trail. They heard gunshots ring out deep within the forest, startling Olivia.

"Gunshots," Olivia frowned, worried for her father.

"We shoot the guns," said Tully. "That probably means they killed it."

"Yeah, your dad is an awesome shot. I'm sure they're fine," Hunter counseled her.

"Why did he have to follow Uncle Dominick?" Olivia was an emotional wreck.

"Because your dad is a hero," Ben answered from the front of the group. "When there is someone in need, he's going to run in and save them. Even if they are the enemy, it's just the type of man he is."

"Enemy?" asked Alistair.

"That soldier, Dominick, this fool traveling with us, they're all employed by Aten, the man who wants to destroy the Seekers and bury our Professor." Ben explained. "I'd call them enemies."

"Why though?" asked Elly. "Why does this Aten guy hate us so much?"

"Not too sure, other than Professor Calenstine has a long history with him," answered Ben.

"Because the Seekers ideologies are foolish," Gerald spoke under his breath.

"I told you, no talking or I'm going to tape your mouth shut," Ben shot Gerald a dirty look. "It's because Aten Corp is evil, money hungry, they don't care how many lives they ruin, as long as they get what they want. They couldn't care less about bettering the world. I hear Aten is a bit off his rocker, I have heard some pretty outrageous claims about his world views."

"He seems like horrible person," Alistair added.

"Look!" Symphanie pointed to the two vehicles parked on the dirt road. "We made it!"

"Okay, kids I want all of you in one of the vehicles and Gerald and I will be in the other. Hang tight until Abram and Dominick return. Just stay calm, and stay in the vehicle."

"Okay," the kids responded. After the events they had just witnessed, none of them were itching to go out exploring.

The group split up as Ben ordered, the kids gathered up in one of the vehicles and settled in.

"Everyone okay?" asked Ben.

"Yeah, we'll be okay," answered Hunter. "Just a little nervous," Olivia added. "Won't be much longer," Ben replied.

"Can you try him on the radio?" asked Alistair. "Check to see if he's okay?"

"I tried earlier, he turned it off, always do when we hunt, don't want to be heard out there." Ben frowned. "I will try again when I get to the vehicle, if I get through I will let you know, I promise."

Ben turned from the kids, shutting the car door. "C'mon," he waved Gerald over to the vehicle.

Gerald breathed a long relaxing breath as he sat in the passenger seat. He pulled down the visor and looked into the mirror. His face was in rough shape, he could barely recognize his own reflection. His nose looked broken, blood stained his face. It wasn't a pretty sight. It angered him, how these fools felt it appropriate to physically handle him with such violence. His hatred for the Seekers deepenec.

"Let's not speak," Ben pulled out his radio.

"Fine with me," Gerald shot back, clenching his fists.

"Abram, do you copy?" Ben clicked the radio transmitter. "Abram, do you read, over?"

There was no reply, just static.

"I'm sorry to tell you this, but Abram and Dominick are as good as dead," Gerald grinned.

"I said, no speaking," Ben flipped up Gerald's visor.

"We're both adults here," Gerald turned to Ben with a devilish grin making his fat lip even more noticeable. "I am sure we can think of something practical to talk about."

"I have nothing to say to you," Ben broke his gaze and peered out his window.

"I would think you would have all sorts of questions about what the hell we're dealing with out there."

"What are you talking about?" Ben frowned. "Do you know something we don't?"

"I know everything; it's why I'm here. Sure, Dominick thinks he's in charge, but he is just the hired muscle. Nothing more than a freelancer Aten uses to clean up our unmentionables."

"Unmentionables?" Ben furrowed his brow.

"When I took my talents over to Aten Corp, my eyes were finally open to reality, a true enlightenment, not like that crap Calenstine taught us. Aten's brilliance far outshines that old fool. Aten Corp sees the big picture, Ben. You may think we're in it just for the money, but there is so much you don't know about Aten's agenda, our goals, and *his* ultimate vision."

"He's a nut job," Ben waved Gerald off. "If you don't have info about this Wendigo thing, you can go back to being silent. If it even *is* a Wendigo," Ben pulled his Seekers journal from the glove box and began flipping through its pages.

"Oh, it's a Wendigo, all right."

"How do you know that? There is not one record suggesting any true sightings. It's Native American supernatural lore, Wendigo's are not real."

"Such ignorance, I can't believe Calenstine thinks so highly of you," Gerald shook his head.

"Spit it out already," Ben slammed his journal shut. "You obviously know more than you're letting on."

"You heard the rumors, those kids saw the plane crash, they reported it to the authorities, witnessed that creature emerge from the wreckage," Gerald explained.

"There was no plane, we scouted the lake."

"There was no plane because Aten didn't want anyone to find it. He flew me in not even twelve hours after our plane went down, gave me an entire team for the cleanup. Aten has taken a liking to me, let's me run his top-secret jobs. I think it's because I gave him so many of your little Seekers secrets."

"I can't believe we ever trusted you and your arrogant family, you were the one who failed at being a Seeker."

"Potato, po-tah-to," Gerald mocked.

"Still doesn't explain to me how you know that thing is a Wendigo," Ben questioned.

"Because you idiot! Aten sent me here to recover his Wendigo! That creature is years of hard work! He created it himself, one of his many little pet projects, part of his epic plan! It's too soon for anyone to find out what he is up to. I am here to retrieve it, keep the damage control down to a minimum. Silence those who threaten our cause… by any means possible."

"He created it?" Ben's mouth fell open. "Is he mad, how?"

"You never question your boss, especially when it's Aten. But, he's shared his dream with me, and it is brilliant. He is wise beyond his time."

"Is that right?" Ben tried to calm himself. "So, what about the kids, why does this grown man have it out for two teenagers?"

"The Kendrick brats?" Gerald chuckled. "Obvious isn't it?" "Watch it, Gerald," Ben grabbed him by his collar, pushing him forcefully against the car window.

"Think about it!" Gerald pushed the grip away. "Their parents tricked Aten. Played him like a fool. He thought he had them in his back pocket, but all the while they were working undercover. They humiliated him. You don't pick a fight with a great white shark when you're nothing more than a couple of clown fish, who do you thinks gonna win *that* exchange? He has a hit out on those idiot children because even with Kendrick's death, he still wants them to suffer. Sabo-taging their plane wasn't enough. He wants everyone they ever loved to pay."

"Aten killed Kim and Jeff?" Ben lost it. His entire body boiled in pure hatred. He jumped across the car seat and grabbed Gerald once more. "You son of a bitch! And you work for this sick murderer!"

"Money is money," Gerald sputtered before getting slapped across the face.

"You're sick!" Ben's hands shook in utter contempt for the man he held smashed against the inside of the car door.

"So what?" Gerald croaked through the pressure of Ben's hold. "You're gonna kill me?"

"No!" Ben let loose his grip. "No..." he took a deep breath. "I am no monster, not like you."

"You Seekers are weak," Gerald wiped the sweat away from his forehead.

"So why tell me all this?" Ben dropped his head onto the steering wheel, trying to make sense of it all.

"Because," Gerald slowly reached into his cargo pocket, cautiously pulling out a lone tranq dart, hiding it within the palm of his hand. He popped off the plastic cover, exposing the poisoned needle. While Ben's guard was down, Gerald made his move, stabbing him in the side of the neck with the needle. "You're not going to live long enough to tell anyone!"

"Son of a—" Ben felt the pain of the needle pierce his flesh, the intense burn of the poison spreading into his blood stream. He became lightheaded, the interior of the car began spinning violently, he tried to fight it off but soon complete blackness swept over him.

"Oh yes, Professor Aten is going to love me," Gerald grinned peering into the review mirror at the children's SUV. "Sleep tight, I will come back to finish you off as soon as I take care of those kids."

Gerald pulled a cellphone from his military jacket, flipped it open and dialed.

"Professor, it's Gerald. No, not yet. Things sort of got out of hand. No, sir, do not fret, I have managed to secure the Kendricks. Yes, of course I did. Do you want them dead or alive? Of course, I understand. Yes, thank you, sir! Of course, I promise the Wendigo will also be taken care of. Thank you, sir," Gerald snapped the cellphone closed.

•　　　•　　　•

"What do you think those two are talking about?" asked Symphanie, staring out the front of the SUV, trying to make out what was happening in Ben and Gerald's vehicle.

"Probably more arguing," Olivia nervously checked her watch. "Where is my dad, it's already been an hour and a half since they left." "They could still be out looking for it, I wouldn't worry," Tully added. "They may not come back until morning."

"That Gerald guy gives me the creeps," Elly rummaged through her backpack, pulling out her Seekers journal.

"Are you really doing homework at a time like this?" Hunter frowned.

"I have to update my journal with all this Gerald stuff," Elly clicked her pen and began writing.

"How cool was it when your dad judo tossed Gerald like that?" Tully slapped Alistair on the back. "You think he could train me to fight like that?"

"I've never seen him like that before, it was kinda scary," Alistair frowned.

"Sorta creepy sitting out here in this car in the middle of these woods, no lights, no nothing," Symphanie slid her hand into Alistair's. "Did my dad give the keys to any of us? Maybe we could listen to the radio or something," asked Alistair.

"No, he kept them," answered Elly. "Probably didn't trust us not to run the car out of gas, or kill the battery."

"Uhhg," Hunter rolled his eyes. "This is going to be so boring!" "How can you be bored when my dad is out there?" Olivia frowned. "I didn't mean," Hunter swallowed hard. What an idiotic thing to say, he knew Olivia was a nervous wreck. "I just wish, you know, we could be out there with them. So we'd know they were safe, instead of locked up in this car with nothing to do."

"Oh," Olivia averted her gaze out the passenger window. "Good one," Tully whispered to Hunter "...smooth."

"Wait, look!" Symphanie pointed to the SUV parked in front of them.

"What, look at what?" Hunter moved towards the front of the vehicle where Alistair and Symphanie sat.

"There's a bunch of commotion in your dad's car, Alistair," Symphanie pointed out.

"Gerald probably opened up his dumb mouth again, and your dad is giving him a beating," Tully smiled at the thought.

"Look, someone is getting out," the SUV's passenger door opened, a dark figure stepped out.

"Who is it? Is it my dad?" asked Alistair.

"Too dark to tell, but he's coming our way," Symphanie answered. "Wait, there was a flashlight back here with the rest of the equipment," Hunter crawled over his seat, rummaged through the goods until he found a large flood light. He crawled back up front with a mischievous smile. "Check this out."

Hunter flipped the floodlight on and aimed it through the front windshield, brightly illuminating the area. The sudden light caught the man off guard, who held up his hands to block the light.

"That looks like Gerald," Tully squinted his eyes.

"What's he doing? Where's your dad, why is he still in the car?" Symphanie frowned.

"He's still coming!" Olivia bit her bottom lip nervously. "Quick, lock the doors, I don't trust him."

Gerald stopped half way, his mouth fell open, eyes wide with terror. "What on earth," asked Alistair? "What's with the funny look?" "It's like he sees—" Hunter tried to interject, but before he could finish, something large smashed onto the top of their vehicle.

"Crap!" Alistair held out his hands, to prevent any whiplash as the entire SUV shook violently from the sudden blow.

"What was that?" Olivia jumped back into her seat, buckling up.

The weight of the creature diving on top of the vehicle caused a huge indentation over the kids head. It sounded like a boulder fell from the sky smashing the top of their car. Then they heard it… the grotesque blood curdling howl from above them.

"Oh, god!" Olivia screamed. "It's the creature!"

"Keep the light on Gerald!" Tully grabbed the floodlight from

Hunter, flashing the bright light back towards Gerald who stood in fear.

"What's he doing?" asked Olivia, who closed her eyes tightly.

"He looks terrified…slowly backing away towards the vehicle," Tully explained.

Gerald spun around and made a mad dash back towards the other vehicle. The kids could feel the amazing strength of the Wendigo as it jumped from the top of their vehicle, causing it to rock violently back and forth. The creature hit the earth, its hooves digging into the muddy ground, swiftly pouncing towards Gerald who was only a few feet from his car door. Gerald fumbled with the handle before jumping out of the way. The Wendigo smashed head first into the side of the SUV with such power the vehicle was lifted off of two wheels. The massive blow made a sickening thud, glass shattered into a million pieces, the frame of the vehicle bent. The Wendigo howled, it was stuck, its antlers pierced through the vehicle, interlocking bone and metal. It wailed violently as it tried to escape, using its long arms to bash and claw its way loose.

"I think it's stuck," Symphanie's mouth fell open in awe.

"My dad is in there!" Alistair turned to Hunter. "We've got to do something."

"Look, he's running towards us!" Tully pointed to Gerald who was running for dear life.

"Any ideas?" asked Hunter.

"Let me in, let me in!" Gerald came crashing against the side of the vehicle, hitting the windows with his fists in a panic.

"What do we do?" asked Tully.

"Let him in, he will die out there!" said Olivia.

"Didn't you tell us to lock him out in the first place?" Alistair gave her a crazed look.

"That was before he was out there with that monster, let him in!" Olivia pleaded.

"You can't be serious!" Alistair turned to Hunter. "He's crazy, right?"

"I dunno what to do," Hunter wasn't fond of the idea of letting

Gerald anywhere near him, or watching him get massacred by the hands of the Wendigo.

"Let me in!!!! Please!" Gerald's eyes were stricken with horror. "Crap, unlock the doors!" Hunter reached over Olivia allowing

Gerald to rip the door open.

"You hesitated!" Gerald pushed Olivia back, jumping into the vehicle and slamming the car door shut as fast as he could.

"It was going to kill me!" Gerald gasped for air, "and you bastards thought about letting that thing get to me, didn't you?"

"We thought about it," said Elly, giving him a deadly glare, "You said we had a bounty on our heads! Why should we save you from anything?"

"Yeah, you're a traitor!" Tully shone the flood light into his eyes.

"You punk!" Gerald's eyes burned, "Turn that off!"

"You left my dad in the car?" Alistair yelled, his eyes swelling with tears, "why would you do that!"

"What?" Gerald grabbed the floodlight from Tully and flipped it off. The last thing Gerald wanted was to be bothered with stupid questions. "Who cares who has the keys, give them to me now! We gotta get out of here," he threw the floodlight back at Tully. "You, keep an eye on the creature, you idiot!"

"What?" asked Hunter. "What do you want the keys for?"

"To get the hell out of here, you little brats. That thing will kill us!" Gerald argued pushing himself forward into the front of the vehicle. He grabbed Alistair by the arm, pushing him out of the driver's seat and over by Symphanie.

"We're not leaving my dad!" Alistair fought back."—Or my dad, or Dominick!" Olivia grabbed Gerald's hair.

"Stop it, you little brats!" Gerald screamed, he shoved Olivia back into her seat. "They're all as good as dead. Give me the keys, NOW, before it's too late!" He climbed into the driver's seat.

"We wouldn't give you the keys, even if we had them!" said Hunter.

"Guys...." Tully held the floodlight on the beast, allowing them to see. "It broke loose."

The Wendigo had freed its antlers from the vehicle. Its bright, evil eyes met with the flood light, and it let out terrifying snarl.

"Turn it off!" Gerald grabbed the floodlight from Tully, but it was too late, the Wendigo had already pounced through the air, landing on top of the hood.

"You're the one who said to keep an eye on him!" Tully fought to get the floodlight back.

"Get down!" Alistair pulled Symphanie down to the floor of the vehicle, directly below the front windshield. They curled up into a ball, Alistair shielding her beneath him.

"Oh, no!" Gerald's eyes widened as he watched the Wendigo in a blur coming for them. It landed on all fours, directly on the hood, its head bearing downward like a bull's, its horns smashing into the windshield.

The creature howled, its eyes peering through the cracked windshield at its prey. Again, its antlers stuck in the windshield, its fists reigning down in a frenzy trying to smash the windshield completely. Each blow cracked the window, until finally one of its horns broke through a large hole; even the bulletproof glass was not enough to withstand the power of the Wendigo. The beast howled, ripping the entire window out, breaking it free from its deathly antlers, and tossed the remains of the windshield into the woods.

"Run!" Hunter opened the rear door and grabbed Olivia's hand. "Follow me," he led her out of the vehicle. The two made a mad dash to the other SUV.

"Where are you-" Gerald went to grab Hunter from fleeing, but instead felt the immense strength of the Wendigo grab his right arm. "Elly!" Tully followed suit, grabbing Elly. The two escaped out the same door as Hunter and Olivia, leaving Alistair and Symphanie literally trapped beneath the struggle between the Wendigo and Gerald. "Let me go!" Gerald tried kicking the Wendigo in its horse-like snout.

"I'm scared," Symphanie cried, tears streaming down her cheeks. "It's okay, don't look," Alistair covered her eyes. Looking above him, he saw the long slender body of the Wendigo hovering over them. It snarled and let out screeches as it held tightly onto Gerald, who was doing much of his own screaming. Alistair needed a plan. Just above his head was the interior lever to open the car door.

"We're getting out of here," Alistair pointed to the handle. "Soon as I get the door open, we make a run for it, into the woods. Understand?"

"Don't lose me," Symphanie frowned.

"Hang on to me," Alistair grabbed her hand tightly. He reached up with his free hand and slowly, so as to not cause any alarm, pushed the handle to unlatch the car door. Symphanie slowly pushed it open. Both kids spilled out into the dirt, freeing themselves from the struggle going on inside of the vehicle.

"I will kill you, you wretched beast!" Gerald struggled to reach for anything in the back of the vehicle to fend off the powerful Wendigo. The creature had a strong hold of his arm and with one mighty tug, the creature pulled Gerald violently out through where the windshield had been. Gerald screamed for help as the Wendigo dragged him from the SUV and out into the road.

"Oh, no…" Olivia turned her head from the scene, burying her head in between Hunter's shoulders.

"Can we save him?" asked Symphanie, who hid behind a large oak tree alongside Alistair.

"Would he save us?" asked Alistair, a deep frown written across his young boyish face.

"Don't watch this, Elly," said Tully.

"It's going to kill him!" Elly fought back the tears.

"He was an evil guy," said Tully.

"No one deserves this," Elly cried unable to tear her eyes away from the violence.

The Wendigo grabbed Gerald with its long bony fingers wrapped tightly around his face, encompassing his entire head. Gerald's arms and legs flailed about, failing to fight the creature off, his screams muffled by the beast's grip.

"What is he doing to him?" Tully frowned, the sight was too much.

"I'm not feeling well." Elly felt the familiar warmth come flooding through her cheeks.

"Don't watch, you'll get sick," Tully said. "No, it's not that."

The creature wasn't clawing and pummeling Gerald like it had the soldier. Instead it held its prey in its hand, using all its weight to keep him grounded. The Wendigo snarled, its eyes slowly turning from bright yellowish to an eerie blue. Gerald's face was now exposed, his screams echoed throughout the forest as his eyes began to glow with the same blue mist.

"My eyes...!" Gerald's screams grew weak, fading to weak mumblings.

"What is it doing?" Tully still had the flood light so he clicked it on and centered the beam on the gruesome sight. The light showed Gerald's now horror stricken, pale face, his mouth wide open, his skin seemingly shrinking around his skull.

"Oh no," Tully quickly switched the light off, allowing the gruesome sight to fade once again beneath the night sky. "I'm so sorry I did that!" Tully looked over to Elly who was face down in dirt, unconscious.

"Elly!" Tully ran to her aid.

CHAPTER 29
MAN—MADE MONSTERS

Elly felt the hot, white light burn through her consciousness, one minute she was watching the Wendigo mauling Gerald, the next she felt her face go flush, and boom! Like a bolt of lightning pulsing through her mind, she awoke in the bizarre world of blue mist, passing from her physical body into the hereafter spiritual realm.

"Not again...!" Elly attempted to get her bearings. The earth was covered in the familiar knee high blue mist, with the sky blanketed over in pure blackness. She could see the ethereal forms of her friends, their spirit shades pulsating through the forest's thick foliage. There in front of her was Gerald's shade, quickly dimming out, dissipating into nothingness, only leaving a faint trail of his essence being slowly pulled from his eyes, mouth, and nose and into the Wendigo. Gerald was experiencing something worse than death.

Standing over the top of his fading life force, was the Wendigo in all its fearsome glory. The creature's shade was nothing like that of her friends'. It burned brighter than anything else around it, glowing a fiery red its eyes the only exception, as they glowed blue, which Elly could only figure was what was left of Gerald's spirit being pulled into the monster.

"You're eating his soul!" Elly gasped at the horrific sight. She could see Gerald's face from where she stood, his mouth gaped open, his eyes bulging out.

The Wendigo jerked suddenly at Elly's voice. "It heard me?" Elly whispered to herself.

The Wendigo arched its back, letting out a low, curious howl. "Oh no," Elly turned to run, but her legs froze in place.

"I...can't...move!" Elly's heart raced. How was the Wendigo doing this? Was she somehow being controlled by it?

The Wendigo cautiously made its way over to Elly, circling around her, stalking her like a frightened animal sizing up its enemy.

"Get away from me!" Elly screamed.

The Wendigo approached hunched over, dropping onto all fours and sniffing her foot.

"Leave me alone!" Elly cried.

"Reach out, place your palm on its forehead," a calmly familiar voice broke through the silence of the forest.

"Nidhogg?" Elly recognized it immediately.

"I cannot show myself, it will frighten the creature," replied Nidhogg.

The Wendigo jumped at the sound of the wyrm's voice. Back on its hind legs, the Wendigo whipped its head up into the air trying to sniff out where the voice was coming from.

"It's frightened of our presence in this realm. This creature is an abomination; an evil hybrid creation, a mix of both our worlds, very rare indeed. You can speak with it, you know?"

"Speak to that thing? I think it just ate that man's soul! It's a monster!" Elly did not like the idea of talking to the blood thirsty Wendigo. She wanted to run to safety, to hide in a safe place until the thing decided to flee off into the forest.

"It cannot hurt you in this realm," Nidhogg explained. "Technically, it's still physically your world. This creature has adapted a unique sense, it is clairvoyant. It can see and interact with the hereafter, but you are nothing more than a shade to it. It can see your presence, smell your emotions, but unless it finds your physical body, you are safe from any harm. You have the upper hand."

"But, I can't move!" Elly explained.

"Oh, yeah, that was me, sorry about that. Couldn't have you go running away again, right? You must be brave; escaping the truth is not the answer. You must find your strength, conquer your fears."

"You did this? How?"

"I am a speaking wyrm, a mystical being that defies time and space. You are surprised I have some magical qualities?" Nidhogg chuckled. "But, it just ate Gerald's soul!" Elly begged. "Please, just let me get away from it."

"You must understand, it wants you to see," Nidhogg pushed her on. "Just reach out your hand, place it on his forehead. The seal will allow you to meld your mind with any living being, man or animal. You can connect with it."

"Its....it's... going to talk to me?" Elly reached out, her hand trembling.

"It cannot speak, but it can share its memories. It will be an overload of images and scenes played out in your head...the creature's memories," Nidhogg explained.

Elly reached out towards the Wendigo, she had never been more terrified in her life. The creature slowly approached, towering over Elly. It lowered its grotesque head down to sniff Elly's fingers. It was even more terrifying up close than she could have imagined. Its long horse like face was stained with blood, its yellow fangs smelled of death. Elly slowly placed her hand squarely at the center of the beast's forehead.

A bright light shot through her head. She lost control of her own thoughts, all the fear and agony she was experiencing diminished, replaced by a series of images and thoughts, terrifying and horrific thoughts... She was now one with the creature's mind, quick sharp images burned into her brain. Memories of being held captive in a lab, painful tests, lab coats and machines always around. Fear and pain summed up the creature's short life, born and raised from a test tube, abused... Glimpses of men chaining it down, arms, legs, even its entire face strapped to a cold hard cement slab. She felt the fear, the pain, the complete agony as they loaded it up into a small plane, locking it up tight in a dark room and injecting some sort of drug into its arms. She saw through its eyes the entire plane crash like a slideshow. Images of how it escaped its cage, was attacked by the men. How it fled into the forest, how its anger and tortured soul turned it insane, hungry for death and madness.

Elly fell to her knees. The raw emotion left her speechless. The

Wendigo stared back at her, letting out a small whimper. There was some connection there. Elly was no longer afraid of the man-made abomination that stood in front of her, she felt sorry for the creature. It never had a chance.

"That's enough!" a man's voice interrupted.

Elly looked up just in time to see a sharp blade explode out from the Wendigo's chest cavity. The creature made no noise, no blood curdling shriek, no spine-tingling howl, nothing, its once terrifying eyes just stared into Elly's.

The blade cut through the Wendigo with ease, its bright yellow eyes faded out, the creature fell to the earth, lifeless. There standing over the creature stood a powerful spirit shade that Elly immediately recognized as King Solomon. He stood, rapier in hand, his slender face hidden behind his silver shimmering hair. He was battle ready, adorned in magnificent golden armor, a mystical knight who had single-handedly slain the abomination with one killer blow.

"That creature was never meant to exist. An atrocity birthed from the inhumane hands of scientists. Its existence disturbed the balance between the realms, too powerful."

"I-it didn't have a choice," Elly's shade walked over to the creature, holding its large horse-like head in her lap.

"It was a blood thirsty monster, ate the flesh of men to sustain its physical body and the soul to sustain its connection to the hereafter. It was never meant to walk this earth."

"He is right," Nidhogg's bright eyes came to life high above one of the nearby trees. The wyrm jumped down with ease, kicking up a cloud of dust.

"What do you want with this young girl?" asked Solomon. "We are invested," Nidhogg explained.

"How are you here, dragon?" Solomon held out his hand to Elly, still looking at the wyrm. She obliged and stood up, wiping away her tears.

"I was given permission, to ensure our friend here would find her way," Nidhogg smiled a toothy grin.

"I have been with her, she is in good hands. She needs no help from a tree and a dragon. She is from my world, no one is more invested in her than I," Solomon added.

"What are you two talking about?" Elly couldn't take her eyes off the Wendigo.

"Your world is one of many of ours. Humanity is the life force of the Universe, have you forgotten all we shared with you?" Nidhogg shook his large head.

"Of course not," Solomon gently put his arm around Elly's shoulder, shielding her from the dead creature.

"Do not feel too bad for the creature, it would have killed you if it found you on the other side," said Nidhogg.

"He is right," Solomon added. "It was created by mankind to kill, eat, and cause destruction, a biological weapon."

"A weapon?" Elly shook her head.

"Mankind has fallen far from the branches of purity. You live in a world spinning out of control, men acting as gods, scientists going unchecked using their knowledge for evil…creating things…monsters like this. Monetary value outweighing good nature, the human soul is suffering from a blight; a dark and bitter stain on the collective human soul." Solomon frowned. "I have sat back and watched it for centuries, turning sour, the evil of men expanding, bubbling over."

"He is correct," Nidhogg frowned. "It's just a lot easier at the current development of your world, for a small group of people to do massive damage to the natural order of the universal balance."

"One flip of a switch away from massive genocide, or worse," Solomon dropped down to one knee to look Elly in the eyes.

"Much worse," Nidhogg added.

"You have my ring, and you have already come a long way to understanding its power. It will not happen overnight. It will take time to further develop your ability to control it. You are the key."

"The key?" asked Elly.

"Just as I was, when my world faced certain doom," Solomon smiled. "You are the modern warrior, the young child who will grow into a warrior woman. You will lead the world to a new order, the evil that threatens the world must fall. You and your friends will be triumphant."

"I do not think I am okay with this." Elly gave Solomon a crazed look.

"There is an immense evil in your world, growing in power by the day. He is just a man, but he has the potential to transcend into something so much more terrifying."

"Aten?" asked Elly.

"Please, do be careful," Solomon shook Elly's hand. "I will be watching over you, protecting you."

"As will I, when permitted," Nidhogg nodded.

"What do I do? I mean, you can't tell me all that and just leave!" Elly frowned.

"Face your fears, never bury the pain, conquer and prevail." Nidhogg rubbed against her affectionately, his big scaly head gently brushing against her. "Continue to learn from your Professor, for he is wise," Solomon gave one last smile before placing his palm on Elly's head. Burning white light once again shot through her head, and then...there was only darkness.

●　　●　　●

"Did you hear that?" Abram held his hand up, signaling for Dominick and his soldier to stand still. A panicked scream echoed through the forest. The group had been tracking the Wendigo for over an hour. Abram did his best to hurry, he knew where the Wendigo was fleeing to, by now Ben and the kids should have made it back to the vehicles, exactly where the beast led them.

"That was Gerald," Dominick winced, pushing back the physical pain.

"Sounded close," the soldier coughed up blood.

"He's getting worse," Dominick held up a torn piece of cloth to apply pressure to the soldier's wound.

"We're almost there, just through that clearing," Abram swung his rifle from his shoulder, reloaded, swapping out the tranqs with bullets and pulled a modification scope from his backpack. "We've got to be smart about this, that thing can't be allowed to live; there is no way we're walking away with this thing captured and alive. This scope's got night vision, so I will be able to make sure the shot is safe."

"Agreed," Dominick nodded. "Just kill the damn thing."

"I'll set up in those shrubs over there. Hopefully we're not too late," Abram waved the group forward. They made their way towards a large shrub near a thick oak tree. Dominick and the soldier found rest against its base while Abram lined up his sights.

"What do you see?" Dominick checked the soldier's wounds.

"It's doing something to Gerald. I can't tell, but I think...I think Gerald's dead."

"We're too late to save him," Dominick shook his head. "Aten is going to be pissed."

"Quiet, the creature just jerked, something startled it," Abram hushed.

"It heard me?" Dominick look confused. "How?"

"I don't know. It seems to be... circling something, but nothing is there."

"Just shoot it already," said Dominick.

"Relax, I gotta make sure the kids aren't nearby. If I miss my shot, I need to know no one will get hit." Abram took his time scoping out the scene looking through the scope in night vision. Both vehicles looked to be damaged, and he noticed an unconscious body of an adult in the closest vehicle. Must be Ben, he thought. At least Abram hoped he was unconscious.

Abram did not see any children, only the lifeless body of Gerald lying prone on the earth. He prayed they escaped unharmed into the woods.

"Okay, aiming the shot," Abram steadied his sight. "Take it...end this madness," whispered the soldier.

"What the hell?" Abram did not pull the trigger. "Take the shot already!" Dominick ordered.

"It just dropped dead." Abram dropped his rifle to his side, staring at Dominick in disbelief.

"What?" Dominick questioned.

"It looked like a hole was blown out from its back all the way through the front, a mortal wound. Dead," Abram raised his brow in disbelief. "C'mon, we've got to hurry!" Abram helped the two men up, making their way down to the dirt road.

"What was that?" Hunter stepped out from his hiding place with Olivia. "It just dropped dead!"

"Dad!" Alistair grabbed Symphanie and ran towards the vehicle. "Kids, everyone calm down!" Abram broke through the far foliage of the forest.

"Dad!" Olivia pulled away from Hunter and ran to her dad's side. "You're hurt!"

"Just a scratch, darling," Abram hugged his daughter tighter than he ever had. "Where is everyone?"

"My dad is hurt!" Alistair screamed.

"Dominick, please check him out," Abram looked to his cousin for help.

"Yeah…" Dominick stood over the dead body of Gerald with a sick look on his face. He turned and limped his way over to the vehicle.

"Help him, please!" Alistair begged. "He's not moving," Symphanie frowned.

"Move it," Dominick lightly shoved Alistair out of the way.

Ben was laid back in his seat, head back and mouth gaped open. Dominick pressed two fingers into his neck, checking for his heart rate.

"He's alive, breathing shallow…" Dominick looked over Ben's body for any sign of struggle.

"Is he going to die?" Alistair's tears falling in earnest.

"No," Dominick noted something of interest between the car seats. He reached over and grabbed an empty tranq dart. He inspected the far side of Ben's neck where the puncture wound was.

"You're lucky kid!" Dominick winced in pain. "Gerald knocked him out with the tranq, he will be fine; he just needs to sleep it off." Dominick handed Alistair the dart. "May take a few days though."

Dominick walked back towards Gerald, where he'd left his soldier sitting in the road.

"Abram," Dominick yelled. "Look at this!"

"Stay here," Abram looked Olivia deep in her eyes. "Everyone is safe now."

"Okay," Olivia smiled.

"What is it?" Abram walked up towards Dominick. "My God..." he frowned upon seeing Gerald's terror-stricken face.

"What happened to him?" asked Dominick.

"I have never seen anything like it." Abram took off his jacket and covered Gerald's face. "I don't want the kids seeing his face like that. It will mess them up."

"I need help!" Tully finally broke through the woods carrying an unconscious Elly in his arms.

"Elly!" Hunter ran towards them. "What happened?"

"That thing where she passes out, one minute she was talking, the next she collapsed to the ground."

"Bring her here!" Abram ran to the kids, meeting them half way. "It's okay," Hunter said. "She does this...," Hunter wasn't sure how to explain. "She just needs to get back to Professor Calenstine, now." "Here's the deal," Dominick broke up the huddle, carrying his injured man. "In ten minutes I place a call to Aten to pick up what's left of my team. Abram, you get your kids out of here, they've been through hell and back."

"I want the Wendigo," Abram added.

"No, it's mine. That's the deal. You know Aten has some things in play that paint a nasty picture for any Seeker, no love lost. Use this time to get out of here," Dominick pointed to the SUV with Ben. "He's been tranq'ed, you're hurt, and the kids are a mess. Leave."

"I can't let you take that thing," Abram shook his head.

"Now is not the time to be stubborn," Dominick gritted his teeth. "I lost two men under my supervision. Aten will kill me if I don't bring him back *something*."

"I think you work for the wrong team," Abram pursed his lips. "Maybe, but it's my team, they accepted me, right?" Dominick turned his back, pulled out his cell phone. "Soldier, without this man's help, you would be dead. When Aten's team picks us up, we were out here alone. Understood?"

"You scratch my back," the soldier coughed.

"Good," Dominick dialed a number. "We need a pick up. I am sending you our coordinates, make it quick. One man down, two injured, medical assistance needed a.s.a.p.," Dominick flipped his phone shut. "Not much longer now, cousin. You should be going."

Abram nodded to the kids. "Let's get moving, we're taking one vehicle. Get in with Ben and hang tight for a second, make sure Elly is comfortable, and keep an eye on her. When we get out of this forest, we'll call the Estate and have a helicopter pick us up. We need medical attention too."

The kids nodded and began to pile into the vehicle. "Dominick," Abram turned back to him.

"You need to leave. They're quick on their response time."

"I am sorry," Abram turned his head away, looking to the dirt road. "You saved two lives out here today," Dominick nodded.

"I am sorry I couldn't save her," Abram frowned while his back was turned and left his cousin behind. He entered the vehicle and drove off. "Soldier, you okay? Hang in there, our boys are coming," Dominick wiped the sweat from his brow.

"I am fine," the soldier lied. "Sir, you look really pale."

"I feel funny…burning up, freezing."

"Sir, you're turning red," the soldier backed up away from Dominick.

"I need help!" Dominick hunched over in pain, his entire body tensed up.

"Hold on…they're coming. Just stay with me…" the Soldier crawled over to Dominick.

"I feel…different," Dominick's vision turned blurry. "If I pass out…the Seekers…they were never," Dominick felt the world spin around him, he vomited what tasted like blood and bile before passing out.

"Oh, God," the Soldier held Dominick in the dirt road. "Please hurry!" he looked up into the sky for any sign of an Aten Corp. helicopter.

CHAPTER 30
THE HAND OF GLORY

Not exactly what we had in mind for the children's first investigation," Professor Calenstine stood over Elly, accompanied by Joe, Abram, and Benjamin.

"No, not at all," Ben replied. "She's been out for how long?" "Four days," Calenstine added.

"What about the rest of the kids? How is Hunter handling the Margot situation?" asked Abram.

"They're doing fine," Joe said. "No one knows of her condition yet." Joe kept a stern face when speaking about the matter. "How are you handling it?" asked Ben.

"Been a rough few days," half of Joe's mouth pursed to a frown. "Still weird to have you standing next to me," Ben slapped Joe on the back. "To think, you died on us, for four hours?" "How did Hunter handle that news?" asked Abram.

"He was excited to see me up and walking again, beyond happy, his face lit up." Joe nodded. "We didn't tell them about that incident either, no clue I died for a bit. He knows something is wrong though. He's a smart kid, or I just suck at hiding my emotions."

"A combination, I assure you," Calenstine nodded with a reassuring smile.

"So, how are you hiding Margot's condition? They aren't allowed to see her?" asked Abram.

"I have spoken with the children," Calenstine answered. "They are under the impression that she is traveling overseas for Estate business."

"Smart," Ben nodded. "They don't need the added stress."

"They had enough emotional turmoil with us," Abram added. "They witnessed some gruesome scenes."

"Yes, your report was thorough. Thankfully everyone escaped mostly unscathed," Calenstine wheeled himself nearer to Elly.

"At least on our side," Ben added.

"That creature wasn't normal, Professor," Abram explained. "If you could have seen the face on Gerald's corpse, I have never...."

"I have my feelings over the matter," Calenstine motioned for Abram to watch his words. "At one-point Gerald was a good man, never without his demons, but he had a good heart, loved his family. Something, or someone got to him, his last few years with us was... unfavorable, to say the least," Calenstine scratched his chin with his bony fingers. "Yet, no matter where your allegiance lies, no one deserves such an end. I feel for his family."

"Do you plan on telling the kids about Margot's condition, at all?" asked Ben. "I mean is she okay keeping this a secret? She is going to get lonely hidden away in the infirmary until God knows when."

"Not until we learn more of what's going on," Calenstine added. "It is time I came clean with certain aspects of her condition."

"What do you mean?" asked Joe. "Do you know more than you're letting on?"

"I have invited someone to join us, to help explain a bit more in depth what we may be up against," Calenstine rolled his way back over to the group.

"Who?" Ben wrinkled his brow. "What's going on?"

"What we are about to discuss does not go beyond the five of us," Calenstine spoke sternly. "It is of grave importance that this does not leave this room, we must contain any panic this may create."

"What's going on, Professor?" asked Abram. "You know you can trust us."

"I am not worried about you or Ben," Calenstine stared into Joe's eyes.

"Since when can't you trust me?" Joe frowned.

"You need to control your emotions, this must not get out, understood?" Calenstine squinted sizing up Joe's mental game. "You will be affected by the truth more than anyone else."

"Of course, c'mon, what's going on?" Joe looked to the others a bit baffled.

"Follow me," Calenstine rolled his wheelchair out of Elly's room and down the hall. The men followed behind. He came to a stop at Margot's infirmary door.

"Why are we heading into Margot's room?" Joe cracked his knuckles, a nervous habit he'd picked up when he was younger. "I left her earlier this morning to rest, she needs her strength."

"Our friend is waiting in here," Calenstine opened the door. Sitting next to Margot's bed was Sebastian, weeping by her side. Margot was attached to a series of machines, cords and wires connected to her, monitoring her vitals.

"What the hell is he doing here?" Joe felt his blood pressure rise. The mere sight of Sebastian made him sick with anger.

"I asked you to behave, Joe," Calenstine gave Joe a fatherly look of disapproval.

"Margot, is he bothering you?" asked Joe. Margot did not move, nor speak.

"She won't respond to you," Sebastian sniffled.

"Why not? What's wrong with her?" Joe's face was overcome with worry.

"I asked Mr. Bell to meet us here," Calenstine explained. "He has something he wants to share with us."

"Is that so?" asked Ben.

"Yes, I....errr..." Sebastian let go of Margot's hand, on a long desperate sigh.

"Wait, answer my question. Why won't she respond," asked Joe? "I was with her this morning, she was in pain, but awake."

"Let our guest explain, please, Joe," Calenstine ordered. "Well...you see..." Sebastian looked to Calenstine for approval; instead he was met with a crippling glare. "He is wasting our time," said Abram. "Out with it," Calenstine nodded.

"I have been working for ATEN for over a year. I started the Order of Shadows," Sebastian blurted out.

"You what!" Joe lost it, completely overtaken by his anger. He took off after Sebastian, and it took both Ben and Abram to hold Joe back, even then, he was still able to break free, tossing both men onto the floor then grabbing Sebastian by the throat. Picking him up off the chair he slamming him into the wall.

"When did he get so strong?" Ben broke his fall. Sebastian gasped for air, his face turning blue.

"Joe!" Calenstine yelled, "Release him, or you will no longer have a place here to call a home!"

"What? Are you serious?" Joe let loose his grip. Sebastian fell to the floor holding his throat. "This bastard is a traitor, and you want to kick me out!" Joe slammed his fist down onto a nearby counter, breaking it in half with one crushing blow.

"Damn!" Abram's eyes went wide.

"Did you just see that?" Ben shot a crazed look over to Abram.

"I am sorry!" Sebastian crawled behind the Professor, his voice raspy from the choke-hold.

"Real nice," Joe smirked, "A grown man hiding behind the Professor."

"There's more to it," Calenstine's voice grew stern. "—And no, I don't want to kick anyone out. Understand, Sebastian is no good to us if we banish him. He may still be of use. He is the closest thing we have to any inside knowledge of Aten. He knows things we are not privy to."

"You know, don't you?" asked Joe. "You know why her arm has turned to stone! Tell me, tell me now!" Joe demanded.

"Turned to stone?" Abram looked at the Professor with disbelief. "Calm down, man," Ben put his hand on his best friends shoulder.

"We know you're upset, let's hear him out. You know the Professor has our best interests at heart."

"Yeah...but..." Joe dropped his head, taking deep breaths. "She is dying, it's spreading so fast."

"Sebastian here got himself into some serious trouble with Declan Aten. He came clean to me a while back when he first got word that he had become a target. I won't pretend to understand why he did what he did, but there is nothing we can do to change the past," Calenstine explained.

"I just wanted a perfect life for Margot and I, I know it doesn't make sense." Sebastian carefully regained his footing, staying a safe distance from Joe. "Aten promised me the world, at first he just wanted me to recruit people here at the estate to spy. No one was getting hurt."

"You're a spineless coward," Abram shook his head. "Pitiful."

"Then he wanted me to find ways to cause havoc, keep everyone occupied. I wanted to be his go-to guy, and he could protect me, pay me more money I could dream of, move Margot and I far away."

"You were behind the Beast of Bladenboro?" Joe looked mad, his eyes practically bulging out of their sockets.

"Calm down, big guy," Ben held out his arms separating Joe from Sebastian.

"Everything changed… he wanted me to…to kill… the Kendrick kids."

"What!?" Ben now joined Joe with the uncontrollable rage, both men looking to tear Sebastian apart.

"Calm down!" Abram kept a cool head. "Let him finish."

"Yes, please, gentlemen. This will be hard to hear, we must control our emotions," Calenstine ordered.

"I mean, I couldn't," Sebastian swallowed the lump in his throat. "I am no murderer. He wanted me to find a way to release that demon. I did everything he wanted. Then when his plan didn't work, he wanted me to…to kill them out there in the woods. Murder them."

"You were behind that demon, too!" Joe threw up his hands in anger. He couldn't believe what he was hearing. "That demon could have killed the kids."

"I know…" Sebastian held his head low.

"So you're okay with causing the events that could have killed them, but not okay with dirtying your own hands?" Abram sighed. "I don't understand why he is standing here, Professor. He is obviously just as evil as Aten."

"No, I'm not, I swear it. I came clean!" Sebastian argued.

"Yes, but for now, he is more valuable to us here. He won't go back to Aten, they're after him, and he wouldn't last a week out there on his own." Calenstine explained.

"How is this fool valuable, again?" asked Joe.

"He has some inside knowledge, knows information that has already proven very useful," Calenstine explained. "We're getting ahead of ourselves. First, Margot."

"Why is she unconscious?" Joe moved over beside her, holding her hand, it was cold and rigid, turned to solid stone. That's when he saw the morbid sight. Tied to her palm was a mummified human hand clutching a single lit candle within its wrinkled palm. "What is that!?" Joe turned to the Professor, distraught by the sight.

"Hold that thought," Calenstine held up his bony hand, silencing Joe. "Fist let me explain the letter."

"What?" Joe sounded panicked.

"We found a letter addressed to her, a green substance was hidden inside the envelope. When she opened it, the powder spilled onto her lap. She inhaled some of it," Calenstine explained.

"They sent it to her because of me," Sebastian bit his lip. "She is dying, turning to stone, because of me."

"We have been studying this substance since its discovery in her apartment," Calenstine rolled his chair over to Margot, who appeared to sleep peacefully. "It's nothing like we've ever seen; some sort of biological weapon, unnatural. I am not sure how Aten could have created such a terrifying thing."

"It actually petrifies the body?" Abram's mouth fell agape.

"Yes, thankfully this strain appears to start off slow, taking its time to spread through the body, allowing us a small window of time. However, Margot waited days before telling anyone of her symptoms. Thus, we lost days of research. Now, the virus has strengthened, the petrification is spreading at an alarming rate through her body. It would have only taken a day, maybe two before we lost her." Calenstine frowned.

"No," Joe felt the warmth of tears budding.

"Our hands were forced. We had to act quickly," Calenstine looked up to Joe, offering a faint smile of hope.

"So where does this old creepy hand come in to play?" Ben couldn't take his eyes off the preserved appendage.

"Not one of our finer possessions," Calenstine frowned. "The Hand of Glory, an ancient relic created in a time much darker than our own. This is the last remaining specimen in the world. The dark art used to create it has been long forgotten, thankfully."

"Hand of Glory?" Joe repeated.

"Been in our collection for as long as I can remember," Calenstine explained. "Our hands were forced. We had to think quickly. This relic's gruesome history may save Margot's life."

"What the hell is it, exactly?" asked Abram.

"This is the severed hand of a thief, put to death by hanging in the gallows. His hand submerged into a very specific concoction of liquid to preserve and mummify the appendage, only a master warlock had the knowledge of the dark arts needed to create such a gruesome relic. It's good for one of two uses; when the owner lights the candle, he can use the hand to open any locked item, or freeze one individual in time," Calenstine explained.

"Freeze," asked Ben.

"Perhaps frozen is not the right term," Calenstine scratched his chin. "After speaking with Margot, and discussing this option, she wished to go under suspended animation. The problem is, the hand is only good once, it can suspend her, but it can't undo the hex. For now her body is safe from the toxin spreading any further, but now we must cure the petrification, and find a way to bring her back once she is cured."

"Great," Ben shook his head. "As if the first problem wasn't going to be hard enough."

"So, she is in a coma?" asked Joe, baffled over what was happening.

"Sort of, yes, you could say that," Calenstine nodded.

"We had to," Sebastian added. "This will give the Professor more time to find a way to reverse the petrification."

"This is insane!" Ben wasn't quite sure what to say...

"The Hand of Glory," Abram ran his hands through his thinning hair. "It never surprises me the wicked things we create."

"We cannot keep her in this state forever, we need to find a cure and fast," Calenstine rolled away from the group. "No one is to know about her condition. Only the five of us may visit her during this time period, understood?"

Joe nodded. He took a seat next to Margot and placed his head on her lap, sobbing.

"Sebastian, let's give them some time," Ben motioned to the door. "C'mon," Abram grabbed him by the arm, walking him out of the room. The group left Joe alone with Margot.

"This is completely insane!" Joe leaned towards her, placing a soft kiss on her forehead. "I feel like the world is falling apart around me."

CHAPTER 31
THE DANCE

Hunter and the boys did their best to return to their normal lives, but that was easier said than done. They rarely spoke of the events that happened in the forest, there wasn't much to say. The atrocities they'd witnessed, the severe brutality of the Wendigo had left them all unsure of themselves. Calenstine even ordered the children to meet with either him, or Patricia, once a week to discuss the events one-on-one. He said it was a crucial step in coming to terms with what they had seen.

Hunter never told his friends, but when he learned that Professor Aten had a contract out for him and his sister, he lost a bit of himself. He was just a kid still trying to cope with the premature death of his parents, trying to find himself in a school where he moonlighted as a potential member of an ancient monster hunting secret society. He couldn't catch a break.

"It's good you're telling me this," Calenstine took a puff from his cob pipe, blowing dark clouds of smoke out through his nostrils. "It's okay if you keep your fears from your friends, as long as you have a supportive outlet like me, your Uncle, or Patricia. Just never bottle those fears up, that's a battle you will never win." Calenstine nodded tapping his boney finger on his large desk. "However, I would encourage you to confide in your friends. You all have been through so much together; I believe you have found a trustworthy and reliable family." "Family?" Hunter frowned. His family was dead, the only one Elly and he had left was their Uncle Joe, and Margot...sort of.

"Yes, I think so," Calenstine offered an optimistic smile. "Don't you? You and Alistair have grown so close, like brothers. You have just met Tully, but has he not proved his loyalty? Are these not the qualities of a family, of brotherhood? Sure, you will find yourselves caught up in silly skirmishes, but when push comes to shove, your friends always stand strong, together, resolute in the face of danger, even when that face comes from a supernatural creature that would send most kids running for the hills. It is your love for your friends that will separate you and your friends from greedy men like Aten and his hired goons. Never lose that, never stop protecting the ones you can, it is who you are, Hunter, a protector."

"I just don't know if I can handle everything," Hunter sighed.

"No one can handle everything you're going through, not alone. That is why you have your support group. Let them guide you, much as you would rush to their aid."

Hunter cracked a half a smile. Professor Calenstine made it sound so easy.

"Have you gone to visit your sister?" asked Calenstine.

"Yes, the moment she woke up," Hunter answered. "We go up every day between our Enlightenment and scholastic classes. She gets lonely in there, you know. I'm hoping she comes home soon."

"Yes, I have spoken with Dr. Wong, she will be out in time for the big dance," Calenstine took another puff. "Tell me Hunter, have you decided if you're going?"

"I dunno. So much has happened, kind of hard to get excited about going to a dance," Hunter frowned. "Plus, the girls were supposed to ask the boys."

"And?" Calenstine cocked his head curiously. "Well, no one asked me."

"I see," Calenstine chuckled. "I think it would suit you and your friends well to go together. It's an important step to getting back to some sort of normal teenage routine. You're going to see a lot of bizarre and macabre things as a Seeker, and it is important to not let those things break you down

"I dunno...maybe," answered Hunter. He had spoken openly to Calenstine about a lot: his parents, the terrifying death of Gerald and the soldier that they witnessed back in the forest, dealing with his

Uncle's handicap and sudden recovery under mysterious circumstances. There was one thing he wouldn't discuss with Calenstine, Olivia.

He felt foolish, with everything going on in his life, how could a simple crush take such precedence over his emotions. Yet, there he was, sitting in front the Professor, completely bummed out that Olivia had not asked him to the dance. He was sure she was going to and everything seemed to work out in his favor. She wasn't with that lame Marcus guy, and she'd been acting really nice to him during the crazy trip. He didn't get it. He swore by the way she looked at him that she liked him, and he liked her. Didn't she feel the same way?

"Well, the choice is yours, of course. You should know, however, your Uncle was the first one to sign up as a chaperone. He is beyond excited."

"He did?" Hunter was baffled as to why his uncle would want to chaperone a stupid dance.

"He did. He feels like he has missed a lot of you and your sister's lives being confined to the wheelchair for over a year. You know how upset he was for missing your first field trip. He wants to be a part of your lives, make up for lost time. Perhaps that may persuade you into at least going for a bit. It's always fun to dress up, plus, you know the Estate caters the most delicious food, all free of course."

"Well," Hunter felt a bit guilty. "I do like the desserts…."

. . .

Elly awoke two days before the big Sadie Hawkins dance, recuperating from the events that caused her to pass out in the Wanigas forest. She was beginning to feel like she spent more time in the infirmary wards then her own dorm room.

She was thankful for Calenstine's nightly visits, she felt like it kept her a sane. There were things she could tell Calenstine that she knew her friends couldn't hear; they'd think she was crazy. Calenstine asked lots of questions, having her go into detail over and over again about her experiences with the hereafter realm. He was in awe of the information, especially about the wyrm named Nidhogg, the Norns who spun the threads of fate, how Solomon killed the Wendigo in the spiritual realm, all the while taking feverishly detailed notes.

The weight of her experiences in the hereafter weighed heavy on her soul. It's not every day a young teenage girl is told she holds the fate of the world in her hands. It was a lot to come to terms with, and she carefully side-stepped those tidbits of information when speaking with Calenstine. Most nights, the burden was so heavy, she cried herself to sleep. She lay on the stiff infirmary bed, staring up at the ceiling, wishing to the heavens she could go back to being a normal kid. She wanted to be worrying about getting her homework done on time, about the cute boy who sat behind her in her scholastic history class…, not about this cursed ring.

It was the night before the big dance when Elly got the okay to be released from the infirmary. Hunter and all their friends came up to assist with moving her back to her dorm.

"I can't wait for tomorrow, Alistair is going to look so handsome in his suit," Symphanie beamed while rushing over to Elly and gripping her in a giant hug. "Don't you think he will be the handsomest boy at the dance?"

"Err, yeah," Alistair blushed. "No need to tell the world that." He'd never been to a dance with an actual date before. He was more than a bit nervous, his last school dance was in a gymnasium and the girls and boys were basically split up on separate sides. He remembers playing basketball for the majority of the dance while the girls stood by and watched. Of course, he was terrible at sports, and felt like a complete idiot the entire time. He told his dad that was the last dance he'd ever go to.

"Wear comfortable shoes," Tully joked, "Symphanie is a dancer, you're not gonna get her off the dance floor for a second. Hope you've been studying up on the hottest dance trends."

"Seriously?" Alistair looked over to Symphanie turning bright red. "Dancing has trends?"

"It's okay," Symphanie smiled. "All you have to do is hold me and sway your hips. It will be fun."

Elly frowned, she was trying not to be irritable, but while everyone else was getting ready for the dance she was stuck in the infirmary. She hadn't even been able to ask anyone to be her date.

"Margot hasn't come to see me," Elly looked to Hunter. "I thought she'd be one of the first visitors."

"Oh, yeah, I guess she went on some secret mission for the Professor," Hunter explained. "Uncle Joe was telling me about it. Not sure when she will come back."

"But, she promised to do my hair and makeup," Elly frowned. It was the one thing she had been looking forward to since her recovery. "I can help you," said Olivia, wading her way through the group to the front.

"You got your hair cut, it's not purple anymore?" Elly noticed. "Yeah... that was silly, what was I thinking, purple? I wanted to go back to my natural color for the dance. I am so excited that we can all go together. We were worried you weren't going to wake up in time." Olivia leaned in, giving Elly a light hug. "I missed you," she whispered. "All Symphanie talks about is Alistair."

"That last one must have taken a lot out of you, huh?" asked Hunter. "You know, the jumping from realm to realm thing you do."

"I guess so," Elly didn't care to elaborate.

"Who are you going with?" Elly asked looking at Hunter, and then over to Olivia with a sly smile.

"Err, um..." Hunter's face grew red. He hadn't been asked, and he'd hoped Olivia would have been the one, but he had not seen her much since they returned to the Estate.

"We're going stag," Tully answered. "Figured we'd just hang out with the group, you know?"

"You didn't get asked out, Hunter?" Elly couldn't believe, it, shooting Olivia a confused glare. Olivia turned her head frowning.

"Well, don't make a big deal about it, not even sure if I am going," Hunter made light of the situation.

"What?" asked Olivia, "I thought we were all going?"

"Oh, we're going! I will *drag* Hunter to the dance if I have to," Tully swung his arm over both Olivia and Hunter.

"Wait, no one asked you either?" Elly asked Tully.

Tully chuckled before responding, "Well, I got asked out, just not by anyone I cared about going with."

"Oh, I didn't mean," Elly turned red.

"It's cool, no worries," Tully patted Hunter on the back. "We've been so busy trying to get everything back in order since the disaster of the "field trip" the dance just kinda seems silly, doesn't it?"

"Speak for yourself," Symphanie frowned. "There's been way too much scary stuff going on. We deserve to act like kids for a change. I'm only thirteen, I want my dance!"

"Okay, sorry," Tully smiled. "I get it; you're excited to dance with Alistair."

The group gathered up the few items belonging to Elly and made their way back to the girls Dorm. There was still much to do before the big dance tomorrow. So the two groups decided to split up and call it a night.

•   •   •

The Sadie Hawkins dance was decorated gloriously, a mix of Halloween themes and Cinderella-esque elegance, gold streamers hung from the ceiling accompanied by a dozen or so fake skeletons and zombie corpses (dressed up in suits, of course), silver balloons danced atop the tables swaying alongside giant rubber bats with bloody vampire fangs.

When the children arrived they stood in awe at the decor. Even the food was perfectly themed with elegant roasted duck in plum wine sauce sitting next to spaghetti zombie brains and meat-eye-balls, delicious blood-red fruit punch chilling next to a fountain of sparkling grape cider. There was more than enough food to feed the entire estate twice over, and everything smelled wonderful.

"This is heaven!" Alistair practically salivated at the sight. The smell of the slow roasted, rosemary pork danced in his nose, his belly already rumbling.

"It's not supposed to be heavenly," Symphanie frowned. "It's supposed to be...you know, scary-ish, and elegant, a perfect mix."

"I think you guys did an amazing job putting this thing together," Tully pulled on one of the rubber bats, it fell and hit Elly on the head. "Watch it," Elly smiled, playfully punching him on the shoulder.

She had felt much better after getting a decent night's rest in her own bed, and a peaceful one at that, with no weird scary nightmares torturing her all night.

"Look, there's Uncle Joe," Hunter pointed to Joe who had a heaping plate of food. He smiled and waved back.

"Sure do wish Margot wasn't on that trip, I am sure she'd love to be here," Elly frowned.

"C'mon Alistair, the D.J. is setting up, let's go ask for the first song," Symphanie grabbed Alistair's hand and pulled him away into the sea of students and faculty.

"...and there she goes," Tully chuckled. "I don't think we will be seeing them for the rest of the night."

"They're going to dance the entire night? I bet you twenty bucks Alistair finds a way out of it," Hunter grinned.

"Dancing, or in the corner making out, one of the two," Tully winked.

"Gross," said Elly. "I don't want to think of those two kissing," she laughed. "I still find them a weird couple, Alistair is so shy."

"Don't you kids look all snazzy," Uncle Joe made his way through the sea of people, snacking with his bare hands on some extra-spicy chicken wings.

"Glad to see you up and walking," Tully smiled. "I haven't seen you since the operation Hunter and Elly told me about."

"It feels good, forgot how it felt to stand," Joe straightened his back pretending to flex his muscles, "Strong as an ox, I tell you. I feel better than ever."

"We're so happy," Elly gave her Uncle a hug.

"You better save me a dance," Joe winked. "I want to get to use these bad boys for a dance or two before the night's over."

"Too bad Margot wasn't here, I am sure she'd love to as well," Elly smiled

"Errr…yeah, of course," Joe frowned, doing his best to dodge anything Margot related.

"So spiffy in your suit Hunter. Glad you decided to make it," said Joe.

"We had to force him," Olivia gave Hunter a dirty look. "Yeah, I dunno, dances aren't my thing," Hunter played cool. "Never was my thing either," Joe nodded.

"Anyway, you kids have fun. I see Symphanie snagged Alistair away already. I promised Ben I would keep an eye out for those two. No funny business," Joe turned, laughing at his own joke.

"I don't see why you were so against going," Olivia pulled Hunter off to the side. "Look how amazing this place looks, and the chefs did such a great job."

"It's not that I didn't want to go. I just," Hunter had a hard time looking at Olivia when he spoke. She wore a beautiful, flowing, darkred dress, and her hair was painstakingly done in a complicated chignon twist with tiny butterfly clips to add a little whimsy to the look. Following the Halloween theme, she added two glued on vampire marks on her neck with a dash of fake blood. She was drop dead gorgeous, by far the prettiest girl Hunter had ever seen. "I dunno, I didn't want to go stag."

"Elly," Tully smiled, he and Elly were left alone standing awkwardly at the entrance of the dance. "I know this is a girls ask the guys type of dance, but because we are both solo, I was hoping you'd be my date for the evening."

"What?" Elly looked utterly surprised. The cutest boy in the entire school just asked her to be his date?

"I mean, you know, as friends and all," Tully's boyish smile brought

Ely's heart to a flutter.

"Oh, as friends, yeah, of course," she said, a bit embarrassed. "When you fainted in the forest, it was so scary. Then I heard what happens to you, you know, when that happens. You're an amazing person, and I was hoping you were going to ask me, but then you know, you never woke up," Tully chuckled.

"It's nothing. Not a big deal," Elly wasn't used to being nervous like this.

"Well, I am glad you said yes. I want to keep an eye on Symphanie, make sure she doesn't scare Alistair away with her dance moves. So I really need a dance partner," he winked, grabbed her hand and led her to the dance floor.

"Oh, look!" Olivia beamed. "Tully is dancing with your sister, how cute!"

"Huh?" Hunter looked over to see the two-slow dancing next to Alistair and Symphanie. "He's a bit old, isn't he? What's he thinking?" Hunter wasn't quite sure how to react.

"Don't be silly, they're only three years apart. Plus, they're just friends." Olivia turned back to Hunter.

"It's been a crazy two years, hasn't it?" Olivia frowned. "I mean, this year isn't even over with, who knows what's going to happen next."

"Yeah, that's for sure," replied Hunter. "I mean, this thing with Aten is just crazy. It's hard you know. I feel like everyone is in danger all the time. Hard to feel safe, even here, right now."

"I can't imagine how you feel," Olivia frowned.

"I am just happy you and your dad seemed to have worked things out," Hunter offered a friendly smile.

"Yeah, things are different...better," she answered.

"I'm glad you're not upset about that Marcus kid anymore, he was a fool," said Hunter.

"Yeah," Olivia looked down towards her feet.

"You *are* over him, right?" Hunter looked confused.

"I let him turn me into someone I don't want to be. I was jealous, hurt, angry. I was mean to my friends, to you, and to Elly."

"Well, I mean we understand," Hunter reached out and held Olivia's hand, a moment of courage, and he wasn't sure where it had come from. "I mean, I have never had a girlfriend, but, I know how it feels, you know, when you have feelings. Like someone, like, in that way and they don't...err...like you back kinda thing," Hunter fumbled with his words.

Olivia only smiled.

"Well…" Hunter let go of her hand, wiped the sweat from his palm on his pants, "I think I am going to go get some food." He turned away. "Hunter," Olivia reached out, grabbing his hand, she pulled him close to her. She placed her warm, soft hand on his cheek and leaned in placing her lips softly onto his. There they kissed for the first time… and for that moment, all the fear in the world, all the pain, the confusion, everything that haunted Hunter's young mind vanished. He stood there kissing the girl of his dreams, and nothing else mattered.

THE END

ABOUT THE AUTHOR

J.L. Hickey was born in Saginaw, Michigan where he has a Bachelor's Degree in Creative Writing through Saginaw Valley State University. He has dedicated his life to writing, focusing on young adult fiction heavy on fantasy and paranormal elements.

Secret Seekers Society
NOVELS

Secret Seekers Society
and the
BEAST OF BLADENBORO

Secret Seekers Society
SOLOMON'S SEAL

Thank you so much for reading one of our **Paranormal Fantasy** novels.

If you enjoyed our book, please check out our recommended title for your next great read!

The Graveyard Girl and the Boneyard Boy by Martin Matthews

"... a compelling and eminently likable cast of characters." *–Authors Reading*